BACKCOUNTRY

Pamela Beason

WildWing Press
Bellingham, Washington, USA

WILDWING PRESS
3301 Brandywine Court
Bellingham, Washington 98226

Copyright © 2017 Pamela Beason

Cover design by Christine Savoie

ISBN-10: 0997642041
ISBN-13: 978-0-9976420-4-9

www.pamelabeason.com

1

Sam Westin stared at the photo on her cell phone. The jagged granite mountains, ivory-barked alders, and cloudless azure sky were so perfectly mirrored in Pinnacle Lake that she couldn't tell the difference between the reflection in the water and the reality of peaks and vegetation above the shoreline.

This picture would make a perfect enlargement to replace the faded print of Table Mountain above her fireplace.

Except that every time she looked at the image, she might cry.

She thumbed the screen back to the selfie that had arrived in her e-mail three weeks ago. Kimberly Quintana, her curly brown hair frizzed around her head, her petite blond daughter Kyla Quintana-Johnson posed in front of her, the lake sparkling behind them.

Kim and Kyla died here.

"They probably sat right in this spot," Sam said aloud, touching her fingers to the rock ledge beneath her. Biting her lip, she turned away from the lake. Behind her, Chase was inspecting a small clearing in the shrubbery. "Who comes to such a beautiful place to commit murder?"

He folded his arms across his chest, his gaze fixed on the ground. "Whoever he or she was, the killer—or killers—didn't leave behind many clues. I can't even tell where it happened."

The word "it" wafted over Sam like a cold breeze. There was

no blood. No outline where the bodies had lain, no yellow crime scene tape. Rain showers had drenched the site since the murders. Dozens of boot and shoe prints were etched into the mud near the lake shore, but they were smudged by weather and trampling; it was impossible to tell when they had been laid down. Sam recognized the tread patterns left by several brands of hiking boots and athletic shoes, but those might have been worn by the law enforcement personnel who had visited the site over the last several weeks.

The trees and bushes were myriad shades of green, only starting to change colors for the coming autumn. The ground cover was the usual mix of grass, lichens, and ferns. There were even a few blossoms left late in the alpine season; fuchsia monkeyflowers and violet penstemons and one lonely white trillium.

The lushness of the surroundings felt almost shameful. Violent death should not go unmarked. But wasn't this what she loved about nature? If left to her own devices, nature could heal all the wounds inflicted by humans. Wasn't that what Kim and Kyla loved, too? Sam hoped they'd had a chance to enjoy the beauty of this place before...

She didn't want to finish the sentence, even in her mind.

Chase lowered himself onto the rock ledge beside her, extending his long legs out to rest his heels in a patch of moss. He wrapped his arm around her shoulders. "I'm sorry I didn't make it to the memorial service."

"You didn't know them. I met them less than a year ago." She'd instantly bonded with the mother and daughter on a trail maintenance crew last November.

Chase studied her face. "Are you glad we came?"

"Glad" was a poor word choice, too. Sometimes human language was simply inadequate. She swallowed around the lump that partially blocked her throat. "I had to see it. Thanks for coming with me."

She and Chase had the place to themselves. They were not supposed to be here at all. The Forest Service trail was officially closed. But years of experience with lack of staff in wild places had taught Sam that there would be no ranger or deputy to stop them. If by chance they had been challenged after passing the "Closed—No Entry" sign, Chase could argue that as an FBI agent, he had cause to investigate a crime site on federal land.

On the way into the trailhead parking lot, they had passed a lone driver, a man in a baseball cap driving a silver Subaru Forester. Others had come as well, at least as far as the parking lot: an informal memorial had grown up by the trail register. Soggy sympathy cards and a heart woven out of grass nestled among two incongruous teddy bears and a pink Valentine-shaped Mylar balloon that had no business defiling a natural area.

Balloons were notorious for killing wildlife.

Both Kyla and Kim would have been outraged to find one here.

A faint scratching sound made her turn to check the rocks that flanked both sides of her. A Townsend's chipmunk, its tail flicking up and down, edged away from her pack and the remains of their brunch. The striped rodent froze, eyeing her. Its cheeks bulged suspiciously.

Sam pulled the leftover crackers and cheese into her lap. The chipmunk dashed to the top of a boulder a few feet away, where he twitched and chittered, loudly broadcasting the news of these giant intruders in his territory.

"Were you here when they were murdered?" she asked the animal. "Did you see what happened?"

The chipmunk leapt from the rock and vanished into the underbrush.

"That's what I figured." Sam stuffed a wheat cracker into her mouth and chewed. "Nobody saw anything."

Nobody except for Kyla and Kim, of course. And whoever killed them.

If she hadn't been in Idaho with Chase at his family reunion, she would have been hiking here on August second with her friends. After conquering all the familiar trails off the road to Mount Baker, they'd been on a mission to explore the trails further south along the Mountain Loop Highway. If she had been here at Pinnacle Lake instead of partying with Chase's Latino-Lakota clan, would Kim and Kyla still be alive?

Chase matched a cracker with a piece of cheese, inspecting both carefully before raising the snack to his lips. "I'm so sorry about Kyla and Kim. But if you'd been here, you might have been killed, too."

Sam didn't respond. As a child, she'd been sleeping, absent from her mother's deathbed. Absent, out kayaking alone when her colleague died in the Galapagos Islands. Absent, away in Idaho when her friends died right here.

In age, Sam was nearly equidistant between Kyla and Kim. But she shared a special bond with Kyla, perhaps because they resembled each other, at least superficially. Like Sam, Kyla was petite with long white-blond hair, although Kyla had warm brown eyes and a splash of playful freckles across her nose, while Sam's skin was uniformly pale and her eyes were a cool gray-green. Also like Sam, Kyla spent weeks at a time backpacking in the wild, while Kim worked behind a desk, escaping only for occasional day hikes with her daughter and Sam.

Kindred spirits were hard to find. The loss of her friends felt like a bruise that might never heal. Sam touched her fingers to Chase's thigh. "You checked the case file for me, right? What *do* they have?"

Chase covered her cold fingers with his own warm ones. "You really want to know?"

She nodded. "It can't hurt any more than it does already."

Letting go of her hand, he pulled a wad of pages from the pocket of his windbreaker, smoothed them across his thigh, and read. "Kyla Quintana-Johnson was shot in the back with a 30-06 rifle bullet. A second bullet, most likely from a .357 revolver, was lodged in her brain. That bullet entered her forehead."

Sam sucked in a breath that made her heart hurt.

"Kimberly Quintana was killed by a single .357 bullet to the brain that entered through her forehead."

At least, Sam tried to console herself, their deaths sounded like they'd happened quickly. The women hadn't been raped or tortured.

"No bullet casings or other bullets were found in the vicinity of the bodies, and unfortunately, those are very common weapons. The surrounding ground was hard and dry; the only footprints found were near the lakeshore. Imprints were taken of those; bits and pieces of trash collected from around the scene, but there are no links to anything substantive yet. The trail register was checked, but the pages were wet and the pencil was missing and no hikers had signed in on that day."

That figures, Sam thought. The registers, which were supposed to be used by the Forest Service to record trail usage by hikers, were rarely collected. Often the pages inside the crude wooden boxes had no place left to write and there was no implement provided to write with.

"No witnesses found so far."

The lake in front of her morphed into an impressionist painting. Sam wiped at her tear-filled eyes but only succeeded in blurring her vision even more. "Can I see the crime scene photos?"

"No." Chase folded the pages and stuffed them back in his pocket. "Trust me; you don't want to remember your friends that way." He checked his watch, then stood up. "We both need to get moving."

Taking his hand, she pulled herself up from the rock. "Was there anything in there about suspects?"

"Christopher Rawlins and Troy Johnson are regarded as persons of interest."

"No way." Sam shook her head. She'd spent time with both Kyla's boyfriend and Kim's husband. Neither seemed remotely capable of premeditated murder. "Troy's the one who convinced me to take this damn job."

"At least it's a normal job," Chase said.

"Is it?" She'd had so many crazy assignments in the past, she couldn't be sure.

In less than three hours, she needed to be back in

Bellingham at the offices of Washington Wilderness Quest. There she would take charge of a troop of troubled teens whose surly attitudes would supposedly be changed forever by a twenty-one-day trek into the backcountry.

"Please, Sam, I'm desperate," Troy Johnson had begged her only a week ago.

Troy was Kim's grieving husband, Kyla's grieving father. Although their talk was supposed to be about business, and they were in a busy brewpub, it was proving to be a painful experience for both of them.

"I can more or less cope with Kim's admin jobs," he confided, sliding his eyeglasses up his nose. The glasses were thickly framed in black, an old style that was all the latest rage. "I can't take Kyla's place out in the field. Our other field guide already left for his teaching job in Montana." He drew a line down the side of his sweating beer glass with his fingertip. "We have several grant applications out right now, and there's no way we'll land a single one if we don't have a full contingent of qualified staff. You'd be a perfect field guide, Sam."

She'd scoffed at that idea. "I am a wildlife biologist, Troy. I have zero experience with counseling troubled kids. Zero experience with kids, period."

If Kim were still alive, she could have told her husband that humans were Sam's least favorite species.

They were seated in a corner of the tap room at Boundary Bay, and the ambient roar was growing as the pub filled with drinkers.

"You have all the skills we need in the field." Troy leaned in to be heard, his elbows on the table as he ticked off the requirements on his long fingers. "You have a college degree. You're a mature, stable adult."

Sam speculated that the "stable" part might be stretching the truth a bit.

"You have extensive wilderness experience in all sorts of weather; and you are a certified Wilderness First Responder for medical emergencies. And since you taught tracking skills for us earlier this year, you already know the system."

"I was only there for a few days," she argued, leaning forward, too.

"We'll teach you some techniques for dealing with the kids. Maya will be with you. She knows the ropes now. Aidan Callahan will be your other peer counselor. He knows what he's doing. The peer counselors carry gear, help set up and break down camp, keep watch on the client kids, and generally do whatever you tell them to. In the field, you're their boss."

Wow. She'd never had assistants before; she was usually a team of one.

"You'll have the backup of the mental health counselors in the office, and they'll take your place for two days halfway through the session to give you a break and check up on the kids."

Lifting his beer, Troy took a sip. Deep lines carved his forehead above weary gray eyes, and his cheeks were hollowed above his carefully trimmed white beard. Like Kyla's, Troy's hair was straight and pale, although his was more white than blond now. "You can't say you're not experienced in working with challenging teens; I see what you've done for Maya."

Sam still wasn't sure how she'd developed such a soft spot for the tough juvenile delinquent she'd met on a trail crew two years ago. "Maya has done everything for herself. It's not like I adopted her. She glommed onto me like a remora."

Just as Sam had feared, Maya Velasquez had been booted out of her foster home in Tacoma only days after she turned eighteen. She'd insisted on living in a tent in Sam's back yard for a few weeks, until Kim Quintana took pity on both of them and gave the girl the summer job as peer counselor with Wilderness Quest.

The edge of Troy's pale eyebrow lifted. "I have no clue what a remora is."

"It's a fish," she told him. "Remoras suction-cup themselves to bigger fish for a free ride."

Setting down his glass, Troy reached across the table to

place his hand on top of hers. His fingers were cool and damp. "My point, Sam, is that Maya accomplished a lot with your guidance, and that's exactly what these six kids need."

Pulling her hand from beneath his, she fingered the beer-stained coaster on the table in front of her.

"It's only for twenty-one days," he continued. "The parents signed their kids up long ago; they're counting on us. It's the last expedition of this year, and there's no way I can find someone to fill the job now. I'll pay you three times the usual salary."

The last was a hard offer to turn down. Had Kim told her husband that Sam's last writing contract had fallen through, leaving her unemployed? Awkward emotions of guilt and shame wrestled with each other in Sam's head.

"You know that Wilderness Quest was Kim's dream," Troy pressed. "She wanted this to be her legacy, helping troubled kids find the right path."

Oh, yeesh. Of course Sam knew; mother and daughter had often sung the praises of the wilderness therapy program Kim had created.

Cupping both hands around his beer glass, he stared into the amber liquid. "I didn't even kiss Kim goodbye that morning. And I hadn't seen Kyla for weeks; when she wasn't out in the mountains with the Quest kids, she was with Chris." His voice wavered, and he paused to swallow before adding, "Kim left a chicken in the fridge to thaw for dinner."

Sam struggled to bring into focus her final moments with her friends.

Kim, her face damp with perspiration after their climb from Iceberg Lake to Herman Saddle. She'd swept her arm across the panorama of Mount Shuksan to the east and Bagley Lake far below them, saying, "This is what cures the kids: nature."

Kyla, laughing with Sam after they simultaneously turned the wrong way during a dance lesson at the Kickin' A Saloon.

At least her last memories of her friends were happy ones.

Troy's tired eyes glistened. "I can't let Wilderness Quest fail. Kim and Kyla..." His Adam's apple bobbed down and back up. "They'd be so happy to know you're taking Kyla's place. That you're helping us go on."

No fair playing the murdered friends card.

How could she say no?

"Summer?" Chase's voice shattered the memory, abruptly dropping her back into the present. He always called her by her given name, insisting that Summer perfectly matched her fair coloring and outdoorsy inclinations. "We really need to go, or I'm going to miss my flight."

Sam gazed at Pinnacle Lake one last time. Shouldering her pack, she murmured softly to the atmosphere, "Kim. Kyla. I miss you guys so much."

Putting a hand on her shoulder, Chase squeezed gently.

"We always said that if we died out in the wild, we'd die doing what we loved," she told him. "But we were talking about being mauled by bears or falling off cliffs or getting swept over a waterfall. We never imagined being slaughtered by a madman."

"No one does, *querida*." He tilted his head toward the trail.

They started down the steep path, the soles of their boots obliterating dozens of other prints from hikers who had trudged up and down this trail over the summer.

The authorities had recovered bullets from the bodies, but no casings from the scene. She'd learned enough about guns from Chase to understand that without bullet casings or the rifle or revolver that fired them, the slugs recovered from her friends' bodies were useless except to explain the cause of death and narrow down the types of weapons used. One 30-06 rifle, one revolver. Or perhaps even two revolvers.

Was the killer a man? A woman? One killer or two? So many unanswered questions. Detritus collected at the scene might contain traces of DNA and maybe even fingerprints, but those were useless without a specific individual to match.

She followed Chase's lean figure down the mountainside. Had the killer hiked this same winding trail? Were they trampling vital evidence? The hundreds of bits of rubbish

ground into each mile of trail would drive any crime scene
investigator crazy. She routinely picked up stray items every
time she hiked, a small good deed to keep wild areas pristine.
On her way up the trail, she'd bagged a button, two candy bar
wrappers, a torn nylon strap with a rusty buckle, and a small
packet of tissues that had slipped unnoticed out of a hiker's
pocket. She knew other hikers who collected garbage along the
routes they traveled. Evidence could easily have been carried
away by environmental do-gooders.

Hell, for that matter, half the debris in her trash bag might
have been transported here by investigators. Dozens of
officials had tramped up and down this trail since that day,
photographing the scene, carrying the bodies, or just coming to
gawk like humans did anytime something exciting happened.

Why didn't perpetrators ever conveniently isolate their
clues from the background mess?

"Too bad the real world is nothing like CSI on television,"
Chase said over his shoulder, reading her mind again.

She needed to change the subject. "I so wish you lived here,
Chase."

"I put down the Seattle office as my OP. But it's a long shot."

Sam understood that meant that Agent Starchaser Perez
had requested a transfer from his Salt Lake City FBI office to
his "office of preference" in Seattle, but the Bureau seemed to
run like the army; agents had little say in where they were
assigned. Today, after a three-day visit, her lover was rushing
off in typical spook fashion to an FBI explosives training
course in a location he refused to disclose to her.

"I'm trying," he added.

Was there was an unspoken "Are *you?*" after that sentence?
She still felt guilty about turning down Chase's proposal to
move in with him in Salt Lake City. Did he truly understand
her reasons, or was he only pretending to be patient because
he hadn't yet found a replacement girlfriend?

There was no time to sort it out now. Chase had a plane to
catch and she had to get to this blasted job. Just thinking about
the assignment knotted the muscles between her shoulder

blades. Twenty-one days, she reminded herself. She couldn't save her friends, but she could help save their dream. Three weeks, and she would be done with this commitment to the ghosts of Kyla and Kim.

She paused to pick up a plastic bottle top and a gum wrapper from the side of the trail.

"Summer?" Chase prompted, glancing back over his shoulder. "I know we came in separate cars, but I want to make sure you get back safely to yours."

"I'm right behind you." Sam stuffed the trash sack into her pack and focused on hustling down the mountainside, keeping a wary eye on the thick forest around them, watching for the glint of a rifle barrel or some obvious sign of evil lurking along the trail.

"Think you can find your way out of here?" he asked as they neared the parking lot.

"I got here, didn't I? My trusty GPS lady helped."

He ran a knuckle over the dark whiskers already starting to shadow his jaw line. "The GPS unit you haven't updated in a decade?"

"Forest roads haven't changed much in ten years either, Chase."

"Touché." He practically galloped to his rental car, but she grabbed him before he slid into the driver's seat and wrapped her arms around him, pressing her ear against his heart and squeezing hard. For a change, he was the first to pull away. "I'll see you again in a few weeks."

"You never know," she murmured. Every goodbye could be the last.

"We'll talk tonight." His kiss was too quick.

They both slid into their cars, and Chase waited until she'd started up her Civic before he peeled out of the lot in a cloud of dust.

Sam shut off her car engine. Walking back to the memorial, she plucked out the Mylar balloon and stabbed it through the heart with a car key before stuffing the deflated remains into her back seat and heading for Bellingham.

2

When Sam arrived at the Wilderness Quest office, she found Troy in the administrator's office. The name *Troy Johnson* had replaced *Kimberly Quintana* on the door plaque.

"It's best not to remind clients of our tragedy," Troy explained. "We were lucky to keep the Wilderness Quest connection out of the news." He grimaced. "Probably helps that Kim never took my last name."

Kim had always maintained that Quintana was a much more interesting name than Johnson, but Sam was not going to share that comment with her friend's husband.

Troy noticed Sam staring at the empty spot where Kim's computer had rested. "The police took her laptop. They took mine from home, too. And my cell phone. They already had Kim's and Kyla's."

She didn't know what to say.

His expression grim, he fingered his beard. "Kim had a hefty life insurance policy, with me as beneficiary. I had one, too, but they'll figure I took that out just to make the situation look less suspicious."

Sam groaned. "Oh, Troy."

"The spouse is always a suspect. I should know." Troy Johnson was a retired deputy prosecuting attorney from the Whatcom County court system.

The kids in her expedition "crew," as Wilderness Quest

liked to call each group of client kids, had arrived in town yesterday, along with their parents. All of them had met with the company's counselors, who reiterated the goals of wilderness therapy—healing old wounds, strengthening family relationships, setting realistic expectations for the future, breaking bad habits. A three-week expedition into the backcountry was a chance for teens to escape the distractions of a perpetually connected world and learn to rely on themselves and find joy in the present. The kids were examined individually by a physician and a psychologist while the parents met with Troy for a frank discussion of their issues and expectations.

Today the kids would be counseled; relieved of personal clothing, jewelry, electronics, drugs, and weapons; and issued uniforms for the outing.

While the staff readied the kids and equipment for the field, Troy installed Sam in an empty counselor's office to watch recorded videos of his interviews with the parents.

The staff had taken photos of the kids as they'd first arrived yesterday, and Sam held them in her hands now to match up kids and parents.

The first video segment was labeled *Olivia Bari, Toledo, Ohio, 16*. In her intake photo, the girl wore a green striped blouse tucked into close-fitting jeans. With her olive skin, long raven hair wrapped in a green headscarf, thick eyeliner, and dangling filigree earrings, the girl resembled a stereotypical gypsy. But Olivia had far more lines engraved on her forehead than any sixteen-year-old should.

Setting the photo aside on the desk, Sam started the video on the computer screen. The camera offered a fish-eye view over Troy's shoulder from the corner of his office. Like their daughter, the Baris' builds were on the small end of average, and they both had bronze skin and dark eyes. The father's hair was graying; the mother's was covered by a paisley scarf.

"Frequent truancy." Troy read aloud from Olivia's file, which lay open on the desk between him and the parents.

Mr. Bari nodded. "She says she goes, but then the school

calls and tells us she doesn't."

"She lies," Mrs. Bari affirmed, her gaze fixed downward.

"She is disrespectful," the father added. His accent—Middle Eastern?—was barely noticeable, but his choice of words were too formal for a native-born American.

"I understand." Troy folded his hands on top of his desk. "Olivia tried to commit suicide by taking pills?"

"It was an accident," the mother assured him, looking up to meet his eyes. "The pills were Tylenol. She had a headache and didn't know how many to take."

Sam leaned away from the screen. *Yikes.* The first kid in her crew was a suicide risk? How many pills had Olivia taken—ten, fifty? She shook her head, already feeling out of her element.

The conversation continued about Olivia's health: good, no allergies, no drug addictions, no smoking, no drinking.

"There will be boys on this trip?" Mrs. Bari looked worried at the prospect.

"Yes," Troy confirmed. "But you have no need for concern. Our field guide and our two peer counselors will keep Olivia safe at all times." He paused, waiting until both parents nodded. "Now, can you tell me what you hope to gain from enrolling Olivia in Wilderness Quest?"

"We want her to be happy," Mr. Bari said. "We want her to go to school."

Pursing her lips, Sam blew out a long breath. It sounded so simple.

Next up: *Gabriel Schmidt, Boise, Idaho, 18.* The photo revealed Gabriel to be a large boy who reminded her uncomfortably of the white flour dumplings she had eaten with stew last night. He wore an extra-large T-shirt and the saggy knee-length shorts that corpulent males everywhere seemed to favor.

The interview video showed that, like Gabriel, both Mom and Dad Schmidt had pasty complexions and were significantly overweight. To Sam's surprise, their issues were all about their son's use of his computer.

"Gabriel won't come out of his room. He stays up all night

playing games."

"He lives in an Internet world."

Troy consulted the boy's file. "Gabriel turned eighteen on August third?"

Both Schmidts nodded.

"You realize that means that our staff, acting on your behalf, cannot compel Gabriel to do anything?" Troy asked.

The point seemed irrelevant to Sam. She'd had a day of coaching by the counselors, but she was pretty sure she couldn't *compel* a teenager, especially one as large as Gabriel, to do anything he didn't want to.

Mr. Schmidt squirmed in his chair. His wife spoke for both of them. "He understands that this is *our* condition for him continuing to live at home."

At least Gabriel had received his high school diploma a few months ago; that put him ahead of the other kids. And there was no mention of drugs or alcohol.

"He's got to come out of his bedroom," Gabriel's father reiterated. "If he's not going to go to college, he needs to get a job."

Sam rubbed her forehead. Why didn't the Schmidt family just take away the computer or game console Gabriel used to feed his Internet addiction? Mom and Dad appeared to be in their late fifties or early sixties, with graying hair. Maybe Gabriel had been a late-life baby. Maybe they were just tired.

If the Schmidts looked worn, Justin Orlov's parents appeared downright elderly. Which was soon explained by their answers to Troy's questions: they were Justin's maternal grandparents. They'd legally adopted Justin at age nine, and changed Justin's last name to theirs. Justin's father had killed their daughter in a drunken domestic violence incident. The father was now eight years into a twenty-five-year prison sentence.

Sam chewed on her thumbnail. Another family coping with murder. In his photo, Justin glowered at the camera, his fists clenched at his sides. He was a tall, muscle-bound boy with a blond buzz cut the Marines would appreciate. A dragon tattoo crawled up the left side of his neck, the beast's snarling head and one clawed foot emerging from the neck of his black T-shirt. Justin was a seventeen-year-old who could pass for twenty-three. Repeatedly suspended from school for bullying. On probation for vandalism and assault.

The Orlovs lived in Los Angeles. They were terrified their grandson was going to end up a professional gangbanger.

With his family history, the kid had probably learned his threatening behavior from the cradle. She made a mental note to keep Justin away from anything that could be a weapon. Sam licked her lips, trying to imagine how she would handle this boy. A stun gun might be a good addition to the standard field guide equipment.

Taylor Durand, Sacramento, California, 16. The teen was a tall angular girl. Her straight blond hair, artistically streaked with strands of burnished copper and platinum, dangled past her shoulders. Her bright red lipstick matched the off-the-shoulder blouse tucked into her skinny jeans. Her face was a matte beige mask that spoke of a layer of heavy foundation.

Sam started the video. Like his daughter, Taylor's father was tall and blond and casually handsome. The mother was of average appearance, with an expensive angled haircut and sophisticated makeup. The problems with Taylor?

"She doesn't think she needs to complete high school," the father said. "All she cares about is becoming a fashion model. And we've found drugs in Taylor's room, too."

"Mainly diet pills," the mother added.

Mainly? Sam leaned back in her chair. Would Taylor be in some sort of quaking, hallucinating withdrawal during this expedition? Sam reminded herself of the promotional video she'd watched on the company website. Kids with drug issues came into the program only after going through rehab. Taylor might be jonesing for a fix during the expedition, but she wouldn't be actively detoxing.

Nick Lewis, Everett, Washington, 15. Sam's youngest draftee, and the one closest to home. Nick's photo showed a slight dark-haired boy wearing a green plaid shirt that was at least two sizes too big, the sleeves turned up into French cuffs, double-buttoned in place around his skinny wrists. As a petite woman who lived in perpetually rolled-up sleeves, Sam knew that trick well. Nick held his hands clasped in front of his stomach as if they were cuffed together. One of the two buttons on his right sleeve was missing; a red thread dangled in its place.

Unlike his son, the video showed Mr. Lewis was a muscular man with thick sandy hair and several days' worth of whiskers on a jutting chin that he stroked throughout the interview. His complaints about his son? Too many school absences. This was obviously a common theme among the clients.

Leaning forward as if to confide in Troy, he murmured, "His mother always said he was 'sensitive,' but really, he needs to grow a pair."

"The file says Nick cuts himself," Troy stated bluntly. "And the doc says some of his cuts appear to be recent."

"Well, yeah, he does that sometimes," Mr. Lewis confirmed. "Why the hell would any kid do that?"

Troy said, "Cutting usually indicates that the child feels a lot of stress."

"Huh." The father's face reddened. He straightened in his chair. "Nick has no reason to be stressed out." He leaned forward again, putting both hands on Troy's desk. "Look, Nick's mom is not in the picture, but he has me. He likes the outdoors, so this seemed like the place to straighten him out. We've been through a rough patch lately."

"Anything we should know about?"

"No." Mr. Lewis shook his head. "No. It was really nothing special. Teenagers, you know?" He grinned, but his smile seemed forced.

Troy nodded. "I know."

"Besides, we can't change the past, right? We all need to put the past behind us; everything is about the future, right?"

"That's what we focus on here," Troy reassured the man. "Acknowledge the past, but embrace the future."

"Nick's basically a good kid. All he needs is to man up."

"We'll take good care of your son," Troy promised.

Sam blew out a long slow breath and twisted her head from side to side, trying to loosen her neck and shoulder muscles. So far, her troop included a suicidal girl, a boy who cut himself, the on-probation son of a violent killer, and a kid who lived inside a video game. Taylor, the would-be model, seemed by far the most normal.

She picked up the photo of the last contestant. *Ashley Brown, Spokane, Washington, 16.* The girl's photo revealed short chestnut hair cut into spiky layers, the tips died purple. Her mascara and eyeliner were so heavy, the girl resembled a raccoon. Her ears were lined with multiple earrings, and a safety pin adorned her left eyebrow. She'd taken scissors to the tight T-shirt she wore, cutting a deep vee to reveal the cleavage between her generous breasts.

Ashley Brown's mother was another single parent. Like her daughter, her body was all curves. The face beneath her blond-streaked hair was pretty. Her words were anything but.

"Ashley is a smart-aleck skank," the mother told Troy. "She dropped out of school. She's run away three times. She's even sold herself on the streets. She's got to straighten up or she's going to end up with AIDS. Or dead."

Sam sucked in a breath. AIDS? Dead? At sixteen?

"Is she close to her father?" Troy asked.

Ashley's mom narrowed her eyes and sat back in her chair with a heavy sigh. "Neither of us is close to her father. He's a snake. I don't know what I ever saw in that man."

Add one teen prostitute to the troop.

The poor parents. The poor kids. With the possible exception of the Durands, none of these families came across as wealthy. Wilderness Quest was a nonprofit, but the costs of maintaining a staff and equipping and feeding all the participants during outdoor therapy were high. Maybe some of these clients had generous health insurance that was paying for this expedition, but she suspected most had scraped together the fee as a last hope of straightening out their kids.

It was depressing.

She didn't want to deal with any of it; she was already depressed enough.

The door opened. Maya stepped in, dressed in her yellow uniform shirt with STAFF printed front and back, quick-dry cargo pants, and hiking boots. "I just wanted to say hi, 'cause we're not supposed to act like we know each other out there. I'm glad you're on this trip."

Sam hadn't seen Maya since the girl started working for Kim. She turned off the computer, stood up, and hugged her teenage friend. "I'm glad *you're* on this trip, because I don't know what I'm doing."

She also realized that she and Maya hadn't had the chance to talk about the murders. Kim and Kyla had been Maya's mentors and colleagues. "I'm so sorry I didn't call you, Maya."

The girl pulled out of her embrace. "You couldn't call, at least most of the time. I worked the trip that ended just a couple days ago."

"I know you're missing Kim and Kyla, too."

A cyclone of emotion tore swiftly through Maya's dark eyes, and she caught her lower lip between her teeth for a second. Then the girl put a hand on Sam's forearm and squeezed. "Shit happens."

She turned toward the doorway, but stopped before exiting to look back. "It helps a lot to be out there, Sam. You'll see." Maya closed the door softly behind her.

Shit happens.

Sam slumped back into the chair. A lot of shit had happened to Maya Velasquez in her eighteen years. She's lost her dad and then her mom to drugs, endured a series of foster homes, and paid for her juvenile burglary convictions through grueling trail work.

Compared to Maya's, Sam's life had been a picnic. When it came to enduring hardship, Summer Westin was a wimp.

Crossing her arms on the desk, Sam lowered her head onto them, envisioned herself back in Boundary Bay brewpub, savoring a cold ESB and a pile of yam fries.

"You're doing God's work," her father had remarked when

she told him she would miss their regular Sunday evening phone calls while she filled in for Kyla at Wilderness Quest.

She'd considered asking him why God wasn't doing his own work, but she knew that Reverend Mark Westin would have an answer that she probably didn't want to hear. She envied him his faith, if not his lifestyle in rural Kansas.

"Ready?"

She jerked her head up, startled.

Troy stood in the doorway with a much younger man beside him. "The kids and the gear are loaded in the van. Ready, Sam?"

"Not really." She stood up anyway.

"Did you watch the videos?"

"Yep. That's why I'm not ready."

Troy covered the distance between them with a few long strides and wrapped her in an awkward hug. "We got lucky this time. None of these kids are too hard core; we didn't have to lock up a single one last night and let me tell you, that's pretty rare."

"Good for them. Good for me."

"You have your notebook with all the exercises; you'll be fine. And Aidan and Maya have done it all before. Speaking of which..." He gestured to the young man to join them. "This is Aidan Callahan."

Aidan's appearance was as Irish as his name. He was nearly as tall as Troy, with reddish brown hair and freckles dotting his face and arms. His cheeks and chin looked freshly shaven.

Troy patted the young man on the back. "Aidan is in his last year of college. This is his third year with us, and we've known him since he was a kid. If he comes back next summer, he'll be a field guide. For now, he's your dependable second-in-command."

Aidan shot Troy an indecipherable look, then turned to her. "I've got your back, Sam."

She shook hands with him. "Glad someone knows what they're doing."

Aidan gave her a little salute, and then turned toward the door.

"You'll be fine," Troy reassured her for the second time. "Remember that you get a two-day break halfway through when the counselors come up to relieve you."

At least she had that to look forward to. With luck, Chase would be able to escape from work again in ten days and they could spend the time together.

Troy gave her a final quick squeeze. "Thanks again, Sam."

"Don't thank me yet. I might march them all off a cliff." Hefting her backpack from the floor, she squared her shoulders and followed him to the parking lot.

"You can't do this to me! Nobody does this to me." The muscular youth hurled a volley of curses in Sam's direction, and then spat on the ground for good measure, narrowly missing the toe of his new hiking boot.

"Yeah," someone else in the group growled, the sound nearly drowned out by the slam of the Wilderness Quest van door.

Sam, bent over her pack, took her time zipping the pouches before she stood up to inspect her clutch of hostile teens. Her crew had made the trip behind a blackout curtain in the windowless back of the van, company policy to ensure they couldn't see the route they were taking. Her two peer counselors, Maya and Aidan, rode in back with them, keeping the kids calm during the trip into the mountains. Sam had accompanied the driver up front.

The teenagers now stood in a semicircle in front of her, fidgeting, fingering their back pockets, sneaking glances at her and at each other. With no cell phones to focus on, they were uncertain about where to put their hands or eyes.

Devoid of cosmetics and jewelry and distinctive clothing, their appearance varied from their intake photos. Each wore an orange bandanna around his or her neck or forehead, or in the case of Olivia, twisted into a headband. Without makeup, Taylor's face was surprisingly freckled, and Ashley, raccoon eyes scrubbed away and piercings emptied, turned out to be a pretty girl whose delicate features could pass for a fourteen-year-old's.

The teens were outfitted in identical boots and multi-pocketed pants. Their long-sleeved blue Capilene shirts had their names printed front and back in bold white letters for easy identification, which seemed a bit ominous in itself.

The spitter was Justin. The boy with the dragon tattoo was a foot taller and probably a hundred pounds heavier than she. With his buzz cut, dramatic tatt, and bulging muscles, he could have recently emerged from a prison yard where he'd pumped iron. Judging from the expression on his square face, the kid wanted to punch her. Wanted to punch anyone, or possibly, everyone. He had the build to inflict serious damage, too.

The other five stood sullen and awkward. Shy Olivia, her long black hair woven into a braid down her back, focused on the ground. The youngest, Nick, whose shirt was again too big, stared at the distant horizon to the north, where the endless peaks of the Cascades blended into the Coastal Range in British Columbia. The other three faces were frozen into defiant glowers aimed at Sam and the two peer counselors on either side of her.

To a naïve observer, the kids in front of her could be mistaken for a teen club. They were actually closer to a chain gang, without the chains. They were essentially prisoners. Her prisoners, for the next three weeks.

She needed an attitude adjustment. Not prisoners, she decided, more like soldiers.

Why had she agreed to be a drill sergeant when she'd never gone through boot camp herself?

The van's engine roared to life, and the driver—Andrew? Anders?—gave Sam a brief wave on the last leg of his three-point turn. *Don't leave me here*, she felt like screaming.

Instead, she sucked in a breath and took a step forward. "I know you've already had a long day."

"Ya think?" snarled Justin, his voice a deep baritone.

Eighteen-year-old Gabriel shook his head. He was as tall as Justin, but puffy instead of muscular, with a spray of pimples across his forehead, and another crop sprouting in the fold between his right cheek and nostril. "I can't fuckin' *believe* they took my tablet. *And* my phone."

"No swearing, please," Sam said.

Fists clenched at his sides, Justin took a step forward. "What the fuck *you* gonna do about it?"

Aidan stiffened defensively beside her. Sam thrust a hand in front of him to signal the college student to stop whatever he was about to do, and then repeated the company mantra. "No swearing, please."

Then she put her hands on her hips in an attempt to appear authoritative. "This is how it's going to go, crew. In your backpacks, you each have a one-person tent, a sleeping bag, an inflatable sleeping pad, and enough clothes to keep you comfortable for the next three weeks."

There was a collective intake of breath among the teens.

"Gawd." Gabriel shook his head. "Did the apocalypse arrive yesterday?"

"This is, like, cruel and unusual," Ashley announced.

Most had probably imagined that they would be stuck in this hellhole for twenty-four hours, or maybe two days, max. With food caches and individual tents and the latest hi-tech clothing, the Wilderness Quest expeditions were actually quite cushy compared to similar youth therapy outings, but these kids seemed unlikely to appreciate that.

Although the August day was sunny, the breeze blowing up the valley was cool, a reminder that September would arrive in a week, along with autumn at this altitude. "If you're cold, unzip your pack and put on your fleece or your windbreaker."

Nobody moved. Maybe they were warm enough, but she suspected they all wanted to appear tough right now.

"You also have items in your packs that belong to the whole group, cooking gear and first aid kits and such. You need to take good care of everything; this is our survival equipment."

"Now, pick up your packs and buckle them on." She hefted her own and slid her shoulder through the strap. "We have five miles to hike before we can eat and sleep tonight, and it will be dark in a couple of hours."

Justin plopped down on the ground. "Fuck. I'm not going."

"Me neither." Taylor, the tall sixteen-year-old, tossed her long blond ponytail in defiance, folded her legs, and sat down a foot away from Justin. "This is bullshit."

Well, crap.

Sam gritted her teeth. She'd expected rebellion along the way, but not minutes into the job. She reviewed her few hours of training. *No pedantic lectures, teach lessons on outdoor skills, no special treatment, enforce personal responsibility, discourage bad behaviors.* What the hell was all that supposed to mean?

"Suit yourselves. The rest of us are going to go have dinner." Her jaw clenched, she strode to the two seated teens and quickly removed a cook set from the bottom of Justin's pack and a bundle of collapsible poles strapped onto Taylor's.

She stuffed the cook set into the pack lying in front of Olivia's feet. The small dark girl's lips twitched as if she might cry, but she remained silent. When she attached the poles to Nick's pack, he said, "Shit."

"No swearing, please." Sam took a dramatic last look at the cloud of dust left behind as the van disappeared down the road, and then cinched her pack strap around her waist. "Let's go."

She set off down the trail, glad to be facing the jagged peaks of the north Cascades instead of the teens. Behind her, she heard murmurs from Maya and Aidan as they flanked the trail, checking that boots were tied and pack straps cinched as their charges passed. The plan called for Maya to step into the middle of the line. Aidan would follow last. Sam felt footsteps behind her. She guessed that the closest would be Ashley, the sixteen-year-old runaway with purple-tipped hair. The busty girl had looked the most alarmed by the foreign environment in which she found herself. Skanks were apparently not outdoorsy types.

Sam chewed on her lower lip. This had to be some sort of record, losing a third of her group on the very first day out.

Hell, she'd lost them in the first *ten minutes.* Clearly she was not cut out for this job. Could she really leave Taylor and Justin behind? Should she turn back?

The clouds to the east and north were already tinged a light mauve by the sun descending below the horizon, but the sky overhead was clear. At this altitude, it would be cold tonight, but there would be stars.

She'd been told that sometimes all the kids complained as they walked; sometimes no words passed their lips for hours. Sam was glad the remaining kids in her group had chosen to suffer in silence, at least for now.

When she rounded a bend of the mountain ridge, she paused. The hikers bunched up behind her. Sam held a hand above her eyes to shield them from the setting sun as she looked back. To her great relief, a lithe silhouette trotted along the mountain trail, ponytail swinging as Taylor jogged to catch up. Twenty yards behind her was Justin's hunched hulk, jaw clenched as he stomped down the path.

"I'm starving," Ashley grumbled.

"Me, too," Sam lied. In truth, she'd had lunch after she had arrived in Bellingham at noon.

It was company policy not to feed the kids lunch on their first day. Hungry hikers were more likely to stick with the group.

"Shouldn't we at least get snacks?" Gabriel whined.

"No snacks." Sam experienced a twinge of guilt about the yogurt-covered almonds she'd consumed on the drive up. "We'll fix dinner when we get to camp."

Aidan stepped aside to allow Taylor and Justin to pass him and join the line of hikers. When her crew was complete, Sam set off on the darkening trail at a faster pace, wanting to arrive before they needed to dig out the headlamps in their packs.

Somewhere to the east, a crack reverberated across the ridges, and the muscles in her neck tightened in response. This trail was in the national forest; shooting was allowed. It was no doubt hunting season for something nearby. The Wilderness Quest jackets and packs were bright orange for that reason.

A second crack didn't follow the first, so maybe it wasn't a shot after all.

Or maybe the sound had only played in her imagination? She was afraid to ask any of the others. They were more than a hundred miles from Pinnacle Lake, two counties north of the murder site. But ever since the deaths of her friends, her brain had been working overtime, conjuring nightmare scenarios. The killer was still out there.

3

They made it the five miles to the first night's camp with only minor grumbling from the kids, but then, it was only five miles. The sun was already below the ridge when they arrived, and the air was rapidly cooling.

Dropping her pack, Sam surged into drill sergeant mode. "Aidan, Maya, show the crew where their tent sites are."

The two peer counselors quickly positioned the teens in a rough oval, each standing on a relatively flat spot in a clearing ringed by firs and pines. Wilderness Quest prepared all their group sites, even creating some new campsites, with the permission of the Forest Service and Park Service.

"Okay crew, we need to set up camp ASAP," Sam told the teens. "Drop your pack on your tent site, pull the headlamp out of the right side pouch and put it on so you can see what you're doing. Have any of you ever set up a tent before?"

After several seconds, Nick tentatively raised his hand.

"Used a camp stove?" she asked next.

Another long pause, and then Nick's hand went up again.

"Teacher's pet poodle," Ashley sneered.

Nick dropped his hand and glared at her through eyes squeezed almost shut.

Justin emitted a couple of shrill barks, sounding like a yappy Chihuahua.

"Knock it off," Sam ordered. "It's getting dark, and it's

getting cold. Pull some warmer clothes out of your packs. You're all responsible for setting up your own tents. And then blow up your sleeping pads and unroll your sleeping bags inside."

A collective groan went up, punctuated by a few muttered expletives.

"Everyone must complete those tasks before we can start on dinner, so help each other as needed. Nick can show you how. Taylor." She pointed to the tall girl. "When that's all done, come tell me."

Sam strolled to her own tent site, sandwiched between two Douglas firs and thankfully positioned twenty yards from the group. Doing her best to ignore the whining and insults flying among the kids behind her, she donned her own headlamp, then quickly assembled her tent frame, snapped the green nylon tent and rain fly onto it, rolled out her sleeping pad and bag, and crawled in on top of them. Pulling a phone, compact power pack, and earbuds from her pack, she hid them beneath her sleeping bag. She extracted her long johns to sleep in, shoving them to one side. She was in the process of pushing her spare clothes into her sleeping bag stuff sack to create a pillow when Taylor approached.

The girl shuffled her feet in the dirt. "Ummm?"

"Yeah?"

"I think they're all set up."

Sam poked her head out, and she and Taylor simultaneously blinded each other with their headlamps.

"Sorry." Sam ducked her chin to move the beam out of the girl's eyes. "You think or you know? It's your job to check."

Even without the benefit of the headlamp, Sam could feel Taylor rolling her eyes. "I know they are."

"Okay, then." Sam slid out and straightened, wishing that she stood taller than Taylor's shoulder. It was a challenge to seem commanding at armpit level. "On to dinner, then." She strode toward the oval of eight yellow one-person tents. "Chore assignments, Maya?"

Maya gestured toward the cooking supplies she and Aidan

had laid out on top of a stump. "Justin, Taylor, fill these two large pots with water from the stream. Gabriel, Olivia, Ashley, you're going to open packages and chop vegetables and sausage. Nick, get the stoves ready."

"What are we having for dinner?" Nick surveyed the supplies.

"Spaghetti with tomato sauce and sausage," Aidan said. "And French bread."

Taylor made a face. "I don't eat pasta. Or bread."

Sam shrugged. "Suit yourself." At least she had the *no special treatment* act down. "Just FYI, all of you, this is the cushy evening, when we have gas stoves to cook on and matches to light them with. From here on out, you'll be making your own fires using the bow-drill method."

Making fire without matches or lighters was a survival skill the kids would learn to be proud of. She'd been pretty proud of herself when she'd mastered it for the first time four days ago.

Justin snorted. "Right. Like *that's* gonna happen."

"You said sausage?" Ashley chimed in. "I don't eat meat."

"You can pick out the summer sausage, then," Aidan told her. "We only have one pot to cook the sauce in."

"Are you *kidding* me?" Ashley's face twisted into a scowl. Several purple-tipped strands of hair were glued to her forehead, transforming her into a teenage gargoyle.

"Nope." Aidan grinned. "And after dinner, you can all help set up the screen around the toilet. We call it the Box with a View. You'll see why."

Sam suspected her male peer counselor might be enjoying his dominant role a bit too much, but the sociology major was the most experienced staff member in camp.

"Let's get cooking," she ordered.

Aidan handed Justin and Taylor each an aluminum pot. "I'll show you the stream."

Justin's pot dropped to the ground with a clang. Folding his arms across his chest, the tattooed teen snapped, "I ain't no slave."

Sam crossed her own arms. She was going to develop an

ulcer in record time. A tension headache was already gnawing at her forehead.

"All right then," Maya said mildly. She faced the others. "Gang, Justin has decided not to eat tonight. Who wants to do his job and get his share?"

Sam mentally blessed the girl.

Gabriel jogged over and picked up the pot. "I'm starving." He turned to Aidan. "Let's go."

Taking two steps forward, Justin ripped the pot out of Gabriel's hands. He tapped Gabriel's headlamp upward on the other boy's forehead, snapping the light off. "I oughta pound that headlight into your brain, game boy." Then he stomped off after Aidan and Taylor.

Gabriel pulled his headlamp back into place on its elastic strap. Now pointed downward, the light cast his moon-shaped face into Halloween shadows. "Game boy?" he shouted after the departing trio. "I'm a Master Wizard!"

"Uh-huh," Olivia drawled from behind him, somehow managing to make the two syllables sound sarcastic. She ripped open a plastic bag of herbs, scattering a few flakes across the toes of her boots.

"I might be impressed if I knew what that meant, Gabriel," Maya remarked. "But I'll be more impressed after you chop this up." She handed him a large onion and a knife and motioned to the plastic cutting sheet unrolled on a stump top.

Shaking his head, Gabriel set down the onion and gave it a vicious chop, halving it. "A Master Wizard is level twelve. There's only thirteen levels to Vebulaze. Everyone knows that."

"Welcome to the real world," Nick hissed under his breath.

"Beam me off this ignoramus planet." Gabriel hacked at the onion, and Sam began to wonder about the wisdom of assigning the big kid to knife duty.

"Uh, Gabriel." Maya moved closer. "You need to take the outer peel off. Nobody wants to eat that brown paper stuff."

"News to me." The boy pointed the knife at her. "I never said I could cook."

Sam tensed, watching the knife.

Maya paused to snap her boot heels together, and then made a salaaming gesture, looping her hand in front of her chest. "If you please, Master Wizard of Vebulaze, may I show you how to remove the outer peel?"

Gabriel actually grinned. He gestured with his knife to the onion. "You may approach."

Together they bent over the onion. Troy Johnson had been right, Maya was a natural at dealing with these kids. It was amazing to think Maya and Gabriel were the same age.

Justin and Taylor tromped back into camp, each carrying a large pot of water. Aidan followed, his arms clasped around a heavy collapsible plastic container.

Sam gestured to the stove, and Justin thunked his pot down on the burner. "Shit, you wouldn't believe how fuckin' cold that water is."

She repeated the company line. "No swearing, please."

Justin loomed over her, using his massive bulk to appear menacing. "Then how the fuck are we supposed to talk?"

The gleam of his headlamp blanked out his features as she peered up at him. "Expand your vocabulary. You're a smart guy. I'm sure you can come up with something."

He rubbed his hands on his shirt for a long minute, drying them, and for a few seconds she worried he might erupt into violence. Then he shouted, "Gex!"

All activity stopped. Everyone turned to stare at him.

Standing straddle-legged, he put his fists on his hips and snarled, "What the gex you guys starin' at?"

Olivia laughed and nodded as she peeled the lid from a can of tomato paste.

"Lurik." Gabriel waved his knife. "I'm finished chopping this lurik onion."

"Then bring that meekam mess over here," Maya directed, waving a wooden spoon at the pot she was dumping chopped peppers into.

Gabriel frowned fiercely at her. "Lurik you!" But then he grinned, lifted the diced onion on the cutting sheet, and walked toward her.

"When the gex will dinner be done?" Justin asked.

Olivia waved a package of pasta at him. "Help me open these onu packages of spaghetti, and it would get done faster."

"Onu?" Nick turned from the stove he was tending. "That sounds like an animal." Switching to a newscaster tone, he held a fist beneath his chin like a microphone. "Today, in an unimaginable tragedy, an entire African village was wiped out by a rampaging herd of onu."

"Those lurik onu!" Gabriel yelped in falsetto.

Aidan waved his hands to encompass the cooking area. "Could we have a little meekam focus here?"

Everyone laughed.

Kyla had told her about these magic moments during expeditions. Sam was surprised and pleased that Justin had created the first one only hours after he'd refused to cooperate with the group.

They formed a circle to eat, sitting cross-legged on the ground. Their first night's camp was in a designated wilderness area; no fires were allowed. In the center of their circle were three candles, their flames creating the focal point that humans seem to crave in the darkness.

Taylor and Gabriel were appalled that the only drinking choice was local water.

"Why don't you have Coke?" Gabriel asked. "Everyone has Coke." His normal voice was higher than she'd expected, given the boy's size. That and his childlike attitude made him seem younger than eighteen.

Sam raised an eyebrow at him. "Do you want to carry a twenty-four-pack for us? There is herbal tea and powdered lemonade mix if you want to make yourself some."

The kid focused on his plate.

"This isn't even bottled water." Taylor shook her Nalgene container. "This is the same stuff that came out of that creek."

Sam noticed she was eating the pasta and the bread, in spite of her earlier objection.

"Aidan and I filtered it," Maya told her. "Tomorrow morning we'll show you all how to filter the water for your bottles."

Ashley studiously picked the sausage from her spaghetti, moving it to the edges of her plate. Beside her, Justin quickly cleaned his plate, and then reached over and scraped Ashley's sausage into his own with a remnant of his bread.

"Hey!" she objected.

He shoveled a bite of sausage into his mouth. "You weren't going to eat it."

"That's rude."

"That's hungry," Justin retorted.

None of the others said anything. After a full minute of glaring at each other, Ashley handed Justin her half-eaten bread. He stuffed the whole piece into his mouth and chewed, his cheeks bulging like the chipmunk Sam had encountered earlier that day.

Gabriel enviously eyed the plates around him, his expression darkening when he saw all were empty.

"Dessert is yogurt-covered almonds," Sam told them. "And then there's dishwashing before bed."

"What about showers?" Taylor asked.

Sam met her gaze. "You can take a dip in the creek in the morning if you like."

"I'll stand guard while the girls wash," Justin volunteered. "To protect their womanly virtue."

Gabriel's headlamp bobbed. "Me, too."

"I'm in." Nick fingered his earlobe, which Sam now noticed sported a pierced hole for an earring.

Taylor snorted, whipping her focus from boy to boy. "In your dreams." Pulling her ponytail over her shoulder, she stroked it like a cat.

Pressing her lips together, Olivia stared at her empty plate.

A small superior smile played across Ashley's lips. Sam wondered what she was thinking.

After standing up, Sam moved behind a tree to turn on the recording function of her cell phone as she'd been instructed. She slid the phone into her jacket pocket, hoping the microphone was good enough to pick up their voices from there, and then walked back to the group. "We are camping in a beautiful place. Before Aidan passes out dessert and you all get your cleanup assignments, I want each of you to appreciate one natural element around you. I'll start." She switched off her headlamp and gazed up. "The stars are incredible here. Without city lights or smog, we can see the Milky Way."

All faces swiveled toward the direction she indicated. "That's the cloudy-looking swipe in the sky there. It's our galaxy, which we share with billions of planets and stars."

"Vebulaze has twin galaxies connected by a wormhole," Gabriel informed them.

Justin set his plate on the ground in front of his crossed legs. "You do realize that's not a real place, don't you, Mister Lizard?"

"Master Wizard!" the pudgy boy corrected.

Throwing her hands out, Maya verbally jumped in to refocus the exercise. "I feel the cool breeze coming up from the valley. I'm glad it's not raining." She gestured to Nick.

The smallest boy glanced around, searching for something to comment on. "I'm glad the ground here is dry."

Sam nodded and shifted her attention to Justin.

"I'm glad I'm not sitting on this gex pinecone." Justin waved one in his hand. "We don't have to use 'em in the shitter, do we?"

"Feel free, Justin. The rest of us will use biodegradable TP." Aidan raised his arms, threw back his head, and addressed the heavens. "I love the silence here. No traffic horns, no backup beepers."

They all listened for a moment to the rustle of the breeze through the trees. Branches creaked as they rubbed together. A raven croaked its hoarse call in the distance. The song of nature.

"No tablets, no phones, no music," Ashley murmured under her breath. "Booorrring."

"You can sing and drum if you like." Sam suggested the options listed in her notebook.

The kids studied her like she'd grown an extra head.

The rest of their observations—the wind was cold, the camp was dirty, the ground was hard—could be categorized more as complaints than appreciation. Olivia offered a positive note, saying the creek water tasted good. At least they all had said something, and nobody had been punched or stabbed yet. Sam decided to count it as progress.

Pulling a leather cord strung with a single bead from her left hip pocket, she continued with her first-day script. "We will be spending three weeks together. At Wilderness Quest, we have a three-step program. Right now you are all classified as Zombies."

That got a laugh from several of them. Ashley stuck her tongue out of her mouth and held her arms stiffly in front of her as she waggled from side to side like an undead character in a movie.

"That means," Sam added, still following her script, "that you are not in control of your destiny, that you let something or someone else push you around."

"Hey!" Justin scowled. "Nobody pushes me around."

Sam raised an eyebrow at him. "Let me rephrase that. Being a zombie means you allow situations and other people to push your buttons. You are not in control of your emotions or your reactions."

The muscles along Justin's jaws clenched. The dragon's head tattooed on his neck looked as if smoke might snake out of its nostrils at any second.

Sam continued, "A Zombie must be accompanied at all times by a staff member. That includes when you go to the bathroom."

"Gawd, no!"

"You're kidding!"

"That's gotta be, like, illegal."

The rule was designed to prevent runaways, but Sam didn't like it any better than the kids did. She held up a hand to cut off the remarks. "When the staff—that's me and Maya and Aidan—all agree that you are willing to take some responsibility without being told and that you are willing to explore different possibilities, you will become a Voyager and receive this necklace." She held it up.

"Big lurik deal," Gabriel remarked.

"It's not fine jewelry," Sam agreed, pushing it back into her left pocket. "It's a symbol of growth."

Aidan chimed in. "Voyagers have the right to use the toilet without a staff member. Some of you will become a Voyager earlier than others. It could happen as early as tomorrow."

"Or never. There's not a set date like a graduation," Maya told them. "You could stay a Zombie for the whole three weeks."

"Finally," Sam took control of the conversation again, "if you show that you are assuming personal responsibility, if you show that you are willing to be a leader, an explorer, a decision maker for your own life, you will become a Navigator. Navigators wear these pendants." Feeling like an inept magician, she pulled out of her right hip pocket a beautifully carved wooden pendant of stars surrounding a compass.

She let the group pass it around, amazed when no smart-ass comments surfaced. After recovering the pendant, she pocketed it again. "Now it's time for our second exercise. We're going to go around the circle, and each of you will say your name and tell why you think you're here. Remember that honesty rules at Wilderness Quest."

She selected Gabriel to start.

"Uh, Gabriel Schmidt." He dug his fingers into the dirt on either side of his legs. "My parents sent me. But I don't really know why."

Taylor leaned forward. "Honesty rules!"

Gabriel blushed and blew out a breath. He fingered the pimples beside his nose, swiping a dark streak of dirt across his face. "Okay, they don't want me to play Vebulaze so much. But I still don't know why."

Taylor rolled her eyes, the whites gleaming in the flickering candlelight.

"Good enough for now, Gabriel." Sam turned to the dark girl. "Olivia."

The teen slouched as if the weight of the planet was on her shoulders. "My name's Olivia, like you just said. I'm here because I skipped school." She paused for a second, then added, "A lot."

"And?" Sam prompted.

Pulling her knees up, Olivia folder her arms around them. "I took some pills, too." When Ashley nodded, Olivia pointed to her.

"I'm Ash," the short-haired girl said, "Not Ash-lee like this stupid shirt says."

"Ass?" Justin chortled. "That's perfect."

She rewarded him with a vicious glare. "Ash! You better watch it, Dragon Neck, I have a switchblade." Embarrassed as she abruptly remembered her current situation, she amended, "Had a switchblade."

Sam's list of kids who shouldn't ever handle a kitchen knife was growing.

"Go ahead, Ash," she said. "I'll try to remember to call you that, but please forgive me if I don't."

The girl finger-combed her purple-streaked hair away from her forehead, making it stand straight up like a rooster's comb. "I'm here because I took some pills too. And shot up some H."

Oh, crap. Ashley's mother hadn't revealed that in the intake interview.

"And I've hit the road a few times." She lifted her chin, a slight smile crossing her lips, obviously proud of being a runaway.

Sam prompted her again. "And?"

Turning her head, the girl gave her a confused look.

Sam wasn't sure how blunt she should be. "The ... er ... customers?"

"Oh, that. Guys pay me for sex." Ashley pretended to be fascinated by a clump of pine needles beside her right leg. "It's no big deal. It's good money."

Sam hated that Ashley was using the present tense. She turned her attention to the next teen. "Nick."

The boy screwed up his lips for a second while he decided what to say. "I'm here because... because my father thinks I'm not masculine enough."

"That can't be a real reason," Justin scoffed.

Nick glared at him. "To my dad, it is. 'Man up,' he always says."

"Why?" Justin leaned forward. "Are you gay or some-"

Sam cut him off with a flick of her hand. "Irrelevant."

Olivia turned to Nick. "What about your mom?"

The fifteen-year-old stared at the ground in front of his hiking boots for a long moment. "My mom left when I was six. She took my sister with her." When he lifted his chin, his eyes were shiny, reflecting the candlelight.

Poor kid. Sam rested her palms on her knees, guru-style. "Justin, your turn. Why are you here?"

He stroked his fingers over the dragon's head on the side of his neck. "That's easy. My dad killed my mom."

The other kids expressed their shock with murmurs of "No way" and "Omigod" and quick intakes of breath.

"But that's your parents," Maya pointed out. "Why are *you* here?"

He folded his arms in front of his chest. "Because I get in fights, I guess."

Aidan leaned toward the candlelight. "You *guess*?"

Justin's gaze glided upward and he regarded the sky for a long moment as if he were counting to ten. "Whatever. So, my grands figured it was here or juvie jail."

According to his intake file, the tattooed kid might still be headed for juvenile lockup if he didn't do well here. Sam gestured to the last teen to talk, Taylor.

"I'm Taylor," the girl began, rocking forward and wrapping her arms around her knees. "My stupid parents sent me here just because I want to be a model."

"That can't be a real reason," Justin complained again. "Honesty, remember?"

Taylor scrunched up her face, showing her annoyance. "So I take a little speed now and then, and there's no point in finishing high school, because I can be a model without that."

The breeze had grown stronger and the kids were starting to curl up like hedgehogs, so Sam decided that was enough therapy for the first night. She handed off authority to assign the remaining kids' chores to Aidan and Maya. Cleanup progressed quickly with most pitching in. From her tent, Sam heard all the expected expressions of disgust as the group set up the nylon screen around the box toilet in the trees, and then Sam left Maya and Aidan to supervise its use, followed by hand washing and teeth brushing and getting the six kids into their tents.

The peer counselors fielded questions about bears (*could be, that's why we hung up the food*) and snakes (*nope, they'd freeze up here*) and wolves (*a faint possibility; if we're lucky we'll hear some*). From her tent, Sam listened to their final conversations.

Aidan: "If you're not sleepy, you can read or write in your journals. But we arise at sunup."

"As in *dawn*? No freakin' way!" Taylor or Ashley, Sam wasn't sure.

"*Arise?* We doin' Shakespeare now? Gex that." Justin, of course.

The breeze gusted through the forest. Something crashed in the dark woods.

"What was *that*?" Ashley squeaked. For all her tough demeanor, she was clearly a city kid.

Maya: "Probably a branch falling from a tree."

"*Probably?*" Gabriel.

Maya again: "You each have a whistle attached to your pack. Blow it if you need help during the night."

"Why would we need help?" Olivia.

"You probably won't." Maya again.

Aidan: "Everyone, put your shoes outside your tent door."

"Why?" Nick.

Maya: "Company policy. No shoes in tents."

"Lurik policy." Gabriel.

"Good night, crew!" A chorus sung in harmony by Maya and Aidan.

After a while, Sam heard rustles and murmured complaints of her campers, and then the soft footpads of Maya and Aidan as they tiptoed from tent to tent. The staff always collected the kids' shoes on the first few nights to discourage runners from vanishing into the darkness.

After changing into her long johns, Sam slid into her sleeping bag, yawning. She already missed her cat, Simon, her faithful sleeping partner and personal heating pad when Chase was not in town. Pulling her smart phone from beneath her makeshift pillow, she flicked it on, and pushed in her earbuds.

Two missed calls had resulted in voice mail messages. She nearly dropped the phone when she read the first caller's name: *Kim Quintana.* For an irrational second, hope flared through her brain. Was it all a mistake? Was her friend still alive?

Then brutal reality crashed back in. The number was Kim's work phone at Wilderness Quest, and of course it was Troy who had called. His voice mail message said, "Remember that you can call the office any time you need help during the day, or call me at night. Thank you again, Sam."

"Stop thanking me," she groaned.

Then Troy unintentionally stabbed her in the heart by saying, "I know that Kyla is with you tonight."

Sam's throat constricted, threatening to choke her. She might have been able to pretend that her friends had simply moved away if she wasn't sleeping in Kyla's tent, shepherding Kyla's delinquents for a company that Kim used to manage, and reporting to Kyla's dad and Kim's husband every day. She felt her friends' absence, not their presence. She'd already stumbled across reminders of Kyla in one of the small pockets sewn into both sides of the tent: a miniscule tube of cold sore cream and a used band-aid. She was afraid to explore the pocket on the other side.

She brought up her phone's list of contacts and changed the entry for Kim Quintana's work number to *WWQ Admin.* She moved the cursor to Kim's personal number, intending to delete it, but then she was seized with an almost unbearable urge to call that number instead. She tapped Cancel. The phone displayed the contact list again, still in the K section.

Oh God, *Kyla Q-J.* Sam highlighted the entry, but again couldn't bring herself to press Delete. How could she intentionally erase both women from her life?

Someone had already obliterated them. Violently. Permanently. She wished she could do something to fill the sinkhole left behind. A colleague had died during one of her previous job assignments, but on that sad occasion, she could at least talk to associates who might provide clues. In this even more personal case, she didn't have a single lead to follow. She'd never felt so useless.

In her mind's eye, she pictured Kim and Kyla by Pinnacle Lake, enjoying the view of crystal water reflecting the mountain on the other side. Then ... did the killer suddenly appear on the trail in front of them? Did he sneak up from behind? Did Kim recognize him? Did Kyla? Or was he a wild-eyed stranger with a gun pointed at them? Correction: a handgun and a rifle. Or maybe it had been two strangers, each holding one gun?

Were there threats?

Was there a *reason*?

All the scenarios were unbearable to contemplate. What she wouldn't give for a glass of wine. Make that a bottle of wine.

When the notice of a text flashed across the screen on her phone, she eagerly switched over to it.

Miss you, Chase had typed. *Wish you were here.*

At bomb practice? Sam responded, hoping he was still online.

He was. *Starts tomorrow. Could practice body searches tonight.*

She typed, *You need practice?*

Always. Stay safe. Love you, Summer.

Love you, too. Good night, Chase.

Stroking a finger across her lips, she relived their goodbye kiss this morning, a twinge of guilt shadowing the pleasant memory. Chase was trying to keep them together, inviting her to share his condo in Salt Lake City. Utah had amazing national parks and monuments, but the state's elected offices were full of people who wanted to take back public lands and burn environmental regulations.

Although she truly loved Chase, she could never live in a place like that. She'd grown up in conservative Kansas, but her environmental spirit had found a home in the ever-green atmosphere of the Pacific Northwest. She had to stay here. With luck, the FBI would let Chase join her soon.

She switched the phone back to voice mail. The second message was from her housemate, Blake. "Hey Sam, just wanted you to know that a deputy sheriff stopped by the greenhouse today to ask about you. I said you were an upstanding citizen. And that I was, too."

What? She sat up, staring at the phone. Since returning from Idaho, she'd been interviewed twice by the Snohomish County Sheriff's Department. Now they were interviewing her housemate?

She unzipped her tent and climbed out. Maya's tent was lit from the inside, the rest were dark and quiet. Pulling on her boots and headlamp, Sam tiptoed away from camp with her phone in hand, switching on her headlamp only when she was hidden from view in the woods. She walked for a few minutes until she reached a group of boulders. Squatting down behind them with the rocks between her and the campers, she turned off her headlamp and punched in her home number. It was after eleven. Good thing her housemate was a night owl.

"Sam? Aren't you guarding delinquents on some mountaintop?"

"I am," she murmured. "That's why I'm keeping my voice low. What's this about a deputy surprising you at work?"

"That's a good way to put it. She surprised my boss, too. I hope he believed her when she told him that I wasn't in trouble."

Sam took a second to untangle the he-she references in her head. "The deputy was a she?"

"Yeah, a Detective Greene, with an extra E." She heard a distinctive hum in the background, interspersed with loud popping sounds. Microwaving popcorn. He had picked up the kitchen phone.

"What did she want to know?"

"Where you were when the murders happened, of course. What you did for a living, how you paid the mortgage, if you were hard up for money. And of course, who the heck I was and why I lived with you."

Was the Sheriff's office working on some sort of conspiracy theory? "Did she think you and I wanted to kill my friends for money or something?"

"I sure as hell hope not. But now that you mention it, Greene did kind of perk up when I mentioned you were unemployed when you went off with Chase. But then I assured her that after this job, you'd have plenty of money to pay the bills for a few months until you got other assignments."

Sam let that information run around her brain for a few seconds. The popping noises on Blake's end grew less frequent, then stopped.

Her housemate made the possible connection sooner than she did. "Oh crap." Blake groaned. "You don't suppose Greene would think that you'd kill to get Kyla's job, do you? I'm sorry."

"There's nothing to be sorry for, Blake. And I don't think they'd seriously consider me a suspect. The job's only for three weeks, and I was in Idaho with an FBI agent, for heaven's sake."

She heard the microwave door open and shut, and then a man's voice asked about butter.

"Is that Claude?" She named Blake's current love interest.

"He's down from Vancouver for the weekend."

"Well, have fun. I better get back to my delinquents."

"Good night, WildWest."

She hadn't heard that one in a while. Wilderness Westin. WildWest. That was the ridiculous nickname she'd been saddled with when she wrote blogs for conservation groups. Back when she'd had writing contracts. Nowadays her former clients posted their assignments on the web, encouraged applicants to compete for free, and paid only for the result they chose. The life of a freelance writer got more maddening each year.

The life of an unemployed wildlife biologist was even more uncertain. As the sheriff's deputy now knew, and was interested in for all the wrong reasons.

Switching her phone off and her headlamp on, Sam made her way to the Box with a View and took advantage of the facilities. The night was cold enough that she could see her breath. The stars were thick diamonds in the black velvet sky. Spectacular heavens were always the best reward for sleeping on mountaintops.

As she returned to camp, she surveyed the tents again. Maya's tent was the only one still lit. Sam could tell by the silhouette that her young friend was reading. Four tents were totally closed up with nylon flaps zipped tight over the black mesh inner doors. Gabriel's tent sounded like a snoring grizzly had denned up inside. Nick's tent was dark, but his rain fly was unzipped and she had the itchy feeling that the boy might be awake, sitting invisible behind the black net screen, staring out into the night. Likewise with Olivia. When she passed Maya's tent, her protégé pulled off her headlamp, twisted around on her pillow and peered out. Sam held up a hand, two fingers in a peace sign.

Maya echoed the sign, holding her fingers up against the netting, backlighting them with the headlamp. Sam was glad to have her on this team. Maya might be only eighteen and might come from a sketchy background, but the girl was smart, tough, and resourceful enough to handle anything this bunch threw at her.

Presumably Aidan knew what he was doing, too.

Day One down. Only twenty more to go.

4

Sam slid out of her tent shortly after sunrise to observe her peer counselors tiptoeing around, returning footwear to all the kids' tents. Nick poked his head out of his tent just as his hiking boots were delivered by Aidan. "Why the gex did you steal my shoes, dude?"

"I took everyone's shoes, *dude*," Aidan responded calmly. "Company policy."

"What if I needed to get up and, you know, drain the hose?"

"You're not coordinated enough to pee barefoot?"

Nick grabbed his boots and turtled back into his tent.

Sam chafed her hands together, longing for coffee. At home, she counted on freshly brewed Italian roast waiting in her programmable coffeemaker when she got up. She rubbed her eyes and contemplated chewing coffee grounds until hot liquid was ready. According to today's training schedule, it might be hours before she'd get any caffeine.

Yawning, she picked up one of the aluminum cooking pans from the top of the stump, then collected the battered metal ladle they'd used for the spaghetti sauce last night. Banging the ladle on the bottom of the pan, she shouted, "Up and at 'em, crew! You all have to learn to make fire before you can eat."

Nothing. She banged on the pan again, and continued to make noise until heads began to pop out of tents.

"You're giving me a headache!"

"Shut the hel...lurik up!"

"I'm gonna take that drum and stuff it—"

Aidan cut off the last speaker. "Get up, get dressed, get out!"

After ten minutes and a lot of cursing and complaining, all six kids crawled out, pulling on socks and boots and fleeces and jackets. Ashley, Nick, and Gabriel finger-combed their hair. Taylor had pushed her tresses into a tight ponytail, and Olivia's mane was still in her French braid from yesterday, now fuzzy with escaping wisps.

"It's freezing out here!" Crossing her arms, Ashley hugged herself.

"Thank you, Captain Obvious," Nick mumbled.

Ashley stuck her tongue out at him.

Justin scratched his chin. His whiskers were thick for a blond seventeen-year-old; he already needed a shave. "Where the gex is breakfast?"

Sam wanted to give the whole crew a timeout, but didn't have a lot of optimism that would work with teenagers. "Before we have breakfast, we must make a fire."

Gabriel glanced toward the cooking area. "What happened to the stoves?"

"They're gone," Sam told the group.

"What?" Taylor frowned. "They can't be."

"They're right there." Raising her hand, Olivia motioned toward the stump, where the stoves rested beside the cook pots.

"You said we couldn't have fires in a wilderness area," Nick pointed out.

Sam huffed out a breath in exasperation. "Crew! We won't be using the stoves any longer. Quest crews have special permission from the Forest Service to build small cooking fires. Now, pay attention. I am going to teach you how to make fire with sticks and stones."

"Yeah, right." Taylor.

"Each of you must make your own fire before you can heat water for breakfast." She knelt on one knee and held up a thick stick about a foot long, a more slender twig a bit longer, a flat piece of cedar, a length of twine, a rounded rock small enough to fit into her hand, and her pocketknife. "To make it easy for you this morning, I have collected the necessary pieces, and you can borrow them after I'm done. From now on, you will have to make your own fire kit, as well as your own fire, so pay attention."

Ashley sat down in front of Sam. The other kids followed. Justin did not give in without saying "gex" first.

"First, make your spindle." Repeating the steps she'd learned less than a week ago, Sam demonstrated how to round one end of the thick stick and point the other.

"Prepare your fireboard and your handhold." With the pocketknife, she dug a rounded hole in the flat piece of wood and made a notch at the side next to it, then used the screwdriver attachment of her knife to gouge a hole into the holding rock.

"You might want to lubricate your handhold with something." She spat into the hole in the small rock a couple of times, and then used a fingertip to work the saliva around the depression.

Olivia screwed up her face. "Gross."

Maya leapt up, realizing what Sam had forgotten. "I'll gather some dry stuff for tinder and find something for a coal catcher."

"Thank you." Sam continued with the lesson, tying the twine to both ends of the slender stick. "Create your bow." She held it up. "See, it should look a bit like an archery bow."

"Now, make fire." After twisting a loop into the bow string, she slipped the loop over the vertical spindle stick, fitted the point of the spindle into the hole on the flat wood, and placed the holding rock between the top of the stick and her left hand to protect her from friction burns. With her left foot on the flat fireboard to hold it in place, she sawed the bow back and forth. The loop spun the spindle stick against the fireboard.

Maya plopped a small piece of wood and a nest of shredded bark and pine needles down beside Sam's foot.

"It's sort of like playing the fiddle." Sam said a mental

prayer. *Please let this work fast.*

Sweat had broken out on her forehead by the time smoke began to snake from the fireboard.

"Oooohhhh," the kids chorused.

"Counselor's a cave woman!"

"Cave woman make fire!"

"I'm not done yet." Sam carefully flicked the smoking ember out onto the coal catcher, then moved it to the tinder and bent over the small bundle to blow on it. It smoked a bit more. She scooped up the nest of tinder with her hands and blew harder, nearly going cross-eyed watching the smoke so close to her face. For an anxiety-filled minute, she was afraid that she'd blown out the heat, but then a tiny flame flared up. Setting the bundle back on the ground, she bent on hands and knees and continued to blow on it, adding a few more shreds until it was a tiny but respectable fire.

"Voila! Now I'm going to make coffee."

"Thank God." Taylor sat back on her heels. "I'm dying here."

Sam stood up. "I'm going to make coffee for *myself.*" She thrust the bow at the blond girl. "Your turn. You'll need to gather some kindling materials first. Make sure they're dry."

Sam had brewed a small pot of cowboy coffee for herself and started heating water for oatmeal by the time Taylor sparked a flame, spurred on by the catcalls of the others. The tall girl beamed at her accomplishment. She handed off the bow to Gabriel. "That's how women make fire here on Earth, Mister Lizard."

It took nearly three hours and many forays into the sparse woods nearby for kindling and new fireboards before Sam's whole crew succeeded in making their fires with assistance from Aidan and Maya. As she had been instructed, Sam celebrated their achievements by handing out packets for hot chocolate in addition to their oatmeal.

"I usually have Coke for breakfast," Gabriel told whoever would listen.

Sam swallowed a gulp of coffee. "None of you will see a Coke or any carbonated beverage for twenty days. Drink choices are tea, lemonade, coffee, and water."

Gabriel crossed his arms on top of his knees and lowered his head onto his forearms. "Lurik."

As soon as the meal was done, Sam stood up. "Pack up, crew. We have ten miles to hike today, and most of it's uphill. Six miles before lunch."

"Everyone bring their dishes over here and wash them." Aidan hovered over a pot of water on his own fire. "Those are your only dishes for the rest of the trip, so keep track of them. You lose something, you'll have to do without."

"As we're hiking today," Sam added, "keep an eye out for pieces for your fire kit. You'll need it if you want a hot dinner tonight. I'll provide the twine and the knife, but you need to find the rest."

"It's the Stone Age all over again." Gabriel walked toward the wash area with bowl and cup in hand. "On Vebulaze, I can just point to something with this finger"—he aimed his right index finger at the sky—"and light it up. That's one of the special powers of—"

"Mister Lizard!" Ashley and Nick sang out. Then they turned toward each other, grinning at their spontaneous chorus, and clacked their upraised spoons together.

Red-faced, Gabriel dunked his dish into the wash water and swished his spoon, then strode to his pack and shoved them in.

While it was nice to see Ashley and Nick smile, it was too bad that it was at Gabriel's expense. If the banter reached the stage of actual bullying, Sam would have to decide what to do about it. Aidan and Maya handed out prepackaged lunches to the kids—crackers, cheese, turkey pepperoni, carrots, dried fruit—then made sure the crew kids put their fires out and scattered all the evidence throughout the woods. The peer counselors supervised as the kids packed up their gear. Sam dismantled her own tent and stowed everything in her backpack.

After pulling a roll of silver duct tape from her pack, she sat down on a log, peeled off her socks, and applied the tape to her heels. "Any sore spots from yesterday?" she asked the group.

"This is my secret. Keeps me from getting blisters." She pulled her socks on over the tape. "Anyone else?"

Gabriel raised a hand, and she tossed the tape roll to him. Three of the others plopped down on the log beside him to wait their turn.

As she'd been told to expect, the whining was nonstop during the second day's hike. Aidan and Maya adjusted pack straps and contents, told the crew to loosen or tighten boot laces. Complaints about carrying a heavy pack or being tired or just being here were ignored.

"Fire starter kits," Sam reminded them after the first mile.

That sparked a few battles over each sturdy stick or flat piece of wood. Nick found a nearly perfect holding stone, just big enough to fit in his palm, with an indentation already hollowed out near the middle. The others obviously coveted the rock, although Gabriel and Taylor pretended they didn't care. Twenty minutes later, Ashley located another small rock that was nearly as good. Sam was amazed that all of them had paid attention to her instructions and that they cared enough to compete for the tools.

The morning was cool, crisp, and sunny, with only a few wisps of white drifting over the jagged peaks of Mount Baker to the south. To the north in British Columbia, clouds were stacking up. The forecast was for increasing clouds in the north Cascades near evening. Forty percent chance of rain, the NOAA prediction said. If it rained, was she supposed to make the kids do their exercises outside, or could they just sit in their tents and write in their journals? She'd have to ask Maya or Aidan what was typical.

They stopped for lunch near a small grove of trees where a log offered convenient, if damp, seating. "You can pull your rain pants from your packs and sit on them to keep your hiking pants dry," she told them.

The girls did just that; the boys seemed to believe that taking Sam's suggestion would make them look like sissies, and parked their backsides directly on the wet wood.

"Completely up to you," she told them. "But if you want to stay warm, it's important to stay dry. Wind goes right through wet britches."

"Britches?" Ashley sneered. "How Little House on the Prairie!"

Sam pulled open her packet of cheese. "As a matter of fact, Ash, I *was* raised on a prairie in Kansas."

"Awkward..." Taylor ribbed the other girl in a sing-song voice.

The uncomfortable moment directed attention away from Nick and Gabriel, who had apparently decided their buttocks were now clammy enough and pulled out their rain pants to sit on. Justin, still in rebel mode, stayed put on the damp mossy back of the log. Sam hoped he'd develop diaper rash.

They munched silently for a few minutes, then a flutter of wings overhead caught Sam's attention as several gray jays landed in the branches of the Douglas fir. "Check this out, crew," Sam began.

Nick too had noticed the visitors. "Whiskey jacks!"

She smiled at him. "Ah, you know them!"

Everyone looked up.

"Crew, these are gray jays, also called Canada jays, or whiskey jacks," Sam told them.

"Whiskey jacks?" Justin laughed. "Are they heavy boozers?"

"I think 'whiskey jack' is a corruption of a Native American name for them."

Taylor put a hand over her brow to shield her eyes from the sun as she gazed upward. "They're cute. So fluffy."

A couple of the birds hopped to lower branches.

"Around here, we call them camp robbers." Aidan stuffed a piece of pepperoni into his mouth.

"Why?" Justin asked. "They don't look too tough to me."

Nick was breaking off pieces of his crackers and cheese, barely managing to stifle a grin.

Sam nodded at him. "Nick, show the crew why."

The boy held out his hand with the bits of crackers and cheese scattered across his palm. Less than ten seconds passed before one of the jays swooped down. The bird hovered uncertainly for a few wingbeats, regarding the offering with bright eyes. Then the jay landed, its tiny claws grasped around the boy's fingers, quickly snatched a snippet of cracker and fluttered back to its perch above.

"That was awesome!" Gabriel breathed.

"Who trained 'em?" Ashley wanted to know.

"Nobody." Sam was pleased to see a smile on every face. "They are wild birds, but for some unknown reason, they are very friendly. Anyone can feed them."

Every kid started breaking off pieces of their lunch and offering them skyward. Olivia and Gabriel and Nick silently beamed when a bird took their offerings. The first time they felt the bird's tiny claws, Taylor squealed, Ashley gasped, and Justin whispered, "Sweet!"

Sam was ecstatic that her crew was so enraptured by the birds' visit; maybe interesting these teens in nature wouldn't be an onerous job after all. "Don't feed them your *entire* lunch, crew. There's no more food until suppertime."

The gray jays were the core of conversation for the next four miles, with the kids tossing in sightings of other wildlife they'd encountered while growing up. Most encounters had been in zoos and roadside parks, judging from their stories.

After arriving at their next campsite and setting up the tents, they all attempted to start their bow-drill fires. After a couple of hours, each camper had a small fire smoldering in front of them, although more than one blaze had been finished by Maya or Aidan. The kids had individual packets of macaroni and cheese to cook, with green peppers and turkey pepperoni to add if they wanted. Carrots and dried fruit rounded out the meal.

Sam slid onto the ground in the circle beside Ashley. "It was a good day, right, crew?"

"Those birds were awesome." Olivia's eyes were still shining.

"We'll probably run into more camp robbers before this trip is over." Sam took a bite of her macaroni. She hadn't cooked it long enough, and had to chew carefully before she said, "A few things before we say good-night, crew. First of all, good job, all of you, on trying the bow-drill fires. I promise that if you keep at it, every one of you will be able to build a fire from scratch."

She scooped up her last bite, and after she'd swallowed it, set down her dish and stood up. "Nick, please stand up."

"Gex, dude," Justin hissed. "What did you do?"

Nick, anxiety stiffening his face, pressed his hands onto the ground and pushed himself to his feet.

"Nick Lewis." Sam pulled a necklace out of her pocket. "Because you have been willing to follow all instructions and because you have helped your fellow crew members without being told, you are our first Voyager."

She placed the pendant around Nick's neck and knotted the leather cord in the back for him. The boy's face was scarlet with embarrassment. He sat down quickly, but Sam could tell he was working hard to stifle a smile as he fingered the bead in the hollow of his throat.

"Congrats, man," Justin slapped him on the shoulder hard enough to make the younger boy wince. "You get to crap alone!"

Sam resumed her place in the circle.

"Lurik, what about the rest of us?" Gabriel wanted to know. "I hacked up an onion yesterday."

Sam said, "You'll all get there. Remember that we're watching for willingness to contribute to the group and assume individual responsibility, as well as your ability to develop leadership skills. Now, I need to remind you that you each have at least one letter from your family in your pack."

Most of the young faces around her assumed wary expressions.

"And you need to use your journal to write a letter to your family sometime during the next two days."

"What the gex are we supposed to write?" Justin asked.

Sam shrugged. "Whatever you want to tell them. Write about what you hope for the future, what we're doing here, about your feelings. It's completely your choice. The letter will be picked up in two days, when the counselors come up to check on you. When they leave the next day, they'll deliver the letters to your families."

Now all six of her crew stared at the ground, shuffling their feet, crossing their arms, clearly uncomfortable with the reminder of the people waiting for them back home. She hated to be the one to bring them down after a good day, but she had instructions to follow. These kids were here to think, and, with luck, to change. Their families were receiving counseling back at the Wilderness Quest office to learn their roles in breaking old destructive patterns.

Reaching into her pocket, she thumbed the recorder on.

"Okay." She rubbed her hands together. "Final exercise of the day before cleanup and bed. I want each of you to say what kind of animal you'd be if you could choose, and why. Me, I'd like to be a crow. They act like they have a lot of fun, and they can live practically anywhere and eat whatever's available. A crow is a very adaptable bird." She twisted her head to the left. "Ash."

"Huh." The girl stirred the remaining macaroni in her bowl for a minute, thinking. Her purple-streaked hair stood up on one side and she had a smudge of charcoal on her cheek, but somehow these imperfections made her more pretty instead of less so. "A leopard. One of the all-black ones."

"Why?" Aidan asked.

"All black so I could be practically invisible." Ashley's gaze bounced around their circle. "And I'd have claws so I could shred other animals when I wanted to." She held up her hands, her fingers curled into claws.

"Leopards are endangered." Nick sounded concerned. "Poachers would want to kill you."

Ashley scrunched up her face as if she'd just tasted something bitter. "That's why I need to be all black," she reiterated, "so I could hide in the shadows."

The girl had prostituted herself, according to her mother. Despite Ash's brave words, maybe she hadn't done that willingly.

"And you'd be a hunter," Nick told her. "You'd have to kill things."

The girl's eyes darkened, a little sad now. "I guess I would."

"Pick someone else," Aidan instructed.

Ashley glanced across the circle. "Gabriel."

"I'd be a voltenark," the chubby boy grinned. "It's a shape-shifter. It can go anywhere and look like anything."

Eyerolls all around the circle. Sam pressed her lips together to keep from laughing. When she'd recovered, she said, "How about an animal from *this* planet, Gabriel?"

"Really? Boring." His forehead wrinkled. "I guess I'd be an owl, then. Owls are cool. And they're wise."

And they're magical and they're in Harry Potter books, Sam thought. An easy answer. Owls *were* cool, and they were real but still magical, some of her favorite creatures on the planet.

Gabriel picked Taylor.

The lanky girl was briefly distracted by finishing the braiding of her long blond hair. When she'd wrapped a rubber band around the end of the plait, she said, "I'd be a peacock."

Justin scoffed. "You'd have to be a pea*hen*."

She aimed an icy glare at him. "We're choosing what animal we want to be, and I want to be a peacock, because it's beautiful."

"Weird," Nick said.

It *was* a bit weird. Did Taylor, who claimed that all she wanted to study was modeling, secretly want to be a boy? An idea crawled into Sam's mind. Taylor was lean and rangy and if she had breasts at all, they didn't show through the unisex crew clothing. Her facial features were androgynous. Was Taylor a transgender girl, and nobody had thought to enlighten the new field guide?

But even if that were true, what difference would it make? Sam considered; she couldn't imagine how she would treat Taylor differently. She had been told to watch out for sexual encounters among her crew, to not allow any two to go off alone. No matter anyone's gender, this was a group date.

Justin volunteered, "I'd be a pit bull, so nobody would mess with me."

"You'd probably end up in the pound," Gabriel said, and then slapped his hand over his mouth to stop himself from saying anything else.

Sam's brain filled in the awkward silence. *In the pound, where nobody would take you home, so you'd be on death row. Sorta like your dad.*

"Olivia," Justin snarled.

The black-haired girl stared at the ground as she talked. "I'd be a lemming."

Maya squinted at her. "A what?"

"It's a rodent of some kind." Olivia briefly looked up and then quickly shifted her gaze back to the dirt in front of her boots. "I'd like to be one because lemmings follow each other, even over cliffs, without thinking at all."

Sam made a mental note to remind Maya and Aidan about Olivia's previous suicide attempt. They'd all have to keep a close eye on her.

"That's even weirder than the peacock," Nick said. "I'd be a hawk. I could soar so high that I'd be out of reach. No hunter could shoot me."

The fifteen-year-old seemed obsessed with hunting. Or was it killing? Sam frowned. She might have expected that from bully-boy Justin, but not from Nick.

The others noticed Nick's preoccupation too. Justin pointed out, "*You'd* be the hunter instead, just like Ass, er, I mean, Ash."

Ashley's hands closed into fists, but she didn't respond. Nick scowled at Justin for a long moment, his jaw clenched, and then turned his gaze back to the coals of his fire still smoldering in front of him. Smacking his foot down on top of the smoking embers, he crushed them into dust with the sole of his hiking boot. The scent of burned rubber filled the air.

Completing the exercise, Maya chose a dolphin and Aidan a chimpanzee, which ended the discussion on a laugh and a less disturbing tone. Why the company psychologists wanted the kids to discuss this peculiar topic was a mystery to Sam. Most likely, she decided, the exercise was designed to make the teens think about themselves and their place in the world.

What would the Wilderness Quest counselors make of her choice to be a crow?

After washing dishes and locking everything away in the metal bear box the company had stationed at this site, Sam gathered them all along the ridge to watch the sunset change the clouds in the west from yellow to gold to fuchsia, then to purple and finally, cobalt blue. Olivia began the conversation by saying her favorite color was that saffron shade. Then the others punctuated the silence with poetic sounding colors as the names occurred to them. Tangerine. Scarlet. Crimson. Amethyst. Mulberry.

"Puce," Ashley contributed.

"Puke?" Justin snorted.

"Puce is kind of a purple-brown color." Nick turned toward the muscular boy. "Similar to mulberry."

"Huh," the boy with the dragon tattoo huffed, for once without a witty retort.

Then they were quiet for a few minutes. Nick sat cross-legged, fingering his Voyager bead. As the sky darkened, he murmured, "Indigo."

As the last colors faded into black, Sam ended the evening. "To your toothbrushes and tents, while you can still find your headlamps."

A collective growl went up.

"It's only a little after eight," Taylor complained.

Maya reminded them, "You can write or draw in your journals, or read."

"And we arise at dawn," Aidan said.

"We arise at dawn!" the six kids instantly yelled in chorus.

Sam laughed. When did they have time to organize that? Kim and Kyla had often talked about special moments when all the kids came together. Camp robbers. Sunset colors. *We arise at dawn.* She'd have a pleasant report for Troy tonight.

5

Day Three. Sam got up before the kids to watch as they emerged from their tents. Nick had been first yesterday, but Ashley beat him this morning, her hair a rat's nest of purple spikes. She was already crouched over her fire kit, bowing as quickly as she could, when Nick slid out of his tent. Before he pulled on his orange windbreaker, Sam spotted a damp red line across his blue T-shirt.

"Nick." She crooked a finger at him, drawing him toward her as she walked a few paces to a private area behind a clump of trees.

He had a hard time meeting her eyes. "Yeah?"

"Show me your stomach."

"What?"

"You heard me."

Resigned, he unzipped his windbreaker and pulled up the T-shirt. Two bright red horizontal scratches adorned his flat abdomen above the fading pink stripes of previous wounds. Blood beaded the top line.

"Why, Nick?"

His gaze unfocused, he slowly untied his Voyager necklace and then dropped it into her hands. His fingers were cold against hers. "I needed to."

She gritted her teeth, experiencing simultaneous urges to slap him and hug him. "Why?"

His thin shoulders lifted and fell. "I just did."

Sam had no clue what she was supposed to say to connect with him. "What did you use?"

Silently, he pulled a sliver of shale from his pants pocket and handed it over, then turned away, shuffling toward the group area and his fire kit.

Well, that was just great. Her first Voyager had already reverted back to a Zombie cutter. She inspected the sharp edge of the shale flake. It was lined with red. She didn't need to keep Nick away from knives; he was a smart kid who could manufacture his tool of choice at any time.

She did not know how to read these kids. Nick seemed happy last night at dinner. What the hell had set him off? It couldn't have been the sunset; he'd been the most enthusiastic about naming colors. The animal discussion? He'd picked a hawk as the creature he admired. She could picture him as a bird now, rising higher and higher, moving so far away that nobody could reach him.

Expect setbacks had been a piece of advice from the counselors, *none of us changes overnight.* Apparently she'd been naïve to imagine that Sam Westin might escape the normal course of events.

She felt slightly more optimistic when pit bull Justin succeeded in making fire on his own for the first time, and then volunteered to help Olivia the lemming with hers.

The gift of the day came in the middle of their nine-mile hike. They'd just resumed their march after taking a lunch break in the middle of a fragrant field of fading lupines and brilliant Indian paintbrush.

"What are those, Cap'n?" Olivia's voice came from behind her on the trail.

Sam stopped, turned. "Are you talking to me?"

The single file of hikers clunked to a halt behind Olivia.

"Yes," Olivia said. "If we're the crew, you should be the captain."

Taylor towered behind Olivia. "Cap'n Sam."

It didn't sound half bad. Maybe Kyla had been Captain Kyla

to her crews. She'd have to ask Maya.

"What are those?" Olivia held out an arm, gesturing across the valley to a ridge on the other side. A sprinkling of white rocks dotted the hillside.

Sam squinted. Two of the rocks moved. "Goats!" She slid off her pack and dug through its pockets for her binoculars. "Mountain goats, crew! Let's take a break to watch them."

She'd never seen goats in this area before. Encountering any sort of wildlife always gave her joy. It was fun to see the kids get excited, too. They set down their packs to relish the moment. Aidan and Maya also carried small folding binoculars in their packs, and the kids passed them up and down the line.

"Are they real?" Gabriel, of course.

"Plastic inflatables," Nick told him. "Rangers use remotes to move them around. They have tiny motors and fans inside."

"I want to see!" Ashley grabbed for the binoculars Nick was using.

"Are they wild?" Taylor.

"Yes," Sam told her. "This isn't Switzerland. We're in a national forest."

"There are three, no, four babies!" For a teen who specialized in beating up weaker types, Justin sounded surprisingly enthusiastic about babies.

"Kids," Maya told them. "Baby goats are called kids."

Justin possessively clenched Sam's binoculars as the goats scampered up a steep rock face. "Wow, can those little suckers jump! How old are they?"

"Three or four months," Nick guessed.

Sam agreed. "That's about right."

"Who is that?" Ashley pointed.

Sam grabbed her binoculars back from Justin. At the fringe of forest across the valley, she spotted a figure in camouflage fatigues.

"Omigod, he has a gun! He's a hunter!" Taylor slapped a hand over her mouth in alarm.

Gabriel groaned. "Oh, dude..."

Justin yanked the binoculars out of Taylor's hands.

"Bastard's not going to shoot one of them goats, is he?"

Sam zeroed in on the stranger. The man, who appeared to be alone, wore his dark hair caught back in a ponytail. His thin face sported at least a week's worth of beard. The rifle had a scope mounted on top and hung from his shoulder by a strap. "He's not aiming his gun at the goats."

They all waited, postures rigid, until the goats hop-skipped up the slope and vanished into the forest some distance from the hunter. The man turned. Swinging his rifle around, he pointed it in their direction and put his eye to the scope.

An alarm siren immediately blared through Sam's head. She was on the edge of yelling, "Hit the deck!" when the hunter let the gun fall back to his side. Then he, too, disappeared into the trees.

Justin spat on the ground. "Shit, that was close. Gex hunter!"

Sam decided to let that infringement go. Her pulse was still galloping through her veins. She hoped she'd been the only one to see that rifle aimed in their direction.

Nick had a greenish tinge and he massaged his stomach as if he might upchuck at any second. Ashley and Taylor were focused on the spot where the goats had vanished. Olivia and Gabriel gazed at Sam, waiting for a cue.

This sort of situation had not come up in her brief orientation. "This is a legal hunting area," she began. "That's why your packs and jackets are bright orange for your protection. But there are rules for which animals can be hunted and where hunters can take them. I don't know what's in season right now."

"*Hunters* should be in season!" Taylor remarked.

Justin shared her sentiment. "Yeah, like maybe they could give them licenses to shoot each other."

Sam winced, jolted into memories of her murdered friends. The conversation was deteriorating fast. Even if she couldn't imagine herself shooting an animal, let alone a person, it was time to play the responsible adult. Surely the hunter had just been looking through his scope, like responsible hunters were supposed to. The guy probably used his rifle scope instead of binoculars.

She took a deep breath. "Look, crew, most of us eat meat. Believe it or not, chickens aren't born in packages on a grocery store shelf, and hamburgers start out on four legs. Hunting is part of our history. Some people do it to put food on the table. You have a right to your feelings about it, but as long as hunters obey all the regulations, they have the right to hunt. And this might surprise you, but hunters are some of the best advocates for protecting wild areas. A lot of tourists never explore beyond the scenic viewpoints, but hunters understand that animals need habitats to live in."

She picked up her pack, relieved to see that her hands weren't shaking. "Let's get moving."

Binoculars stowed, they continued, reaching camp by early afternoon, in time to make an early supper.

Mealtime was an exercise in frustration as the kids all tried to spark fires with their kits. Only three succeeded on their own this time—Nick, Taylor, and Olivia. Discouraged, Justin snapped his spindle stick in two and flung the pieces into the forest, swearing. From personal experience, Sam knew it took a lot of practice to consistently start a fire with the bow-drill method. After observing for a while, Sam let them share the three fires the crew had managed to start.

The meal was freeze-dried chicken and noodle mix. Taylor wrinkled her nose, but kept her opinion of the pasta to herself.

They were camped in a relatively flat spot on the top of a ridge, their tents scattered among a cluster of tall firs. According to her instruction book, it was time for another exercise. The six client kids watched with perplexed expressions as Sam stretched a rope approximately five feet off the ground between two trees.

"The object," she explained, "is for everyone to get over this rope. No going under, no going around, no hanging on the rope."

"Shit." Justin studied the situation. "I mean, 'Gex!' How's that gonna happen?"

"Every crew before yours has done it." Sam intended to

ignite a spirit of competition. "Including all-girl crews."

Ashley stood up and walked over to inspect the line. "Probably the all-girl crews did it fastest."

The others rose to their feet.

"We could vault," Nick suggested, inspecting the surroundings. "Except there's no pole. But I think I could just jump over it," he said. "Like a high jump."

Taylor snorted. "You'd land on your head and break your neck."

A spark of panic ignited in Sam's gut. Surely she wasn't supposed to allow that.

"Any ideas, Olivia?" Justin asked.

Staring at the rope, which was at her eye level, Olivia shook her head.

"I have one." Justin scooped the small girl up from the ground and tossed her into the air, up and over the rope.

Olivia's shriek ended abruptly as she crash-landed on her hands and knees. Aidan, Sam, and Maya all ducked beneath the rope and rushed to her.

"Jesus!" Aidan's hands hovered above her back, as if afraid to touch her. "Are you okay, Olivia?"

The girl pushed herself stiffly to her feet, swiping dirt from her hands and the knees of her cargo pants. Then, to Sam's amazement, she grinned. "Next?"

Justin pivoted toward Ashley.

"No, Justin. No more tossing anyone," Sam ordered. "This is supposed to be an exercise in teamwork, not in throwing people around like bags of horse feed."

"Well, it's not like little Martini there is gonna be able to catch any of the rest of us," he grumbled.

Martini? Olivia. Olive. Martini. Justin had been the first to call Gabriel Mister Lizard, too. Was his habit of assigning nicknames a gang tendency she should discourage? Olivia's expression was pleased; she didn't appear to mind the new name. It did imply a certain acceptance.

"Someone can stand on my shoulders," Olivia offered. "I'm stronger than I look. Ash could. Then when she's over, the two of us could hold the next one."

"I got it," Nick said. "Justin, you and Mister Lizard stand close together."

Sam was surprised that the two large boys let Nick pull them into place.

"Ash, turn around and face them."

Sam watched as Nick positioned Ashley, then showed her how to step up on their thighs. With each of the larger boys clasping one of her hands and placing another hand under her thighs, they boosted her over the rope.

"FYI world, Sparky here is not exactly a lightweight," Justin remarked in a loud voice.

"Hey!" Ashley objected. "Muscles weigh more than fat!"

Sparky. Sam was glad that Justin had replaced his former designation of "Ass" with a friendlier nickname for Ashley.

Nick helped to place Ashley's feet on Olivia's shoulders. When the boys let go, Olivia nearly fell backwards. Ashley jumped off. Both girls ended up on hands and knees, but seemed fine when they stood up.

"A big guy next," Nick said.

Groaning dramatically, Taylor, Nick, and Justin boosted Gabriel into the air.

"Oh God." Ashley stretched her hands up over her head to hold him.

Olivia begged, "Please don't squish us, Mister Lizard."

The two girls managed, barely, to hold up his torso, staggering backward under Gabriel's weight. The toe of the pudgy boy's boot snagged on the rope as he went over. Nick freed it, and Gabriel's feet dropped onto the ground on the other side a second before the girls lost their balance. The three teens clutched at each other to stay upright.

Next they decided to get Justin over. Grumbling, Taylor and Nick boosted him by the buttocks.

"Oh yeah, Sweet T," Justin crooned. "Feel free to caress the junk. Nicky boy, you keep your hands to yourself."

"Let's just throw him," Taylor said. She and Nick shoved Justin over onto three sets of upraised hands.

Four teens on one side of the rope. Two on the other. "Now what?" Taylor turned to Nick. "Maybe I could boost you up on my shoulders."

Nick shook his head. "I'm going to boost you."

Taylor eyed him doubtfully. The boy was seven inches shorter and probably forty pounds lighter than she was.

"I'm really strong," Nick assured her.

"But even if you can lift me up, then how will *you* get over?"

"Limbo!" Ashley suggested from the other side, leaning back, her arms held out to her sides. She shimmied, her breasts jiggling, as if she was about to dance under the rope.

Justin's eyes lit up. "Go, Sparky! Shake 'em! Show us what you got!"

"Justin! Ash!" Sam was appalled.

"No going under," Aidan reminded them. "Or around the trees."

Nick told Taylor, "I'm going to kneel down and you're going to climb onto my shoulders, and then they'll grab you and pull you over while I hold your legs and you make like a plank."

The tall girl shrugged. "It's your sacroiliac."

Sam had nearly forgotten that Taylor's father was a doctor.

Nick squatted, and Taylor slid her legs onto his shoulders and held his hands. With a major effort, a beet-red face, and several staggering steps, the slight boy managed to get to his feet and pass Taylor over the rope.

"Okay." Nick stretched his arms above his head and waggled his neck to relax the muscles. "I am gonna fly over this rope. And you guys will catch me, right?"

That sounded like a dangerous plan. Sam caught Maya's gaze, and then Aidan's. They didn't look as alarmed as she felt.

Nick examined the faces of the five teens on the far side of the rope. "You'll catch me, right?" he repeated.

The girls and Gabriel nodded. Justin refused to commit.

"I think you need to back up a little. And raise your hands." Nick briefly held his own in the air to demonstrate.

The four backed up a couple of feet. The girls raised their hands, and after a few seconds and a sideways glance at Justin,

Gabriel did, too. Justin stood stubbornly in place, refusing to obey instructions.

"Four's enough." Nick paced backward several yards to get a running start. "Here I come!"

Sam had the sickening feeling this was not going to end well, but before she could stop him, Nick raced forward and launched himself into the air, hands outstretched in front like Superman. Then, in an astounding cooperative effort, the rest of the crew caught him, including Justin, who joined the others at the last second. Sam wished she'd captured the moment on film.

"That was amazing." Maya applauded. "Most of the other crews ended up climbing the trees."

The kids stopped their high-fiving to stare at the trees to which the rope was tied. One fir had a branch low enough to jump and grab. A couple of bare spots showed where the bark had been worn off by the boots of hikers climbing up.

Aidan grinned. "We said you couldn't go under the rope or walk around the trees, but we didn't say you couldn't climb a tree to get over."

For a few awkward seconds, a disappointed silence reigned over the campsite. Sam mentally cursed her peer counselors for spoiling her crew's best bonding moment.

"Wimps," Justin growled. He flexed his arms in a strong man pose. "This crew's got muscles. Plus, we got Lightning." He slapped Nick on the back.

"We don't need no stinkin' trees," Olivia growled in a deep voice.

The laughter and the hand slaps began again. Aidan untied the rope and put it away.

Digging into her pack, Sam handed them small bags of dried apricots as prizes. "Sunset watch!"

Their groans seemed good-natured now as they moved away from the trees and faced the west. She decided to award Voyager necklaces to all her Zombies before bedtime. Even Justin, although she'd have to talk to him about his temper and his recalcitrance. And she'd have to pull Nick aside before bedtime and make him promise not to cut himself.

6

On Day Four, Sam led her group down a rocky overgrown path that was barely more than a game trail. They saw no other hikers, but when the disturbing crack of a gunshot echoed in the distance, they all stopped to survey the peaks around them.

"Another angel gets its wings," Justin remarked morosely. "Gex hunters."

"We don't know what that was," Sam snapped, trying to reassure herself as well as her group. "There are a few mines around here; that might have been a dynamite blast. It could have been target practice. In any case, no worries, crew; it sounded pretty far away."

Her suggestions didn't help. She could tell by her crew's faces that their minds were fixed on possible targets. Baby goats. Hikers. She felt chilled the rest of the day as Kim and Kyla haunted her.

They hiked to a small mountain lake where they would stay for two nights. The sun was warm when they arrived in early afternoon, so Sam announced it was time for bathing and washing clothes. They strung up lines among the trees to hang wet clothing, and Aidan took the three boys off for a tracking lesson while Sam dug out the biodegradable soap.

"Oh thankyoubabyJesus," Taylor breathed, pulling up her T-shirt. "I don't care how cold that water is; I can't even stand myself, and the rest of you reek like rotting fish."

Ashley laughed. "My mom would say I have achieved a new level of skank."

Taylor suspiciously regarded the small tube of biodegradable soap Sam extracted from her pack. "That is *it*? No, no, no. I need decent shampoo and lots of conditioner." She flopped her ponytail over her shoulder from back to front to emphasize the point.

Olivia and Ashley waited to see what Sam was going to do about that.

"The fish and other critters that live in that lake don't need shampoo and conditioner," she reminded them. "And we are invading *their* world."

"Critters," Ashley murmured under her breath, as if memorizing the word. She cast a wary glance at the surface of the water. "What other critters?"

"Anacondas, probably," Taylor said. "You know, with global warming and all, they're crawling north to Canada."

"Frogs and waterbugs are more likely," Sam said.

Olivia shivered. "Waterbugs?"

"Pond skaters, water striders mostly," Sam clarified. "You know, those spider-like insects that walk on water."

Olivia clutched a hand to her chest. "Spiders?"

Sam had no patience for humans who were scared of benign insects. "They're not really spiders. They're harmless. In fact, they're incredible. Some people call them Jesus bugs because they walk on water."

"Uh, conditioner?" Taylor reminded her.

Maya instructed, "Comb your hair first and be careful not to snarl it when you soap up. Watch Sam if you don't understand." She grinned as she ran her dirty fingers through her short locks.

After carefully combing out her French braid and pulling off her clothes, Sam waded into the lake with Maya, gasping. The first six inches had been warmed by the sun, but below that, the water was glacial. As the crew girls watched from the shore, Sam and Maya soaped their bodies and then their hair. Sam smoothed soapy fingers over her scalp and squeezed suds through her long tresses.

It was an effort to keep her teeth from chattering. Raising an arm, she beckoned. "Come on in, the water's fine!"

"You'll love it!" Maya shouted in encouragement.

Taylor and Ashley dashed naked into the lake, squealing as the water deepened. Their young bodies were beautiful, Ashley curvaceous and Taylor with small high breasts. Sam was embarrassed for having ever imagined that Taylor might be trans. Olivia followed the others, still wearing her bra and panties, declaring, "I'm going to wash these while I have them on."

As Sam tossed the tube of soap to Taylor, something slick brushed across her ankle bone. A fish, blundering blindly through the silt she'd stirred up, or perhaps coming to check if she was edible. The feel of its slippery skin against her bare foot instantly transported her back to a farm pond in Kansas, a happy time skinny-dipping with Chase on a hot summer night. Cicadas singing, cows quietly chewing as they observed her and Chase in each other's arms. Had they ever been as light-hearted since that evening?

A stream of soap slithered over her eyebrow and slid into her right eye, stinging. She deserved that. She wanted to teach these kids to focus on the here and now, and her own mind was forever slipping into the past.

"Agh!" Ashley yelped, flailing and splashing. "Something just touched my foot!"

"Anaconda," Taylor suggested again.

"Relax! It's only a fish." Sucking in a breath, Sam ducked underwater and swished her head in the icy liquid to rinse off, then followed Maya as she ran back toward camp. The three crew girls washed quickly, gasping at the chill, then shot out of the water and galloped in unison for the shore like seals pursued by an orca.

When the girls were dressed again, Sam showed them how to use a water-filled tarp laid in a depression to wash out underwear and T-shirts. "Don't wash everything," she warned. "These could take a while to dry."

The bath and laundry did wonders for the mood in camp, and the girls laughed and talked as they helped each other comb out wet hair and dry it with their tiny camp towels. When the boys came trooping back, it was the girls' turn to march over the hill.

A small tarn awaited them at the bottom of the slope, little more than a large puddle now at the beginning of September. The still water mirrored the blue sky overhead, and Sam was uncomfortably reminded of Pinnacle Lake.

Maya squatted on her haunches a couple of feet from the edge of the tarn. "This mud is perfect for finding animal tracks," she told the other girls.

Sam dragged her brain back to the present. "Do you recognize any of the prints?"

Aidan and the three boys had left multiple boot impressions in the mud. Another uncomfortable reminder of Pinnacle Lake. No. She headed off the memory, unwilling to let her mind wander down that dark path again.

"I know exactly what sort of critter left these." Ashley waved her hand over huge boot prints recently pressed into the damp soil. "It's a voltenark!"

Maya giggled.

"I don't know." Olivia studied the prints, pursing her lips. "Those are awfully similar to pit bull tracks."

Taylor nodded. "Could be voltenark; could be pit bull. I never realized the two species were so closely related. Who knew there was interplanetary travel between Vebulaze and Earth?"

"Moving on," Sam interrupted the comedy routine. "What are these?" She indicated several sets of animal tracks.

All the girls recognized the many deer tracks.

"How about these?" Taylor bent over a dried patch of prints. "They're bigger, and the toes—hooves?—point out instead of in. But they're not all so big. There are some small ones here, too."

"Excellent observation, Taylor." Sam studied the girls' faces. "Any guesses?"

"Elk?" Ashley ventured.

"Good guess, Ash, but elk tracks would be even bigger," Sam told them.

"Moose?" Olivia guessed.

"Still bigger," Maya said.

"It's hard to be sure when tracks are in squishy mud, because mud slides around and doesn't give us a perfect impression," Sam said. "But I believe these prints belong to mountain goats, like the ones we saw a couple of days ago."

Her brain conjured the hunter they'd spotted along with the goats, and she couldn't prevent herself from taking a quick glance at the surrounding hillsides. Nobody there. She quickly tamped down that disturbing image.

Ashley put her hands up in front of her face as if she was holding a cell phone, and tapped a spot on the pretend device. "Taking a mental photo, Cap'n."

As they circled the tarn, Sam pointed out the tracks of small rodents, birds, and cat paws that most likely belonged to a bobcat. She stopped near several impressions of four toes surrounding a triangular lobed pad. "How about these?"

Olivia smiled. "Another bobcat!"

"No, check the bobcat track and then examine this one again."

The trio walked back to the bobcat prints and bent over them. They returned after a couple of minutes and kneeled down close to the new tracks. "These have claws!" Taylor remarked.

"Right." Sam added, "All felines except for cheetahs can retract their claws, so generally, claw marks won't show up in cat prints. Canines, on the other hand, can't retract their claws. This track belongs to either a coyote or a dog that came up here with a hiker."

"Another hiker. I knew it. I thought I felt someone watching us when we were naked in the lake," Ashley said.

The other girls regarded her with horror.

"What?" A chill whispered over Sam's scalp. "Why didn't you say something?"

Ashley shook her shoulders. "I suspected it was the boys. No big deal; give 'em a thrill, you know?"

Was this only teen bravado invented to compete with Taylor's anacondas? Sam couldn't decide. Wilderness Quest reserved their group campsites and tried to use less popular paths, but it was always possible that other hikers were in the area. And hunters often traveled cross-country, away from the trails. She wouldn't be able to completely relax until she led her crew out of the national forest into the safer preserve of North Cascades National Park.

"We haven't seen any other hikers today, and I'm pretty sure Aidan wouldn't let the boys spy on us." That better be true. "Back to our animal tracks," she urged.

"Look at this one." A few yards away, Olivia dropped into a squat close to another print, her long black braid swinging over her shoulder. "It must be a Saint Bernard!"

They joined her and studied the elongated pad and four oval-shaped toe prints that ended in claw points.

"Oh." Maya's gaze slid sideways to meet Sam's.

"These prints belong to a bear." Sam gestured to several impressions in the soft earth.

A collective intake of breath whispered around their circle.

Ashley clasped her hands together. "There really are bears here?"

"We told you that on the first night," Maya said.

"Bears." Olivia's facial muscles stiffened into a grimace.

"That's part of the reason we hang our food when we don't have those metal safes in camp. Why did you think we call those things bear boxes?" Maya glanced around their little circle.

"I guessed you were just trying to scare us." Olivia clasped her braid with both hands like a lifeline.

"Bears live in these mountains," Sam reminded them. "It's always wise to be careful, especially with food, but there's no real reason to be afraid. You've been out here for the last four nights, and so have they." She stood up and dusted her hands off on her pants legs. "Live and let live, you know."

"As long as the bears remember that," Taylor commented.

Sam checked her watch. "I think it's safe to go back to camp now."

When they'd all gathered in the group campsite again, Aidan reminded them about the letters they needed to have written to their families by tomorrow morning.

"Here are envelopes for you to put them in." He doled out six business-size envelopes, one to each teen.

Olivia stared at hers, holding the rectangle of white paper out from her as if it were contaminated. "What if we don't want to write anyone a letter?"

"It's completely your choice," Sam explained. "No judgment. But you might want to remember that your families agreed to go through counseling while you are out here, so they're spending this time thinking about you and how they want their relationships with you to be in the future."

"I doubt that," Ashley scoffed. "I guarantee my mom's not thinking about anything but work."

"Ditto for my dad." Nick raised a fist and Ashley bumped knuckles with him.

"If you don't choose to write anything," Sam continued, "the staff will send a note to your families telling them that, so they'll know we didn't forget a step in the process or leave one of you out."

At that news, the previous good cheer on her crew's faces faded into gloom.

"You have the afternoon off to write those letters, work on your fire building, write in your journals, or read. You can also explore around the shoreline, but if you walk out of our camp area, you have to tell Maya or Aidan and you have to stay in sight." She checked her watch again. "We'll reconvene at six to start supper."

Her crew crawled inside their tents. Olivia and Gabriel stayed there. The other four emerged with journals and pens in hand and scattered around camp to write. Nick chose to perch on a rock facing the lake to draw in his journal, his hands moving in long strokes and zigzag motions.

All six envelopes were grudgingly filled by suppertime. Four kids succeeded in making their own fires, and they all seemed resigned to the freeze-dried cheese ravioli pouches and carrot and celery sticks she issued. Personally, she was already sick of reconstituted food every night, and the Wilderness Quest stash in this camp's bear box was nearly empty. Tomorrow, new supplies would arrive with the counselor. Did she dare wish for fresh fruit or a taco for dinner?

The kids all seemed to dread the arrival of the company's mental health counselor.

"Do we have to talk to her?" Olivia.

Gabriel: "Why can't you guys just let us *be*?"

Taylor: "Things are good now, and you're going to ruin it again."

Feeling like the stern teacher all schoolkids hated, Sam reminded them that they were not on vacation. "This program is all about change. The counselor is here to talk to you about how you feel about what you're going through."

"I'm changing into a butterfly." Taylor thrust out her arms and flapped them. "I feel, well, like I'm going to be a really big butterfly."

"I'm changing into a coyote." Justin threw back his head. An unearthly howl emerged from his mouth.

Sam was startled when the other five crew kids quickly joined in. Maya and Aidan added their voices, too.

As their rip-rip-ahrooooo faded, an answering call came from somewhere beyond the surrounding ridges. Real coyotes.

Justin grinned. "That's sick!" He howled again, and then waited. After a second, the coyote pack answered back.

They all howled several more times in growing crescendo until Sam couldn't tell which noises were her crew and which were the wild canines. Finally, she cut off another round before the howl-fest could slide from awesome to annoying. "Cleanup time. Before bed, you can read your books or write in your journals or play games."

She expected Gabriel to especially appreciate the last suggestion, but instead his expression grew dismal. "Games?

How? We don't even have phones."

"Before computers were invented," Sam told the group, "way back when dinosaurs roamed the earth, humans created games that they played with each other. In person."

"No duh," Justin snorted. "My grandparents play cards all the time. Boring. Besides, we don't even have cards."

Aidan stepped in. "There are all kinds of games that are super simple. Marbles, for example. You can use little stones instead of glass marbles."

Ashley dismissed that idea. "Kid game."

"There are mind games," Maya suggested. "Where people have to guess what you're thinking." She suggested that each one pick an animal to start. "But not the one you already said you wanted to be. Pick an animal you think nobody would ever guess. Sit in a circle so we can go around and each person can ask a Yes or No question. First one to get three correct answers wins."

"What's the prize?" Gabriel wanted to know.

Maya considered for a minute. "Staff will wash breakfast dishes for the winner tomorrow morning." She glanced toward Sam, who nodded in agreement. "Unless, of course, Aidan or I win, in which case you all get to wash our dishes. I've already got an animal in mind. Someone ask me a Yes or No question."

"Does it have four legs?" Nick asked.

"Yes."

"Does it have fur?" Taylor.

"Yes."

Sam was pleased by how quickly they all dived into the game. After Justin correctly guessed a skunk, Ashley questioned whether Maya had given the correct answer to "Is it more than a foot tall?" The majority ruled that a skunk was probably shorter than that.

"I vote for Sparky to measure the next skunk we run across." Justin poked Ashley in the arm.

"Me next," Gabriel urged, waving his hand. "I have a really cool animal. From Earth, I promise. It's really cool."

Sam wanted to hear what the animal turned out to be, but

with eight in the circle, she knew this game could take forever, and she needed to make notes for her daily report, and then climb to the top of the ridge to get a cell signal and transmit her daily text report to Troy.

As she walked back down the slope after finishing her duties, she heard the voices of her crew going back and forth around the campfire. These kids were discovering coyotes and birds and goats and each other, and learning that they could not only survive in, but actually enjoy a world without smart phones and game consoles.

Returning to her tent, she shook her hair out of the French braid she usually wore when camping. While searching her tent pockets for her comb, a sharp object stabbed her finger. She pulled it out. It was a broken earring, a small silver filigree dangle on a broken wire. Entangled with it was a soft, rolled piece of paper that appeared as if it had been wadded up in the pocket for some time. She unfurled it carefully. The tiny ribbon of paper turned out to be a prediction from a Chinese fortune cookie: *You will meet a stranger who will change your future.*

Good God. That prophecy had come true with a vengeance for Kyla. Sam felt like setting a match to the creepy fortune. But maybe it would mean something to Troy. She pushed the earring and scrap of paper back into the tent pocket.

7

Sam's instructions were to stay in place the next day, which was fine with her. The clothes they'd washed still felt too damp to pack, and she was content to have a day of rest near the lake. The old logging road from which the counselor would hike in was less than two miles away, but the kids had no way of knowing that. To lessen the danger of a runaway, the field guide and peer counselors were forbidden from showing the crew a map or pointing out roads.

Sam was teaching the kids what she knew about the local geology when one of the Wilderness Quest mental health counselors, David Berg, strolled into their camp at ten-thirty a.m. Her mouth dropped open when she recognized his companion: Kyla's boyfriend, Chris Rawlins. Chris was first mate on a fishing boat, and she'd believed he was still working in the Bering Sea.

"I was," he said in response to her question. His face was reddened from recent exposure to wind and sun. "But the boat's in for an engine repair, so we've got a break until that's done. Troy knows I'm here."

She'd seen Chris only once since the murders, at the memorial service. Today, his expression was nearly as morose as it had been then. With reddish-blond hair and beard and weathered face, he resembled a young Robert Redford, although now his beard was ragged and his hair needed a trim.

For a few days in the wild, she'd managed to push the murders to the back of her mind, and she wasn't exactly happy to have his presence bring them to the forefront now. She was uncertain about how to greet him, but when he opened his arms, she gave him a quick hug. "How are you doing, Chris?"

He eyed the teens surrounding them. "Can we talk, Sam?"

Berg had already taken Taylor off for a one-on-one chat; she could see them sitting on the far bank of the lake. After ensuring that Maya and Aidan would keep an eye on the rest of her crew, Sam led Chris over the ridge to the tarn. Two crows were busily dipping their beaks at the water's edge, but took noisy flight as the humans approached. She and Chris parked themselves on the two least uncomfortable rocks near the small pond.

Chris's intense blue eyes met hers. "I need you to give me a character reference."

"Oh." Sam knew Chris mainly from her friends' conversations about him; she'd spent only a few hours in his company. Kyla had always been the bridge between them, with Kim occasionally offering motherly opinions about her daughter's relationship. "What's going on?"

His gaze focused on the water in front of them, and he rubbed his index finger across his chapped lips. The back of his hand was crisscrossed with scratches and cuts. "I did something really stupid, Sam."

An ominous opening statement. She waited.

"Before ... it happened, I had three guns."

She nodded. "I remember that Kyla said something about that." Her friend had detested having weapons in the house.

"Yeah. A rifle, a Remington 700, and two handguns, a Smith & Wesson .357 and a Glock 19."

Goosebumps crawled down Sam's spine. "Is that rifle a 30-06 caliber?"

"Yeah." His shoulders sagged. "I know how that looks."

Kyla and Kim had been murdered with two of those same caliber weapons. No wonder Chris had been listed as a "person of interest." She wasn't sure about the models, but the names sounded familiar. "From what Chase tells me, those are common guns, right?"

"Right."

"And I'll bet the police have tested them, right? So they know they weren't the ones." *Please let the answer be yes.*

His expression was grim. "Here's the stupid part." He sighed heavily. "After Kyla died, it just didn't feel right having guns in the house. I mean, these things *killed* her. So I sold all three guns. On Craigslist."

She could see how that might look bad to the police. "Well, Chris, I can understand—"

Slashing his hand through the air, he cut off her expression of sympathy. "It gets worse. I didn't even get the name of the buyer." His forehead puckered. "It was just some guy. He said his name was Robert, and he gave me cash."

"Jeez, Chris." She was appalled on multiple levels. Did people sell guns that casually all the time?

Moving his hand to the back of his neck, he massaged the muscles there as he stared over her shoulder into the distance. "I know, I know. I wasn't thinking. I bought 'em that way, no papers or anything. But my friends, well, I guess they told the cops I had 'em, because we've been out target shooting together a few times. And when I told Detective Greene all this, I could tell she didn't really believe me."

Detective Greene again. Sam had to meet the woman as soon as she could, find out where this investigation was headed. But the odds were not good that anyone in the Snohomish County Sheriff's Department would talk to her; she didn't even live in their jurisdiction. "I'm not sure what I can do, Chris, but if Greene asks—"

"Oh, she's asking everyone about everything. Remember about a week before Kyla's birthday, when we were all in the Kickin' A?"

When they were in town, Sam and Kyla, and once in a while even Kim, went to the saloon to take western line dance lessons. Sometimes Chris showed up, too, to shoot pool, drink beer, and two-step with Kyla.

"Yes," Sam said, although she couldn't put a finger on the exact date Chris was talking about. She had a whole group of line dance friends, and she always sat and chatted with whoever was there on any given evening.

"Greene's been out there, asking the manager and the staff about all of us. She even got hold of a photo of you and me sitting at a table with our heads together while everyone else was dancing."

"Really?" Sam didn't remember a moment like that.

"Greene showed it to me. She wouldn't say who took the picture, but I'm guessing it was that girl Janey."

"Jamie," Sam corrected. Jamie was a regular at Kickin' A. She lived for drama and was always spreading rumors about who was lusting after whom, stirring up trouble wherever she could. Sam avoided her as much as possible.

"Like I said, it was about a week before Kyla's birthday. She was on the dance floor and I was asking you what I should get her."

Sam nodded. "Now I remember."

"Greene asked what you and I had going on."

Shit. Was Detective Greene working on some sort of conspiracy theory? First asking Blake and Troy about Sam's new job as field guide, and now inventing an affair between her and Chris? Sam imagined what Greene would make of them sitting here together right now.

She exhaled slowly and rolled her shoulders, trying to release some of the tension there. "Thank God I have an FBI agent for an alibi."

Chris's attention was still focused on her, his blue eyes shiny, his lips tight with worry.

"Weren't you already gone fishing?" she asked. Neither of them could bring themselves to talk openly about the day Kyla and Kim were murdered, but it was almost more painful to talk around it like this.

"The boat left Bellingham that evening. At the time..." He paused, ducked his head, ran his fingers through his shaggy hair. "I was home. Alone."

"Dammit, Chris."

His chin jerked up. "Kyla told me she was going hiking with her mom. I had to pack; we'd already said our goodbyes. I knew I wouldn't see her until I got back. I didn't know I would never see her again." On the last word, his voice cracked and he raised a fist to his lips, then bent his head and closed his eyes. Opening his fist, he spread his fingers, pressing against his closed eyelids.

"Chris, stop, or in a second you'll have me crying." She rested a hand on his knee. "Thanks for telling me all this. I'll do what I can to set the record straight. I know you'd never hurt Kyla or Kim."

A tiny gremlin nagged at the back of her mind, reminding her she knew no such thing. She ignored it. If Chris had ever been violent with her friend, surely Kyla would have ditched him.

"Thanks." He took a shaky breath, and then stood up. "I wanted to tell you in person."

"I appreciate it." They started back up the trail to the lake.

"How long do you think this counseling stuff is going to take?" he asked.

"Probably most of the day," she guessed. "You can just hang with the rest of us till David's done." She pondered that for a minute. "Say, are you good at knot tying?"

"Couldn't work on a boat otherwise."

She stopped and turned to him. "I'm supposed to teach the kids outdoor skills every day. We have plenty of clothesline we can cut up. Could you show the kids how to tie some knots?"

"Love to." He actually smiled, revealing a dimple in his right cheek, and Sam remembered how much younger he'd looked before Kyla's death.

The crew kids were fascinated by the newcomer. They vied for Chris's attention, striving to achieve the fastest, most perfect bowline, half-hitch, and more complicated trucker's hitch. As one teen came back from a counseling session, Aidan or Maya would show that kid what he or she had missed. By three p.m., all of the kids had been through their one-on-one

sessions with David Berg. Chris was enthralling them with
harrowing stories about fishing in the Bering Sea when Berg
pulled Sam away for a private chat.

"How'd it go?" She wanted him to reassure her that she was
doing an adequate job as field guide.

"About like I expected. Gabriel is an open book, although
it's a pretty kooky open book."

They both chuckled.

"But the rest of them?" David shook his head. "None are
ready to give up all their secrets yet."

"Am I supposed to find a way to make them do that?"

"No. Just be grateful that you don't have to deal with the
families, too. Speaking of which..." He waved at Chris and
pointed to their backpacks, now emptied of the supplies they'd
carried. "Don't forget to ask the crew about their feelings, and
make them write in their journals and share tonight. It's
important."

"I'm on it."

The two visitors buckled on their packs. Sam said goodbye,
thanked Chris for making the trip, and wished him a safe
outing on his next fishing expedition.

He grimaced. "That assumes I make it back to Alaska."

As soon as the two visitors had left, Sam sat all the kids
down, asking them how they felt about talking to a counselor.
The opinion was unanimous: they were angry.

Justin picked up a rock and lobbed it hard toward the lake,
where it splashed into the shallows. "I'm pissed."

"Me, too," Taylor said.

Nick crossed his arms, his expression irritated. "We were
having a good time out here."

Ashley glared at Sam. "And then up comes the lurik shrink,
bringing up all the shit again."

Sam frowned back at her.

"Shit is not a swear word," the girl snarled. "Crap isn't a
swear word, so why should shit be?"

"Why can't you just leave us alone?" Olivia whined.

Sam wanted to tell them that the counseling visits weren't

her idea; that she would have been happy to simply lead them around the mountains and revel in nature for three weeks. But that wasn't the job. "The program is structured this way."

"You could unstructure it," Justin suggested.

"And like, add some better food." Gabriel, naturally.

"Here's the thing, crew," Sam explained to the circle of sullen faces. "I'm thrilled that you're enjoying being out here, but none of us can stay forever. We all have to go back to our regular lives. That's why you're supposed to work out a contract with your families."

Groans all around.

"What's the most important thing about a contract?" she asked per her instructions. It made her feel like the proverbial high school substitute who asked stupid questions. The clueless teacher everyone made fun of.

She was rewarded by six stony glares.

"What's the most important thing about a contract?" she repeated. "I'm going to keep asking until someone answers."

Gabriel gave in. "Both sides have to promise something to the other."

"Thank you, Gabriel. So think about what you want your families to promise you, and what you are promising them in return." She waited a beat for that to sink in, and then told them, "Tonight after dinner is sharing time."

More groans.

"No more gex *feelings*," Justin complained. "I'm all felt out." He shot a suggestive sideways glance at Ashley. "I'd rather be felt up."

Maya jumped in. "Sharing doesn't have to be talking about feelings, although that's always good. You can write something to share, or lead a song, or dance, or...well, whatever." She spread out her hands to demonstrate how wide open sharing could be.

"Stories and jokes are good, too," Aidan added.

Sam straightened. "Until dinner, you are free to write in your journals and think about what you want to share with everyone. Tell staff if you're leaving this group area, and stay where we can see you."

They all rose, issuing complaints as they separated.

"Sharing? Gex that." On his way back to this tent, Justin kicked a tree to punctuate the statement.

"I told Berg *he* needed to get his own shit together," Taylor told Gabriel.

Parking her butt on the ground and her back against a log, Sam made a few notes in her own journal and kept an eye on the crew as they scattered.

After each had pulled his or her journal out of a tent, the six kids huddled to discuss something. Sam couldn't hear what they were saying, but Taylor seemed to be the initiator, or maybe it was Gabriel. Aidan watched them from a distance and didn't seem concerned.

Maya lowered herself to the ground next to her. Sam fretted about what sort of conspiracy might be hatching. "It was all going so well before... I really don't know what I'm doing."

Leaning her head close, Maya murmured, "This has happened after every counseling visit on the trips I've been on. Didn't make any difference who was in charge."

Nick and Ashley retreated together to the far side of the lake with journals in hand. The other four chatted for a few minutes, and then Olivia and Gabriel ducked into their tents while Taylor and Justin picked out spots along the near shore with their journals in their laps.

The conspiracy turned out to be haikus for sharing that evening. That was unexpected; Sam would not have predicted that most of these kids knew what a haiku was. As they formed a semicircle around a small fire, she nearly asked permission to record their performances, but then realized they'd rebel if they knew the sound track was destined for the Wilderness Quest counselors back in the office. Reaching into her pocket, she surreptitiously clicked on the recorder as Haiku Night began.

Gabriel volunteered to go first. He stood up, lending his performance a more dramatic tone. "The sky is so vast, the bright stars are infinite, and I am so small."

All was quiet for a moment as he sat down again.

"Powerful," Ashley complimented him.

Sam agreed. Mister Lizard could be eloquent when he wanted to be.

"Me next." Taylor pushed herself to her feet. "I wrote this for my parents." She positioned herself on center stage, just beyond the fire. "I'm tall and I'm strong. Strong enough to say you're wrong. I will be myself."

"Right on, Sweet T!" Justin waved a fist.

Olivia rocked forward into the firelight. "You tell 'em, Taylor."

Next up was Justin, who prefaced his performance by saying, "I need two, to tell the whole story. The first is about my girlfriend, Anna." He scrubbed his spiky blond whiskers with dirt-rimmed fingers as he chanted, "Oh, baby, baby; I miss your soft silky lips; but I'm on a trip."

Nick choked down a laugh.

"Yeah, baby!" Gabriel snapped his fingers twice. Sam didn't know whether he intended to imitate beatniks or an old television show or something else.

Justin smiled, his teeth flashing white in the darkness. "Here's the second." He counted off the syllables by touching his thumb to his fingers as he said, "You ain't seen nothin', until you've see the somethins, that I've seen out here." He turned toward Sam to check her response.

"I'm impressed," she told him.

"Yay, Justice!" Taylor nodded in his direction.

So now Justin had a nickname, too. Sam wondered who had come up with that one.

Olivia shot to her feet. "Here goes." She studied her toes for a long minute, then raised her head and peered off into the trees above their heads. "I'm finding myself; with goats, whisky jacks, and friends; you won't stop me now."

She stepped around the fire back to her place. "That was for my parents, in case you couldn't guess." Then she shook her head. "No, maybe it's for the whole world."

Ashley patted her on the back, and Nick leaned toward

Olivia. "That was really good, Martini."

There was an awkward pause while all her crew regarded each other uncertainly.

"Nick? Ashley?" Sam named the two who hadn't yet spoken.

Nick reluctantly rose to one knee, and then to his feet. "Well, I don't want to go last, because I'm pretty darn sure this is crap."

"Was that it?" Aidan snickered. "Very original."

Nick shot him an exasperated look.

Maya counted off the words on her fingers. "That *was* seventeen syllables."

They all laughed. Nick's face grew dusky with embarrassment.

"Okay," he told them. "Now for my *second* haiku." He shook out his hands, cleared his throat, and then began. "I never meant to, I've done some terrible things, want to make it right."

That instantly sobered the group into an uncomfortable silence.

Sam interjected, "Thanks for saying what we all feel sometimes, Nick."

The boy's eyes were glistening with tears when he sat down. Of all her crew, Nick seemed by far the most sensitive. Or at least the most sad. She'd need to be sure he didn't start cutting again. Ashley patted Nick's arm, and then stood up.

"And now, for the final piece of crap." She strode to the other side of the fire, and motioned to Justin, Gabriel, and Maya as she said, "Gex, lurik, meekam, perfect words for my past life." She folded her hands together and bent her neck in a thank-you gesture, then raised her head and focused on the distance as she finished, "Now I look ahead."

Flattening one hand on her diaphragm and one behind her back, she bowed dramatically, the purple tips of her hair dipping briefly into the firelight. Everyone clapped.

"That was wonderful, crew," Sam told them. "I could listen to this every night. You are all natural poets."

Maya clasped her hands around her knees, grinning. "That's

the absolute best sharing I've heard out here."

Aidan agreed, and then reminded them, "We've been here two nights; that's enough rest. Early wakeup tomorrow for a long hike."

Sam clicked off the recorder as they all stood up to disperse for bed. The evening would have been perfect if only Kyla had been here.

Chase was frustrated. Sitting at the desk in his hotel room, he reviewed the slides on his laptop, committing the images to memory. Twice he had failed to spot vital pieces of bomb-making material in the staged scenarios. If he was ever called upon to save a crowd from a potential explosion, he'd probably be standing right next to a parking meter or a water fountain when it blew him to confetti along with everything else in the area. He was glad that none of his colleagues from Salt Lake was in his training group. Tomorrow was the last day of practice, and he had to do better. He had to stop thinking about Sam and her murdered friends and focus.

At least she wasn't in a foreign country this time, but she was in a remote camp in the wilderness. With juvenile delinquents who had God knows what kind of criminal records. Was she always going to embroil herself in dangerous situations so far from any help? Whoever had killed her friends was still out there. He called up the latest data on the murder investigation and read through it. There were several troubling entries. He texted Sam, asking her to call when she could.

His cell buzzed as he was brushing his teeth. "*Querida*," he breathed into the phone, then spat into the bathroom sink.

"Was that some sort of sexy Lakota greeting you've never told me about? Express your love, and then spit to ward off evil spirits or something?"

"Sorry." He wiped his mouth on a towel. "I figured you wouldn't be able to hear that. Toothpaste."

"How goes your training?"

"You know those Kevlar Michelin Man suits that the bomb

guys wear? I'm ordering one for everyone I know. I'll do my best to find a petite size for you."

"I'm sure it's not that bad."

If she wanted to believe he was perfect, who was he to shatter her illusions? "How's the Camping with Criminals program going?"

"They're more troubled kids than actual criminals." She sighed. "I think we're mostly moving in the right direction. At least I hope so. Chase, have you had a chance to check into the murder investigation?"

"Yeah. Ever since you told me, I've been keeping up with the case. Since it's on federal land, the file is available to the FBI."

She interrupted him with, "I saw Chris today, and he said a deputy was after him. So they haven't zeroed in on anyone yet?"

"Not yet." He didn't like the fact that a prime suspect now knew exactly where she was camped. "Summer, he's the reason I texted you. I want you to beware of Christopher Rawlins. He has a record. Assault and battery in a bar fight five years ago, illegal weapons discharge before that, along with possession of enough pot that he was probably selling it."

"Before pot was legal," she guessed.

"Obviously. But it's not legal everywhere, and it's not legal to sell it anywhere without a license." According to federal law, it still wasn't legal to sell marijuana anywhere in the nation, but he wasn't going to get into that sticky issue now.

"I remember Kyla saying Chris had some drinking issues in the past, and I know things get pretty rough sometimes on the fishing crews in Alaska. But none of that seems really major."

She was always too willing to give everyone the benefit of the doubt. "That's all major enough. Other charges could be missing because Rawlins hasn't been *caught* at anything else," he reminded her. "You said you didn't know him well."

"I don't. But I know..." Her voice caught in the middle of the sentence. "I knew Kyla."

"We can never know what's in another's mind, Summer. We can only judge by what they tell us."

During the brief pause that followed, he heard his own pedantic tone, and he felt insulted on her behalf. What a jerk he could be.

But then she only said, "Message received," and changed the subject. "Guess what? So far we've seen mountain goats. And gray jays that ate out of the kids' hands. And wildflowers are still blooming up here."

"Nice. I wish I could see all that." He loved this about Summer. She was so alive, she lived in the moment. She appreciated every flower, every bird, every animal, even the bugs. When he was away from her, his brain got bogged down by all the bad things that had ever happened and all the bad things that still could.

He heard only a staticky silence on her end. "Are you still there?"

Nothing. "Summer?" Had she lost reception or something? "What's going on?"

"Shhh!" she shushed him. That was followed by another long pause. Finally, she said, "I was listening to something moving through the woods."

His heartbeat sped up. "What?"

"Don't worry. It was probably a deer, or maybe a bear. I was afraid it might be one of my crew on walkabout, or maybe someone else camped nearby. One of the girls said she felt like she was being watched today."

"You mean there are strangers out there with you at night?"

"I suspect Ashley made it up. But yes, Chase, there might be other backpackers out here. We can't reserve the whole mountain range. But I'm pretty sure it was only some sort of critter."

"Pretty sure?" That meant she hadn't actually laid eyes on whatever had made the noise.

"Yes, Mr. FBI, I'm reasonably sure. Humans are not the only species that wander around here, you know. Anyway, whatever it was is gone. You can holster that pistol now." He could feel her smile through the phone. "Are you going to be able to come back here for my break?"

He groaned, hating to disappoint her. "The ASAC denied my request; I'm not on her favorites list right now. Gotta be back in Salt Lake working then. Sorry."

"That's okay. I'm only off for only a couple of days, and I can't keep asking you to come out here anyway. You're not made of money. After I get paid for this job, I'll come to Salt Lake, or we can meet somewhere in between when you get time off."

"We'll work it out," he reassured her. "Summer, be careful out there."

"Always. I should go make sure my teenage criminals are still in their tents. *Te quiero, mi amor.*"

He was happy to hear her say she loved him. He hoped it was only his imagination that she sounded a bit sad at the same time.

8

The next morning, they were all ready to move on, and Sam led them up a narrow trail over a steep pass. Then she asked Maya to lead the group down the valley to a long lake while she brought up the rear, pausing now and then to glance back on the trail. Ever since Ashley mentioned the feeling of being watched, Sam couldn't rid her mind of that disturbing idea.

The highlight of their hike was the discovery of a lush crop of ripe huckleberries. The time of year was right, so when she first noticed the red-tinged leaves, she checked for the small dark fruits that were mostly hidden near the ground. Taylor was the first to glance back and notice Sam pushing the berries into her mouth.

"Are those edible?" the tall girl asked.

"No." Plucking another berry, Sam popped it between her lips.

Taylor snorted and then squatted to begin her own search. "Blueberries, guys!"

They all stopped.

"Huckleberries, to be precise," Sam told them. "Close cousins to blueberries."

Gabriel trotted toward them. "Save some for me!"

"Look around," Aidan advised.

After scanning the area for a few seconds, Olivia exclaimed, "They are *everywhere!*"

"They just grow out here?" Justin asked.

The naiveté of the urban teens never ceased to amaze her, but Sam managed to stifle a sarcastic retort. Instead, she reminded them that all food came from the wild before humans domesticated animals and plants.

"Can we, like, graze, Cap'n?" Gabriel's lips were already tinged blue with juice.

"Like, why not?" she said. "Set down your packs, crew, and we'll feast on nature's bounty. That's the beauty of being out here. Our schedule is determined only by the sun and the weather, and me, of course. Today we have time to savor each moment. All we have to worry about is getting to camp before dark."

Taylor inhaled, thrusting out her chest. "These berries even smell purple."

"Like grape Kool-aid." Justin sucked in a breath and held it like he was toking on a joint.

"That's actually the lupines." Sam waved a hand at the mostly wilted stems of purple flowers that bloomed in bunches along the side of the trail. "They're past their prime, but still fragrant. And this—she waggled the white furry seed head of a plant between her thumb and forefinger—"this is pasqueflower, which has pretty white flowers earlier in the season. At this stage, it is sometimes affectionately called 'mouse-on-a-stick.'"

"On a stick? Ugh. Someone call the SPCA." Ashley shoved another handful of berries into her mouth.

They'd been sitting in the sunshine for nearly an hour among the huckleberries, collecting and eating handfuls, when Sam noticed Nick's gaze was glued to a spot halfway up the opposite hillside. The boy's expression was solemn; she couldn't decipher the emotion underneath. She followed his line of sight, and spotted a dark shape half hidden in the vegetation on the other side of the lake.

Nick's eyes met hers. She raised a finger to her lips, indicating that this was a secret between them, for now.

It took another ten minutes for anyone else to notice. "Wait a minute!" Ashley abruptly stood up and stared in that direction. "Is that a *bear*?"

Justin pushed himself to his feet. "What was your first clue?"

Ashley shoved him. "Uh, it looks like a bear, doofus."

"Don't call me a doofus."

"If the blue lips fit—"

Justin pursed his lips at her and made a kissing sound.

Olivia was staring across the valley, her face anxious. "It's moving!"

"Bears do that a lot." Nick.

"It won't come over here, will it?" Olivia wadded the hem of her T-shirt in her hands.

"Not likely; not while we're here," Maya reassured her.

Gabriel squinted. "Is it a grizzly?"

"What do you think?" Sam asked. "What's the difference between a grizzly and a black bear?"

"Grizzlies are brown," said Justin.

"Some black bears are brown," Aidan informed him. "Or red. Or even blond."

Justin frowned. "No shit?" He tossed a chagrined look Sam's way. "I mean, no gex?"

"Grizzlies have humps," Nick said. "And they're usually bigger, and their faces are dished."

"Dished?"

"They sort of dip in between their foreheads and their noses." Nick demonstrated by swooping a hand down from his hairline to the tip of his nose.

Taylor turned to Sam. "That right, Cap'n?"

"Nick is correct. Black bears have straighter noses and no humps on their shoulders. So which kind is that?" She handed Taylor her binoculars.

The girl studied the bear for a minute. "Black bear. Yikes! It's staring right at me."

"Probably not," Sam told the group. "Bears have pretty poor eyesight. That bear might be facing you and it might hear us or even smell us, but from that distance it probably can't tell what we are. And just for your information, crew, we have very few grizzlies in the Cascades. We'd be lucky to see one."

Olivia shivered. "I hope we're not that lucky. I saw a TV show about a woman who had her arms eaten off. I don't want to go on solo tomorrow."

Day Seven was the first of two overnight periods when the kids were supposed to be spaced out in their individual tents to spend twenty-four hours alone.

"You'll have your whistles, and Aidan or Maya or I will check in with you to make sure you're okay."

"But will you check in with Martini *before* or *after* the bear does?" Justin smirked at Olivia.

"Enough," Sam said. "We have had bears all around us for the last week. No problems, right? What do you think that bear is doing right now?"

They all stared at the bear for a moment, and then turned to stare at her.

"Planning its attack strategy?" Justin suggested.

"Yeesh, you guys! That bear's eating huckleberries, just like we are. Get a grip."

They watched as the bear ambled up through the vegetation and shuffled over the crown of the hill.

"Oh, crap." Maya stood up and held a hand over her eyes to shield them from the sun as she focused on the area to the left of where the bear had disappeared.

Gabriel followed her gaze. "Is that the same hunter?"

A camouflage-wearing man had climbed to the top of a boulder across the way. Sam grabbed her binoculars back from Taylor and pressed them to her eyes. She couldn't be absolutely sure it was the same guy, but this man was slender and he had a long dark ponytail, just like the previous hunter they'd seen. The rifle and scope slung over his shoulder looked the same.

She tried to reassure the group. "I can't tell if it's the same man. If he's traveling across country, like hunters often do, it's not so unusual that he might see us again." Although they had hiked many miles of trail, they actually had stayed in a fairly small area in terms of square miles.

Aidan was glued to his binoculars, suddenly as rigid as a guard dog.

Even with her binoculars, Sam couldn't see enough detail to be sure, but it seemed as if the hunter was staring right at her. He raised a hand into the air, signaling that he saw them.

Her stomach did a somersault.

The man's rifle remained dangling from the strap over his shoulder, clearly in safety mode, but just seeing the hunter and weapon again made the hair prickle on the back of her neck. Was he by himself? Did he have comrades hidden in the brush? If she were hiking alone, she'd hike fast and far to lose him. But now she was painfully aware that she was responsible for the safety of eight young people, including four beautiful teen girls. She couldn't hustle them an extra five miles and hide them all in the bushes.

Her crew kids' heads were swiveling as if they were following a tennis match: they faced the hunter on the ridge and then anxiously glanced back to the other teens. Nick appeared to be holding his breath. Olivia was chewing her thumbnail.

The hunter lowered his hand and then slipped down off the boulder, vanishing from view.

"It's okay," she told everyone. "He's being responsible. He waved to let us know that he sees us and won't shoot in this direction." *Please let that be true.*

The stranger could be a friendly, conscientious hunter. However, even if that *was* the case, it seemed likely that he was tracking that bear, and she had no desire to see him kill it. She didn't want the kids to witness that, either.

"C'mon, Aidan." She tapped him on the shoulder. He finally lowered his binoculars, but his expression was still tense. "Stand down," she told him. "He's gone."

She shouldered her backpack. "Grazing time is over, crew. Pick up your packs and let's move on toward camp."

* * * * *

No gunshots interrupted their evening, so apparently the hunter had either not seen the bear, wasn't out to kill it, or had hiked in the opposite direction. Sam hoped for all three.

After breakfast the next morning, she prepared the crew kids for their first solo campout, handing them plastic garden spades, packets of food, and coils of parachute cord. "You have your fire starter kits, you can heat up food in your metal bowls. You all know how to make a fire now. There are no bear boxes where you'll be staying, so follow the same rules we used in the camps where we needed to; don't leave any food or anything that smells like food out, seal it in your Kevlar bag and hang it up high."

Gabriel leaned toward Taylor and growled, "Bears."

"Keeping your food out of the reach of mice and coyotes is every bit as important, Gabriel," Sam chided him. "One of us will come to check on you during the daylight hours, and we'll come get you to regroup at noon tomorrow. If you get into trouble, blow your whistle and we'll come running. None of you will be very far away, but stay close to your tent. Enjoy this time alone."

"Can't wait." Justin's voice dripped with sarcasm.

Olivia regarded the spade in her hand. "Is this what I think it is?"

"Probably," Maya told her. "That's a personal dig-your-own toilet kit."

Ashley drawled, "Yippee."

"But what will we *do* out there?" Gabriel whined.

"Spend your time writing in your journals. You might plan something to share with the group," Sam suggested. "You should also think about the contracts you're going to make with your families. Envision where you want to be in five years and plan how you're going to get there."

Justin snickered. "Mars, spaceship."

Sam pushed the remaining supplies back into the bear sack. "Aidan, Maya, please take Justin and Ashley to their solo camps. I'll stay here with the rest until I see you coming back."

As soon as she spotted Aidan returning toward the camp,

Sam led Olivia to her assigned site in a small copse of alders near a stream that fed into the lake.

The girl seemed fearful. "What if a bear comes into my camp?"

"That probably won't happen, but if it does, you know what to do."

"Bang on a pan, yell?"

"That's right. And if it doesn't go away, blow your whistle." Sam didn't tell her those instructions would most likely work with a black bear, but might not scare off a grizzly. The odds of encountering a griz here were slim.

Sam, Maya, and Aidan left the crew kids in their solo camps for eight hours, then divvied up the task of visiting them all before dark. Sam chose her two favorites, Nick and Ashley.

She found Nick's camp neatly set up, his tent on a small rise away from the trees. The boy had collected stones to make a fire ring. A few coals smoldered within the small circle when Sam arrived. She found Nick sitting cross-legged in front of a downed tree. The dark rotting wood was covered with ruffles of bright orange fungi, and Nick was sketching the scene.

She studied the drawing in his journal. "That's really good."

"You don't need to check on me." He didn't look up.

"We're checking on everyone, just like we promised."

Abruptly, he leapt to his feet, tossing his journal to the ground. Yanking up first his shirt and then his sleeves, he showed her his flat abdomen and his forearms. "I'm not cutting."

"I didn't expect you to, Nick. You promised me you wouldn't."

"Yeah." His frown was defiant. She had no idea what was going on in the boy's head. She was glad she didn't have one of these mercurial teens waiting for her at home. Cats were mysterious enough.

After asking if he had any questions or wanted to talk—no and no—she wished Nick a good night and left for Ashley's camp.

At first she couldn't find the girl anywhere close to her tent.

She searched the nearby woods. No sign of Ashley. She circled the area. Shit, had the girl taken off? The counselors had warned her of this possibility. Why hadn't she seen it coming? She was pacing back and forth, working herself into a panic when a small crackling sound caused her to raise her head.

Ashley had shimmied up the trunk of an alder that leaned into two upright trees. She sat on a branch overhead, an amused expression on her face.

Sam took the same route up and perched a few feet away.

The girl had painted muddy stripes across her cheeks that transformed her into a slightly crazed warrior woman, especially in combination with her purple-tipped hair. She grinned at Sam. "Almost got away with it."

"Yes, you did."

"Hunger Games," Ashley said.

Fortunately, Sam understood the reference. The movie heroine had climbed a tree to avoid a group of killers. "Good thing you're not really on the run, isn't it?"

Ashley made a scoffing sound and stared off into the distance, where three thin columns of smoke rose into the sky. "Looks like the others are cooking dinner. Guess I'd better get to that."

They climbed down.

"Are you okay alone?" Sam asked.

"I've been alone most of my life."

Sam had a sudden impulse to hug the teen, but took her leave instead.

After Sam reunited with Aidan and Maya, the three staff members shared stories of what the crew kids were doing in their individual camps.

"Gabe is creating the story line for a new game," Aidan told them. "I barely escaped hearing about all the subplots for Episode Three. He'll probably be up to Episode Ten by dawn."

"What's it about?" Maya asked.

"You'll both hear all about it before this is over, I'm sure."

"I think Olivia's going to fast or eat her food cold so she won't have to come out of her tent," Maya said.

Sam frowned. Would the shy girl be terrified camping alone in the dark?

"We've had a lot of others stay inside their tents all night," Aidan told her.

Maya nodded her agreement. "They don't all have to be brave explorers. They just have to find the strength to endure twenty-four hours by themselves."

"Justin's creating a rock pyramid," Aidan reported. "He promised to knock it down tomorrow."

Taylor was making lists in her journal of things she planned to do in the future. She seemed to be the only teen with any noticeable ambition.

Sam and her two peer counselors enjoyed a quiet evening by themselves. While Sam and Maya talked and explored the immediate area, Aidan collected some long grasses, then sat with his back against a tree as he braided them and then proceeded to deftly stitch the braids together with more grass, creating a small circular mat.

Sam peered over his shoulder. "Coaster?"

He tilted his head to the side. "Unless I keep going, in which case it could be a placemat. Or even a doormat."

"Interesting. You should teach the kids how to do that." It would relieve her of some teaching duty, in addition to giving the kids something else to do in their spare time.

He nodded. "I will."

The sunset was largely hidden behind the tall mountains surrounding the lake, but the three of them stayed on the shore, watching the stars come out until they got cold and crawled into their tents, Aidan and Maya to read and Sam to write up her notes.

When she got up to pee, Sam was treated to a meteor streaking across the black velvet sky. The August Perseid shower was over, but she was happy that a few stragglers were still rocketing through early September. It would be nice if some of the crew kids were seeing them now.

She sat on a rock by the lake shore for a moment, grateful that no whistles had sounded. If only Chase were beside her.

With him unwilling to give up his job and Sam unwilling to join him in Salt Lake, they seemed doomed to slip into each other's lives like asteroids temporarily caught in a planet's orbit, then slingshot away, alone in the vastness of space.

Did that mean they didn't love each other enough? Should one of them be willing to make a major compromise? Her only other long-term relationship had been years ago with self-absorbed newscaster Adam Steele. He had definitely expected all compromises to be hers.

As her crew regrouped the next day, the talk was all about what had happened during their solo campouts. Nick recounted the small animals and birds he'd seen. "I heard a great horned owl, too."

"Something a lot bigger than that was prowling around my tent," Ashley said. "A bear."

Justin and Gabriel rolled their eyes. But Maya, who had brought Ashley back, confirmed the story. "There were bear prints about thirty feet away from Ash's tent."

Ashley looked smug. "I threw a rock at it, and I heard it run away.

"Omigod," Olivia gasped. "I don't know what I'd do if one came close to my tent."

Maya's mouth turned up at the corners. "There were bear prints in your camp, too."

"For real?" Olivia's brown eyes were huge. "I went out to pee when a bear was there?"

"Huh," Justin huffed. "It was probably too afraid to come to my camp. I was ready for it."

"The point is," Sam said, "that bear was around but left us all alone. Nobody had to blow a whistle. You should all be proud of yourselves."

Ashley turned to her. "I saw your light. You guys didn't really need to come check on me."

The muscles between Sam's shoulder blades tightened. "I didn't, Ash. You saw a light?"

The girl nodded. "Headlamp or flashlight. In the woods, not too far away."

"Me, too," Taylor said. "I figured it was one of you." Her gaze bounced from Aidan to Sam to Maya.

Could it have been that hunter? Or another backpacker? Wandering around after dark in the mountains was not a common activity. She considered how close together the solo camps had been, how Ashley had observed smoke from several of the cooking fires.

"Maybe it was one of your friends here," Sam suggested, checking their expressions. "Was one of you skulking around in the dark?"

Did Nick look troubled? Was that a flash of guilt she saw on Justin's face? She simply couldn't tell. Her entire crew professed their innocence, swearing they'd all stayed in their own camps for the entire time. Sam didn't know what to think; they all had headlamps and they'd all had plenty of time on their hands during their solo campouts.

She'd been warned about teens hooking up for sex. Had one of the boys been sniffing around Ashley's and Taylor's tents?

Their faces revealed nothing.

If one of them was guilty, he or she was hiding it well. She had no evidence against anyone. "Anyway," she summarized, "you all survived. Now, gear up; we're moving ten miles today."

At their next camp, she instructed Aidan and Maya to set out the food and pots for dinner and then find something else to do. Aidan perched on a log, a minuscule sewing kit beside him, and set about stitching up a rip in his pants leg. Maya braced her back against a tree and focused on a book in her lap. Sam sat not far away from her, reviewing her guidebook and keeping an eye on her crew.

Gabriel was the first to notice that dinner preparations were not underway. "What's supposed to happen here?" He spread his hands out to indicate the supplies. "Who's supposed to do what?"

Sam yawned dramatically. "Staff is tired. It's the crew's turn to cook from here on out."

"Huh." Taylor's expression was annoyed, but she walked over to the supply area to survey the dinner ingredients. "It looks like goulash tonight."

Shaking his head, Justin reached for the largest pot. "I'll get the water. Lightning, wanna come with me?"

Nick grabbed another pot, and snatched up the water filter, and they turned toward the creek they'd crossed a short time ago.

They argued about who was supposed to do what and girls' chores versus boys' chores, but the teens managed to cook dinner with a minimum of scorching and when it was clear that the staff was no longer responsible for doing dishes, either, the crew also cleaned up afterwards. She had to remind them to hang the remaining food from the trees, but overall, Sam imagined that Kyla would be proud of her group.

Sam reported the successful solos to Troy that evening. He congratulated her on how well her expedition was going, but he sounded despondent.

Maya was right, it helped to be away from Bellingham, in the backcountry with a job to do. The tasks Troy was doing every day would remind him of his dead wife and daughter. "How are you, Troy?"

"Day to day," he responded. "And thank you again, Sam."

"*Please* stop thanking me. I'm only a third of the way through this gig." She could hardly believe she was saying that; it felt like she'd been out here for at least a month. "Have the cops been by? Is there any news?"

She heard Troy slowly inhale and then exhale just as slowly, and guessed he was trying to keep his voice under control. Finally he said, "A Detective Greene from Snohomish County was here yesterday."

"What did Greene want?"

"She asked about Chris and what we knew about him, and

she wanted to know all about the company history and
finances, what Kim did at Wilderness Quest and what I'm
doing, how long you had worked here."

"Did she ask how much you were paying me?"

"Yeah, she did. I explained that these were extraordinary
circumstances."

"No kidding." She felt slightly guilty about the deal she'd
made with Troy, but she needed that extra money. And this
was an extraordinarily stressful job that she would never have
taken under normal conditions. "Do you have a clue what the
authorities might be thinking, Troy?"

His laugh was bitter. "They're checking out me, Chris, you,
everyone I ever prosecuted."

She hadn't considered *that* pool of possible suspects: Troy's
job with the Prosecuting Attorney's Office had no doubt earned
him many enemies. "Are there any suspects there?"

"I suppose there's one or two. Over the years, I received
several notes from one guy by the name of Hockney. He got
five years for his third DUI; he was upset, to say the least. He
lost his job, of course, and his wife and kids left him while he
was in lockup."

"Those sound like self-inflicted wounds."

"It's a common story. There's another one, a Martha
Sheldonack, who hates me because the guy we prosecuted
didn't get sent away. It was a case of road rage, and the guy
sideswiped their car and killed her husband and daughter. But
there was also a deer that ended up entangled in the wreck,
and the defense made it sound like Bambi caused the accident
instead of the maniac who forced the Sheldonacks off the
road."

Sam was grateful that it wasn't her job to handle all those
sad cases. "Do you think either of those two is so determined to
get back at you that they would hurt your family?"

"Seems like a long shot."

"Do they live in the area?"

"Hockney is in Ferndale and Sheldonack lives in Deming."
He named two towns in Whatcom County, each less than

twenty miles from Bellingham.

She was glad she was up in the mountains away from the crazies.

"My best guess, Sam? The cops are grasping at straws, hoping the right one floats by on the stream."

"That's the feeling I'm getting, too. Stay strong, Troy."

"Remember that your break is coming up in a few days; we can talk more then."

"I'm ready for some time off." She concluded the phone call.

As she lay in her tent that night, she dreamed fitfully about hazy threats that never quite materialized. In her nightmare, she was hiking with her friends in dense fog when a rifle barrel appeared out of the mist.

She tried to shout a warning, but her voice didn't work right and Kim and Kyla couldn't hear her. Sam woke to find the corner of her sleeping bag had flopped over her face as she slept. The word "Kyla!" was still echoing in her head.

9

Sam didn't find the note until she had stuffed her sleeping bag into its sack. The small slip of paper, previously smashed under her makeshift pillow, skittered across the floor of her tent. She flattened it with her fingers.

KLAPTON WAS HERE.

All caps, scratched in blue ink on the back of a sales receipt. Squinting at the faded print on the other side, she made out the words *Glacier, OJ*, and *ter jrk*.

Looked like the writer had stopped at the convenience store in the small town of Glacier and purchased orange juice and...teriyaki jerky? But how the hell had the note appeared under her pillow? Goosebumps spilled down the back of her neck at a sudden vision of a hand snaking into her tent as she slept.

She rarely zipped the exterior rain flap; being completely closed up made her feel like she was sleeping in a sandwich bag. Had she left the net door unzipped, too?

She backed out of her tent and inspected the ground around her knees. She'd obliterated whatever marks were immediately in front of the door by crawling over them, but she located several prints a couple of feet away. Two mostly whole prints, a couple of heel and toe marks. Men's boots, most likely. Not big enough to be Justin's or Gabriel's, too big to be Nick's. The prints looked about Aidan's size.

He was bent over his pack, stuffing in cooking gear, when she tapped him on the shoulder and shoved the note in front of his face. "Did you do this?"

He pulled his head back a few inches and stared at the note for a minute. His forehead wrinkled, and he pursed his lips. Then he took the note from her, lowered it in front of his chest and scanned the message again. Flipping it over, he studied the receipt side for a few seconds.

"What's up with this?" she asked again, pulling it from his hands.

Finally he raised his eyes to hers. "Am I supposed to have an answer to that?"

"Is it some sort of joke?" she persisted.

He quirked a sandy eyebrow. "If it is, nobody let me in on it. Who's Klapton?"

She shook her head. "I haven't got a clue. The only Clapton I know is the guitar player, and his name is spelled with a C."

Maya joined them. "What's going on?"

Sam showed her the note. "Someone left this in my tent."

"*Inside* your tent?" Maya asked, her eyes wide. "When?"

Sam abruptly realized she'd only *assumed* the note had been left as she slept. "I'm not sure."

Now that she thought about it, it could have happened anytime after the tents were set up. She hadn't been standing guard, and as Voyagers, the kids were allowed to wander around camp. If one of them had pushed the note beneath her pillow yesterday evening, she could have easily overlooked it until this morning.

Maya raised an eyebrow just as Aidan had. "Who's Klapton? Or is it a what?"

Sam shrugged. "Beats me. There were boot prints outside my tent, too."

"And *that's* a surprise?" Aidan asked. "We're all wearing hiking boots."

The three of them inspected the area. Aidan stepped next to one of the prints, bounced on his feet, then stepped away. "See, those are mine. Timberlands. There's the tree circle logo." He spiraled a finger above a smudged circle in the prints.

To Sam, Aidan's seemed slightly larger than the first prints, but then, he'd bounced to make a deep impression in the soft ground. "Why were you standing outside my tent?"

Aidan rubbed his stubbly jaw, thinking. Then he snapped his fingers and pointed his index finger at her chest. "Remember, I came over here yesterday to ask you about dinner?"

It seemed unlikely that his prints would have remained intact with all her comings and goings since then, but she wanted to believe him. "I remember now, thanks."

Maya's brow was still furrowed. "Wait. Aidan, wasn't Klapton the guy that Kyla talked about?"

"Was it? I don't remember." His expression was perplexed.

"You know," Maya persisted, "on the day we got back from the last expedition. Remember, we were in the locker room and she got a Facebook message from him?"

Aidan scratched his head. "Sorry. Girl chat doesn't register with me. Just ask my sisters."

Sam faced Maya. "What did Kyla say about Klapton?"

Maya pulled on an earlobe, thinking. "I'm trying to remember. I think he was some sort of long-lost boyfriend that got into drugs, big-time. She didn't know what to do about him."

Justin nudged his way into their trio and stared at the ground, too. "What are we lookin' at?"

How easy it was to make others look by simply gazing in a certain direction. Sam shifted her eyes to the boy's face. "Nothing of interest," she told him, hoping that was true.

Justin jerked his head toward the cluster of the other five crew kids, who stood talking to each other, their packs resting on the ground at their feet. "We're ready."

"Then I'd better get a move on. Be there in a minute."

When he'd walked out of earshot, Aidan asked, "You're using Kyla's gear, right? Are you sure that note wasn't stuck to the bottom of the sleeping bag or something?"

Sam was starting to feel foolish.

"Might be some sort of crew prank, too," Aidan added. "Although I still don't get it."

"Want me to grill them?" Maya asked.

Sam considered. If any of the staff asked and the teens hadn't been in on the joke, they would naturally be curious about the note. After twice seeing the hunter and Taylor and Ashley's reports of lights in the woods during their solo, the suggestion of someone skulking around in the dark while they slept would definitely freak everyone out. Sam was a little freaked out herself. "Don't say anything to the kids; we'll see if one of them gives us a hint."

Her peer counselors nodded and walked toward the waiting crew. Sam crawled back into her tent and began to shove her belongings outside toward her pack. The note felt like some sort of junior high prank designed to scare, like rattling a door knob and then vanishing into the night. She needed to be the adult here and not overreact.

Someone was probably trying to spook her. Or maybe Aidan was right, the note had been in her gear the whole time. The small slip of paper could have been inside Kyla's pack or stuck to the sleeping bag or stuff sack. But she couldn't rid her mind of the image of a hand slipping inside her tent as she slept. In her imagination, that hand belonged to that long-haired camo-wearing hunter. Had he been holding the light that had flashed through the woods on the solo campouts, too? Was he following them? Was he *stalking* them?

Was it only her imagination, or had Aidan reacted oddly when she showed him the note? It had seemed like he was stalling for time. Were those boot prints his, or a stranger's? She shuddered.

Crazy thoughts? Had she become paranoid because her friends had been murdered?

Maybe.

Possibly.

Probably.

Who wouldn't be paranoid? She had killers skulking around her brain.

She unclipped her tent from the frame and snapped the poles into a bungee-corded cylinder.

Get a grip, Westin. It was only a note. The prints came from common boots. Most likely Aidan's boots. She was spooking herself with all these speculations. Someone was probably playing a joke. The real joke was that *she* was expected to be the voice of reason and sanity on this expedition.

Rolling up the tent and ground sheet, she stuffed them into the tent sack. The next camp was twelve miles away. If nothing happened there, she would know she was imagining threats where none existed.

None of the kids revealed anything about the note. If it was a prank, they kept the secret well. Sam still didn't understand what the words were supposed to mean, and when nothing more happened in camp, she suspected the Klapton note was no more meaningful than the fortune cookie scroll—just old detritus from an often-used tent.

The night before the staff break, the scheduled exercise was intended to get the crew to start talking about feelings, since the counselors would be staying with the kids for the next two days to discuss their emotional and behavioral progress and their work on the family contracts. As was now their habit, they all sat in a circle, this time with the candles in their midst for a focal point. Firewood was scarce in the area. Partially because of that, and partially to temper the discomfort of having the counselors in charge, the group would be allowed to use stoves for cooking during the staff break.

Sam flipped on her still-hidden recorder, then started the evening discussion. "I know you all had a lot of time to think during your first solo. Our exercise tonight is to state what you're feeling now." She hesitated a moment to let that sink in. "Here are the rules: no judgments, there are no right or wrong statements, any of you can comment as long as you're respectful."

The response almost seemed planned as the teens groaned in unison.

"I'll start so you can have a minute to think about it." She took a breath, and then placed a hand on her chest above her heart. "I feel happy that I get to share my love of nature with you all. And I hope that the experience of being out here makes a difference in your lives."

Then she pointed to her right, at Gabriel.

The boy squirmed for a minute, his face solemn, then crossed his arms and looked up. "I feel like a lot of others are getting to level thirteen while I'm out here communing with birds."

Justin snickered, but when Sam glared at him, he fisted his hand in front of his mouth and changed the sound to a cough.

Aidan leaned forward, peering around Justin to ask Gabriel, "So what if they do?"

While Gabriel considered the question, they heard only the whispering of the candle flames as they flickered in the slight breeze. Then the boy's shoulders lifted and sagged, and a calm settled on his face. "Yeah, so what if they do?"

Aidan was a born counselor. She was grateful to have him along.

Next up was Olivia. The girl studied her hands, which she clasped in her lap as she mumbled, "I feel like nothing will change when I get back."

This time Ashley leaned in. "Can't *you* change, Olivia?"

A glimmer of satisfaction began to glow in Sam's belly. This was how things were supposed to go. The kids were learning, and so was she.

Taylor added, "If *you* change, that'll change the equation, right?"

Olivia, a doubtful frown on her face, responded by pointing back at Taylor. "Your turn."

The lanky girl straightened her spine and placed her hands on her knees, somehow managing to make the position look authoritative. "Okay. Here's what I feel: I'm not going to take it anymore. *I'm* going to change the equation."

Sam wanted to ask what this mysterious equation was, but her instructions were to stay quiet unless a fight erupted.

Ashley said, "I like it here. The food may be crap but the

rules are easy, and there aren't so many people in my face all the time. I'm afraid that when I go back home I'll start doing all the bad stuff all over again." Before anyone could comment, she held up a hand like a cop stopping traffic. "But I'm going to try my best not to, because I don't want to be like that anymore."

Instead of meeting anyone's eyes, Nick drooped forward over his crossed legs and poked a finger in the dirt. He pinched up a little, rubbing the soil between his index finger and thumb. "I feel like I've got to find a way to get beyond this thing with my dad."

Several of the kids nodded, but nobody offered any advice.

Dropping the dirt, Nick rubbed his fingers on his pants leg. "But I can't think of any good way to do that."

Sam wanted to know what "the thing" was with Nick's dad, but nobody else seemed curious about that. Maybe all teens had "things" with their parents. Heaven knows she'd had issues with her own father.

When it was his turn, Justin began by flexing his biceps and cracking his knuckles. "I feel like I'm strong out here. I mean, I've always been strong." He struck a bodybuilder pose and flexed again for emphasis. Ashley snorted in response, and Nick shook his head.

Relaxing his posture, Justin continued, "But out here I'm strong *with* you guys, not against you. Like that rope thing, how we all did our part to get over it."

"Way to say it like it is, dude." Aidan offered Justin a fist to bump.

Sam was allowed to sum up the exercise. "I feel like you guys are getting smarter by the hour. The world can be ugly or cruel, or just plain stupid, but you realize *you* don't have to be ugly or cruel or stupid. Things around you can fall apart, but you can keep yourselves together."

Sam was sure she sounded incredibly wise.

Taylor rolled her eyes. "You don't remember what it's like to be sixteen."

Several of the others muttered a "yeah," seconding Taylor's statement.

Sam lifted her chin. "I was sixteen once. My mom died when I was nine, so it was just my dad and me, and he didn't understand me very well."

Crap. She had just fallen into her crew's typical routine of blaming others. Too late, she corrected herself, "We didn't understand each other very well."

Maya volunteered, "When I was sixteen, I was convicted of burglary and some other stuff."

All the crew faces swiveled to stare at her.

"Yeah." She ran her fingers through her spiked ebony hair, nodding. "And I was in my fourth foster home." Her gaze slid skyward for a beat, then back down. "No, my fifth."

They all turned to look next at Aidan. He chuckled and bounced his shoulders. "I got nothing, sorry. Hey, someone has to do the two-parent, middle-class thing. Else what would you guys have to compare against?"

"And that's an excellent stopping point." Sam stood up. "I have notes to write and plans to make. It was a good day, and now good night, all."

The kids dispersed to their tents. Sam strolled off into the dark woods to answer a text from Troy, confirming their location and approximate time for the pickup and staff exchange tomorrow. After she'd done that, she skipped down to a new line and typed *The name KALPTON mean anything to you?*

As she waited for a response, she leaned against a cedar. With little air movement, the evening was quiet, the hush almost velvety. Her eyelids felt so heavy she could hardly keep them open. The abrupt buzz of the phone in her hand startled her so badly that she nearly dropped it.

WWQ Admin lit up the screen.

"Troy?" she answered quietly.

"Where did you see the name Kalpton?"

She told him about the note she'd found. "It was actually Klapton; I can't type worth a darn on this thing. It was probably some kid's idea of a joke, but it also might have come from Kyla's pack or sleeping bag."

"Klapton with a K?" Troy sounded breathless.

"Yeah. Is that important?"

"Can you describe this note?"

"Uh, blue ink, all caps. It's on the back of a receipt from the convenience store in Glacier."

"Glacier?" There was a beat of tense silence before he asked, "Is there a date?"

"Just a second, I've got it in my pocket." She pulled out the slip of paper. "I can't see in the dark. I'm going to turn on the flashlight mode on this cell; if I disconnect you, I'll call back." She scanned the note and raised the phone to her lips again. "No, if there ever was a date, it's been torn off."

"Sam, are you in the same place as you were when you found that note?"

"No, that was this morning. We hiked twelve miles today."

"That's good. Did you see any other hikers along the way?"

She mentally rifled through the day's events for a minute. "No."

Several quick breaths rasped across the airwaves. Troy sounded like he was hyperventilating. "Sam, bring the whole crew down to the trailhead tomorrow, first thing after breakfast. We're going to relocate everyone."

Now she felt like *she* was on the verge of hyperventilating. "What's going on, Troy?"

"I have to go; I've got a lot of arrangements to make. Please don't say anything to anyone else."

"Troy?"

"I'll explain everything tomorrow, Sam. Be extra careful tonight." He hung up.

"Gex!" she hissed, staring at the phone. What the hell? Chase was right when he said that she didn't know the Quintana-Johnson family well enough. Troy Johnson was hiding something.

10

Sam considered calling Chase. After checking the time, she realized it would be nearly one a.m. on the east coast, if he was still there. Earlier in Salt Lake if he was home, but there was no way he could shed any light on whatever was going on, anyway. She settled for texting *Miss you* to him, then punched Home on her call list.

"Whazzup?" her housemate Blake answered.

"Since when do you talk like that?" she asked.

"I figured you'd be fluent in teenspeak by now. Although I think Hannah says "S'up?" when she's trying to be cool. Or whatever they say instead of 'cool' now. Rad? Sweet? Sick?"

"Don't ask me." Hannah was Blake's daughter, fifteen years old a few weeks ago. It was comforting to hear her housemate's usual banter. "I assume it's my duty to teach these kids adult English."

"So, same question—s'up, Sam? How's life in the wild?"

"Well, like you might expect, it *is* wild from time to time. The food is pretty awful, and now that the crew is cooking it, it's burned half the time. And you should have seen my biggest kid throw the smallest one over a five-foot-high rope."

"And some people worry about bears."

"We did see a bear. And some mountain goats. Gray jays. And a couple of hunters." *Or maybe the same hunter twice.*

"I'm impressed." After a pause, he added, "I *am* supposed to be impressed, right?"

Blake was not a wilderness type.

"Yes. Those critters are not so unusual up here, but it's always sweet to spot them. How's Simon? How's Claude?"

"They're both soft and purry when they want to be, and all teeth and claws at other times."

Sam laughed. "I hope it's the former most of the time."

"It is, thank God. Although you need to come home ASAP, because Simon's taken to sleeping on my head, and Claude says that is not a good look for me."

She laughed again.

"Maya okay?" he asked.

"Everyone's okay so far. It's just been a little stressful for me; you know I'm not a natural caretaker."

"You mainly kill house plants. And maim perfectly good groceries now and then."

"Right. Anyhow, I just wanted to hear your voice. I'll be home tomorrow night. Just for two nights, though."

"Tomorrow? I'd better vacuum up the dust bunnies. They're more like jackrabbits now. I'm pretty sure they mate in the wee hours of the night. And Simon can sleep on *your* head for a change."

"I'm glad you're there to take care of everything, Blake. I always feel better after I talk to you."

"Then I'm impressed all over again. And if you get eaten by a bear, I still get the house, right?"

"As long as you keep cooking and paying rent, you'll stay in my will," she promised.

"Ah, cooking. Let me think about that."

She knew he would. He took nearly every culinary class the community college offered each quarter. Eating great meals was one of the benefits of living with her housemate. "Night, Blake."

For a minute after she turned off the phone, she stood still, listening to her surroundings. Something cracked a short distance away. A branch dropping to the ground?

A footstep on a twig?

Klapton?

She waited, listening to her own heart pounding, holding

her breath, but there was nothing more, and her heart rate slowed back to normal.

Damn Troy. That phone call had put her on edge. But Troy was a cautious man. If some danger was lurking in the dark, surely he would have sent in reinforcements, even if they had to travel in darkness.

Wouldn't he?

She told herself he would.

The camp was quiet when she returned, with all lights out. An owl hooted softly in the woods. In the serenity of the night, it seemed melodramatic to worry about a piece of paper, and she cursed Troy for being so mysterious about that dang note. Unzipping her tent, she slithered into her sleeping bag, being careful to pull her door zipper tightly closed. She stashed her headlamp under her pillow and opened her jackknife and placed it within reach. If a hand slipped into her tent tonight, the intruder was not going to escape unscathed.

Every tiny sound of the forest woke her up. By dawn, she was exhausted.

"What? *Why* are we relocating?" Aidan wanted to know. "We've only done that once before, when there was a threat of forest fire." He scanned the sky around the campsite.

"I don't know exactly," Sam hedged. "Maybe some sort of Forest Service directive? I'm sure Troy will fill us in later."

"He'd better. This doesn't make any freakin' sense." He stomped off to pack his tent.

Sam whispered to Maya, "Why is Aidan upset? We move almost every day."

"I don't know. He's been sort of in a mood lately. Maybe because he's going back to college in a couple of weeks? I think he's worried about paying the tuition."

That might explain his erratic behavior; Aidan's job here ended after this expedition. "I understand about money issues. Does he have a job lined up at school?"

"Dunno. I think he tutors sometimes."

Maya would soon be out of a job, too. And Sam Westin would be unemployed again, too. As they broke camp, Sam considered where she might look for work.

As usual, the staff didn't tell the crew kids where they were going. The group got excited when they crested the hill and saw the company van in the lot below.

Justin pointed at the parking lot. "What the gex?"

"Was the twenty-one day threat just a bluff?" Ashley.

Taylor suggested, "Time off for good behavior?"

Olivia stopped in her tracks, causing the three kids behind her to halt, too. "I'm not ready to go back home."

Sam, bringing up the rear, was surprised to spy Troy Johnson leaning against the front bumper of a Jeep Cherokee, scanning the slope with binoculars. He seemed to be training them above their location on the mountainside. She glanced over her shoulder. Nothing but empty trail behind her as far as she could see. What was he watching for?

"Nobody's going home yet," Sam informed her crew. "But like I told you earlier, the counselors are going to take the place of me, Maya, and Aidan for a couple of days. They're bringing you chocolate and letters from your families."

"Good news on the chocolate," Ashley drawled.

"And you'll get the counselors' help to work on your contracts with your families," she reminded them.

"Gex counselors!"

"Lurik contracts!"

"Meekam families!"

"Onu, onu, onu!"

At least the last refrain from Olivia got a chuckle from everyone, so her crew sounded lighthearted as they reached the parking lot.

Troy explained to the group that the Forest Service had asked the company to move this crew to a different location for the duration of their field trip. They forgot about their annoyance at being shepherded by three counselors for the next two days when he added, "And the big news for you all is that the van will stop at a restaurant on the way to your new location. You can order whatever you want."

"Cheeseburger, cheeseburger, cheeseburger!" Justin yelled.

"A giant fresh salad with veggies and crunchy croutons and ranch dressing." Taylor's eyes were half-closed, her expression dreamy.

As they climbed into the company van, they eagerly discussed what they would eat. After the outgoing field crew conferred briefly with the incoming counselors, Troy directed Sam, Maya, and Aidan to the Jeep. He jerked his thumb at the van, which was backing up to turn. "They're going south to Highway Twenty; we're going back to Bellingham."

After tossing her pack into the cargo area, Sam slid into the passenger seat beside Troy. Aidan and Maya climbed into the back seat.

"What's really up, boss?" Aidan asked.

Troy started the engine. "Like I said, some Forest Service thing. It's happened before. Annoying how they never bother to give us enough notice." He shot Sam a sideways look that said *we'll talk later.*

As much as her two peer counselors said they were looking forward to a break from their teen charges, the crew was all they could talk about on the way back. Aidan and Maya discussed liaisons they saw developing.

"Justin and Olivia," Maya suggested.

Aidan countered with, "Taylor and Gabriel."

Sam twisted in her seat to glance back over her shoulder. "Seriously?"

"Trust us," Aidan responded. "Nick and Ashley."

"Call me Ash," Maya poked Aidan in the arm with an index finger. "Or you get this knife I no longer have."

"Don't threaten me; I'll send a vortenex after you."

"Voltenark!" Maya exclaimed. "Don't you pay attention to anything? Vortenexes are pussycats, while a voltenark could rip you to shreds."

"What *is* all that?" Troy asked, frowning at them in the rear view mirror.

"You had to be there, boss," Maya told him.

Aidan's funk seemed to have lifted, at least for the moment. As her two assistants laughed together, Sam turned her face to the side window and silently watched the scenery slip past. After ten days in the backcountry, all the cars zipped by too fast, and there were way too many of them. The tiny village of Glacier seemed crowded, and the larger settlement of Maple Falls, with two gas stations and neon signage for several fast-food restaurants, seemed downright garish.

What was Chase looking at right now? She wished she could go out to dinner with him tonight, then relish hot sex and happy dreams while cuddling in her bed.

But maybe it was just as well that they were apart. Chase would not approve of the activities she had planned for the next couple of days.

Troy drove to the Wilderness Quest office. Maya and Aidan deserted them in the parking lot.

"Showers, then party time," Aidan told Sam. "Cheeseburger, cheeseburger, cheeseburger!"

"No, pizza!" Maya argued, then turned to wave from the window of Aidan's silver Subaru Forester as they drove out of the lot. "See you day after tomorrow!"

Sam watched her two peer counselors vanish down the road, something about Aidan's car tickling her memory. But silver Foresters were nearly as common as squirrels in Bellingham.

"Maya's still bunking in the staff house, I take it," Troy observed.

"Guess so." Whatever was bugging her about Aidan's car refused to come into mental focus. She wearily picked up the pack at her feet.

"Our summer rental house closes down after this expedition," Troy warned.

Maya would be unemployed and homeless. Again.

Troy unlocked the door of the office and held it open for her. "How's the expedition going, Sam?"

"Slowly." She followed him, curious about why the building was vacant until she remembered it was Sunday. Troy led her into the company break room, where Sam plopped down at a round table, grateful to sit in a chair for a change. He pushed a bottle of orange juice into her hands. She eagerly opened it.

Troy helped himself to a cup of water from the filter gizmo attached to the faucet. On the counter between sink and refrigerator rested a large bouquet of pink carnations and daisies. Behind that, a photo had been taped to the wall: a fish-eye portrait of Kim and Kyla, standing side by side, smiling in their jeans and tees. The glittering water of Pinnacle Lake filled the background. Kyla's arm extended off to the left side of the photo. The selfie.

Suddenly there wasn't enough air in the room. Sam sucked in a painful breath.

"I know." Troy slid into the chair across from her, blocking her view of the photo. "I wouldn't let the staff put it in the public areas, but they really wanted to have something in here."

"That's where..." she began, her voice little more than a whisper.

"I figured. Kyla sent it to me on the day."

"She sent it to me, too." She leaned to the left to study the happy photo again. Kim and Kyla had such an affectionate relationship; mother and daughter had truly enjoyed each other's company. Sam ached with the knowledge that her own mother hadn't lived to see her grow up. They'd never had happy times as adults, never had a photo like this. In fact, she barely remembered any days before Susan Westin became an invalid.

This was not the time or place for self-pity, she reminded herself, straightening in her chair and focusing on Troy. The poor man seemed thinner than he had ten days ago, and the lines across his forehead were deepening into crevasses.

His gaze was on the cup of water in his hands. "We have to remember that Kim and Kyla were friends with all the staff, too."

She nodded, afraid that her voice might crack if she tried to talk.

He took a sip of his water. When he set the cup down, he met her eyes. "Everyone here in the office thinks you're doing a fantastic job, Sam."

She almost choked on a swallow of orange juice. "Really?"

"Really. We listen to all your recordings, you know, and read your reports."

"As you know, there have been a few ..." she struggled for the right word, "...incidents."

"There are always ... incidents," he said, imitating her cadence. "There'd be no need for this business if these were well adjusted kids. It's amazing how well your group seems to be getting along. We especially appreciated the poetry. Were the haikus your idea?"

She shook her head. "I'd love to take credit for that, but the crew came up with poetry night on their own."

"Even more amazing. Keep doing what you're doing." He stood up and rolled his shoulders back. Vertebrae cracked, and he raised a hand to the nape of his neck. "Well, I'm sure you're anxious to get home."

"Oh no, you don't!" She grabbed at his arm. "What the hell's going on, Troy? Start with Chris. You know he came up to tell me about his guns and ask me to vouch for him?"

"I know; I told him it was okay."

"And then how about this Klapton thing?"

"We'll get to that in a minute. First, about Chris and the investigation."

"What's all this about Detective Greene?"

"She's tenacious, I'll give her that. Unfortunately, she seems to be the only one. I get the feeling that nobody knows what to do with this case."

Those comments were not reassuring. "You don't believe Chris could be guilty of anything, do you?"

Troy crooked an arm toward the hallway. "Come with me to my office."

Orange juice in hand, Sam followed him down the hall. After she was seated in his guest chair, he handed her the news section of a local paper. An article on the front page featured a grainy photo of Troy and Chris perched at a tall table in a dimly lit bar. In front of them were half-filled beer glasses, along with one empty beside Chris's elbow. At the side of the photo was a server with a tray, dressed in a crop top and skimpy shorts that showed an abundance of cleavage and long legs. The two men appeared to be staring at the scantily clad girl.

"I think the original photo was focused on the singer on stage." He pointed to three-quarters of a woman sitting on a stool with a microphone in hand. He was right, it looked like the photo had been blown up and cropped; the texture was coarse and the singer's right side was missing.

The article text was brief, but questioned why the murder victims' husband and boyfriend had been out ogling girls at a bar a month before the women were killed.

"I still can't believe this." Troy shook his head. "We weren't 'ogling girls,' for chrissakes. We were talking. I picked that place because it was close to the marina where Chris was working, and I asked him to meet me there."

She waited.

Troy raked his fingers through his hair, making it spike out on one side of his head. "This will sound like it's coming from the nineteenth century, but I wanted to know his intentions toward my daughter."

Sam drained the last sip of juice from the bottle.

"Kyla adored Chris, you know," he said.

"I know." Kyla had made Christopher Rawlins sound like the ideal man.

"She hoped to marry him. But I knew he hung with rough company sometimes on the fishing boats, and I just wanted to make sure he was on the up and up."

"Plus, he had a record."

Surprise froze Troy's features.

"The police told me about a couple of charges," she lied. Troy didn't need to know she was checking up on everyone through Chase.

"I know about the bar brawl in Alaska, five years ago," Troy muttered. "Like I said, he hangs out with some tough characters."

"You don't really think that Chris had anything to do with Kim and Kyla's murder, do you?"

He slumped in his desk chair. Sliding his fingers under his glasses, he pinched the bridge of his nose and closed his eyes. "I don't know what to think anymore, Sam."

Sam squirmed, feeling an unexpected pang of missing her crew kids. At least she might be able to help them. She didn't have a clue what to do to help Troy. The only thing she could think of was to locate this Detective Greene and find out what the woman knew. She stood up. "I'll go in a minute, Troy. I'm sure everyone would appreciate it if I took a shower. And I'm *so* looking forward to clean socks."

"I'll bet." He wearily let his hand drop to the desktop.

"But first, what about that Klapton note? Seemed like it put you in a panic."

He leaned forward. "Did you bring it?"

"I found all of these in Kyla's tent." She unzipped the outside pocket on her pants leg, fished out the broken earring and the two curls of paper and handed them over.

He set the earring aside on his desk, then unfurled the fortune and read aloud, "You will meet a stranger who will change your future."

"Good Lord." He scrunched the tiny Chinese scroll into a ball and tossed it into the wastebasket beside his desk.

"You don't want to keep that?" The idea that it might be some weird sort of evidence crossed her mind.

Troy lifted an eyebrow. "A fortune from a commercial cookie? Kyla was addicted to those things. She always had a box of those cookies in her cupboard and fortunes in her pockets." He used his fingernails to roll out the other piece of paper.

Sam had read about people blanching before, but she'd never seen it until now. The blood simply drained out of Troy's face. He stared at the note in his hand as if it were a scorpion. "My God. I was so hoping..." His voice trailed off into silence.

"Who is Klapton?" she asked.

"When did you find this?"

"Yesterday morning. In my tent. At first I thought it was a joke of some sort, or maybe just an old note that got stuck to Kyla's equipment."

He turned over the receipt and moved it into the pool of light under his desk lamp, squinting behind his glasses. Then he pulled open a desk drawer, removed a magnifying glass and held it over the note, reading the printed receipt. "No date," he murmured to himself.

"Who is Klapton?" she asked again.

Troy returned the magnifying glass to the drawer and then scrubbed his hand across his bearded chin for a long moment before saying, "Klapton is Erik Heigler. My nephew. My sister's son. We...I haven't seen him for nearly ten years. We assumed he died in Mexico or Central America or some Third World drainage ditch."

Sam flinched at the callousness of Troy's last statement.

He locked his hands together in front of his chest and rocked back and forth a few times. "Oh God, please tell me this is not true."

An alarm buzzed in Sam's head. "What's not true?"

"Erik's been an addict for as long as I can remember. Meth, coke, heroin. Buying, using, selling." Troy stared sadly at the crumpled receipt on his desk. "He burned through the whole family before he left the country."

She waited for the rest of the story.

"He'd be around thirty now. When he was nineteen, Kim convinced me we could rescue him."

"That sounds like something she'd do," Sam said.

His gaze bounced up to connect with hers. "Erik stole our debit card and emptied our checking account. We would never have gotten Wilderness Quest off the ground if I hadn't had a regular paycheck at the time."

It was a disturbing story, but one that happened a long time ago. It seemed improbable that this character could be haunting her in the mountains. "Why would Erik come to our camp?"

"He might be looking for Kyla."

"That doesn't make sense, Troy."

He shook his head. "Kyla was too young at the time to grasp everything that Erik was up to. He did have a certain slick charm, and he played a mean guitar. Hence the Klapton. With a K, to match the K in his first name. Kyla thought her cousin was cool. When I threw him out, she was devastated." He swallowed hard. "So if Erik decided to show up again, he might visit her instead of Kim or me."

It still didn't make sense. "But Kyla's been...gone...a while." More than a month had passed and she still couldn't say it.

Troy considered for a minute. "Erik might not know about Kyla and Kim. I doubt he watches the news or reads the papers."

How could Kyla or Kim have never mentioned this guy?

Troy answered her unspoken question. "We believed Erik was gone for good ten years ago."

"Does Detective Greene know about Erik?"

"I'll make sure she does."

Sam pointed to the note. "It could just be a coincidence, couldn't it? Anyone could write that. I sort of suspected Aidan did it."

He lifted an eyebrow. "Aidan?"

"He acted kind of funny when I showed it to him."

"Well, you have to admit it's an odd thing to be asking about."

That was true, but still... "You said you'd known Aidan 'forever'?"

"The Callahans live a few houses away from us. Aidan mowed our lawn when he was in high school. He's always been a good kid."

"So he was in the neighborhood when Erik stayed at your house?"

Troy picked up the shred of paper again. "Nobody outside our family knew about the Klapton nickname."

Sam suspected that Troy might be a bit naïve about what his daughter had shared as a teenager. But if Aidan knew about

Erik and the Klapton nickname, why would he hide that information from her? Troy was right, unless Aidan was pretending to be Klapton for some unknown reason, the idea that he would sneak the note into her tent seemed far-fetched.

"Maya told me Kyla talked about Klapton contacting her."

Troy's head jerked up, his glasses reflecting the overhead light. "What? When?"

"The last day of their last expedition, in the locker room here. Maya said it was a Facebook message and that Kyla didn't know what to do about him."

Troy pulled at his beard. "Oh, God! I always told her Facebook was dangerous. She'd 'friend' anyone who asked." He used air quotes to enclose the word "friend." "Oh, damn. I'll tell Greene to look for that on Kyla's phone."

He focused on the note again. "This does look like Erik's handwriting, at least what I remember of it. He always printed in block letters; I used to wonder if he'd ever learned cursive. But the truly damning factor is that, after I threw him out, we'd find notes just like this, in the mailbox, stuck behind a windshield wiper, pinned to the back door." He shuddered.

"Creepy," Sam agreed. "But do you really think he could have tracked my group down in the north Cascades?"

Troy sucked in an audible breath, thinking. "Erik's not stupid. Kim was starting this company at the time he was staying with us. If he was skulking around here again, he might have phoned the office and asked for Kyla. When you called yesterday, I realized I'd never changed her name on the schedule because the client parents all had a list of the crew leaders and I didn't want to upset them with our ... last minute change. We use an answering service after hours, you know. If asked, the evening operator would probably say Kyla was out in the field with a crew."

He rocked a couple more times. "Our website says we take our groups into the north Cascades."

"That's a whole lot of territory to get lost in," Sam reminded him. But then her brain seized on the train of thought that was likely rocketing through Troy's brain. "You always tell the

Forest Service and the Park Service where your groups will be, and when."

He nodded. "It's a safety issue, with hunters and forest fires, and we never know when we might need their help to evacuate a sick or injured camper. Anyhow, that's why I relocated your crew." Using a pen, he slid the note to the side of his desk and placed his stapler on top to hold it in place. "I'll call the sheriff's office and make sure they get this."

"What does Erik look like?"

"He's about my height—five ten or so, with black hair. Last time I saw him, he was rail thin, like most addicts. It's likely that he'll be unkempt, needing a haircut and a shave."

The hunter came to mind. Thin, long dark hair. She made an effort to relax her jaw, reminding herself that description could fit thousands of men in the immediate area. Still, the coincidence was frightening.

"Women say he's good looking, and pretty much everyone thinks he's charming. He could always worm his way into all sorts of deals." Troy raised his arms and raked both hands through his hair, his eyes unfocused. "Oh sweet Jesus, did Erik kill my wife and daughter?"

"You mean... You think he might be the one?" Sam pointed out, "Ten years is a long time to wait for revenge."

"Don't assume he's operating in a logical manner. He has racked up at least two convictions I know about, one for assault and one for armed robbery. The night we threw him out ... correction, *I* threw him out, Kim didn't want me to ... he threatened to kill us both."

Lowering his hands, Troy chafed his upper arms as if he had a sudden chill. "I can't think of a better way for him to hurt me than killing my family."

Sam picked up the orange juice bottle again, but it was empty. She couldn't argue with that logic, but Troy's scenario didn't make sense. "But if Erik was responsible for ... that, then he wouldn't be wandering around the north Cascades looking for Kyla."

He grimaced. "I don't want to think he might go after some

of my employees, but I can't discount the possibility."

A homicidal maniac might be stalking her crew?

"But you're safe now," Troy tried to reassure her. "I instructed the whole staff, and our Forest Service and Park Service contacts, not to give out any information about your field trip. And now the authorities will be looking for Erik."

As she drove back to her house, Sam wondered what other secrets the Johnson family had hidden from her.

At home, she tossed her clothes into the washing machine, then slipped into a hot bath. Her cat Simon perched on the tub rim to keep her company until she pressed the button to start the motor. She rarely used her whirlpool tub, but today the jets of water felt luxurious. The ring of dirt left behind when she pulled herself out was mortifying. She scrubbed it off before emerging from the bathroom.

Simon insisted on sitting in her lap and head-butting her arm as she mangled a text message to Chase, asking him to check into Erik Heigler's background. From the moment she'd arrived home, the cat had followed her around the house. She gently rubbed his silky ears. He purred and closed his eyes as she stroked a fingertip down his brown nose and scratched his chin. She was already feeling guilty about leaving him the day after tomorrow to return to the mountains.

Blake arrived home with one bag of handmade mushroom raviolis and one of various greens he'd no doubt "pruned" from plants in the greenhouse where he worked. Walking into the living room, he bent and briefly kissed the top of her head. "So I haven't inherited the house after all?"

"Not yet."

"No Chase?"

"Nope. No Claude?"

"*Non. Il*...went...*a Montréal.*"

"Conjugation got you down?"

Her housemate snorted. "In more ways than one, *cherie.*"

"I sympathize. Your Frenglish is as bad as my Spanglish. Fortunately, tonight we have no need of either; we can speak our native tongue."

"Deal." He pointed to Simon. "And *he* nests in *your* hair tonight."

Blake whipped up a creamy sun-dried tomato and cheese sauce for the raviolis while she put together a salad. They shared a bottle of wine and commiserated about relationships with teenagers and missing lovers.

As he poured them both a second glass of merlot, she said, "You know something, Blake? You are my rock."

He handed her the glass and picked up his own. "Ditto, Sam." He took a sip. "It's kinda sad and wonderful at the same time, isn't it?"

11

The next day, when she should have spent time in front of her computer, trying to line up contract work after the expedition, she called the Snohomish County Sheriff's Office and asked for Detective Greene.

"She's out. Want her voice mail?"

Sam left the detective a message, asking if they could meet and discuss the Quintana-Johnson case. She didn't have a lot of confidence that she'd hear back. Then she drove to Christopher Rawlins' address. Maybe he could fill in some details.

When she pulled up at nine a.m. in the driveway of the small rental house he had shared with Kyla, she parked alongside a dark sedan with a Snohomish County Sheriff logo, and next to a cruiser from Whatcom County.

The front door of the house was standing open. Chris was slumped morosely in a plastic chair on the sagging porch, sucking on a can of beer.

She slipped into the vacant chair beside him. "What's going on?"

"Search warrant." He motioned to the pages he was holding down with his left boot.

A loud thump from the wall behind them caused Sam to turn toward the house. Whoever was in there was dumping out a box or emptying a bookshelf. "What do they expect to find?"

He shook his head. "God only knows. The missing guns? Bloodstains on the carpet? A skeleton crammed up the chimney?" Crumpling the beer can, he tossed it into the bushes, where it landed beside another. She didn't blame him for being upset, but this couldn't make a good impression on the law officers. Was it normal for Chris to drink so early in the day? Could Kyla have fallen for an alcoholic?

He narrowed his eyes at her. "You know anything?"

"I was hoping you'd update *me*."

He jerked a thumb over his shoulder toward the interior of the house. "Update: they think I killed my girlfriend and her mother. And oh, by the way, they also think you and Troy may be in on the conspiracy."

"What are our motives?"

"I can only guess. Mine, to get hot and heavy with you."

"Yeesh, Chris, I'm nearly old enough to be your mother." She did a quick calculation. He was probably nearing thirty, and she was rapidly approaching the big four-oh. Nope, only around ten to twelve years between them. "Well, your older sister, for sure."

"Your motive is to get Kyla's job."

"Yeah, I've always wanted to babysit a bunch of delinquents for minimum wage." Then she remembered that Troy promised to pay her triple the usual amount, and her cheeks flushed.

"And Troy?" Chris stared at the driveway. "Who knows? I haven't figured that one out yet."

"That's because he doesn't have any motive. Chris, do you know anything about a guy called Erik Heigler, nickname of Klapton?"

"Klapton." Chris grimaced. "He's a cousin, I guess. Major druggie, according to everyone. He contacted Kyla, right before... He hasn't been around for a long time, but he was going to be up here and wanted to see her." He shook his head. "She was actually *considering* meeting up with him. I told her no way should she respond at all. You never want to even pretend to be friendly to a junkie." His brows came together, and he turned toward her and said, "You don't think that guy could have..."

Sam returned his questioning look. "I don't really know anything about their history or the guy. His name just came up."

A brown dog emerged from the side of the house, joining them on the porch. Short legs ended in large white paws. A long tail with a white tip wagged uncertainly. Its ears hung nearly to the ground. A mix of basset and something else, maybe beagle. Squatting on its short hind legs, the pooch watched them with huge soulful brown eyes that reminded Sam uncomfortably of someone.

"Who is this?" Sam asked Chris.

Chris lifted a shoulder. "Some stray. Kyla was feeding him."

She studied the dog carefully. "It's a her, not a him." Yeesh, those eyes reminded her of Kyla. "Who's feeding her now?"

Another shrug. "Sometimes I do."

"Sometimes?"

"When I'm home. But he ... she's not my dog. Kyla was trying to find out where she belongs, but nobody's claimed her. I'm surprised the neighbors haven't called Animal Control."

Sam leaned over to pat the dog's head, and the pooch licked her hand with a soft tongue. Those eyes were so sad. She wore no collar. The dog seemed sweet, surely she hadn't been dumped.

A man in a Whatcom County Sheriff uniform preceded a woman out the front door. She was carrying a cardboard box. She stopped, staring at Sam. "And who do we have here?"

The dog rose to her feet, wagging her tail uncertainly at the newcomers.

Sam stood up too. "Sam, er, Summer Westin, Officer ..."

The woman was not in uniform. The box she carried hid the shield that was no doubt hanging from the leather strap around her neck.

"Detective Greene."

Ah, the elusive, persistent detective from the Snohomish County Sheriff's Department.

Greene handed the box and a sheet of lined notebook paper to Chris. "Compare the list and sign here." She pointed to a space on the page and then stood in front of him, her feet spread apart, hooking her thumbs in her back pants pockets, her right elbow crooked over the pistol on her belt. Greene couldn't have been more than five foot four.

She swiveled toward Sam. "I was told you were up in the mountains." Greene pushed a strand of dark brown hair into the bun at the nape of her neck.

"I'm on a two-day break. I have to be back up there tomorrow afternoon."

Detective Greene eyed her. "I want to talk to you."

Chris rifled through the box in his lap, then looked up at the detective. "My family photos? Really?"

"You'll get them back."

"My timesheets from the boat? My laptop?"

Greene turned to wave goodbye to the departing Whatcom County deputy and waited patiently until Chris had signed the list. "Mr. Rawlins, we're done here. For now."

Chris disappeared into the house. With a sigh, the dog flopped down onto the porch.

The detective turned to Sam. "My car. Let's chat."

After depositing the box in the back of her county car, Greene opened the side door. A computer took up most of the passenger space, and radio equipment and a locked compartment occupied part of the floor.

"Uh." Sam eyed the cramped quarters. "I think my car has more space. At least we can slide the seats back."

"Good idea." Greene slammed the door shut. "Let's do yours." When they walked to the Civic, the detective held up a hand. "Hold on a sec." Jerking open the door, she bent her head inside, opened the glove compartment, scanned the area beneath the seats, then pulled her head back. "Okay."

When Sam was in the driver's seat and she was in the passenger's, Detective Greene put her head back against the headrest and closed her eyes. "Sorry. Had to check."

"I understand," Sam said. "I could be a dangerous criminal."

Greene opened her eyes—they were hazel, with enviable long dark lashes—and looked at Sam. "Seems unlikely, but you never know. So," she said, leaning back again. "Ask me whatever you want to, and then I'll ask you my questions."

Why are you wasting your time investigating me and Troy and Chris when the real killer is out there somewhere? What makes you think I wanted this job?

Instead, Sam said, "Kyla and Kim were my friends."

"I know. And you would normally have been hiking with them, but on that day, you weren't."

Arrow right to the heart.

Sam frowned. "True. I feel terrible about that, like if I'd been there, I might have been able to change things."

"Really?" Greene peered intently at her again. "What would you have been able to change?"

Was the woman waiting for Sam to reveal that she knew the killer and would have been able to stop him, or—? It was no wonder that Chase told her never to talk to law enforcement; she sucked at this. Every word that came out of her mouth sounded suspicious.

"I know that I probably couldn't have changed anything," she admitted. "I feel guilty because I was having fun at a family reunion in Idaho with my boyfriend. Man friend. Oh, you know—" She waved a hand in exasperation.

Greene rolled her shoulders as if they hurt, and then twisted her neck, stretching. "Awkward, isn't it, how we still don't have a term for any unmarried relationship over thirty?"

"Yeah, it is. Lover sounds sort of sordid, and partner isn't right, either, when we're not even living together." This conversation was going nowhere fast. "Do you know anything new?"

"What counts as new?" Greene asked.

Gad, the woman was cagey. "Why do you suspect Chris? He loved Kyla, and she loved him."

"Mostly looks that way," the detective conceded. "I'll bet you envied her. Good looking fiancé, good job, loving parents."

Sam weighed her words carefully. "I believed Kyla was happy, and Kim was, too. And so was I. The three of us always had a good time hiking together. And Kyla and I did line dancing together, too."

"You were happy even though you were unemployed?"

Now *that* was annoying. "I'm not destitute, Detective."

"But Troy Johnson offered you triple the usual salary for taking Kyla's place."

Sam had to admit that sounded bad. "That's because I didn't want to take the job, and he was desperate."

"So he says." Detective Greene studied her for a minute more, and then reached for the door handle. "Guess that's it, for now."

"You didn't tell me a single thing!" Sam protested.

"You noticed." Detective Greene slid out of the passenger seat, shut the door and walked around to the driver's side. Leaning down to Sam's level, she said, "I will tell you this. Your FBI guy, Perez, is a hunk. So you really have no excuse for lusting after Rawlins."

Greene waited a beat for a response. When none came, she said, "Have a nice day, Ms. Westin."

Sam's mouth was still hanging open when the detective slid into her sedan. Then she jumped angrily out of her car and ran up to Greene's vehicle. "Wait a minute!"

The window slid down.

"Did you get the word about Erik Heigler?"

"I did," the detective said. "We're checking into him."

"And the Facebook messages?"

The detective grimaced. "We already got the messages on Kyla's phone, at least the ones that weren't deleted. Harder to check an entire history and confirm ownership details, but we'll get Facebook to cooperate. Eventually." The window slid up.

Sam fumed for a few minutes before returning to her car. It was all so unsatisfying. And how the heck did Detective Greene know that Chase was attractive? Or was she simply fishing for information?

That thought reminded Sam that she'd planned a fishing expedition of her own. She started the engine.

On the porch, the dog stood up, watching. Her tail wagged, once.

"Oh, for heaven's sake." She leaned over and opened the

passenger door. "Come on!"

The basset-beagle trotted over, floppy jowls and ears swinging. The dog paused for a minute in the doorway.

"I said it was okay," she told the pooch, and the dog awkwardly jumped onto the floor, scraping her belly on the door frame. "Stay down there." She leaned across and closed the passenger door.

The dog climbed onto the seat and checked the view out the window. When she turned her head, Sam could have sworn she was smiling.

"Oh, whatever," she said. "Just behave yourself."

With the dog riding shotgun, she drove to the address she'd found in the Whatcom County Assessor's records, two blocks away from Kim and Troy's home. While Kim and Troy's neighborhood was modest but obviously maintained with pride, this block appeared worn. Older cars took up the lawn space in many of the patchy front yards, proving that the houses were most likely rentals occupied by university students from Western.

Sam cracked a window for the dog, locked her car and then walked up the front steps of a small gray house. The welcome mat told her she was in the right place: *The Callahan Clan*.

The woman who answered the door wore a headset with a tiny microphone poised in front of her lips. Into it, she said, "Your subscription should arrive within two weeks. Thank you, and have a nice day." She crooked a finger and pulled down the microphone. "Yes?"

Sam introduced herself. "Sorry for dropping in like this, but I wanted to know if there was some special snack Aidan particularly likes. I want to take treats back for my peer counselors as well as the crew kids."

"I'm working, but come on in." The woman waved her into a small kitchen. On the table was an open laptop with a form on the screen. She pulled off her headset and tossed it on the tabletop. "I've had some crappy jobs in the past, but this one is the worst."

"I know what you mean," Sam said.

Mrs. Callahan tossed her a doubtful look. With light brown hair and freckles, there was no mistaking the family resemblance between the mother and her son.

"I've done mostly contract work," Sam told her. "Unpredictable, isn't it?"

"You can say that again. And no benefits."

Sam knew that song all too well, but she wasn't here to commiserate about the job market. "I want to tell you that Aidan's doing a wonderful job. He's really helping me out."

His mother put her hands on her hips. "You know this is his third year with Wilderness Quest?"

Sam nodded. "He's an excellent peer counselor."

"We were sure he'd be promoted to field guide this summer, which would have meant more money and been a great plus for his resume, but noooo." She stretched the negative out into three syllables. "Of course, Kim gave that job to Kyla." She folded her arms across her chest. "We should have expected that. Keep it all in the family, right?"

The woman sounded bitter. Did Aidan feel he'd been cheated out of a job when Kyla came on board? Had he resented Kim and Kyla?

"And now, here *you* are," Mrs. Callahan added, her blue eyes fiery.

That sounded like a challenge. Was it possible that Aidan expected to get Kyla's job if she was no longer around?

Sam pressed her lips together, trying to keep her mental meanderings from showing on her face. "I don't know anything about the way jobs are assigned. I'm sure Aidan would make a good field guide."

Motive, means, opportunity: the trinity necessary for proving guilt in any crime. Aidan and Kyla would have been between expeditions at the same time. So Aidan had opportunity. Maybe he had a motive in wanting Kyla's job. Did he have the means? "Does Aidan know anything about guns?"

Mrs. Callahan stiffened. "What does *that* have to do with being a field guide? Why are you asking that?"

Sam had never been fluent in chit-chat; she clearly needed

to work on her segues. She dismissively flapped a hand. "It's not really important. It's just that we ran across a hunter up there, and Aidan was trying to identify the guy's rifle," she lied. "So I was curious."

The woman uncrossed her arms and fingered the headset on the table. "I guess that makes sense. We don't own guns, but Aidan's gone hunting a couple of times with friends. I don't think he enjoyed it much. He's an animal lover."

So Aidan had at least a passing familiarity with guns. A twinge of anxiety for Maya's safety zipped through her head. Had Detective Greene thoroughly checked the background of all the WWQ staff? Could Aidan have a gun at the summer staff house?

She struggled to re-focus on the task at hand. "I understand that you've known the Johnson family for a long time?"

"Years. But I can't say I really know them. The connection was Aidan. He mowed the neighbors' lawns, and he knew everyone, but he especially liked the Johnsons. Kyla was a few years older, but he was infatuated with her when they were teenagers."

Sam had never heard Kyla mention Aidan, so that attraction had to be one-sided. "Do you think he still is infatuated?"

"How can he be?" The woman's expression went rigid again. "Kyla's dead."

At least *she* could say it. Swallowing against the lump in her throat, Sam asked, "How's Aidan taking it?"

"He doesn't wear his heart on his sleeve. But I haven't seen him much since then." Mrs. Callahan clucked her tongue. "Such a horrible thing to happen. Do they know anything yet?"

"Not that I'm aware of, but the police don't really talk to me. Mrs. Callahan—"

"Judy."

"Judy, do you remember the Johnsons' nephew who lived with them for a while when Kyla was a teenager?"

Judy nodded. "I don't remember his name, but I met him once on the street. He seemed like a nice boy. But he wasn't with them for very long."

"Does the name Klapton mean anything to you?"

"Was that the nephew's name? I was thinking it was Ethan or Evan or something like that."

"Erik."

Judy's chin came up. "His name was Erik Klapton?"

"No." Sam explained that Klapton was a nickname. If Judy remembered Erik, then Aidan might, too. But the Klapton name hadn't meant anything to Judy Callahan, just as it hadn't meant anything to Aidan. Or so it had seemed when she asked him.

"The answer is pears."

"What?" Sam was startled.

"You wanted to know a favorite food to take to Aidan. He loves dried pears."

"Oh." She smiled. "That's easy." She stood up, and then remembered the pooch in the car. "Say, you don't know anyone who's missing a dog, do you? A brown and white basset mix?"

The woman shook her head.

"Do you want one?"

"Like I want a root canal," Judy Callahan responded. "One boy who takes five years to get through college and two girls waiting in the wings are more than enough to deal with."

"I'll bet," Sam said. "Thanks for your time."

As she pulled into her driveway at home, she realized that she'd wasted most of the day and learned only that Chris was drinking too much and Greene still suspected everyone. Plus, she'd ended up with a dog she didn't have a clue what she was going to do with.

The pooch was happy to eat Simon's dry cat food, and much to the cat's dismay, laid down in the corner of the living room as if planning to stay there. When Blake came home from work, the basset-beagle transferred her sad-eyed gaze to him, lying in front of him with her muzzle on top of his foot.

"He looks like a Barney," Blake decided.

"We can't keep *her*."

"Correction: she looks like a Sophie. And how can you resist that face?"

The dog's focus transferred from Blake to Sam. Her heart lurched. Those were Kyla's big brown eyes, definitely.

She reminded her housemate, "I'm going back to the mountains tomorrow. I'll be gone for ten days. Could you take her to the animal adoption center?"

Blake patted the dog's head. "I'll deal with Sophie until you get back. Look at that face!" The pooch gazed lovingly at him.

From the arm of the couch, Simon slitted his green eyes, glaring at the canine intruder. Blake stretched out an arm to pet the cat. "I still love you, Simon. You're the best cat in the whole house."

Simon jumped off the couch and stalked regally into Sam's bedroom.

Blake turned to her. "Anything new on the case?"

"Not really." The only possibly useful information she'd gleaned from her meanderings today was that Aidan had a grievance against Kim and maybe Kyla, too. She pulled out the business card that Detective Greene had handed her and called. She got the detective's voice mail again.

"You should check out Aidan Callahan." She summarized the Callahans' resentment of the Quintana-Johnson family. "Aidan knew Kyla's schedule because he worked with her." Then a wave of anxiety rose up and smacked down over her, and she hastily added, "Please don't let on that you got this tip from me. I will be camping in the mountains with him for the next ten days."

Had she accomplished anything? She briefly considered driving south to the Pinnacle Lake trail and hiking up and down that mountain until she stumbled across something that could be a clue. Which, after another minute, seemed a stupid idea born of desperation.

No wonder law enforcement seemed inept. At this point, they probably were just as clueless as she was. The only promising lead, if anything could be said to allow even a glimmer of a clue, was that Erik Heigler, a criminal with connections to and a grudge against the Johnson family, might be back in the country.

Could Kyla have been in touch with Heigler? Troy said she'd admired Klapton in her younger years. Although Chris had advised his girlfriend to keep her distance, like Sam, Kyla was not the obedient type.

A new possibility occurred to her. Could Chris have slipped the note into her tent? He had hiked up with the counselor only a few days before. It would be easy for Chris to find out where the group was camped, and he'd know by its color which one was her tent. The cops were continuing to investigate him, but she didn't believe they were keeping him under surveillance. With a good headlamp, he could probably hike in and out the same night and be back in his bed before anyone noticed.

While possible, that scenario seemed improbable. What motivation would Chris have to place that note? The only plausible reason she could come up with was to shift suspicion from himself to this Heigler character. Troubling.

Everything about that note was troubling. It seemed highly unlikely that Heigler would be tracking them in the mountains, but she couldn't shake the image of that hunter out of her head. And the roving light the kids had reported on the solo campouts. Klapton?

It was terrifying to think that a violent criminal might have been tracking her expedition through the backcountry. Thank God Troy had relocated her group.

Still, she favored the idea of Heigler as a suspect over Chris. Or Aidan. She didn't want to believe that she might *know* her friends' killer. Or be working alongside him.

12

That evening, Chase told her something even more alarming.

They were Skyping, which was still unsatisfactory, but at least she could see him. He leaned toward the screen as if sharing a secret. "Heigler's a known coyote."

Her wildlife biologist brain was momentarily bewildered by his statement. Then she clued in that Chase wasn't talking about wild canids. "You mean he smuggles illegal immigrants across the Mexican border?"

Chase nodded. "Well, he did at least once, according to the group he abandoned in Organ Pipe National Monument. But Heigler himself wasn't actually apprehended."

That was bad news on multiple counts. A coyote who smuggled people into the country through a national park probably had backcountry skills. And obviously knew how to slip into the country undetected. And no doubt could get his hands on weapons, although that was obviously a no-brainer in the U.S. for anyone with ready cash. Probably in Mexico, too.

Chase gazed intently into her eyes or, she reminded herself, into his laptop camera. "Coyotes usually have connections to Mexican drug cartels. I don't want you going back up to the mountains tomorrow, Summer."

"And I don't want you going back to Salt Lake," she retorted.

"I *am* back in Salt Lake. I'm calling from my condo."

"I know; I can see your kitchen behind you." She squared

her shoulders and sat back in her chair. "My point is, here we are, Chase, both doing our jobs. My crew has been relocated to a new area. Troy and the kids are depending on me. And the nation is depending on you."

He snorted. "It's not as grandiose as that." After taking a sip from the wine glass that sat on the table beside his elbow, he added, "And I hope it will never be." Then he cast his gaze down at the table top.

She knew that look. "What, Chase?"

"I have some more bad news to tell you." He sipped again at his wine. "My ASAC found out I was sniffing around about job possibilities in Seattle. So she suggested I transfer soon."

Sam's mood brightened. "How is that bad news? I can't wait for you to be closer!"

"She suggested I transfer soon to North Dakota."

"Gex!" she yelped. Their relationship couldn't be stretched all the way across the country.

His eyebrows came together. "Gex?"

"Never mind." She waved a hand as if erasing the word from a blackboard. "Chase, you can't go to North Dakota! Please tell me that's not happening." Salt Lake City had been at least a consideration. It was in a state that had mountains and streams and five national parks, not to mention a variety of amazing natural monuments and other wild places. But North Dakota! Her rational mind knew she wasn't giving that state a fair chance because she'd never been there, but her imagination instantly filled with endless windy prairies and drifting snow.

"It's not official," Chase said. "She was demonstrating how irritated she was that I was disloyal enough to want to leave."

"She wouldn't really have you transferred, would she?"

"I think she'll let me stay; Nicole promised to put in a good word for me."

Nicole Boudreaux was another FBI agent who often worked cases with Chase, a woman who was smart, well-spoken, and always immaculately groomed. In other words, instantly annoying to someone like Sam who suffered from foot-in-mouth disease and wore dirt on her face more often than makeup. "Aren't FBI agents allowed to have personal lives?"

His expression was pained. "They're expected to drag their families with them wherever the Bureau assigns them."

Sam understood Chase's dedication to the FBI. She also knew Chase wasn't precisely referring to how she'd turned down his offer to move in with him in Salt Lake City, but his words felt like a dig nonetheless.

She gritted her teeth. Wildlife and greenery were essential to her sanity; she had no desire to live in any big city. There were days when even mid-sized Bellingham felt far too crowded. She needed space. But she would no longer be able to use *that* excuse if Chase was transferred to the remote stretches of North Dakota.

The next morning, Sam, Aidan, and Maya reunited with their crew in a wilderness area dozens of miles south of the one they'd left. The crew kids were glad to see them back, but they seemed to be in foul moods. That was normal, the counselors warned Sam, after a couple of days of intense therapy to make them reflect on their histories of bad behavior. She was thankful that her job was to teach outdoor survival skills and guide these kids through the backcountry, not to teach them how to navigate the morass of teen emotions and family issues.

Throughout dinner, all six of her crew complained about the counselors' insistence on working on their contracts. Even more irritating to them were the letters they'd received from their families offering support *only* if the teens changed their behavior.

It seemed to her that they *were* changing, learning to appreciate each other and the world around them. But out here that didn't include school attendance and family expectations. She had to constantly remind herself that she was dealing with only half the equation; the company counselors were talking to both parents and kids, trying to pave a constructive path to the future.

The exercise she was instructed to lead that evening seemed designed to prolong the painful process.

After surreptitiously activating the recorder in her pocket, she sat with the kids around the campfire and read from her instruction book: "Come up with one word to describe what you want to achieve when you're back home. No explanation or response needed."

Her request resulted in expressions ranging from annoyance to confusion on the faces of the six client teens.

"For example," she added, "I would say 'tranquility.' I'd like to achieve tranquility when I return home. Who wants to go next?"

"Revenge," Ashley blurted. "I want revenge."

That was new. All heads turned toward the girl, questions on their faces.

"Not you guys," she said impatiently. "It's a family thing."

Sam wondered if the Spokane paper would be reporting a domestic violence incident at Ashley's home in the near future.

Gabriel said, "Respect. That's what I want."

"Reincarnation." Justin.

Interesting. And sad.

Olivia quietly murmured, "Peace."

"I want freedom," Taylor said.

Nick twisted his lips, then finally said, "A do-over. That can be one word, right, with a hyphen?"

What a downer exercise. All their answers were disturbing to Sam, but poignant reminders that everyone involved with this expedition had real problems to face back home. It was depressing to think about, even to her. The reality she was returning to wasn't so rose-colored, either. She was going back to unemployment and the need to widen her circle of friends, now that Kyla and Kim were gone and Chase wasn't likely to join her any time soon.

"Enough of that," she told them. "Let's do something fun now. Maybe a game?"

All six kids eagerly leapt to their feet. "We've got it, Cap'n."

Over the staff break, her crew had somehow found time to

escape thinking about reality too much, because they'd planned to act out a short scene from the video game Gabriel was creating. The role assignments were not what Sam would have expected. Olivia and Taylor played diabolical alien queens.

"In the game, we're twins," Olivia explained, gesturing between her small dark self and willowy blond Taylor. "You have to use your imagination. Our species plans to exterminate the inhabitants of Planet X."

"We totally screwed up the environment on our own planet," Taylor added, "so we need a new place to live."

Nick and Ashley were rebel warriors from Planet X, battling the invasion. "Imagine a whole horde of rebels behind us." Ashley brandished a broken branch like a sword.

Sam frowned at the weapon, but the counselors had assured her that the teens had been on their best behavior for the last few days.

Justin was a cyborg on the rebel side, but it was clear that everyone doubted his loyalties because his programming could be hijacked at any time by the self-serving president of Planet X, who was played by Gabriel. His role seemed to be to manipulate everyone into doing his bidding.

Aidan and Maya were extras, Gabriel explained, motioning the peer counselors to stand up. "You'll have to ad lib or just keep your mouths closed." He assigned Aidan to the role of an invading warrior and Maya was recruited to the rebel defense.

Sam found the scenarios difficult to visualize, but the kids filled in the backstory. After the horrific and deadly invasion, the cowardly Planet X president made a deal with the evil alien queens, selling out his people in exchange for saving his own family and reaping the rewards of riches and property.

Gabriel was appropriately despicable in his role of the puppeteer president, which Sam guessed might be close to that of a Master Wizard on Vebulaze. Olivia and Taylor were masterfully evil and Aidan appropriately subservient, although at times his tone seemed mocking.

To soften the sharp divisions of good versus evil, Gabriel

explained that if the aliens' mission failed, their species was doomed to die in the frigid expanses of outer space. The rebels—Nick, Ashley, Justin, and the recently drafted Maya—demonstrated courage and conviction in their valiant resistance to the invaders and to their own corrupt government.

Justin swore his allegiance in a mechanical voice that sounded as if he were mouthing whatever he'd been programmed to say. He also made a few unrehearsed comments, judging by the annoyed expressions that flashed from Nick and Gabriel as the cyborg character spoke.

Then, just when Sam was really getting into the performance, the cyborg ran completely amok as Justin grabbed Ashley and bent her over backward, kissing her roughly. Ashley struggled, beat her fist against Justin's arm. "Get your hands off me!"

Not in the script, obviously. Sam shouted, "Hey!"

Maya and Aidan rushed toward the grappling pair.

Nick's stick sword accidentally whacked Aidan in the back as the college student stepped into the fray, and Aidan turned, wrenched it out of Nick's hand and shoved the small boy down on the ground.

Nick raised both hands into the air toward Aidan. "Sorry, dude, that was an accident! I was aiming for the stupid robot."

Her face twisted with disgust, Ashley wiped her lips with the back of her hand and growled at Justin. "Idiot! Don't ever try that again."

Justin raised his hands in the air, grinning sheepishly. "What can I say? My cyborg programming has a few bugs in it."

"Shithead," Taylor remarked. "You ruined it."

Sam debated whether or not to demote Justin to Zombie again. "The play was good up to that point, Gabriel."

Gabriel gazed sadly at Justin. "I think I'm going to fry the cyborg's circuits in the next chapter."

"Oh, no, dude," Justin objected. "The cyborg is the coolest character."

"The cyborg is clearly out of control," Sam said. "Apologize to Ashley, Justin."

"I ... am ... sorry ... Sparky," Justin recited in a robotic voice. "Fun ... though."

Ashley narrowed her eyes at him, but a trace of a smile played across her lips. "Bad cyborg," she scolded.

"That's it for tonight." Sam stood up. "Gabriel can write whatever he likes, but there will be no more acting during this expedition. You should have been working all this time on your contracts with the counselors, anyway."

Scoffing and eyerolls all around.

"There were only three of them," Taylor explained. "And six of us. We couldn't all be in therapy"—she put the word in air quotes—"all the time."

Sam kept her expression noncommittal. She and Maya and Aidan were also a staff of three. Was a mutiny imminent?

"We spent a lot of time writing in our journals." Nick's sarcastic tone implied that they'd been working on the story instead. He then proceeded to prove her right by showing her his drawings depicting the characters.

"Wow." Sam flipped through the pages. The aliens had reptilian features but managed to be exotically attractive at the same time. The rebels were more human in shape but covered in dramatic tattoos and clothing that mainly consisted of leather straps and metal. "These are fantastic, Nick."

His face glowed with the praise.

"I want my scales to be blue-green," Taylor said, flicking her tongue out like a lizard. "But Gabriel says gold, because we're queens. What do you think, Cap'n?"

Yeesh, she wasn't going to side with one over the other, especially not in so trivial a matter. "That's not my call. Personally, I've always loved chameleons. They can change into almost any color, and even create patterns on their skin."

Gabriel's face lit up. He slapped a hand on his forehead. "Omigod," he squealed, sounding like one of the girls. "That's perfect!"

The teens buzzed about how chameleon abilities would

make the aliens able to hide out among the Planet X population and how the queens could change colors for different events. Sam became aware of Aidan and Maya staring at her. The crew kids were excited and enjoying themselves, but they were off in an imaginary world instead of grounded in this one.

She'd lost her commander mojo over the break.

"Speaking of colors." She stood up. "Get your jackets and hats if you want them, then let's enjoy the sunset before we turn in."

They scattered to their tents. When they regrouped ten minutes later, Sam noticed there were only nine of them.

"Where's Aidan?" she asked Maya.

"Don't know." The girl swiveled her head, checking the surroundings, and after a minute, pointed to a figure walking out of the woods toward them. "Here he comes."

"Visiting the facilities," he told Sam.

Sam pursed her lips. If he'd come from the toilet, he'd taken a roundabout path to get back. She decided to let it go, for now.

As the group sat in a line on a ridge, she tried to keep the conversation on the scene before them, naming colors and talking about cloud shapes. The cumulous clouds stacking up near the Canadian border were purple gray and ominous, but the incoming front was predicted to stay to the north.

The skies in their immediate vicinity were mostly clear. Sam did allow a few brief diversions in their talk about how the colors and shapes in the sunset sky could play into their Planet X game. Everyone needed a little fiction now and then.

She managed to connect with Chase that night. He was in Bonner's Ferry, Idaho, investigating a possible drug ring. But he was also staying current with the Snohomish County investigation.

"I've got the file on the screen now," he told her. "Nobody's been able to track Erik Heigler yet," he told her. "There's no record of him coming across from Mexico."

That wasn't too surprising, with the sleazebag's record as a coyote along the southern border. "How about that note?" she asked.

"Never got to AFIS. There were so many prints all over it that they were all mucked up."

Flashes of her own fingers on it, then Aidan's and Troy's, zipped through her head. How could she have known the dang piece of paper might be important?

"The convenience store owner in Glacier couldn't remember who bought jerky and orange juice. According to him, those are common purchases by hikers and hunters in the area."

"Damn," she muttered. "So we don't even know if the note really came from Heigler, or if he's around at all."

She didn't know where any of this was heading. The counselors had reported seeing only a couple of other hikers in the new area last night. No hunters. Nothing suspicious or frightening had happened during the break. She wondered again if Aidan could be responsible for the Klapton note. "Nothing else on the case?"

Silence dominated the cell phone atmosphere for a second, and she understood he was reading. "Why'd you ask Greene to check out Aidan Callahan?"

She could hear the worry in his voice. "No particular reason, Chase, other than he knew Kyla and Kim. And Aidan could have met this Heigler character years ago. So, did anyone check him out?"

"Aidan Charles Callahan, twenty-four years old. Minor drug possession—Oxy, but only two tabs that he didn't have a prescription for. Last year, couple of speeding tickets. Mediocre grades at Washington State. Dad works for Burlington Northern. Two sisters. Family went through bankruptcy a few years ago. All fairly common stuff for a college kid his age."

"Good," she said, although the Oxy possession was troubling. "Say, Chase, does that case file you're looking at include photos of boot prints near Pinnacle Lake?"

"I think so. Hang on. Gotta switch windows here." She heard keys clicking as he typed. After a minute, he said, "Okay, I'm looking at several photos of prints from the lake shore."

"Do you see any boot prints that have a circle logo stamped in the tread?"

Another pause. "One has a circled number 11 on it; I'm pretty sure that's the size."

"Sounds like it."

"Here's another that looks like a stalk of cauliflower inside a circle."

Her pulse quickened. "Could it be a tree?"

"Probably more likely than cauliflower."

"A circled tree is a Timberland logo."

"And?" he prompted.

If she told him that Aidan wore Timberlands, Chase would freak out. She shouldn't have asked him about the prints. "And ... nothing, really. Timberlands are a common brand. I was just showing the kids animal tracks and so I was looking at boot treads and noticing all the different prints they leave."

"Uh-huh." His tone was dry; he knew her too well. "You suspect Callahan of something."

"He thinks he should have the job I'm doing right now."

"Kyla's old job?"

She knew what he was hinting at. "Yes. But he admired Kyla, and he worked alongside her all summer."

There was no response.

"Really, Chase," she reassured him, "Aidan's been great to work with, and this is the last expedition of the year. Anything else on the case?"

"They still have nothing on Chris Rawlins, so he went back to his job in Alaska," he told her. "I suppose you're back up there in the mountains."

In spite of the fact that I asked you not to go hung in the airwaves between them. He knew by now that she was not the obedient type.

"Yep. Nine days to go," she told him. "Everything is quiet. Troy relocated us to a whole different section of the north

Cascades. We'll be okay."

"You better be," he said. "Watch your back."

"*Te quiero,* Chase."

"I love you too, *querida*. I don't know what I'd do without you."

How ironic. They spent most of their days separated from each other. She ached to kiss his handsome face, run her fingers through his straight black hair, lay her head against his muscular chest, and listen to his steady heartbeat.

Chase had already been shot once before on assignment, and he nearly died then. What if she never saw him again?

What if he decided to look for someone more accommodating to his career? His work was important, while these days she was more often unemployed than not.

Maybe she could live in Salt Lake City. She could still hike; there were incredible mountains and canyons. She could take trips to kayak on the rivers. Maybe she'd learn to love the high desert and not miss the Northwest's thick evergreens, ferns, ocean inlets, and islands.

Could she ignore the anti-conservation politics?

Shouldn't she at least try?

13

The brown-speckled bird slowly emerged from its frozen state, first twitching only its head, and then slowly shifting one feathered foot. It took another hesitant step, bobbing its head, and stepped out from beneath the huckleberry bush. The bird was the size of a small chicken. The feathers of its belly were white, while its wings and back were a dull gray brown pattern.

Olivia twitched her boot in the dirt. That miniscule sound was enough to make the bird freeze again. Gabriel slowly raised a hand and extended a finger, pointing to another bird hiding in the shrubbery a few yards away. Then Taylor sneezed, and those two birds, plus another two they hadn't yet spotted, leapt into the air with a noisy whir of feathers that startled everyone.

"Sorry." Taylor apologized, wiping her nose with the back of her hand. "It's the wind. I think I might be allergic to something."

"I hope not." They'd all been healthy so far. Sam wanted it to stay that way. Only a few more days; the end was in sight. She stood up and stretched, amazed that her entire crew had been able to sit motionless and silent for as long as they had.

They'd had decent weather for the last four days, but now the breeze was increasing, and the clouds scuttling overhead made the afternoon chilly. So far the sky remained more blue than gray, though. Unfortunately, the front predicted to come in was moving down from Canada and she wouldn't be able to see the northern skies until they achieved the ridge.

"Those birds were awesome," Nick commented.

"What do you call 'em again?" Justin wanted to know.

"Ptarmigans," Sam told him. "White-tailed ptarmigans, to be precise. Members of the grouse family. Ptarmigan begins with a P, in case you ever want to look it up. P-t-a-r-m-i-g-a-n."

"That's weird," Ashley said. "Puh-tarmigan."

"They turn completely white in the winter so they can blend into the snow," Sam said. "Right now they're half-way between winter and summer plumage. The biggest one was the hen, and the other three were probably her chicks for this season, almost grown now." She stood and picked up her pack. "Let's get a move on. The clouds are gathering and we still have several miles to go, but I want to show you the lookout. You're going to love it."

She was leading her crew to one of her favorite spots in the north Cascades, an historic fire lookout. The ripe huckleberries were nearly gone along this high trail, but the leaves on the bushes still glowed with colors ranging from mulberry to crimson, a stunning view against the sharp gray and white granite rocks and chartreuse lichens covering the flanks of the mountain. To the east rose the impressive snow-covered pyramid of Mount Baker.

"Mount Baker is the name given to it by European explorers," Sam explained to the group. "The native name for that volcano is Koma Kulshan, or just Kulshan."

"It's an active volcano, one of five in Washington State," Maya added, clearly proud of possessing that information.

"It's active?" Justin studied the mountain. "When will it blow?"

"Not in our lifetime, I hope," Sam told him. "It does puff out gas now and then, so we know there's still geologic activity inside it. And sometimes it launches debris flows down the sides into the creeks and valleys."

"Earthquakes also happen. They're pretty common in the Cascades," Nick added, reminding everyone that he was from western Washington, too. "Mostly little ones."

That prompted a discussion of the earthquakes that Justin

had felt in California compared with those experienced by Aidan and Maya and Nick in Washington. Justin was sure that California won in the dangerous earthquake category.

"I heard that Oklahoma now has more earthquakes than any other state," Taylor added. "It's the fracking from all those oil wells."

"But we had Mount Saint Helens," Ashley argued. "My mom told me the ash cloud turned Spokane into, like, a wasteland, and I've seen pictures of how that mountain collapsed, too. California might have earthquakes, and even Oklahoma, but Justin, you never had an erupting volcano."

"I think Hawaii is the clear winner in the American volcano eruption contest right now," Sam told them, ending what seemed like a senseless competition. "Get moving."

Forty minutes and several hundred feet of elevation gain later, they stood at the end of the trail. The old fire lookout rose above them. "Let's leave our packs down here and take a look around."

"Sweet!" Gabriel dropped his pack, then galloped up the rickety wooden steps to the deck. The rest of the crew followed more slowly.

The lookout perched on the edge of a steep cliff, its deck overhanging the valley below. The view in all directions was spectacular. Mount Baker dominated the east and dozens of other Cascade peaks rippled over the horizon in the south and west. To the north, down the valley, lay the wooded site where they were scheduled to camp this evening.

"Uh-oh." Maya groaned, only a second before Sam would have. A turmoil of clouds churned along the Canadian border, thick, high, and dark. Worse, the towering thunderheads were rolling swiftly southward down the valley toward them.

A jagged streak of lightning flashed in the distance. The resulting boom made them all jump.

Not so distant, then.

"Let's get inside, crew." She practically shoved the kids into the lookout building. Less than a minute later, the first balls of hail pinged off the roof above their heads. Within seconds, the hammering was so loud they found it impossible to talk. The torrent of hail was punctuated by bolts of lightning and booms of thunder.

The kids were glued to the large windows, watching the spectacle. The sudden storm was both magnificent and terrifying in its ferocity.

Maya jogged Sam's elbow. "The packs."

"Crap!" She cursed herself for leading her crew up here, for not keeping better track of the weather. The teens had been cooperating and she'd enjoyed the recent days for the most part. As a leader, she'd gotten lazy, and now they were all going to pay for it.

As soon as the hail stopped, the deluge began. Rivers of water streaked down the windows, blurring the vista beyond. "Uh, crew, I need volunteers to go down with me and grab our packs."

They all turned to stare at her, dismay written on their young faces. She'd have to draft a couple of them.

Then Justin's hand shot up. "I'll go."

Ashley and Taylor volunteered next. Then they all gave in.

"What the heck, let's all go and grab our own packs," Sam told them. "Three at a time, so we can speed up and down the steps. Justin, Ashley, Taylor, you volunteered first, so you three go now."

The trio dashed out the door, swearing and squealing as the rain hit their heads. In less than five minutes, they thundered back up the steps and through the door, clothes and packs dripping onto the rough plank floor. The others cleared a wide path for them.

"You look like a voltenark fished out of a sewer," Ashley told Justin as she shimmied out of her pack.

Justin set his pack on the floor, leaning it against the wall. "And you're a rat that swam up through a toilet."

"I'm the only one who can battle the storm and emerge looking like a fashion model." Taylor struck a pose, thrusting out a hip and tossing strings of long blond hair over her shoulder in what would have been a seductive manner had water not been dripping from her eyebrows and the end of her nose.

They all laughed.

"Well, now or never." Aidan moved toward the door.

Justin wiped the back of his hand across his forehead. "Cap'n, it makes no sense for everyone to end up like a drowned voltenark."

"We're already soaked," Taylor agreed.

Ashley said, "We may as well get the other packs, too."

Sam beamed. "That's a heroic gesture! Thank you, Ash, Justin, Taylor. You three have just earned Navigator status."

The three soaked teens high-fived, grinning, and then dashed back out the door.

"I was ready to go," Gabriel complained. Olivia and Nick grumbled that they were prepared to go out and get wet, too.

Sam stifled a smile, inordinately pleased that half her crew had been willing to sacrifice their comfort for others, and the remaining half regretted their missed opportunity to be heroes.

When her three Navigators had made two more trips and all packs were leaning against the wall, Sam told everyone to face away as Ashley and Taylor changed into dry clothes, then repeated the instruction for Justin.

"Oh, let 'em look," Justin said. "Everyone deserves to see this body."

Sam was adamant. "Nope."

"Just the dragon," Olivia suggested.

"It is awesome," Gabriel commented, reminding her that the boys had all bathed together several times during the trip.

"Got your pants on, Justin?" Sam asked.

"Yeah. Your loss, women of America. But you can still behold the dragon."

They all turned to inspect Justin's upper half. Turning his back to them, he flexed his muscles. The dragon tattoo, black and red, stretched from his neck across his broad back. Its tail curled up just above his belt.

The girls all made appropriate sounds of appreciation.

"How much did it hurt to finish that dragon?" Sam wanted to remind the kids of the cost of a tattoo.

Justin looked at her over his shoulder. "About a month's worth of burn."

"Shirt on, Dragon Man," she instructed.

The rain continued with no letup. They slid to the floor, sitting with backs against the walls, everyone eyeing the lone twin bed in the center of the lookout. The sparse furnishings appeared to be as historic as the building itself. In one corner was a small table and a chair. A rusty Coleman stove and an old journal sat on top of the table. The only modern touch was a large plastic bucket with a lid in one corner of the room.

"People stay here?" Olivia asked.

"It was originally built to be a place for a firewatch volunteer to live in during the summer. But now, the first hiker to claim it each night can stay here," Aidan told them. "I slept up here once. Pretty cool, except for the thundering hordes of mice—"

"Mice?" Taylor studied the floor around her feet.

"Seemed like there were thousands," Aidan said. "If you read the journal over there"—he indicated a small notebook that lay open on top of the table—"you'll see that all the visitors complain about them."

Ashley pushed herself to her feet, grabbed the journal, and sat down again.

"That bucket is to store food in." Aidan jerked his chin toward it.

"I guessed it was a bucket with a view," said Taylor.

"No," Aidan answered. "The toilet facilities are down the steps, across the field, and up the hill in the trees."

"Swell," Taylor said.

"The place did come with a shower, Sweet T," Justin observed.

Taylor slapped his arm in response.

Lightning flashed, brightening the room like a spotlight. A clap of thunder reverberated loudly, rattling the small building.

"Guess we're in for the night, crew," Sam told them. "When you need to visit the toilet, put on your raingear and headlamp first, and Aidan will show you where it is." She shot him a look to show that was an order. "Now, someone set out some pans to collect water."

Olivia jumped up.

Nick headed for the Coleman stove. "I'll see if this thing works."

"I'll sort out dinner," Gabriel volunteered. "Where is it?"

Sam gulped. "Here's the bad news. The new food stash is in the bear box at the campsite where we're supposed to be, which is another couple of miles down the valley."

Gabriel gazed wistfully in the direction that Sam pointed. "It's just rain. We can do a couple of miles in under an hour. It's only water, right?"

Maya made a face. "And a whole skyful of electricity just waiting to zap us. Not to mention that you might remember that it's a really steep trail with a lot of rock steps, and this rain will make it uber slippery."

"Maybe we could rappel down," Ashley suggested.

"Yeah," Justin seconded.

They'd done climbing and rappelling practice yesterday. Ashley and Justin had been particularly enthusiastic, and it was a nice mood pickup after the last visit by the counselors to check in with the kids and deliver more letters from their parents. Only four days after tonight. Search and rescue lessons; wilderness first aid, last solo campout, more exercises to focus on constructive plans for the future. The finish line was so close; Sam could almost taste the steak waiting for her at home.

"No, we can't rappel down," she said. "We left the harnesses and most of our rope in the bear box back at the last camp. And we're not going to chance hiking down the trail in the dark, either. So, for dinner tonight, we've only got, well, whatever we've got." She crawled the short distance to her pack. "I have a bag of nuts and some carrots left over from lunch, and a couple of instant soup packets." She placed them on the desk next to the stove.

Aidan contributed a pack of crackers and cheese and the few dried pears he had left from Sam's gift, and Maya added her gift bag of yogurt-covered raisins.

"You guys been holding out on us!" Gabriel accused, then, his cheeks growing red, guiltily pulled a small pack of M&Ms from his jacket pocket. The counselors must have bribed the kids during their sessions.

Nick paused in pumping the stove to slap down several celery sticks left over from his lunch, as well as a half-eaten granola bar.

Justin found another soup packet, and Ashley and Olivia contributed crackers.

With Taylor supervising, Gabriel divided up the small smorgasbord into nine equal offerings. "We can make a cup of soup for everyone, maybe?" He looked at Nick.

Aidan stood up and fished a lighter out of his pocket.

"I knew it!" Justin said. "And you make us create fire like cavemen."

"This is only for emergencies. You should be proud of yourselves. Not many people could make a fire with only sticks and twine." Aidan held a flame to a rusty burner as Nick twisted the knob. They both jumped back as the burner abruptly flared up with a whoosh.

"So there *is* some gas left in this thing," Nick commented. "We better get the water on while we've got heat."

Olivia retrieved a pan filled with rainwater from the deck outside and placed it on the burner, then began to hand out the small piles of food by scooping them into her drinking cup and offering them to each person. Most held out their hands to accept. Sam pulled out her bandanna to use as a plate. Ashley used her own drinking cup.

"Shades of Anne Frank," Taylor said as she accepted the meager offerings from Olivia's cup and spread them on her outstretched thighs. A flash of light and loud boom from outside made the atmosphere seem more Halloween than Holocaust.

"God bless us, every one." Nick's voice slipped into falsetto for a Tiny Tim imitation.

"If this continues, we'll have to decide who to eat," Gabriel predicted.

"We can't eat the Cap'n; we need her. Olivia's the next smallest." Justin grinned at the dark girl.

"Which means we are both excluded," Sam told him. "It would be most efficient to eat the largest person, wouldn't it? Bigger meals for everyone, and the largest consumer removed from the group."

"Yeah!" Nick heartily agreed.

Justin frowned. "Well, gex!" He sank back into his spot against the wall, promising, "I'll be so tough to chew that you'll be sorry, though."

After everyone had consumed a cup of soup apiece in addition to their portions of the snacks, Sam made a little ceremony out of bestowing Navigator necklaces on Justin, Taylor, and Ashley. Where two weeks ago these kids would have sneered at the honor, now they blushed with pride as they fingered the pendants she fastened around their necks.

She was tempted to do the same for the other three teens, but decided to wait until morning to allow her first volunteers time to bask in their glory. To finish, she handed around one chocolate covered peanut each from the stash she'd saved in her pack and they toasted the occasion by tossing them simultaneously into their mouths.

"I'm liking this." Maya unzipped her pack and extracted her headlamp and a book, then returned to her position against the wall and buried her nose in the pages.

Sam lit the lone oil lamp on the desk. She could hardly believe how well the kids had accepted their situation.

Outside, the thunder gradually diminished but the deluge continued.

There was not enough room inside the lookout for all nine of them to stand, rummage in their packs, and dress. After taking turns sitting on the bed to don their rain gear, everyone trooped off to the toilet, then squished their way back over the soggy ground. While the others remained outside on the deck huddling as best they could under the narrow roof overhang, Sam instructed the first five to go inside, strip off and stow their rain gear, take a seat and then call out for the remaining four. It was a laborious process.

"No stars tonight." Ashley stated the obvious, staring at the sheeting rain over the dark mountains. "And I'd say the overwhelming color of the sunset is wet."

"Nature in all its glory." Nick's words sounded like a comment, not a complaint.

Finally they were all back inside and sitting around the walls again.

"There's not enough space to set up our tents in here," Taylor observed from her spot near a corner.

"No shit, Sherlock," Justin teased.

Taylor slapped his arm again. "Shut up, Holmes."

"Figure it out," Sam said.

Olivia studied the room. "There's enough space for nine sleeping bags if two go on top of the bed."

"Maybe." Justin eyed the floor space. "Someone might have to sleep underneath it."

"Oh, joy." Gabriel pulled off one of his boots. "How do we decide who goes where?"

"Olivia and I will sleep on the bed," Sam announced.

"Why?" Ashley asked.

"Why do you think?"

After a few seconds had passed, Nick said, "Because it's a small bed, and they are the two smallest."

Sam touched the tip of her nose and then pointed at him to show he'd gotten it right.

"Poodle," Ashley hissed under her breath.

After what seemed like an interminable game of What Animal is It? (a flying squirrel) led by Maya, they finally retired to their sleeping bags. The kids had worked out that if four of them slept with their feet under the bed, the space was adequate. Aidan rolled his sleeping bag out in front of the sole exit door.

"Aidan, please swap places with Gabriel," Sam instructed.

Her peer counselor frowned. "Why?"

"I want to move that buzz saw as far away from the rest of us as possible," she lied. "Sorry, Gabe, but in case you don't know, you snore a little."

Gabriel hung his head, embarrassed.

Aidan's jaw was set, but he murmured, "Your wish is my command, Cap'n," and then gave her a sloppy salute.

She wanted to tell him to ditch the sarcasm. He wadded up his sleeping bag, and the two switched places. Gabriel slid into his bag, planting his backside up against the door. That was more to her liking. Twice in recent days, Aidan had been unaccounted for. The crew kids had been given more freedom, so the peer counselors could roam more, too. Sam suspected he was using the cell phone he had in his pack, which was supposed to be reserved for emergencies. Tonight, she could make sure Aidan would not slip out unnoticed.

Sam and Olivia lay in their mummy bags, feet to nose on the twin bed. The mattress was surprisingly comfortable, but the ancient metal frame squeaked every time either one of them moved.

The lamp had been snuffed out for only a few minutes before the skittering began. A muffled squeal came from the corner where Taylor lay. "A mouse just ran across my chest!" she whimpered.

"And many more." Aidan sang the usual follow-up verse to "Happy Birthday" in a minor key.

Justin growled, "Suck it up, Tee."

"Hey, we could eat them instead of Justice. Mouse on a stick!" Gabriel.

Olivia pulled the sleeping bag over her head.

"Good night, all!" Sam insisted.

She woke before dawn. Rain still sheeted down the windows, but the thunderstorm was over. Outside on the deck, boards creaked. The sound moved around the deck from the front steps to the back side that overlooked the drop-off.

Her heart sped into overdrive as her brain conjured the hunter who had been following them. Klapton? They were sitting ducks in here, all lined up for execution. She wriggled carefully out of her sleeping bag, then quickly stepped over the inert forms of Gabriel and Nick to reach the window.

She peered outside in the pre-dawn gloom. For a long moment, her eyes could not identify any shape other than the deck railing, but then she saw a movement below the window.

Was a sniper lying in wait on the deck? Her heart hammering in her chest, she pressed her face against the glass.

A tawny black-tipped tail twitched across the deck boards, and then flicked back out of view.

Cougar.

Smiling, Sam tiptoed back to bed. Did that mountain lion routinely use this lookout as a perch, or had it come here to escape the deluge? She hoped there would be paw prints in the morning to show her crew.

As daylight filtered in, the kids sat up, stretching. Aidan and Maya extracted themselves and quietly rolled up their bags.

"A dozen mice slept with me last night." Nick lifted the flap of his bag to inspect the interior.

"I could eat a dozen mice." Gabriel licked his lips. "Charbroiled. Or chocolate covered."

At that moment, Olivia screamed. Her arm shot out, index finger aimed at the window. The cougar, hearing the noise inside, now stood with his paws against the glass, curiously peering in.

Chaos erupted. Everyone shouted at once, and although most were still hampered by their sleeping bags, the crew tried to crawl away from the window the big cat had chosen. The cacophony was too much for the cougar. The cat dropped down to the deck. The noise made by her crew covered the swift padding of the lion's exit.

Sam grinned. Food rationing. Mice. Thunder and lighting. Hail. And now a mountain lion, up close and personal. This was a story the kids would tell the rest of their lives.

14

The rain had slowed to a gentle drizzle by the time her crew was ready to hike down the mountain. The normally small tarns on the plateau below the lookout had merged into larger ponds, and as they sloshed down the muddy trail, they could hear rushing water in creeks to all sides. Mist obscured Mount Baker, so it was either still raining or snowing at altitudes that were only slightly higher. The clouds overhead were thick, but with luck, the major precipitation would stick to the slopes of the volcano.

After reaching their scheduled camp, they breakfasted on last night's dinner, which vaguely resembled spaghetti carbonara. Then Sam awarded Nick, Olivia, and Gabriel their Navigator necklaces, for their adult behavior and contributions last night to the welfare of the group. She wanted all her crew kids to finish on the highest level; they deserved it.

Precipitation continued in the form of sporadic drizzle, but Sam decided that was part of the outdoor experience, so they all donned their rain gear and spent the day learning search techniques. These mainly consisted of spiraling out from the place last seen as best as possible given the rough terrain, marking off search quadrants and exploring new ones. She divided them into three teams, with Nick, Olivia, and Gabriel as leaders.

"Safety first," she stressed. "You never want to lose a search volunteer."

"Good thing we don't have any *volunteers*," Ash said.

Aidan and Maya took turns getting lost, and the whole crew seemed to enjoy finding them again, blowing their whistles to alert everyone else when they did. Ashley was astute enough to look up and spot Maya in the branches of tree, and Nick and Taylor, a team of two, simultaneously discovered Aidan hiding between boulders.

The search exercises were strenuous but fun. Sam was proud of her crew. They'd been on their own for hours during the day, and they'd all shouldered the responsibility well. Reflecting back to their first day together when Justin and Taylor had been so uncooperative and the rest so hostile, she knew they'd all come a long way.

In the evenings, around the campfire, came the most difficult times. Sharing, urging the kids to plan for their futures. The exercises were carefully sequenced by the company counselors to prepare the teens for the end of the program.

Taylor, Gabriel, and Justin seemed reasonably optimistic about getting back to the real world. Nick, Olivia, and Ashley were unwilling to share their plans, but Sam believed they were strong enough now to at least begin coping with whatever awaited them at home.

After dinner, they sat in their usual circle, struggling with the daily matter of entertainment for the evening. Gabriel suggested the question game again, which was quickly vetoed. Then they discussed marbles, but dismissed that as well because of the lack of appropriate pebbles in their location. Swordfighting with sticks was proposed by Justin and seconded by Nick and Ashley.

"No way," Sam said. "The first one to pick up a stick gets demoted to zombie."

Taylor stood up, dusting off her pants. "Bocce!"

They all stared at her.

"Bocce ball," she said. "I've played it before. There's even a court in my neighborhood. It's sort of like bowling, except without the pins. All you need is four balls apiece and an extra one that looks different for a marker."

Gabriel, Nick, Justin, and Olivia pushed themselves to their feet and started the hunt for bocce ball-sized rocks. Maya and Aidan rose to keep them within sight.

"No, no," Taylor said in the distance, "Best would be baseball size rocks."

Ashley elected not to participate and instead sat with her back against a log, frowning, her journal open in her lap and a pen in her hand. Sam went to her tent and pulled out her own notebook to write about the happenings of the day.

Within a half hour, the crew had marked the boundaries of a bocce ball court with twigs, located a mostly white rock that Taylor called the pallino, and were enthusiastically tossing their rocks toward it. The three rocks that ended up the closest to the pallino scored a point, and the teens had decided that ten points won the game. There were occasional arguments about which balls belonged to whom, which was not surprising given that the "balls" were all rocks, and most rocks in the area were similar. When Sam looked up, Taylor was in the lead with seven points, followed by Justin and Gabriel, both with six. Olivia and Nick had four.

Nick lobbed his rock toward the white one, but tossed too hard, and overshot. His rock collided with another on the outside of the mass and then ricocheted away, ending up completely off the makeshift court.

Justin guffawed. "Gex, Lightning, that was pathetic. You couldn't hit an elephant if it was standing on your foot!"

Clenching his jaw, Nick snatched his last rock from the ground beside his feet and pitched it hard overhand at Justin. The rock struck the larger boy squarely in the forehead with an audible thud.

"Shit!" Justin dropped to his backside in the dirt. Blood gushed from his face.

Holy crap. Sam rolled to her knees, dumping her notebook into the dirt. In her peripheral vision she saw Maya and Aidan running toward the bocce game.

Justin was on his feet again before Sam or her peer counselors could reach the kids. Taylor and Olivia rushed

toward their tents, Ashley and Gabriel froze in place at the side
of the court, and Nick stood his ground as Justin charged and
punched him in the face so hard that the smaller boy fell
sideways to the ground.

Sam's pulse was galloping as she positioned herself between
the two boys. To think that only a few minutes ago she had
been congratulating herself on how well her crew was getting
along.

Maya helped Nick up, then dragged him off into the woods.
Aidan and Sam restrained Justin, each hanging onto one of his
arms, until he unclenched his fists. Then Sam doctored the big
kid's face as he sat on a stump. Her hands were trembling as
she cleaned the gash with antiseptic, closed it with butterfly
bandages, and then taped a large gauze rectangle on top. The
gauze patch was quickly dotted with seeping blood. It was
scary how copiously facial wounds bled.

"You'll have a big bruise." She placed the last piece of tape
next to his left eyebrow. "But that will just add to your brawny
appeal, Justin. Goes with the dragon tattoo."

Justin's fists were clenched in his lap. "That little shithead.
He's gonna pay."

How quickly that situation had gone to hell. Probably
wasn't a good idea to encourage games that involved rocks.
And who would have guessed that Nick would strike the first
blow?

She examined Justin's eyes with a penlight. Equal pupil size
right and left, thank heavens. "We've got almost three days to
go, Justin. Three days you and Nick have to spend together."

Reaching a hand up, he pressed his fingertips to the
bandage on his brow, wincing. "I'll pound that shrimp into the
dirt."

She rested a hand on Justin's shoulder. Her fingers were
weak from adrenaline; but under her grip the boy felt like a
solid knot of muscles. "I can understand why you feel that way,
and you have reason to be mad. But you did insult him first.
And what would beating up Nick accomplish?"

He glared at her like she was a dimwit. "Respect."

"I know about your past, Justin. Do you want to end up in jail?"

He bristled. "I can't let anyone get away with—"

"Justin, do you respect your father?"

The teen scowled at her for a moment more, his eyes burning. Then he lowered his gaze to his lap. His pants had dark splashes of blood on the thighs. "Gex."

After a few minutes more, Nick and Maya were back, both uncertainly watching Justin. The smaller boy's cheek and jaw were swollen, the blotchy redness already giving way to purple. Maya, her gaze fixed on Nick, jerked her chin toward Justin.

"Sorry." Nick's voice was barely audible.

"You should be," Justin snarled. He stared over Nick's head into the distance.

"I wanted you to see that I can aim," Nick said.

Justin snorted and faced the other boy. "I was *kidding*, for chrissakes. Why the gex are you so *sensitive*?"

Nick turned on his heel, shooting a look at Maya. "I'll be in my tent." He strode off.

Sam pondered for a minute whether or not to insist that Justin apologize to Nick for punching him, but decided to leave the situation alone. After kicking apart the bocce ball court to keep the campsite as pristine as possible, the kids read or wrote in their journals and eventually went to bed.

Sam fretted. Should she take away the two boys' Navigator status? Would she be held liable for Justin's and Nick's injuries? Would Troy? The poor man had enough trouble. She didn't want to tell him what had happened, but postponing the news could potentially get her in more trouble, so after asking Aidan to check on Justin during the night to be sure he wasn't concussed and unconscious, she carried her phone into the woods to report in.

"Don't worry," Troy reassured her. "As long as they're ambulatory when we give them back, the parents are usually grateful. We had one who ended up in a sling after dislocating his shoulder."

"It all happened so fast. I never expected it." She felt for the parents of these teens. "Nick is so quiet most of the time."

"You have to remember that they're broken when we get them, Sam. And neither the parents nor the kids are ever totally honest about all their hot buttons." There was a pause. "Kim was better at drawing them out than I'll ever be."

Sam knew how he felt. The rock throwing incident would probably not have happened if Kyla had been in charge. "I never saw it coming, Troy. They were all getting along so well. And we're so close to the end."

"Sometimes that's when they're the most self-destructive, Sam. Some of them don't want to go home."

"Is it safe to do the final solo campout tomorrow night?"

"That's the program. Put Nick and Justin as far apart as you can. And then watch 'em like a hawk."

Lovely, she thought. She stashed her cell phone back in her pocket and began the trudge back to camp. She studied the sky. The clouds had briefly risen during the evening, but now they'd lowered again. There would be no stars and no moon visible tonight. The dreariness matched her mood.

She was a very weary hawk.

15

Sporting multicolor bruises and scabs on swollen faces, Justin
and Nick circled each other warily the next morning. Sam kept
a close eye on them throughout the rainy day's lessons on basic
first aid. Feeling a bit like a first grade teacher, she assigned
Olivia and Taylor to work with Justin on splinting and
bandaging, and teamed Ashley and Gabriel and Nick.

She had two real injured victims to use as patients, so she
showed the crew how to dress the cut on Justin's head with
butterfly bandages and an overlying gauze pad, and how to
check for concussions and brain injuries such as strokes.
Justin clearly enjoyed the extra attention. Nick seemed
embarrassed.

"But if the person can't hold both arms up," Taylor asked,
pressing down on Justin's arms as he sat with his eyes closed,
"what are you supposed to do with them?"

Excellent question, and this was probably why these lessons
weren't part of the backcountry first aid course. Sam wasn't
sure what the answer was. "Give them aspirin and call for
help," she hedged. Or was that the recommendation for heart
attack?

"But we don't have cell phones," Gabriel reminded her.

"If you can't call, and there's more than one of you who is
still ambulatory, send one person for help and have one person
stay with the victim to keep the victim warm and awake."

"What if something happens to the person who goes for
help?" Ashley asked. "It would be just my luck to be stuck with

you," she complained to her victim, Nick. "While Gabriel got eaten by a bear on his way to get help."

"And they lived happily ever after, all alone in the deep woods," Nick warbled in a high voice.

"But seriously," Olivia said, "what if there are only two of you left?"

"Make the patient as comfortable as possible, and then save yourself and try to get help," Sam said. "You just have to do the best you can."

"What if someone gets attacked by a bear?"

"What about when someone gets shot?"

Yeesh, the constant questioning was irritating. How did parents do this? By noon, she was eager to send her whole crew on their second and last solo campout.

She and Aidan and Maya led the crew off one by one, careful to position Nick and Justin as far apart as possible. Which wasn't far enough for Sam, plus it put Taylor and Ashley too close to Justin for comfort, but it couldn't be helped. She reminded them all about the possibility of bears and mountain lions prowling after dark, hoping that would keep them from wandering. She and Aidan and Maya would just have to check on them several times during the twenty-four hour solo period instead of only once.

Chase Perez sprawled across the hotel bed to focus on Summer's return call. As usual, earlier he had to leave her a text message. She didn't call him back until it was nearly eleven his time.

"Sorry," she puffed in his ear. "I had to climb to the top of the ridge to get a signal. "Where are you?"

"Kalispell, Montana. See, we're getting closer, only one time zone apart tonight. I've got an interesting case, investigating drug smuggling from Canada down though the Flathead Reservation.

"And you're with your people."

"Drug smugglers?" He knew she was referring to his Lakota

heritage, but Lakotas and Flatheads were as different as coyotes and wolves, and he couldn't resist giving her a hard time.

"Well, no, of course not! Sorry, Chase, I didn't mean to imply..."

"Stop apologizing, Summer, I'm just yanking your chain. It's interesting to see how different tribes live and govern." He wished he were more at ease on reservations. Having been raised in the suburbs of Boise with a Lakota mother and a Mexican father, visiting a "rez" made him feel like a pretend Indian. "How's the Camping with Criminals program going?"

"The kids are on their last solo campouts tonight. Then we've got one more night together, and I'm done. Last night one kid beaned another with a rock, but today is going better than I would have expected."

"Maybe you've found a new career," he suggested.

"No way. It gives me a headache just to think about that. And both Maya and Troy tell me I got a pretty easy bunch to deal with."

"No sign of Heigler?"

"No." They'd seen no hunters since moving. "I guess the relocation fixed that. If he was ever really here at all."

"What do you mean by that?"

She didn't want to explain her suspicions about Aidan placing that note.

"And Callahan? You're getting along with him?"

"He's disappeared a couple of times, which pisses me off, but never for long. Probably talking to a girlfriend or something; he has a cell phone. And frankly, I've wanted to disappear more than once, too. This twenty-four hour togetherness grates on my nerves."

"Good to know," he murmured. He'd had dinner this evening with the head of the resident FBI agency, Rueben Farmer, and his wife, Jenny. When Chase had remarked on the variety of places the Farmer family had been posted to, Reuben's wife had smiled and patted her husband's arm affectionately, saying, "That's what I signed up for."

Her devotion to her husband and his agency career was depressing.

On the other end of the phone conversation, Summer was apologizing again. "I didn't mean togetherness with *you*, Chase. We both know how to give each other space."

"Yes, we've each got plenty of space." She had the mountains and coastline and the mild weather and political climate she favored; he had a job that involved roaming over three states.

"You're scaring me," she said. "I promise that I will come see you in Salt Lake as soon as I'm done here."

"That sounds good. When I'm home." He wanted to see her *every* time he was home. He loved his job, but maybe there was some sort of equivalent, if not in Bellingham, at least in Washington State. He'd check the Homeland Security website; see if he could surreptitiously search for openings and not irritate his ASAC any further.

"We'll make it happen, Chase. Somehow. I've been thinking about it. Maybe we could do a trial run; maybe I could stay in Salt Lake for a few weeks and see."

"I don't want you to sacrifice anything for me." The words sounded a bit sarcastic, even to him, although he knew he meant them.

After a pause, she said, "*Te quiero*, Chase. I mean that. I love you."

"I love you, too, *querida*. Stay safe."

As she trudged her way back to her tent, Sam heard pebbles skittering behind her. She froze, turned, pushed up her headlamp to shine its beam into the distance. Another crack sounded in the trees off to her right, a branch breaking underfoot. She twisted sharply and saw a flash of movement in the woods, pale, then dark.

Whatever it was vanished. She replayed the vision in her brain, but couldn't bring it into focus. First dark hide, perhaps, then the flash of white. A deer she'd spooked, most likely. But cougars also had white bellies and fronts, tails with black tips. Not a bear, anyway. Something running. Fleeing from her. Running away from the humans, not toward the group camp. She hustled back to her tent.

Sleep was hard to come by that night. Sam dreamed about looking for lost people: she'd snatch a glimpse of them but could never quite catch up to them. Disembodied voices shouted "Sam!"

Waking up with a start, she stared at the green nylon overhead. What was that about? Teaching search techniques earlier today, or because she had recently lost friends, or because she was afraid she was going to lose Chase?

"Sam!" the urgent voice murmured again.

Maya was crouched outside her tent. Damn, she hadn't dreamt it after all.

Sam rolled over and peered out. "Yeah?"

"Nick and Olivia are gone."

16

Alarm bells went off in Sam's head. She quickly pulled on her clothes and scooted out into the damp morning. At four a.m., it was still dark. Dense fog snaking between the trees made it seem even darker.

She walked with Maya to the solo camps. Olivia's and Nick's tents were empty. Olivia's pack was gone, too.

"Shit!" Sam cursed, staring at the vacant campsite. "Aidan said they were all in their tents when he checked at ten p.m. What made you get up and check, Maya?"

The girl shrugged. "Just a feeling. The closer we get to the end, the less Olivia's eating and the quieter she gets."

Sam had noticed that as well. "I've been worried about Nick, too."

"When I saw Olivia's tent was empty, I went to the next, Nick's. The others are all still there."

"We got runners?" Aidan's voice came from behind them, startling them both.

"How could they?" Sam couldn't believe it. Troy and Maya had told her about other expeditions where kids hightailed it during the wee hours. She'd halfway expected escape attempts by Ashley and maybe Justin, but Nick and Olivia? And why now? Only one more one day and night remained in their expedition. They were so close to completing this journey. "I thought they were both preparing themselves."

"Guess they were." Aidan scratched his beard. "You never know what they're thinking."

Sam's stomach was roiling. The dark. The fog. The teens could fall off a cliff; that happened to hikers walking in the dark in unfamiliar terrain. They could drown in a river or creek; every stream was swollen and swift after the storm, they were camped near several watercourses. They could meet that cougar from the lookout; they were probably still in its territory.

"You've had runners before?" she asked Aidan and Maya.

"Yeah," Aidan said. "We usually call the rangers and the highway patrol and we catch up with them sooner or later, usually hitchhiking on the nearest road."

Sam groaned. "We're a long way from any road."

"We've never lost anyone permanently," he assured her.

She couldn't lose two kids. Kyla had never lost two kids, had she? And Nick and Olivia? They both seemed so responsible. They couldn't be runners.

"We're not calling 9-1-1," she told her peer counselors. "At least not yet."

She yanked at the cord around her neck, pulled the whistle up out of her shirt and blew it long and hard. "Aidan, go get Taylor and Gabriel. Maya, you get Ashley. I'll take Justin." He was camped in the closest solo site. "Make them dress appropriately and grab their headlamps and a water bottle, too. Make sure they have their whistles around their necks. Meet at the group site ASAP."

"What the gex is going on?" Justin's voice was even deeper than usual as he crawled out of his tent.

"Get your headlamp and water bottle. This is your chance to be a hero, Dragon Man."

"Can't I do that later? Noon might work for me." He yawned dramatically as he stuffed his shirt into his pants.

"Put on your boots and jacket, and follow me."

As she was grabbing supplies and their remaining rope from the bear box in the group site, the rest of her crew emerged out of the mist. Ashley's hair was wild, Gabriel hadn't tied his boots and Taylor had jammed the zipper on her rain jacket. Sam handed them each a packet of granola bars.

"What is this, a fire drill?" Justin yawned again.

Gabriel guessed, "Alien invasion?"

Taylor and Ashley shifted from foot to foot, chafing their arms to warm up.

"This is not a drill," she told them. "It's a real search. Nick and Olivia are missing."

Justin raised both eyebrows. "Lightning and Martini ran away? Sweet."

"It's not sweet, and we don't know that they ran away," Sam told them. "They might be in trouble somewhere."

"Oh, they're in trouble all right," Aidan said.

"They need our help, crew. Gabriel, tie your boots; you're with Aidan. Ash and Taylor, you're with Maya. Justin, you're with me. Aidan, Maya, carry your cell phones."

"What? They have cell phones, too?" Gabriel was astonished. "Didn't you tell us only the captain could have electronic?"

Sam ignored him. "Let's go find them."

Unfortunately, they were camped near a T intersection where a side path met the main trail they'd taken the day before, so there were three options about which way the two escapees had fled. Sam assigned Aidan's team and her own to head in opposite directions down the trail the kids had traveled for the last two days, reasoning the runaways might pick the most familiar route. "Blow your whistles if you find them, and call me on my cell. Maya, you and Ashley and Taylor take the intersecting trail. We'll search for an hour and a half, and then check in before going farther."

"Copy that," Aidan said.

Maya nodded. "Got it."

It took eighty minutes of stumbling around in the brush, darkness, and fog before Sam heard a whistle. Then two more whistles.

Sam's cell buzzed. "Got 'em," Maya said. "We're at the creek."

"Are they okay?"

"Mostly."

"What does that mean?"

"You'll see. You've got the rope, right?" Maya asked.

"In my pack. Call Aidan and keep blowing your whistles so we can all find each other."

"Roger that. Hurry."

It took nearly another hour for Sam and Justin to follow the whistles back to the creek. Maya stood with Taylor and Ashley on the crest of the river bank, gazing down into the narrow channel the river had carved.

"Damn," Sam said. "The trail's completely gone."

The creek channel was known to be unstable, especially in periods after heavy rain. The soil was extremely soft and sandy here, ground into powder by ancient glaciers. Conditions shifted with the seasons. Most years, the trail had to be rebuilt to cross the creek. She had planned to take the long route around this area to their last campsite at a lake.

Nick and Olivia were on all fours about fifty feet down the steep slope, their hands and feet invisible, buried in the soft earth. A boulder rested a few yards down the slope from them, perched on the edge of a sharp vertical bank that dumped into the raging creek. The water surged beneath them, as wide and deep as the main river now, carving out a huge chunk of the sandy bank as they watched. As the earth collapsed into the stream, the boulder slid further down the slope. So did Olivia. Shrieking, she reached for Nick's ankle above her, and they both slid a foot closer to the roiling water.

"Every time they move, they slide," Maya said.

Aidan and Gabriel arrived just as Sam was pulling the rope out of her pack.

"Well, crap," Aidan observed. "That's quite the predicament."

"And the falls are downstream." Maya moaned.

"Shh." Nobody had ever survived the long drop onto the rocks below those falls.

She tied the rope to the closest tree. "Olivia, keep hold of Nick," Sam shouted to the kids below. "Nick, try to grab this rope."

She flung it toward him. The end snapped into the dirt a

foot above Nick's head. But when he pulled his hand from the sand to reach for it, he and Olivia began to slide again. Nick pinwheeled his arms, trying to swim upward through the sand for the rope, but slipped even further downhill. Olivia screamed until they stopped moving, then dissolved into hiccupping sobs.

Sam felt like screaming herself.

Taylor stated the obvious. "The rope's not long enough."

Gabriel took a step closer to the edge. The sand beneath his feet slumped, and Aidan grabbed the boy by the back of his shirt just in time to keep him from tumbling down the slope to join the other two.

"Everyone step back, now!" She hated to lose sight of Nick and Olivia, but the rest of them were in danger of collapsing the soft sand hill into an avalanche that would bury the two kids below or shove them over the bank into the raging stream.

Six pairs of eyes focused on her, waiting for instructions.

Shit, don't look at me, she thought, *save yourselves*! She paced. There had to be a way.

She couldn't see any branches long enough and stout enough to be helpful. Cut down a tree? Right, with what? Her pocketknife? All she had was a rope that was too short and a paralyzed audience of six horrified people.

Six strong horrified young people, plus one middle-aged terrified field guide. Each with two good arms. The standard Wilderness Quest uniform was high quality, with belted pants and Gortex rain jackets. She uncapped her water bottle, took a swig to wet her throat, then untied the rope from the tree.

Below them, Olivia shrieked again. Sam prayed she and Nick were not being swallowed by the river. "Nick! Olivia! Hang on, don't move. We're coming!"

She turned to the others. "Okay, crew. We're going to form a human chain. Justin, take off your jacket, loop it through your belt, and then use it to tie yourself to that tree."

He hesitated, confused.

"I need you at the top of the chain because you are the strongest, but you can't hug a tree and hold us at the same time."

Nodding, he did as she asked. "Gabe, take off your jacket, loop it through your belt and hand the sleeves to Justin to hold you."

She positioned the rest of them, the boys at the top and the girls toward the bottom, linked with jackets and belts. Maya was the last link she added to the chain, because she knew Maya would stay calm even if the worst happened. She tied one end of the rope to the belt around her young friend's waist and the other around her own.

"Now, we're going to walk, or more likely slide, down that slope. I'm going to grab Nick and Olivia. And you guys will pull us back up. Ready?"

Although their faces were tense with anxiety, they all nodded.

"We're going over to the left side. We don't want to push more dirt down on top of them. Got it?"

Six heads bobbed again.

"Here goes. Everyone, hold on. Maya, play my rope out gradually, and wait until the rope goes tight before you follow." Sam stepped over the crumbling edge. Her feet sunk into the soft sand, which gave way beneath her. She slid a yard down the slope before the rope jerked her to a halt. A river of sand shifted beneath her boots, sliding down and over the edge of the bank, sloshing into the roiling water.

The boulder resting on the edge tilted sideways. So did Olivia and Nick. The pink light of the sunrise over the flank of Mount Baker revealed the terror in the eyes of the two teens.

As the steep bank slid away from her, adrenaline coursed through Sam's veins. At this rate, half the hillside would give way and they'd all go in. Sam sank onto her backside, shifting only a little sand. Better. She inched her way down the slope on her butt until she reached the end of the rope. Her boots were at least twenty feet from Nick's outstretched hands.

"Okay, Maya," she yelled up the slope, "sit as carefully as you can on the edge and slide down slowly. Everyone sit down as you come over, and move as slowly as you can."

The progress was slow, but as Sam felt slack in the rope at

her waist, she inched downward. Rivulets of sandy earth piled up behind her backside and slithered down beside her legs as the pressure on the slope above increased with the weight of the human chain.

"That's it!" Aidan yelled from above. "That's all we've got."

Sam's left foot was still above and to the side of Nick's hand, a good eighteen inches away. The boy's expression was no longer terrified. Instead, he looked resigned to his fate. She had no idea what Olivia was thinking. The girl's entire focus was on her own hands, gripped tightly around Nick's ankle above his boot.

"Crew, stay strong," Sam yelled up the slope. "Hang onto each other, no matter what."

She turned to the fifteen-year-old. "Nick, I'm going to take off my jacket now. That's going to be our rope. When I say, I am going to toss it in your direction, you're going to grab onto it, and hold on for dear life. You got it?"

"Got it." His voice was hoarse, little more than a whisper.

She peeled off her jacket, knotted a sleeve around her right wrist and passed it through her fist. "Ready? Now!"

She flung the jacket in his direction, reaching as far as she could. The loose sleeve slapped Nick's shoulder. He pulled his hands out of the soil to grab it. The earth beneath him shifted, and Olivia shrieked as the ground slid away from her. The landslide shoved the boulder beneath them over the edge. As the huge rock tumbled, it pulled more dirt with it, and suddenly the whole bank was moving beneath them.

Everyone in the human chain screamed.

17

Sam was astonished when all the teens managed to hang on. How long they could keep it up was a totally different question. Pain sliced through her body. The belt at her waist was cutting off her breath. The jacket stretched between her and Nick threatened to pull her shoulder out of its socket.

She dug her heels into the soft soil to push as best she could. "Pull us up!"

The only movement she felt was more sand giving way beneath her.

"Pull, crew! Give it all you've got!" Pain shrieked through her shoulder; it felt like it was being torn apart. Her belt threatened to cut her torso in half. The kids above her had to be in the same predicament. She closed her eyes and clenched her jaw.

This was going to be the biggest disaster in Washington Wilderness Quest history. Instead of losing two kids, most of the kids in her crew were going to slide into this damn stream and if they didn't drown first, they'd be bashed into pulp over the falls downstream.

Summer Westin would be famous for poor planning and failed leadership. Sort of like George Donner, whose inept guidance caused half his party of pioneers to perish on their trek over the Sierra Nevadas.

Why was there always so much time to think when death was imminent? For mercy's sake, the final lights out should be instantaneous, not drawn out like this, leaving too many moments for regrets.

Sorry, Kyla. Sorry, Kim. Sorry, kids. Troy. Sorry, Chase. Sorry, Dad, Blake... She'd almost reached the end of her list when her belt jerked tighter beneath her ribs and she began to move uphill, sand snaking down the back of her pants and into her boots.

"Yes, yes!" She dug in with her heels, finally making some progress, inching backwards. Nick and Olivia were face down in the dirt, but she could see they were trying, too, digging in the toes of their boots.

Their uphill progress grew swifter as more kids reached the top of the slope and could help pull. As their chain straightened, Sam could hold onto her jacket sleeve with both hands, lessening the strain on her right shoulder. But everything still hurt like hell. Her waist, her ribs, her hand, her wrist, her elbow, her shoulder.

Nick's knuckles were white, and so were Olivia's. Sam noticed for the first time that the girl still had her pack on her back.

By the time she reached the top of the slope, Sam's pants were so full of sandy soil that she probably weighed twenty pounds more than usual. She didn't care. She whooped as Justin and Gabriel yanked her over to firm ground. As soon as Nick's hand emerged at the top of the bank, the boys grabbed him by his arms and hauled him up. Olivia clung to his leg like a snapping turtle.

Then the entire group collapsed at the top of the ravine, some sitting against trees, most spread-eagled on the ground, all breathing heavily.

Sam watched the stars above dissolve into the pinkish gold of dawn, breathing shallowly, waiting for the pain in her ribs and wrists and shoulder to dissipate. She could hardly believe all nine of them were present and alive.

Finally she sat up, rubbing her shoulder. "Excellent effort, crew."

"And I thought the night at the lookout was memorable," Maya drawled.

Justin laughed weakly.

Sam turned to her two runners. Nick lay on his back on the ground, massaging his hands. Olivia had pulled off her pack and sat with her legs extended and her eyes closed, her back against a slender alder. Her face and dark hair were coated with dirt. "Nick, Olivia, you've got some explaining to do."

Nick sat up. He untucked his shirt. A shower of sand slid out. The bruises on his face were even darker now, although some of the duskiness was probably dirt. Licking chapped lips, he croaked, "It's my fault."

Ashley, the closest to him, handed him a bottle of water, and he gulped down several swallows. After wiping his mouth with the back of his hand, he continued. "I felt like taking a walk, and I made Olivia come, and then we got into trouble."

"No, no, no." Olivia shook her head violently. "That's not the way it went at all. I was alone. When I got here, I couldn't figure out how to cross. I sat down on that boulder and then the bank gave way. I knew I was going to slide into the river. Every time I moved, I slid down farther. And then Nick showed up."

Sam wearily pushed herself to her feet and pulled at her waistband. Rivulets of sandy soil coursed down the insides of her pants legs and spilled out over her boots. Yeesh, she had dirt in her bra and dirt in her underwear, but she resisted the urge to pull her panties away from her butt cheeks in front of the kids.

She wanted to burst into a halleluiah chorus at her relief that everyone had survived, but she needed to look fierce, so she put her hands on her hips. It hurt to curl her fingers into fists. "Were you two running away?"

"No," Nick said. He shook his head and then winced, touching dirty fingers to the swelling near his eye.

Olivia gazed at him, her eyes clouded with doubt, lips parted, as if trying to make up her mind what to say.

Flapping his shirttail to dislodge more sand, Nick said, "I heard Olivia get up in the night to...you know... She walked by my camp; she probably didn't even know I was there. But then she didn't come back, so I went looking for her."

"Olivia?" Sam asked. "I can't help noticing you have your pack with you."

The girl focused on the ground. "I was thinking about not going home, but when I got here, I changed my mind." Her eyes flicked up and she shifted her gaze from one person to the next. "I'm sorry. Thank you for saving me."

She stretched out a hand toward Nick. "And Nick, thank you for coming. You kept me from sliding into the river."

"Are you kidding me? I nearly pushed both of us in. I nearly killed both of us."

"I would have given up if you hadn't been there," Olivia insisted.

Nick rubbed dirt from the uninjured side of his face. "If I'd only had a rope..."

Nobody said anything for several minutes, and Sam realized the whole group was waiting for her to instruct them. "Can everyone walk?"

They could.

"Back to camp for breakfast, then. But first, take a minute to check out Mount Baker." With dawn, the fog had lifted. The group pivoted toward the volcano. Only its triangular summit was visible above the sharp ridge that separated this valley from the mountain, but its glaciers were covered in new snow. Sunrise painted the entire landscape in rose and gold.

After dragging all their gear from the solo camps to the group site, Sam rewarded the kids by letting them use a lighter instead of making their bow-drill fires. Which probably proved her sense of discipline was going to hell. But she wasn't sure she could make her arms and hands work well enough to create her own fire. What kind of a leader was she, anyway, who hadn't noticed that Olivia was the most likely to take off? Had the girl truly decided to turn around before she'd tumbled down the slope, or only after her escape was foiled?

Sam wasn't sure she believed Nick wasn't running, either,

although evidence hinted that he was telling the truth. Olivia's pack had been full, but Nick had only the clothes on his back.

"We'll still make it to the lake tonight, right?" Aidan asked, his brow furrowed. "Because if we don't, we'll never arrive back at headquarters in time."

Sam sighed. She wanted to stay in place and rest, but the schedule had gotten mucked up after the storm at the lookout and last night's drama. Scraping together her remaining energy, she carried her coffee and a protein bar up to the ridge to get a decent signal. Troy was silent during her description of the dramatic events, but seemed remarkably unperturbed after he found out everyone had survived relatively unscathed.

"Sounds like it was quite the adventure," he said.

"That's one way to put it. Thank God tomorrow is the end."

"You haven't seen the hunter again? Or gotten any more notes?"

"No. Maybe that was Aidan's idea of a joke after all."

"Aidan? You mentioned that before. Why are you saying that again?"

She didn't know how to answer that. The college student still seemed a bit "off" to her.

"Aidan's not causing any problems, is he?"

"No, forget I said that, Troy. We haven't seen that hunter and nothing else weird has happened." She grimaced at her own words. "Well, nothing else more weird than what we've been through the past couple of nights. What should I do to Nick and Olivia?" she asked. "Take away their Navigator pendants? Or just Olivia's?"

"I'll back you, whatever you decide," he said. "Will you still make it to the lake tonight? The families will all be here tomorrow afternoon for the final ceremony. I need the kids to show up on time."

Some help he was, more concerned about tomorrow's meeting than about her current situation.

"Yes, Troy, we can still make the lake tonight. Everybody's ambulatory. I'll hustle them out on the trail as soon as we finish breakfast."

The kids couldn't stop talking about the rescue. Olivia and Nick were chastened and embarrassed that they had been the cause.

Sam decided to let the group decide Nick and Olivia's fate.

Gabriel was the first to speak up. "I don't think they should be demoted. I mean, Nick actually tried to save her. And Olivia"—he stared at her, frowning—"I think she's sorry she tried that, and she won't do it again."

"Everyone deserves a second chance. You gave Nick and me one." Justin crossed his arms. The bandage on his brow was dirty, and dark bruises shadowed his right eye, giving him an outlaw aspect.

"And we only have tonight, so she wouldn't have a chance to earn it back," Ashley added.

Sam had expected them to be more competitive. Instead, they were unanimous. Then again, these were kids who had grown up in an era when every participant got a ribbon. "All in favor of Olivia and Nick keeping Navigator status raise their hands."

Four hands shot up, then six as Aidan and Maya added their votes.

"All right then. It's decided. Clean up and pack up. We've got a lot of miles to cover today and we're behind schedule. Remember that tonight is our final night for sharing. I'm not going to ask about contracts or future plans."

A cheer went up.

"That will happen tomorrow after we get back to Bellingham."

The groans were louder than the cheers had been.

"Tonight we will enjoy each other's company and friendship and savor our last night together in the wilderness. I want to hear a statement of something you're grateful for, and then I want you to share something with all of us."

Maya held up her cup and nodded at Sam. Aidan simply looked relieved. He was already a few days late getting started at Washington State University, and he'd probably been worried that they might not make it out on time.

* * * * *

It was a long tough hike on a rarely used trail to get to their last night's camp. They had to climb over two downed trees and push their way through overgrown patches. The kids were silent for the most part, winding down after the adrenaline rush of the early morning hours, brooding over reuniting with their families tomorrow.

Aidan and Maya were probably contemplating where they would live next week and how they'd earn money after this final paycheck. Sam was fretting about the latter, making a mental list of all the conservation nonprofits she'd worked for in the past year.

They'd just emerged from a tangle of brush to a small clearing when Ashley pointed across the valley. "Hey! Check it out!"

A small herd of goats dotted the steep hillside there. Two of the smallest goat kids chased each other, scampering up and down the rocks while their mothers grazed.

Justin studied the hills around the herd. "No hunters."

"It's like a good omen," Taylor happily summarized.

18

Despite the beautiful setting of their camp on the bank of a long mountain lake, on the last night of their expedition the atmosphere was melancholy. The six crew kids would be glad to get back to their beds and the food they liked, but they seemed unanimously worried about returning to their families.

Sam wrapped her arms around her midriff. They had not encountered other hikers all day, but she still couldn't rid her brain of the itchy feeling that their camp was being watched. Just a case of nerves on their final night, she told herself. Understandable after last night's drama. Why did Troy have to ask her about that hunter again? Tonight, she was the one who needed to be watching her crew. Tomorrow the kids would be reunited with their parents, which meant that her work would be judged by six sets of parents.

Before they began their sharing exercise, Aidan pulled Sam aside and asked if he could make cocoa for everyone as a final reward.

Sam nodded. "Great idea. Thanks, Aidan."

As they formed their usual evening circle, he disappeared into the darkness toward their makeshift kitchen area.

Sam elected Gabriel to start the exercise.

His pimples had been replaced by a ragged beard and a tan, and he was no longer such a flabby boy. "I'm glad I met all you guys, even if you did make fun of me."

Several of the others looked away, uncomfortable with the reminder.

"I'm grateful that my clothes are almost falling off now." He hitched up his pants for effect. "I'm glad I got to work on my new game story. That was fun to do with you guys."

He pulled out a wrinkled sheet of paper. "So here's my share with you. This is the synopsis for my game."

He proceeded to read a convoluted summary of the conflict between the rebels and the invading aliens, with fierce battles and dirty tricks on both sides. Sam expected the rebels to triumph in the end and expel the aliens, but to her surprise, Gabriel said, "I'm gonna structure the game so that the best result is a peace agreement where both species share the planet."

"A future where cyborgs will be treated with respect," Justin interjected, the trace of a smile on his lips.

Gabriel glanced at him uncertainly. "Okay." He looked back at his piece of paper. "And you all get a copy of the game for free."

They clapped at that.

Nick stated that he was grateful for the whiskey jacks and the bear and goats and the sunsets. "And for making new friends." He ducked his head, suddenly shy. "Here's my share for you."

He handed each participant a drawing. They were remarkable sketches of scenes during the expedition: the whole group as seen from the back, mesmerized by the goats on the opposite ridge; everyone focused on the visiting whiskey jacks; the group effort of passing Justin over the rope; a couple of pictures of the characters acting out Gabriel's play; rappelling and studying tracks and trying to make bow-drill fires.

Now she knew what the boy did in the spare time allowed for journaling and writing letters and notes for contracts. "These are absolutely amazing, Nick."

Taylor looked up from the drawing in her lap. "I want all of them. Can we swap e-mails and make copies and send them to everyone?"

Sam considered. "I can do even better. If you want to trust me with your drawing, I'll get the Director to copy them tomorrow and give you each a set."

Olivia eyed her sketch, which depicted her playing the alien queen in front of the campfire. "I want to keep mine, just for tonight."

The other crew kids decided to do the same.

"This is an incredible gift, Nick," Sam told the boy. He tried to maintain his cool demeanor, but he failed to stifle a grin as he sat down.

Justin reluctantly took his turn. "I don't know how I can follow that, Lightning, but here goes. Um, gratitude. Those gray jays—camp robbers, whiskey jacks, whatever you call 'em—sitting on my hand. Those little tiny bird feet—that was unbelievably sick! And the sunsets, the way we all named the colors; I'll never forget that."

"As for sharing, Sparky, Martini, Sweet T and I are making a joint effort, so first we're going to finish the gratitude thing. Spark?"

Ashley stood up. "The thing I like most about being here is that there's time to just be, you know? I had time to think."

Murmurs of agreement rippled around the circle. Sam hoped they'd all remember the peace that came from being unplugged from cell phones and Internet.

"I'm not done," Ashley told the group. "I wrote another haiku."

Clasping her hands in front of her stomach in an antiquated performance posture, she took a deep breath and then recited, "I thought it was a sentence, as in jail. But I found it was a gift, as in jewel."

Sam had to fight back tears. "Wonderful, Ashley! Thank you."

"I liked the storm at the lookout the best," Taylor said. "Even with those meekam mice."

Olivia took her turn next. "I camped with a bear. I still can't believe I did that. And slept only a couple of feet away from a mountain lion! But most of all, I'm grateful that you guys let me be me. And that we never got around to discussing religion."

"Were we supposed to?" Sam murmured to Maya beside her.

Her protégé shook her head.

The four teens put their arms around each other's waists. Ashley counted down. "One, two, three." Then they belted out a unique rendition of *You'll Never Walk Alone*. Justin had a rich baritone and others did their best to harmonize, with Taylor and Ashley slightly off-key as they sang:

> *When you hike through a storm*
> *Hold your head up high*
> *Even though you're afraid of the dark*
> *In camp after the storm*
> *You'll get food that's dried*
> *And the haunting howl of a voltenark*
> *Hike on, through the wind*
> *Hike on, through the rain*
> *Till you smell like a corpse fly-blown*
> *Hike on, hike on, with that contract in your head*
> *And you'll never pee alone!*
> *No, you will never pee AALLLOOOONE!*

The five audience members applauded as the four singers bowed.

Taylor beamed. "I'm especially proud of the 'corpse fly-blown'."

"The 'haunting howl of a voltenark' was all me," Justin boasted.

"Very poetic," Sam told them. "And a fitting end to our final sharing exercise."

"Everyone, grab your cups!" Aidan held up a pot of cocoa. The teens scattered to their tents and then quickly regrouped to accept their share. After he poured the last cupful into her mug, Sam's cell phone in its jacket pocket vibrated against her hip, and she turned to retreat into the woods.

"Aren't you gonna drink that?" Aidan tilted his head toward the cup in her hand.

"Of course. I've just got to go confirm pickup plans with the office." She took a small sip to show her appreciation. "Thanks for the cocoa, Aidan. That was a really nice gesture to end the group session."

He dipped his chin. "My pleasure, Cap'n."

"You and Maya will make sure everything gets buttoned up for the night?"

Maya emerged from the darkness from behind her. "Don't we always?"

"Thanks. I know I can count on you two." She made her way into the woods to be out of earshot from the camp.

"I believe we can make it there by one o'clock," she confirmed to Troy. "We're all extra grubby, but I guess that's normal."

"The parents wouldn't think they had gotten their money's worth if their kids didn't return filthy and hungry."

"Then we've nailed it," she told him.

"We'll have a few extra hours at the office for the ending ceremony and good-byes. And then you'll be done, Sam."

"I'm looking forward to the end and dreading it at the same time." She was tired of being a responsible adult and making the damn bow-drill fires and eating crap every day, but— although she'd never dreamed she would admit it—she was going to miss all the kids.

"That's what Kyla always said, too."

She pondered for a moment whether to ask him about the investigation, then decided that could wait. "See you tomorrow, Troy."

After stuffing the phone back into her jacket pocket, she picked up the cup of cocoa and pressed it to her mouth. A slimy skin of cooled milk glued itself to her upper lip before the cocoa even reached her tongue. Ugh. She wiped the scum off her mouth with a finger and then poured the rest of the cold liquid onto the ground and then scuffed dirt over the damp spot.

The camp was quiet, with all tents dark. She wasn't surprised. It had been an exceptionally long day. She was so tired her body felt like it belonged to someone else. At the lake's edge, she rinsed out her cup. Her right shoulder burned, and probably would for days. Beneath her ribs, her abdomen hurt where the belt had bruised it, and the skin there was chafed and sore. Her hands still ached from clutching that jacket sleeve this morning, so she soaked them in the frigid water until numbness set in.

The clouds had cleared and the starry heavens were mirrored in the tranquil black lake water. She wished Chase was here to share this view with her. What was he looking at right now? Most likely a boring television screen in a hotel room somewhere.

The atmosphere was cold and clear. There'd be frost on the ground in the morning. She loved hiking in autumn, but the weather was unpredictable. In the north Cascades, hikers never knew when the trails would be buried for the winter. Last year she and Kim and Kyla had hiked well into October, but this year, this camp might be buried under a foot of snow within a week.

She stared at the diamond-studded sky. Could heaven really exist up there? Personally, she liked to believe that some spirits of the dead became the wind, some the glittering stars in the universe. She whispered to the night, "Well, Kim, Kyla, it's almost over. I did my best. I'll always miss you guys."

She walked to her tent and slipped into her sleeping bag.

A few hours later, a low rumble awakened her. She lay still, listening intently. A rockslide on the mountain across the lake? The pitch of the sound grew higher and louder, changing to a whining buzz. It didn't sound like the whop-whop cadence of the helicopters flown over this area by the Border Patrol. Had to be a small plane, flying low through the valley. Then the sound faded into the distance.

Weird. Like the plane had buzzed their mountain lake, which seemed like a dangerous thing to do in daylight, and almost suicidal on a moonless night with high peaks all around.

Sam pulled on her pants, boots, and jacket and slid out of her tent with flashlight in hand. Her breath steamed in the cold night air. All was quiet, except for Gabriel's snoring. Aidan's tent was unzipped, its door flap hanging loose. Walking to it, she thumbed on her flashlight and aimed the beam through the net door. His sleeping bag was empty. Had he been awakened by the noise, too?

Flicking off the flashlight, she strolled through the trees to the shoreline. Moonset had preceded sunset tonight, sinking behind the peaks to the west in the early evening. The shadows around her were dense. Selecting a rock, she sat, scanning the surroundings. Had the plane been searching for something? Had it even been here at all? She wasn't sure now that she hadn't dreamed the sound of an aircraft passing overhead.

A movement at the water's edge halfway down the lake caught her attention, but her eyes couldn't translate the shapes in the darkness. A mountain goat coming down for a drink? An elk? She squinted. No, the patch of black was more bear-shaped. Or perhaps human-shaped. Aidan? Whoever or whatever it was melted back into the forest.

She moved a hundred yards in that direction, but then was stopped by a gigantic downed log that blocked the easy path around the shoreline. Aidan might be out for his last solo ramble in the mountains before heading back to college. She couldn't hold that against him.

If the shape hadn't been him... Did she really want to enter the woods at night in pursuit of an unidentified creature? It would be just her luck to encounter one of the rare north Cascades grizzlies. She could see the headline now: *Clueless Trail Guide Eaten by Bear on Last Night of Expedition.*

A step sounded behind her, and she turned.

Suddenly a hand snaked over her mouth and a muscular arm whipped around her throat, jerking her backward.

19

She wrapped her hands around the arm, trying to tear it away from her trachea, but she was off-balance, heels dragging in the dirt, clutched tightly against the attacker's chest.

Her heart hammered in her chest. Her first thought was: *Please God don't let him have a knife.* Her second was: *Aidan?*

"Don't scream, okay?" a deep male voice rasped in her ear.

That voice did not belong to anyone on her crew.

The hunter.

Why did they always say "Don't scream?" Of course you would scream if you could. Wasn't that the most logical response unless there was a knife pressed against your throat? *Was* there a knife pressed against her throat? She didn't think so. She slid her hands up the offending arm to be sure.

The arm tightened, choking her. Her attacker took a couple of steps backward, dragging her so she couldn't regain her balance, hiding them both in the shadow of the forest. "That fucker Troy, trying to keep you from me. I can't believe it took so long for me to find you again. Why didn't you give me better clues? Now we only have tonight…"

Black spots danced across her vision. She tugged frantically at his arm, trying to get even a tiny breath of air.

"You calmed down now, Kyla?"

She would have answered if she could breathe. Instead, she stopped struggling and made herself go slack, sagging against him. Maybe he'd believe she was unconscious. She wasn't far from it.

The arm rasped away from her throat. The hand slid away from her mouth and he spun her around, clamping her arms with both hands to hold her up. "It all came together, Kyla. We'll be okay now, right? Just—"

He stopped, grabbed her higher, digging his fingers into the tender trapezius muscles between shoulder and neck. "Kyla?"

The stranger thrust his face close to hers until their foreheads nearly touched. His breath smelled like he'd been feasting on road kill. Then he shook her, hard. "Shit, *you're* not Kyla. Who the hell are *you*?"

Rubbing her throat with one hand, she managed to croak, "Her replacement."

Her whistle was around her neck, under her shirt. If she could somehow just unobtrusively pull it out...

Spittle flew from his lips as he demanded, "Why are you pretending to be Kyla?"

Sam flinched. "I'm not." She curled her hands around his wrists. "Let go of me!"

His grip was as strong as a gorilla's. She couldn't shift his hands. His fingers were pinching nerves; her arms were going numb.

He stank like a burger left out in the hot sun; even the long dark hair that hung down around his face smelled like it hadn't been washed for six months.

"What the hell did you do with Kyla?" he growled, sending more foul saliva her way. "Is this a trap?"

Grungy camouflage fatigues covered his wiry frame. A knife was sheathed on his belt, and the strap of his rifle was slung over his left shoulder, the tip of the barrel protruding from behind his back. A scope was attached to the barrel. He was definitely the hunter who'd been following them earlier.

"Are you Erik?" She wiped the back of her hand across her face. "Klapton?" She could feel the whistle against the skin of her chest, and tried to slip her fingers under the cord to pull it out. Why hadn't she ever studied self-defense, for godsake?

"How do you know that? Are you in on the deal, too?" He shook her, digging his fingers into her shoulders again, holding her at arm's length so she couldn't reach his chest. "Where's Kyla?"

"In on what deal?" He'd started to say something about what Kyla had told him. "What did Kyla tell you?" she croaked.

Letting go of Sam's shoulder with his right hand, he grabbed her by the throat, his thumb and fingers digging into the soft flesh on both sides of her trachea. He demanded, "Where is Kyla?"

She slapped at his fingers around her throat. He loosened his grip enough for her to gasp. She coughed twice. "What the hell is wrong with you? What do you want?"

"Where's Kyla? Tell me!" He grabbed the front of her jacket this time.

"Kyla's dead." So she *could* say it. The word fell out of her mouth and thudded onto the ground between them.

He stared at her for a moment, bloodshot eyes gleaming in the faint starlight. Then he shoved her backwards, slamming her into a tree trunk. "What the fuck?"

She rebounded off the tree and staggered forward, rubbing at the back of her head, one hand held out to fend him off. Troy had been right when he said that Erik Heigler was not in his right mind. This maniac wasn't even trying to be quiet. Surely one of the crew kids or Aidan or Maya would hear their ruckus and show up soon. "Erik, Kyla and Kim were murdered a month ago."

"What? What!" Wild-eyed, he pulled at his greasy hair. The rifle strap slid off his shoulder.

She wanted to run, but assuming the rifle was loaded, he could probably shoot her in the back faster than she could get away. And then he could go to the camp, to the sleeping teens...

Her heart was pounding so loudly in her head that she could barely hear him. She had no idea whether she was whispering or talking in a normal voice. "Kyla and Kim were murdered a month ago," she repeated.

"No!" He shook his head as if he could cast off the fact. Snatching his knife from his belt, he pointed the tip at her left eye. "That fuckhead Charlie." He let the leather strap slide down his arm and swung the rifle around with his left hand, pointing it in her direction with his other hand.

She was nearly cross-eyed, trying to focus on the knife and keep the gun within view at the same time. The roar of blood in her head was deafening. Charlie?

When Heigler looked at her again, his eyes were shiny with tears. "Who killed them?"

"Nobody knows."

"Troy? That douchebag Chris? Kyla wrote me. He's the one, my ass."

She repeated, "Nobody knows."

"Is this for real? Are you shittin' me?" He lowered the knife tip to her throat. With one quick thrust of his hand, he could kill her.

Were those footsteps she heard coming their way? Heigler turned his face toward the sound. She stepped back, reached into her shirt, yanked out the whistle.

The maniac swiveled around, caught her before she could get the whistle between her lips. "I'll kill all you motherfuckers." Snatching the whistle from her fingers, he jerked hard. The cord yanked her head forward, slashing into the back and sides of her neck before it snapped. "Why couldn't you be Kyla?"

She took advantage of her own forward momentum to knee him in the groin. When he crumpled, mumbling "Bitch," she grabbed the rifle with both hands, shoving the barrel to the side. He pulled back. She twisted the barrel along with his arm, yanking the strap off his arm, but he held on and grabbed for the trigger.

The rifle discharged. Heat shot through the barrel under her hands and the boom instantly rendered her deaf, but she kept her grip tight and managed to slam the butt into his chest. When he staggered back a step, she ripped the rifle from his hands and slung it in a wide arc out over the lake. It splashed into the water thirty feet from the shoreline.

"Shit!" He shoved her again, so brutally this time that her

head snapped back against the tree trunk.

Fireworks exploded in her brain. She slid down the trunk, ending up on her backside, black spots closing in on her vision. A rock stabbed into her thigh.

He'd pull out his knife now to finish her off, and then he'd be after her crew. No, she couldn't be absent again when someone died. She grabbed for the rock beneath her leg, realized it was her whistle, managed to cram it between her lips and let out a long piercing blast with the last of her breath.

His cursing was the last thing she heard before his fist slammed into her head. Her vision faded to the sound of his footsteps running away. Pain flooded out from behind her eyeballs to wash over her brain, leaving only blackness in its wake.

She came to slowly, confused by blurry black spots dancing in front of her eyes. They slowly resolved into fir branches overhead. Why was she sprawled on the ground? How long had she been out? The murmur of a footstep on gravel scratched close by and from the corner of her eye she caught a glimpse of the toe of a hiking boot.

Klapton! The knife! Panic came rushing back. She clawed her fingers into the dirt and struggled to a sitting position.

"You okay, Cap'n?" Aidan asked. "I heard your whistle."

She peered up into a flashlight beam so blinding it felt like a bolt of lightning darted through her brain. She ducked her head again and pressed a hand against her brow as a shield. "Get that flashlight out of my face."

He complied, and then held out his hand to help her up. "Is that blood running down your neck?"

Gaining her feet, she swayed for a moment like a drunk. Gingerly rubbing her fingers over her neck, she felt the sting of raw flesh and wetness running down into her shirt collar. "Did you see him?"

"See who?"

"Klapton. I mean Heigler—Erik Heigler. Our hunter."

Aidan tilted his head. "You okay, Sam? You're not making any sense."

She squinted to bring him into focus. Like the other boys, Aidan's face was scruffy now, with more than a week's worth of reddish whiskers. In the dark, the shaggy beard lent him a menacing aspect.

"I just got attacked by the guy who left that Klapton note," she said. "He's the hunter we saw twice before."

"Really?"

"Think I'd make that up? Turns out Klapton is Troy Johnson's nephew. He was looking for Kyla."

"What? The hunter is Klapton? Wait—didn't he have a gun?" Aidan glanced around nervously.

"A rifle. It's in the lake. He had a knife, too."

"Should we call 9-1-1?"

A snort escaped her lips. She loved the wilderness for its lack of civilization, but that same aspect rendered it dangerous in emergencies. Even when cell phones worked up here to summon help, no assistance would arrive for hours, maybe even days. "I think he's gone now."

"Why would you think that?"

"Because I'm not Kyla?" That sounded weird, she knew. "But it sounded like he came here for her, and now he knows she's not here. He seemed upset that she was dead."

"Really?" Aidan ran his fingers through his ragged hair. "What a freak."

What an odd thing to say. But then, this was a very odd conversation in a very odd situation. Wincing, Sam touched her cheekbone where the maniac had punched her. "Or maybe he ran off because I threw his rifle in the lake and blew my whistle."

Aidan glanced at the lake and then turned back to her, tilting his head to one side. "What are you doing out here in the middle of the night, anyway, Sam?"

She moved her hand to the back of her head. Although there was a sizeable lump there, she was relieved that she didn't feel any blood. "I'll ask you the same thing, Aidan. That plane woke me up, and when I got up to check the camp, you were gone."

"I couldn't sleep. I was sitting down by the lake when that plane flew over. That seemed weird, so I walked down the shoreline to see if I could spot what the pilot was looking for."

"Did you find anything?"

He shook his head. "Nada."

Her peer counselor was trying too hard to appear nonchalant. *That fuckhead Charlie.* Aidan Charles Callahan. She'd bet he was involved in tonight's events somehow.

She sucked in a long slow breath and then blew it out again, clearing enough of a space in her brain to get a sudden vision of Heigler circling back to the group site with that knife.

"We've got to get back to camp."

20

Sam and Aidan walked toward the group camp together. With every step, his boots made a squishing sound, and Sam noticed for the first time that Aidan's pants legs were wet. His sleeves were, too. He had a bandanna wrapped around his left hand, stained dark with something that also spotted his jacket cuff.

"What happened to you, Aidan?"

"Stupidity." He blew out a breath in a huffing sound. "I was whittling on a stick, just trying to shut down my brain so I could go to sleep, and I slipped and cut myself. The blood freaked me out, so I waded into the lake to wash. It's okay now. The cold water helped to slow the bleeding." He shook his head. "It was stupid to stand there like that. I even dropped my damn knife somewhere in the water. My feet are like icebergs. I'm here to tell you, that lake is freakin' cold. I'm glad we're hiking out tomorrow, because I bet my boots will still be wet when I wake up."

Sam doubted Aidan was telling her everything. How could he not have heard her wrestling match with Klapton? He'd only mentioned the sound of her whistle.

"Didn't you hear the gunshot?" she asked.

After a brief pause, Aidan said, "Jesus, was that a gunshot? I heard a loud bang right before your whistle."

"And you didn't see Klapton?"

"I think I'd remember that," he said dryly. "I'm sorry you tangled with him."

She suspected Aidan's story was mostly lies. But her head

was throbbing hard, an ache that echoed each step she took. It was hard to focus on anything else.

Everything in camp was quiet. The crew kids and Maya were all in their tents. She unzipped three of the tents to make sure the inhabitants were breathing. Olivia, Nick, and Maya didn't even roll over when the beam of her flashlight rolled over them. How had they all slept through the plane and the scuffle? The gunshot. Her whistle?

"Guess you weren't so loud after all," Aidan said. "And after last night, we're all pretty zonked."

Except for you, she thought. They stopped in front of his tent.

"You really think that guy's gone?" he asked.

"I hope so. He ran away when I blew my whistle. He made it clear that he wanted Kyla, not me." That's all she could say for sure. How far Heigler had run was anyone's guess.

"Then it's bed for me." Aidan yawned. "But I'll sleep lightly. I always do. If that creep shows up again, I'll know."

She studied him as he stretched, then knelt and untied his hiking boots. Given the evening's events, he was unusually calm. It seemed probable that Aidan Charles Callahan somehow *knew* Klapton was gone. Sam found that oddly comforting, but wasn't sure she should.

"I've got to make a quick phone call," she murmured. "Tell Troy what happened." She noticed that her head didn't ache quite so much when she stood still.

He looked up. "I'll come with. You need a guard."

"No," she said. "I'll scream if I need you."

She walked toward the dark woods, but after she was certain she was cloaked in the shadows, she stopped. Turning, she watched Aidan crouch in front of his tent. He removed something from his jacket and tossed it into his tent before climbing in.

It was nearly two a.m. She hated to wake up Troy. She heard only two rings before he answered.

"Sam?" he gasped. "Are you okay? Are the kids okay?"

"Yes and yes. Sorry to call in the middle of the night. Take a breath, Troy."

She heard him inhale deeply and exhale slowly before he said, "But you're calling at two in the morning."

"Don't panic, Troy, but I need to tell you what went on tonight." She told him about the plane and the probable drug drop.

"Damn, Sam. Double damn," he said. "I can't believe it. I've heard that stuff happens up there, but as far as I know it never happened on our trips."

As far as you know being the operative phrase here.

"And you said Aidan was gone from camp?"

"Yes. That's why I went out looking. And then I ran into Heigler."

"What? God, Sam, how is that possible?"

She told him about the encounter and the fight. "He seemed to think I was Kyla; that's why he's been following us."

"That makes no sense."

"I hope it will, eventually. The drug drop is probably in the mix somehow, but I think that now he knows about Kyla, he'll leave, Troy. He certainly took off in a hurry when I blew my whistle. But he might come after you or Chris; he seemed to blame you somehow. I'm going to call Detective Greene now and tell her, too."

"Sam, how can you be sure Erik's gone?"

She had trouble zeroing in on a coherent thought amid the waves of pain that kept sloshing around inside her head. "We'll keep watch tonight, and we'll be out tomorrow." She didn't specify who the other part of "we" was.

There was no response from the other end of the phone for a long minute, and then he said, "Maybe I could get the rangers up there in a helicopter."

"We both know that couldn't happen before dawn. The kids are all sleeping; they're all in their tents." She considered telling him her suspicion that they'd been drugged, but decided that could wait. She was so tired. "I'll see you tomorrow as scheduled, Troy."

Next she called Detective Greene's number, but of course

her call went to voice mail. She left a detailed message about Heigler and potential threats against Troy Johnson and Chris Rawlins, and a possible connection with Aidan Charles Callahan. After ending her message, she contemplated calling 9-1-1, but couldn't imagine any events that would happen afterwards that Greene wouldn't handle much more efficiently tomorrow. Or later today, actually.

Sam ended the call and stood, breathing quietly, listening to the forest. Silence. Was Heigler really gone? She didn't feel his presence. Then again, she couldn't feel much except for her throbbing head, the burning slashes along her neck, and the ache of her wounded shoulder and bruised ribs from yesterday. Heigler had spoken as if he was done with her, but then, the man didn't seem exactly rational. She tried to take comfort in knowing at last sight, he was running away from their camp, not toward it.

She walked back to camp and surveyed the array of tents and the still blackness of the lake beyond. Aidan's tent was zipped tight. He'd hung his pants and socks outside over the tent peak in an attempt to dry them. She could hear him inside, a whistling almost-snore.

Aidan had been amazingly cool about the night's activities. Almost as if he'd been expecting things to play out like they did. Was he in league with Heigler?

His casual demeanor suggested that he wasn't worried about Heigler showing up in the vicinity. As if he knew for certain that Heigler was no longer a threat. What had he taken from his jacket and tossed into his tent? He'd been uncharacteristically nice to make that hot cocoa for the entire crew on their last evening. Damn lucky she'd poured hers out.

Lucky? Maybe not. Ignorance of everything she'd experienced tonight would have been nice. She chewed on her thumbnail, fretting. Every muscle in her entire body ached. She had no proof of anything and it could be dangerous to openly accuse Aidan with no backup.

An unwelcome vision flooded her imagination: Heigler strolling into camp and spraying the tents with bullets. No, his rifle was in the lake. He hadn't been carrying a handgun; she would have felt it on his skinny frame. But he still had the knife. Her waking nightmare of Heigler was followed by the image of Aidan emerging from his tent with a gun and doing the same thing.

If the teens were drugged as she suspected, she wouldn't be able to rouse them now. She unzipped her tent and pulled out her sleeping bag, grabbed her water bottle and first aid kit, then closed the tent door again. Sinking to a sitting position with her back against a big fir, she wrapped the sleeping bag around her. She dabbed the slashes on her throat with antibiotic cream, which somehow made them burn more hotly than they had before, and swallowed three aspirin. Leaning against the tree, she resolved to stay awake until daylight. A dull pain at the back of her head informed her of the lump still growing under her scalp.

Sometime later a skittering noise above her sent her pulse into race mode. Looking up through the branches, she was rewarded with bits of bark showering onto her face. Were those *eyes*?

She glanced quickly at the kids' tents. The camp remained dark. She risked advertising her position by flicking on her flashlight, and spotlighted a pointed furry face peering down at her.

At this distance and in the dark, she couldn't be absolutely sure, but she guessed her companion was a fisher. She'd read that the fierce weasels were making a comeback in the Cascades, but until now she'd seen only stuffed ones in museums.

She chose to believe that keeping company with a rare "tree wolverine" was a good omen.

"Nice to see you, buddy," she whispered. Turning off the flashlight, she gazed back at the crew tents and surveyed the surrounding woods. "If I fall asleep, please jump down here and bite me, would you?"

21

Before wakeup call at dawn, Sam assigned Aidan and Maya to take the big water bottles down to the lake and filter water for the hike out. First Aidan looked surprised, then his mouth hardened in annoyance. By the end of an expedition, the crew kids were supposed to take on all these tasks. But he left without saying anything, Maya trailing behind him, tossing concerned glances back over her shoulder as she walked. The girl knew Sam well enough to guess that something was up.

As soon as her peer counselors were out of camp, Sam crawled into Aidan's tent. He'd already stuffed his sleeping bag, but she squeezed the cushy roll to be sure nothing other than down was inside. Then she crawled back out and checked his pack. In the top and outside pockets, she found only the clothing and the gear he'd been assigned to carry, and the disc of woven grass he'd created.

She held the coaster for a few seconds, turning it over in her hands. Something about weaving, something about Aidan. Her exhausted brain failed to snare the elusive thought. She put the coaster back and moved on.

Unzipping the bottom pocket, she discovered two plastic bags rolled up inside his rain pants. Grainy off-white powder had been double-bagged, duct tape covering the zip-lock closures for good measure.

Damn. All her suspicions had been correct. Was Aidan part of a drug smuggling operation? Like Troy, she'd heard about drug drops in the north Cascades, small planes dropping loads containing avalanche beacons that a hiker with the corresponding transceiver could easily locate. For all she knew, tracking could probably be done with smart phones and GPS apps these days.

They were camped less than twenty miles from the Canadian border. The plane had come from the north; these bags of whatever it was were probably headed south for distribution across the States.

She poked the bag with a finger. Hundreds of dollars worth of drugs? Thousands? She'd bet it was only one of many Aidan and Heigler had stashed in the woods last night. What was in the bag—cocaine, meth?

"Looks like H to me."

The voice startled Sam so much she nearly fell over.

Ashley squatted down beside her. "Where'd you find it?" The girl's eyes were glued to the bags and she licked her lips, a sharp reminder of her history.

Sam gathered up the bags. Damn. Now she'd have to decide what to do next, and quickly. She hadn't found a weapon in Aidan's pack. If he had one, it was on his person or stashed nearby. Sam debated what to tell the girl and whether or not it was wise to confront Aidan. Then the decision was abruptly made for her as Aidan materialized in front of her, his arms full of water bottles, Maya by his side.

He set down the water bottles and fiddled with the fresh bandage wrapped around his left hand.

Maya immediately focused on the bags in Sam's hands, her eyes wide. "Is that what I think it is? Where'd that come from?" Then, "Damn, Sam, what happened to your face?"

Sam gingerly fingered the swelling on her left cheek that had partially closed her left eye. "I collided with a tree last night." She stood up. "And only Aidan knows where this came from."

He looked up. "I..." A fast-moving storm of emotions flashed over his face. First, fear, or maybe simply shock at being discovered. Second, denial raced through so quickly she barely noticed its shadowy form. Third, he signaled the improbable thought of flight as his gaze skittered around the nearby woods. Or did he have a weapon stashed in the trees? Was he hoping for help from a partner?

Sam's skin prickled at the idea that Heigler might be waiting nearby with his knife, but she resisted the urge to follow Aidan's gaze and kept her eyes on the college student.

Finally, Aidan settled on a strategy and turned back to Sam, his mouth grim under his red-blond whiskers. "I found that last night. When that plane flew through here, I was pretty sure it had to be a drug drop."

"Where's the rest of the load?"

He fidgeted a second longer. "I buried it. Well, I didn't have a shovel, so I hid it under a log, so the mules couldn't find it."

Drug lingo. "Was there a signal device of some kind?"

"Avalanche beacon. I tossed it into the lake." He rubbed his wet hands against the thighs of his pants, calmer now that he'd decided on his story. "I figured I'd take these back to the cops as evidence." He pointed to the bags. "And then I'd lead them back to the rest."

"Why didn't you tell me about it last night?"

His face blushed a darker shade of red. "I was worried about you and that guy. He had to be here for the drugs. You were bleeding and shook up. I didn't want to pile on anything else."

Ashley and Maya turned to Sam, their expressions horrified. "What guy?"

Aidan was making himself out to be a hero. He'd been with Kyla on the last trip. Had there been a drug drop then? Had he drugged the group beforehand like he had last night? Her peer counselor, the young man she'd believed was a natural for this job, was also a drug dealer.

Gabriel was up now, emitting dramatic sound effects as he yawned and stretched. Nick emerged from his tent. Taylor and Olivia crawled out minutes later.

Taylor towered over Sam and Maya. "What's going on?"

"Damn, Cap'n, what happened to your neck?" Justin joined the crowd. "Someone try to hang you?" He stepped around to look at the other side of her face. "Who have you been fighting?"

"Everything's fine, crew," Sam reassured them, stuffing the bags of drugs back into Aidan's pack. "There was a little incident last night, but it's over. Let's focus on breakfast and then we'll get you back to your families. Aidan, keep everything moving, okay?"

She waited until he gave her a nod. When he walked away, she finished searching his pack. No weapons. If he hadn't lost his pocketknife in the lake last night as he'd told her, it had to be on him.

"Maya, could I talk to you for a minute?" She led the girl far enough away that they couldn't be heard.

"What the hell, Sam?" Maya raised a hand toward her tender neck abrasions.

Sam blocked that hand before Maya could touch the stinging slashes.

"Klapton." Sam watched her young comrade's face carefully. She didn't want to suspect Maya, but the girl had been on the previous expeditions with Kyla and Aidan.

"Kyla's old boyfriend, the guy from Facebook she was worried about?"

"He's that hunter we've seen twice."

Maya's eyes widened. "*He's* Klapton? He attacked you?" Her gaze darted around the forest that surrounded them. "Is he still around?"

Sam touched the girl's arm. "He believed he was following Kyla."

One of Maya's ebony eyebrows dipped. "What? That's crazy."

"Well, so is he," Sam said. "But I want to know about Aidan. You were on the last trip with him and Kyla, weren't you?"

Maya's expression turned cautious. "Yeah. Why?"

"Do you remember a plane or helicopter flying over at night?"

The girl shook her head. "But I sleep like the dead out here, you know."

"Does Aidan always make cocoa on the last night?"

"If there's enough left. I think it's a sweet thing to do." She paused, frowning. "Wait, you don't think..."

Maya had been involved in some sketchy things in the past, but Sam was convinced by her protégé's demeanor that Maya was innocent this time.

"I do think, Maya. But we're not going to say anything until we get everyone out of here."

Maya put her fists on her hips. "You want to tell me what's goin' on, Sam?"

"Not yet." She patted the girl's arm. "I promise that I will when I can. C'mon. Only a few more hours to go, and we're done."

Sam replaced the gauze patch on Justin's forehead with a clean one so that he wouldn't frighten the staff or parents, then instructed Aidan to lead the group back to the parking lot while she brought up the rear. She didn't want to turn her back on him, and she was determined to keep all the teens in view, too. Maya walked in the middle of the line of hikers, occasionally tossing questioning glances over her shoulder at Sam on the turns and slopes when they could see each other.

As Sam walked, her fragmented thoughts about Aidan converged. The woven grass coaster. There'd been a heart woven out of grass at the makeshift memorial at the Pinnacle Lake trailhead. His silver Subaru Forester—wasn't that the car she'd seen driving out of the trailhead parking lot?

She knew that sometimes murderers revisited the scene. Was Aidan a killer who came back that day to savor the memories at the site of his bloody handiwork?

She had good reason to suspect Aidan was involved in the drug drop. Maybe Kyla was the one who didn't drink the cocoa on the previous expedition. Maybe Kyla had witnessed Aidan collecting drugs.

Icy slush slid through her veins. She'd lived and traveled with Aidan Callahan for three weeks. She was sure now that Aidan was a drug dealer. Was he a murderer, too?

By the time they reached the parking lot, odds were good that all of the kids would have metabolized and sweated away any drugs Aidan had added to the cocoa. She needed to talk to

Detective Greene. If these suspicions were crazy, the woman would probably tell her so.

She wished she could channel Kyla. What did her friend know about Aidan? About Klapton? At intervals Sam turned to look over her shoulder, unable to rid her mind of the creepy vision of Erik Heigler following her crew back to civilization.

22

Like her crew kids, Sam anticipated the reunion with their families with an emotion somewhere between dread and excitement. According to Maya and Troy, the ceremony was always a poignant one, but often had a few bombshells tossed into the celebration of success. And now she had the whole Aidan situation to deal with, too. After the kids and peer counselors were loaded into the van for the trip back, Sam delayed the driver long enough to walk fifty yards away, call Troy and report the drugs Aidan was carrying, and then leave the same message on Detective Greene's voice-mail.

After being reunited at Wilderness Quest headquarters, crew and staff and families came together in a big circle. The September afternoon was pleasantly warm, so Troy had decided to hold the ceremony outside, in the big grassy area in back of the office building. Folding chairs had been set up, crew kids in a cluster on one side, families in a semicircle around them. Sam was surprised to see two USFS rangers sitting in chairs against the back of the building, observing the ceremony. Both wore pistols on their belts.

She glanced at Troy to see if the rangers' presence was scheduled. His hand came up with fingers curled in an okay sign, so everything was going as he'd planned. She guessed the rangers were there to collect the drugs and information from Aidan after the ceremony. Troy wouldn't want the Quest clients to learn about any of that.

With Aidan and Maya seated on her right and Justin on her

left, Sam sat with her crew. The six client teens were
unwashed, their hair mostly uncombed, and they remained
dressed in their stained and battered expedition clothing to
show what they'd been through in the last three weeks.

Taylor's carefully streaked blond hair now revealed its
brown origins at the roots. The purple tips of Ashley's short cut
had faded with sun and repeated lake washings to only the
faintest tint of lavender.

Aidan, Justin, and Gabriel sported ragged three-week
beards. A thin mustache was valiantly trying to sprout on
Nick's upper lip, and on his chin, there was what might, with
the help of a magic marker, pass for a soul patch.

Olivia was physically the least changed. She'd pulled her
kerchief over her ebony hair, which was dull with dirt. Her skin
was a shade darker from three weeks in the sun.

They drew numbers to see who went first. Nick Lewis drew
number one, either winning or losing, depending on how one
regarded the situation. The boy was visibly nervous as he
stepped into the center of the makeshift circle and faced his
father. One side of his face was still purple and yellow with
bruises.

"Zap 'em, Lightning!" Justin urged in a loud voice. Sam laid
a hand on his arm to quiet him.

Nick studied the toes of his boots, swallowed hard, and then
raised his eyes. "Dad."

"What the hell happened to your face, Nick?" his father
asked.

Nick raised his hand to his multicolored cheek. "Don't
worry about it. It's okay."

"Dad," he said, starting over. He took a breath. "I feel sad
because you don't know me. And I don't think you want to
know me."

Tom Lewis sat with his hands clasped together in his lap,
his face strained. His lips parted, but no words emerged.

Nick continued, "I'm never going to look like you. I'm never
going to be like you, Dad. I'm small like Mom; that's how I'm
built. I love the outdoors like you, but I want to see the animals

alive. I don't ever want to hunt again." Toward the end of the sentence, his voice cracked.

His father quickly leaned forward, seeming panic-stricken at what might emerge next from his son's mouth. "That's okay, Nick. No more hunting." He started to stand up.

Nick held up his hand to signal his father to stop. Lewis sat back on the edge of the chair.

"I like art. I like books. I like music," Nick said. "I know you're afraid I'm gay, but I'm not." He glanced over his shoulder at Ashley, who gave him a thumbs up and an encouraging smile. Then he turned back to his father. "I'm one of those 'intellectuals'"—he gave the word air quotes with his fingers—"you always say are ruining the world."

Tom Lewis frowned. "I don't think I ever said that."

"Yeah, Dad, you did. Lots of times."

"Way to go, Nick," Sam murmured under her breath, proud of the way the boy was standing up for himself.

Tom Lewis rubbed his hand over his trim beard as he glanced around at the other parents, clearly uncomfortable at being in the spotlight. Then he focused again on Nick. "I'm sorry I didn't accept you for what you are. I do want to get to know you; I will try harder to accept you as you and not try to make you into a mini-me. From now on, we'll keep the past in the past, and look only to the future. That'll be our contract, Son."

Nick gave his father a last doubtful look, but then he nodded and collapsed into the empty chair beside his father. Everyone clapped, but the clustered parents all wore worried expressions now; no doubt concerned about what private matters their teens might reveal in front of the crowd.

A verbal agreement had been made between Nick and his father, but Sam felt there were still secrets lurking behind the hope for a happier future.

Next up was Taylor Durand. The girl's posture was stiffly erect as she walked close to her mother and father, and Sam was reminded of her performance as the haughty alien queen.

Crossing her arms in front of her chest, Taylor radiated

confidence, even defiance as she started her speech. "I'm
frustrated because you keep telling me what I should be. You
know, just because I'm tall and, you know, I have no boobs, I
don't have to be a basketball player or a fashion model. I can
be anything I want to be."

Her father opened his mouth to say something, but Taylor
held up her hand just like Nick had. "I'm smart, too. So maybe
I'll be a model, but I think I also want to be an attorney, maybe
for some organization like the Sierra Club, because our crew
has been to so many beautiful places and we need to protect
those places from getting the trees chopped down and mining
and hunting and pollution and all the animals losing their
homes. When I get enough money, I'll buy some boobs if I
want to."

"So." She paused to take a breath and flip her ponytail over
her shoulder. "Here's the contract I want. I'm going to eat what
I want, and I'm not taking any more diet pills. I promise I'll go
to school if you promise you'll quit telling me what I should
be."

She thrust out a hand, palm up, to her parents, signaling it
was now their turn.

Mrs. Durand licked her carefully painted lips before saying,
"Heavens, Taylor, sweetie, I never meant you couldn't be other
things, too, just that you'd be perfect for basketball or
modeling."

Taylor aimed her index finger at her. "This is exactly what
I'm talking about!"

Her mother clamped her lips together, then lowered her
eyes and raised a hand to pat down her already smooth
coiffure.

Mr. Durand stood up, making it obvious where his daughter
got her height. "Taylor, I'm proud of you. I'll be proud of
whatever you choose to do. And I'm really happy you want to
go back to school. I'll help you with whatever it takes to go to
law school or whatever you want to do. And—er—we can talk
about that other thing, too. I love you."

"Yay, Sweet T," Justin murmured softly beside Sam.

Mr. Durand embraced his daughter. Taking her hand, he pulled her forward to sit beside him.

That felt like a communications breakthrough. Sam hoped it would stick.

Gabriel shuffled forward to stand in front of his parents. After twenty-one days in the wild, he was a different teen than the flabby boy who had started the expedition. He'd lost weight and gained muscle tone, and his skin had cleared up. Now, with his longish hair and whiskers, Gabriel Schmidt resembled a hermit from the backwoods.

"I get it now, Mom and Dad," he said. "I'm sorry I was such a lurik goof-off. It's just that Vebulaze is so much fun, and I'm so good at it. I'm so close to level thirteen, you know; I'm a Master Wizard."

He glanced over his shoulder at the kids still seated behind him, expecting them to chime in with "Mister Lizard." Justin and Olivia complied by mouthing the words. They high-fived together, and Gabriel grinned.

The elder Schmidts exchanged looks, dismay written on their faces.

Gabriel turned back to his parents. "But you know what? I'm good at other things, too. I can make a fire without matches and I can carry super heavy loads, and I can figure things out faster than other people can."

Mr. Schmidt found his voice. "Yes, Gabe, you've always been smart."

"We want you to do something with those brains," Mrs. Schmidt chimed in.

Gabriel, embarrassed, scuffed the toe of his boot against the grass. "Yeah, I get it." He shoved his hands into his pants pockets and raised his eyes to regard his parents again. "So, here's the deal I want to make. I don't want to go to university right now because I'm super tired of studying."

The parents swapped sideways glances again. Gabriel took a step toward them. "But maybe I'd like to take a few classes at the community college, like computer programming and visual art, because you know, making computer games is really big business, and I think I'd be good at it and I could make a sweet living that way."

Leaning forward in his chair, Justin whispered, "Way to go, Lizard Brain."

"And for now," Gabriel continued, "I'll get a part-time job, maybe at Home Depot or somewhere that they need some muscle, because I'm scary strong."

The parents grinned and nodded enthusiastically.

Gabe's last request came out in a rush. "And I want you to not let me use my game stuff except between nine and midnight."

Sam pressed her lips together to stifle a smile, knowing that was a difficult request for the teen to make. The elder Schmidts appeared confused.

Gabriel dramatically rolled his eyes. "I'll show you how." Then he slid into the seat next to his mother.

Olivia stood up.

"You can do it, Martini," Justin quietly encouraged. "You have camped with bears."

Plucking nervously at the scarf that now covered most of her hair, Olivia approached her parents. The poor girl was visibly shaking. She didn't raise her head as she said, "I'm scared to tell you this."

Mrs. Bari's eyes grew huge, and she raised a jeweled hand to her throat. "What is it?"

Olivia clasped her hands together. "I don't want to be Muslim anymore."

Sam was stunned. She'd been expecting Olivia to admit to her attempt to run away. She had no idea the Bari family was Muslim, although now that she thought about it, some clues had been there.

There was an audible intake of breath around the circle, and Mrs. Bari reached toward her husband. He twisted in his chair to take her hand between both of his.

Olivia lifted her chin. "This is the United States. I'm an American. We have freedom of religion. And I choose not to be Muslim."

Her father stared at her, his mouth slightly open, clearly horrified.

"I want to go to college out of state, and I will no longer pretend to be Muslim there."

Dropping his wife's hand, Mr. Bari leaned forward and finally spoke. "This is very dangerous, Olivia. It's apostasy."

Sam flinched inwardly, hating that word. She'd only ever heard it from the strictest of religious types, in reference to the ultimate, unforgiveable sin.

Mrs. Bari said, "When you are born a Muslim, you are al—"

Olivia shook her head so hard her bandanna slid back, revealing more of her wavy black hair. "I don't buy into that. I just don't. So if you want to kill me for that, I guess you should go ahead and do it." Wrapping her arms around herself, she bowed her head as if awaiting the death blow.

Sam had read about Muslims issuing death threats to those who left the religion, but she didn't know if those threats were ever actually carried out. She'd read about escapees from other fundamental religions who feared for their lives, too. If the threat was real, Olivia's bravery was nothing less than astounding. Whether Olivia wanted to quit being Muslim because it was just too hard in the United States or because she had become a nonbeliever, it took guts to announce that decision. It would take even more courage to carry it out.

The poor girl was still quaking despite the warmth of the afternoon sun, but she was also standing her ground. Sam wanted to go to her and wrap her in a hug, but that would interrupt this battle of wills.

Mr. Bari's gaze bounced around the clusters of parents seated in a semicircle around him. Most of the other adults in attendance focused their attention elsewhere, probably praying that their kids wouldn't ever act out in public like this. By the time his focus landed on his daughter again, his face was mottled with purple. Sam expected steam to emerge from his ears and nostrils at any second. "Olivia, do you respect your parents? This is dangerous for us, too."

Raising her head again, Olivia looked him in the eye. "I

know that, Papi. And that's why, until I go away, I agree to act and dress Muslim, as long as you agree to let me go after I graduate from high school."

After a silent tense staring match that seemed to go on for an hour, Mr. Bari dipped his chin, and then held out his hand toward his daughter. Olivia didn't take the hand, but sat down beside him, wilting now after her bold request. Had the Baris agreed to Olivia's contract? Sam couldn't tell.

Ashley Brown leapt up from her chair, then turned and embraced Justin, the last teen remaining in the crew section.

Justin hugged her back. "Go, Sparky. Give 'em hell."

Ashley strode over to her mother. Sam's expectations had been thrown off-kilter when Olivia provided the shocker of the day, but Ashley quickly tossed her own emotional hand grenade into the mix. "Mom, you know that I was molested when I was six."

Mrs. Brown's hand flew to her mouth, and she glanced right and left. Then she pulled her hand away and sat up straight, gripping the sides of her seat. "Your father was such a sleazebag. I should never have let you visit him at all."

Ashley pointed at her mother, stabbing her finger in the air. "You know it wasn't him. It was his friend Henry. Dad got rid of him as soon as he found out."

Mrs. Brown argued, "But he let it happen. And he never said anything."

"You let it happen, too," Ashley confronted her. "And you never said anything. And you never let me talk about it!"

Mrs. Brown covered her face with her hands and exhaled loudly into them, then lowered them to her lap. "What good would that do? You were just a little girl; you didn't understand what it would mean."

Ashley crossed her arms and shifted her right foot sideways, widening her stance. "That's where my college fund came from, didn't it? Henry. I know Grandpa didn't have the money to leave me a huge amount like that."

Her mother huffed out a breath. "Do we have to talk about this now?"

"Yes!" Ashley insisted, thrusting her chin forward for emphasis. "Here's the deal, mom. You're going to let me see Dad whenever I want to; I'm grown up now and I can protect myself. And you're going to stop saying all those horrible things about him in front of me. I'll stay home and I'll finish high school or at least get my GED. And then I want to join the military."

"The military? Where is this coming from?" Mrs. Brown glared at Troy, and then her angry glance fell on Sam.

So did everyone else's.

Sam was glad she'd washed her face, tied a kerchief around her battle-scarred throat, and slapped some makeup over the bruise on her cheek. She could have told Ashley's mother that her daughter's field guide was just as surprised as she was. There had been no discussion of military service on her watch. Counselor Berg was so right when he'd said that all these kids kept secrets.

Ashley continued, "Probably the Navy or the Air Force. But maybe I want to be a Marine. And you'll save that money for me until I want to use it. For whatever I want to use it for."

Mrs. Brown leaned against the chair back and folded her arms. "Oh, Ashley—"

Ashley wasn't giving her mother an inch. "Do you agree, Mom?"

Mrs. Brown's cheeks puffed as she blew out a long breath, considering.

"Do you agree, Mom?"

Finally Mrs. Brown said, "As long as you stay home and stop the drugs, and finish high school or get your GED."

Ashley concluded the bargain. "Then we have a contract." Stepping forward, she held out her hand.

Her mother shook it, and then Ashley told her, "And by the way, I love you, Mom." She bent forward to give her mother a quick hug, and then slid into the chair by her side.

Sam could finally breathe again.

"Okay." Justin stood up, rubbing his hands together.

"Good luck, Justice." Sam patted the boy's forearm.

He approached his grandparents, and then shook his hands out, flexed his fingers, and squared his shoulders. Emulating Ashley, he positioned himself straddle-legged in front of his guardians. "Here goes."

He took a breath. "I'm sorry I gave you such a hard time about coming to this thing, Gran and Pop, because I really loved it out there. I made Navigator."

He pulled the necklace away from his chest and bent close to show them. "Turns out I'm a natural leader."

His grandparents beamed. Mrs. Orlov put a hand on her husband's arm. "We're proud of you," she said. "But what happened to your head?"

"It's not important. I'm fine. Don't distract me." Justin straightened. "Like I was saying, for the next year, I'm going to focus on leading instead of fighting. There's this anti-bullying group at school; it's called STOP. I'm going to join it. As a matter of fact, I'm going to lead it because I have better ideas than they do."

Sam stifled a laugh at the incongruity of Justin bullying his way into the anti-bullying group. But she knew he was sincere and as he'd said, he'd learned to be strong with others, not against them.

His grandfather could not have been more pleased. "Wow. I'm impressed, Son."

Justin wasn't done. "But to be honest, I think I'm going to miss fighting."

The joy on his grandparents' faces melted a little.

Justin turned to glance at David Berg. The counselor dipped his chin, and some sort of signal passed between him and the boy.

Justin faced his grandparents again. "So I want to do karate or boxing or something competitive like that."

Mrs. Orlov's expression lifted again. "Karate sounds good. I bet you'll be good at that."

"And maybe if I have time, I could get a part-time job doing construction or landscaping or something like that, because, as you know, I'm super strong. And you know how they're going to make a community garden on that lot down the street? I think it would be sweet to work on that. I'd like to grow things. Could you help me with that?"

Mr. Orlov leapt up and wrapped his arms around the big kid, ducking his balding head beneath his grandson's chin. "That sounds fantastic, Justin."

Sam couldn't listen to the concluding remarks from Troy. She was too busy trying to keep tears from welling up. Although she was glad to be relieved of the responsibility, she was going to miss these kids.

Now she understood how much Wilderness Quest had meant to Kim and Kyla. She hadn't helped find their murderer, but she had at least helped keep their dream afloat for a little while.

She was collecting her car keys, ready to go home and sop up a few glasses of wine to recover from the day's emotional roller coaster, when Troy informed her that her duties weren't quite over yet.

"We always let the kids say goodbye," he told her. "Wait in the break room."

Sam drew a cup of water from the tap dispenser, trying to relax her face back into a neutral expression. When she turned to grab a paper towel, she was confronted with the photo of Kim and Kyla on the wall. Today, a bouquet of sunflowers was positioned beneath it. Phrases like *Miss you!* and *We'll never forget* were scrawled in a variety of ink colors across a sheet of paper taped to the countertop.

She gulped.

Aidan came in first to shake her hand. "You're a natural field guide, Sam. I'm honored to work with you."

"You were really good with the kids, Aidan."

He pulled back and ducked his whisker-stubbled chin to meet her eyes. "But you weren't too sure of me, were you?"

She took a sip of water before answering. She still wasn't convinced he'd told the truth about his relationship with Kyla or Eric Heigler, but she'd leave the final decision on that up to law enforcement. "To be honest, I didn't know what to think, with the drugs and all."

"To be honest," he mimicked her words, "the thought of keeping them for myself did cross my mind."

She stared into his blue eyes.

"But only briefly," he quickly added. "I knew they were worth thousands. But then I tried to think about how I could sell them, and I couldn't come up with any strategy that wouldn't land me in prison or get me killed." He grinned. "Thank God I came to my senses."

"Thank God," she echoed. She suspected he would have made a different decision if she hadn't discovered the drugs in his pack.

"I'm going back up with the rangers now to show them where the rest of the stash is hidden."

"That's good." Troy must have arranged this while the company van was driving her group back to town.

"The crew kids will come in now, to say goodbye before their final counseling sessions." Aidan turned on his heel to leave, then stopped as he caught sight of the memorial. Turning back, he stared at the photo for a long moment, then raised his right hand and gave Kim and Kyla a final salute before heading out the door.

Sam expected the kids to enter en masse, but instead each came in individually, closing the door to say a private goodbye.

Taylor hunched over to give her a hug, making her feel like a dwarf. "Thanks, Cap'n," the girl said to the top of Sam's head.

As they separated, Sam held Taylor's hand long enough to say, "Don't ever forget that you're beautiful, no matter what you choose to do."

Taylor's eyes shone. "You too, Sam."

Olivia entered next. Since the teen was only a couple of inches taller than Sam, their hug felt more natural. "Thanks for taking me out there, making me into a wild Martini. Who knew I could fly over ropes and rappel down mountains?"

Sam laughed. "The Martini bit was all Justin. And the wild part, well, you always had that in you."

"I camped with a bear."

"Yes, you did, Olivia."

"And thanks for...you know..." Olivia sucked in a breath. "For giving me a second chance yesterday. I didn't deserve it."

"We all believed you did, Olivia. Stay strong."

"I'll try."

Justin grabbed Sam in a bear hug that threatened to crack her ribs. "Gex! I don't want this to end! Gex, lurik! What was the other one?"

"Meekam. And don't forget the rampaging onu."

"Never. Or the goats, or the bear, or the whiskey jacks eating out of my hand. The lion looking in the window—nobody's ever gonna believe that! And that termigen."

"Ptarmigan. Justin, all those things are still out there for you. California has a lot of wild places."

His expression was doubtful. "I don't think my regular friends are gonna go for that."

"Then ditch them. Look at all the new friends you made in the last three weeks."

"Yeah." His tone was questioning, as if the idea had not occurred to him before.

"How's your head, Justin?"

"Hard," he answered. And then his lips spread in a grin.

"Your probation officer will get a complimentary report from me," she told him. "And I think David Berg will put in a good word for you, too."

"Sweet," he said. "Thanks."

"Everyone deserves a second chance. But the future depends on you, Justin."

His face clouded over again.

"Find an outdoor club to join, Dragon Man," she suggested. "You could start with the Sierra Club; they have branches almost everywhere. They can always use extra muscle to help maintain trails."

He brightened. "Sierra Club. Sweet, I'll do that." He held up a fist. "Wish me luck."

She bumped his fist with her own. "You'll make your own good luck from now on, Justice."

Gabriel's face was tanned and weathered instead of doughy now. And when she hugged the boy, she felt muscles and even a rib or two.

"You've turned into a he-man, Gabe," she told him.

"I stepped on the scale in the changing room. I lost twenty-six pounds out there!" he whispered in her ear. She guessed he didn't consider it masculine to talk about weight. "Thanks for all that lurik food."

She snorted. "It was pretty bad most of the time, wasn't it?"

"No, seriously, thanks for the adventure, Cap'n Sam. I've never been on a real one before."

"You can have all the real adventures you want to, Gabriel," she reminded him. "But you can't have a single one at home in your room."

He rolled his eyes. "Yeah, I get that. I'm still going to level thirteen on Vebulaze, but I'm not going to play games so much anymore. I'm going to invent them."

"A worthwhile goal, Mister Lizard." She hugged him again. "You have the smarts and the creative talent, and with some more education, I know you'll do it."

He turned to go out, tossing "Just watch me!" over his shoulder before he left the room.

Nick was dressed in the clothes he arrived in, the too-big green plaid shirt. As he raised his arms to hug her, she noticed again the piece of red thread dangling from the spot where a button should be. That missing button seemed so sad. Not only did Tom Lewis never bother to learn his son's true size, apparently nobody in the family knew how to replace a button, either. But the remaining buttons looked like mother-of-pearl instead of the usual plastic imitations, so maybe they were hard to match.

The boy's face was dark with emotion as well as bruises, and he seemed speechless, his gaze shifting from her face to the tile floor and then back again.

"I really enjoyed having you in my crew, Nick." She held out her arms, and he stepped in for a hug. "You contributed so much, and we all loved your art. No matter what your dad says, you don't need to 'man up.' You're perfect just as you are."

"Thanks." He mumbled so softly she barely heard the word. As Nick stepped back, his eyes were shiny with tears. While he tried to compose himself, his gaze darted around the room, stopping on the photo of Kim and Kyla.

His whole body went rigid. He leveled his index finger at the photo. His voice was little more than a whisper when he asked, "Did you know them?"

Nick lived in the same county where her friends had been murdered. He had no doubt heard the story of the murders and probably seen photos of Kim and Kyla in the paper and on television.

"They were my friends," she said. "They both used to work here."

"Really?" His Adam's apple slid up and down his skinny throat. "I didn't know..."

She put a hand on his shoulder. "It's okay. We didn't want to remind anyone."

He pressed his lips together, nodded, swallowed again, then quickly trotted out of the room.

Poor kid. The world was not kind to sensitive boys. Sam closed her eyes and took several deep slow breaths, trying to compose herself.

When Ashley appeared, tears streaking her newly applied mascara down her cheeks, Sam clamped her jaws together to keep from bursting into tears herself. How had Kyla done this over and over again?

"I learned so much from you," Ashley said into Sam's neck, her arms clasped tightly around her. "You just kept going, no matter what. You kept pointing out all the good things, you just kept teaching us. And that human chain! We totally rescued Nick and Olivia."

"We did. All of us, working together." Sam still had a sore shoulder and bruises at her waistline to remind her.

"Like Nike says, just do it. And you do. You just do it."

Sam hugged the girl back. She didn't know exactly what Ashley was trying to say, but it sounded like high praise.

"Ash." She peered into the girl's tear-filled eyes. "You are one of the strongest women I've ever met. I mean that. Just figure out where you really want to go. Set your sights on that, and you will get there."

"I think maybe I can now." With a final quick hug, Ashley sniffled her way out the door.

Sam grabbed a tissue from a box on the desk to wipe her eyes. She was blowing her nose on it when Maya stepped in, a duffel bag slung over her shoulder.

"Oh God, not you, too." Sam groaned.

Maya gave her an exasperated look. "You and Kyla." Her gaze slid to the photo on the wall and then back to Sam's face. "Peas in the soup."

Sam nearly choked, making a strangling noise halfway between a sob and a chuckle. After clearing her throat, she said, "Peas in a pod, you mean."

"What's the diff? What do you mean, 'not me too'?"

"Coming to say goodbye. I don't think I can take any more."

"Good thing." Maya cocked out her hip and put her hand on it. "Because I just wanted a ride home."

Oh, yeah. The staff house would be closed now after the last expedition of the year, and Maya's tent was still in Sam's back yard. Sam picked up her own duffel. "C'mon."

As they left the break room, Sam spotted Troy in his office, talking to a woman seated with her back to the door. Dark hair was knotted at the nape of her neck. Detective Greene?

Troy spotted Sam through the open doorway, and he and Greene both paused to turn and nod in her direction. Sam changed course, eager to unload on the detective all the details from last night. Troy rose from his chair to shut the door between them, ending any possibility of her joining the conversation.

Fine, she thought, *be like that*. She was satisfied to leave the matter there for now. She was completely drained—mentally, emotionally, and physically.

Maya led the way to the parking lot. "Blake's making enchiladas and guacamole and a huge salad with fresh everything. Cherry crisp for dessert."

That news gave Sam a jolt of new energy. "You talked to Blake?"

"Why wouldn't I?" Maya asked across the top of Sam's old Civic.

As she pulled the driver's door open, Sam grinned. Her remora was back, glomming onto her life, hitching a ride without waiting for an invitation.

23

After a shower and dinner, Sam longed to go to bed, but she made herself go to her office and write down every detail she could remember about Aidan's behavior and her encounter with Heigler. She called Detective Greene's number and left a voice mail message to tell her she had documented all that information. The woman apparently never answered her phone, but she did listen to voice mail and showed up at Sam's house the next morning to hear her story.

From her seat at the dining room table, Greene told Sam, "Callahan led the rangers to where he claimed to have left the stash, but the drugs were not there."

"Erik Heigler took them," Sam told her. "Or Aidan Callahan hid them somewhere else."

"We're checking out all the probable scenarios," Greene assured her. "So far, we have no evidence to link Callahan to Heigler or the drug drop." She tapped the two pages of description that Sam had printed out for her. "And we have only your word that Heigler was there."

Sam gritted her teeth in frustration.

Greene picked up the coffee cup Sam had given her, saw that it was empty, set it down again. "We ran out of daylight yesterday, but two rangers are headed back this morning to search the area thoroughly."

"Good. Will you let me know what they find?"

The detective sat back in her chair. "If and when it's appropriate, I will."

She'd have to settle for that. Or get Chase to check the case file for her.

"I can tell you that Facebook delivered the records from Kyla Quintana-Johnson's account, and from Klapton's as well." Greene pulled out her phone and spent a couple of minutes tapping around on the screen. "There were only three messages back and forth between them. The first, from Klapton to Kyla, was '*Hi, Cuz.*' That was sent three days before the murders. The next day, Kyla responded, '*Where are you?*'"

So Kyla had been in communication with Erik Heigler. But it didn't mean she wanted to see him. *Where are you?* could indicate she was worried about her cousin coming after her family.

"Then, on that same day, Klapton messaged her back, '*Working in your area soon, can I see you? 555-459-2772.*'" Detective Greene looked up from her phone. "Unfortunately, that's a prepaid cell, traceable only to the store that sold it for cash."

That was the last Facebook message between them. There the trail ended.

"There were no phone calls to that number from Kyla's phone. But it doesn't necessarily mean their communication ended," Detective Greene told her. "They might have verbally exchanged numbers on different phones."

"Can't you get recordings of all calls to that 555 number?"

The detective chuckled. "You've been watching too much TV. If some shady entity is wiretapping every phone call across America, they haven't bothered to let law enforcement in on it."

"Maya told me that Aidan borrowed Kyla's phone frequently because he was always forgetting to charge his own. She said he borrowed it on the day they all came back from Kyla's last expedition."

Greene nodded. "Two days before the murders, on the day Kyla and Aidan returned from her last field expedition, there was a call from Kyla's phone to the Callahan house. Aidan's mother verified that her son called home on that day. Seems pretty innocent to me."

"But Aidan could also have opened Kyla's Facebook messages and copied down the Klapton number on that day," Sam argued.

"Maybe," Greene acknowledged. "But we have no evidence to prove that."

Sam told the detective about her suspicions surrounding Aidan and Pinnacle Lake—the Timberland boot prints, the woven grass heart at the trailhead memorial. "I don't want to think that Aidan could kill anyone, but—"

Greene cut her off. "Callahan already told me he visited the memorial. Plus, he has an alibi on the day in question. His mother verifies that he was helping her fix the fence in their back yard on that day."

"This is the same mother who resents Kim and Troy for not hiring Aidan as a field guide?"

Detective Greene studied her face, waiting for more. The woman's direct gaze was unnerving.

"I talked to Judy Callahan a couple of weeks ago, on my break," Sam told her. "Remember, I said she was bitter about her son not getting the supervisory job this year. I put that all in there." She gestured to the statement she'd written.

"Interesting." Greene rose from her chair and gathered the pages from the table top. "Thank you for these. I may have more questions later. I'd appreciate it if you did not speak again to anyone in the Callahan family. I'm sure you need to spend your time searching for work."

Sam felt like she should have a witty response stored up for this situation, but she was at a loss for words.

Two days later, a new twist developed.

"The rangers didn't find any drugs, but they found a corpse in the lake," Troy informed Sam from his seat on her couch. He'd stopped by her house to deliver her paycheck. "It was Erik. He'd been stabbed in the throat. Someone had tried to weigh down his body with rocks, but I guess the stones weren't heavy enough."

That explained so much. Aidan's wet clothes and boots, the cut on his hand, his calm demeanor on their last night of the expedition. He'd known that Heigler was gone for good. Surely the authorities would be able to put Aidan and Heigler together now.

Then she remembered that Erik Heigler was Troy's nephew. The poor man had already lost so much family.

"I'm sorry, Troy," she said.

Removing his glasses, he began to polish them with the tail of his shirt. "I wish things had worked out differently. But at least now we know where Erik is."

"True." She couldn't generate a kind thought for the maniac who had attacked her.

"Erik had a cell phone in his pocket. It was ruined, of course, but they were able to recover the SIM card." Troy slid his glasses back on. "There were multiple texts that looked like they came from Kyla. And a couple from Charlie, who apparently was a friend of Kyla's. Erik believed he was going to meet up with Kyla. But the messages couldn't be from Kyla; they were all sent after..." His voice trailed off.

"They're all from Aidan," Sam told him.

Simon leapt onto the couch beside Troy and head-butted the man's arm.

"The authorities can't find any evidence that Aidan ever communicated with Erik." Troy's voice was sad. He stroked the cat. "I don't want to believe that Aidan's mixed up in this."

"Believe it, Troy. I'd bet Aidan got interested when Kyla showed him the message from Klapton about working up here. Aidan doesn't strike me as a user, so he probably intended to sell heroin. His mother hinted that times were hard in that family."

If Troy was having a tough time believing that Aidan had known about the drug drop, she doubted that he'd realized that Aidan most likely killed his nephew. She decided not to bring that up. "Did the rangers find any other cell phones? Did they find the knife that Erik was stabbed with?"

Simon climbed into Troy's lap and curled up there, purring. "I told you everything I know, Sam."

She'd have to ask Greene, or maybe Chase about Aidan's knife.

The status quo was maddening. The events had coalesced in her head, but she didn't have anything more than speculation to offer; there was no way to prove any of it. Aidan had turned in the drugs he was carrying. He'd been cooperative, leading the rangers to the supposed drop area. Then he had simply gone back to school.

The front door opened and Blake came in, trailed by the basset dog. He'd been taking Sophie to work with him. Now she waddled over, toenails clicking on the hardwood floor. She sat in front of Sam and then, with a sigh, flopped to the floor, her head resting on Sam's shoe. Simon raised his head to glare at the canine, and then hissed to show his disgust. Having made his point, he laid his head back on his paws and closed his eyes.

Troy said hello to Blake, then looked back to Sam. "You have a dog?"

"Sophie's a stray." Sam reached down to pat the basset's head. "Kyla was feeding this girl, and I couldn't leave her there when Chris went to Alaska."

Blake said, "She's the quietest dog I've ever known. She seems depressed, but maybe it's just her sad brown eyes."

Kyla's eyes. Sam wondered if Troy saw that, too. She lifted the dog's silky ear and stroked it, let it flop again. "She's very sweet. I can't believe nobody in Bellingham has claimed her."

"Maybe she's not a native," Troy suggested. "I read once about a dog that ended up halfway across the country."

Sam laughed. "With Sophie's short legs, that would take about twenty years."

In a phone call two days later, Chase read to her from the case file. "The autopsy showed that Heigler had only a few months to live. His liver was mincemeat." He was back in Salt Lake for what he described as a "quick bounce" between cases.

"If Heigler knew he was dying, that might explain why he was so desperate to see Kyla again." Sam shuddered, thinking of the demon's hands on her, his spittle in her face. "She was probably the last relative who would speak to him."

"According to Greene's notes, Callahan claims he knew nothing about Klapton or Erik Heigler or about a planned drug drop. He said he was out for a nighttime stroll and it just fell into his lap. He also told them about cutting his hand and losing his knife in the lake. The rangers haven't found it, but Callahan wasn't very clear about where he'd dropped it."

"Damn convenient that it all happened at that particular lake on that particular night when everyone was drugged," she'd responded. "Everyone except for Aidan. And me, but that was a surprise to him."

"So far, that's only your suspicion."

She hated Chase's habit of reminding her when she had no real evidence. "He probably went back for the heroin after the rangers were gone."

"No. Campus police are keeping tabs on him at Washington State University. He hasn't left the area."

It was not a lot of comfort. "He could have had someone else pick the rest of the load up."

"Maybe. Or maybe Heigler had associates who collected the drugs."

It was a disturbing idea, to think that other criminals may have been lurking close by in the darkness as her crew slept on that last night. Was investigation always this nebulous?

"I know," Chase said. "It's frustrating."

"Seems like Aidan is going to get away with murder." Sam bit her lip. "Maybe with three murders."

"I doubt you'll find this helpful, Summer, but about a third of murder cases in the U.S. are never solved. Or at least, never prosecuted."

"You're right, Chase. Not helpful. Or comforting."

* * * * *

Another week went by with no more progress anywhere, or at least none that anyone shared with Sam. She searched for contract work and tried to interest Sophie in playing with a ball or going for walks, but the dog seemed to want something from her that she couldn't decipher. Blake started taking Sophie to the greenhouse on the days he worked, which was a relief from having to stare into those mournful brown eyes.

Chase had not found time to come to Bellingham for a visit or meet elsewhere for a rendezvous. The last time she spoke with him, he said, "I have something I want to tell you about."

"I'm listening," she'd said.

"It will have to wait, Summer. This is something I need to do in person."

He refused to give her another hint. She tried not to interpret that as ominous. His voice didn't offer any clues about what might be coming. The transfer to North Dakota? An ultimatum to commit to living together, or else? A break-up?

Now, she hadn't even talked to him for three days, which always ratcheted up her anxiety level. The last time he'd vanished from communication, he'd almost died in the Arizona desert and nobody had thought to inform her.

Between job search stints at her computer, Sam worked on volunteer trail maintenance crews and paddled her kayak around the nearby islands. In the evenings, she read with Simon in her lap, trying to push away unwelcome visions of being left on the platform as all trains pulled out of the station. Nobody seemed to need her right now.

Not even Maya, who packed up her tent and informed Sam she was moving into an apartment with a couple of college kids.

"A social worker told me about a grant from this extended foster program," Maya explained as she stuffed her sparse belongings into a duffel. "Housing subsidy and some college money for a year. As long as I have a part-time job, too."

"Sounds complicated." Sam's reaction flashed back and forth between relief and disappointment. She wouldn't have to worry about Maya freezing outside in a tent or taking up her couch space over the winter, but freeloading remora or not, she would miss having the girl around.

Maya's young forehead puckered. "Yeah, it is sorta complicated. I only get the money as long as I work and take classes and have a place to live. My first class at the community college is tomorrow."

"What do you plan to study?" Maya had a sharp mind, but the girl had barely graduated high school. Whenever anything more interesting cropped up, she had always been quick to ditch class.

The girl shrugged. "We'll see. To begin with, I'm taking American Sign Language and English Composition and something called The Biological World." Maya made air quotes with her fingers around the last class name. "And starting in two weeks, I'm working at REI on weekends."

Sam never expected Maya to be so motivated. "You're really pulling your life together."

The girl grimaced. "I heard a lot of lectures this summer. Where do you want to be in five years, et cetera, et cetera. It makes a girl think."

Sam pursed her lips. She had personally delivered that lecture during the expedition and she didn't have a clue where *she* was going to be in five years. Where did she *want* to be? Gainfully employed and still romantically involved with Starchaser Perez. She wasn't making much progress on either front.

Maya shouldered her duffel. "I don't want to be living in a tent in your back yard in five years. But maybe I can still come to dinner sometimes?"

"You'd better." Sam hugged her. As she let go, she noticed the cell phone in the back pocket of her friend's jeans. "Say, do you by any chance have some of those crew kids' e-mail addresses? Like Olivia's and Nick's?"

"Yeah," Maya eyed her curiously, as if she thought Sam should have collected that information herself. "We exchanged."

Pulling out her phone, she gave Sam the two addresses before she left.

Sam sent quick messages to both teens, asking how their contracts with their parents were working out. Olivia responded quickly: *I think we have a deal, but won't really know until college.*

Sam was relieved that the girl was okay. Nick didn't respond. But the boy had seemed more interested in pencils and paper instead of electronics, so maybe he wasn't glued to a cell phone or tablet like most teens.

The calendar reminded Sam of a hike she'd scheduled with Kim and Kyla. She'd been eager to introduce them to one of her favorite hikes, the Maple Pass loop on the boundary of North Cascades National Park. Early October was the perfect time to enjoy that trail. Sam decided to hike the spectacular trail solo before snow closed it for the winter, promising herself that the journey would be her way of saying a final goodbye to her murdered friends.

When she pulled out her day pack for the outing, she found the small trash sack left there from her hike to Pinnacle Lake with Chase. Still thinking that trail could hold some clue about the murders, she was reluctant to dispose of the debris she had collected. She spread out a newspaper, dumped out the little bag onto it, and sorted through the collection, using a pen to separate the items.

The torn candy wrappers might have a fingerprint. The broken strap might match another vital piece of evidence yet to be discovered. Damn, why had she thrown away that Mylar balloon she'd taken from the memorial? The killer could have left it there.

The off-white button could be important, couldn't it? It wasn't big enough to catch much of a print, but it was a button made of shell, not a common white plastic one. A single red thread looped through its holes.

That button felt like a puzzle piece she should recognize. She turned it over in her fingers several times, willing a memory to surface.

One finally bobbed up: Nick Lewis was missing a button like this from his shirt sleeve.

What were the odds that this was his button? One in a million?

Maybe not that low. Nick lived near Everett, which wasn't all that far from the Mountain Loop Highway and the Pinnacle Lake Trail. He said he and his dad hiked from time to time. All the litter along the trail once belonged to someone hiking there. There were only so many trails in the Cascades, and enthusiastic hikers could explore many of them in a season. She often spied names of friends in the damp pages of the register at a trailhead.

She slipped the button into a sandwich bag for safekeeping. She'd find Nick's address, take the button to him one day soon. It would provide a good excuse to check up on the teen; make sure he was not cutting himself again.

24

She drove two hours from Bellingham to North Cascades National Park to tackle the Maple Pass loop. As she climbed the trail, delighting in the kaleidoscope of autumn vegetation surrounding the lake below, she heard the sharp whistles of not one, but three different pikas. Pausing to search for the small round-eared mammals in the rock-strewn mountainside, she murmured, "Kyla, Kim, can you hear this?"

Pikas were declining in all mountain ranges. They needed cold weather and their populations were falling victim to global warming. They'd already disappeared in some parts of the Rockies. It was heartwarming to find a healthy pocket of these tiny rabbit cousins here in the north Cascades.

The huckleberry bushes were at the height of their glory, their crimson leaves delicately edged with white frost from the night before. The short needles of the alpine larches were brilliant yellow. In a few short weeks, the branches of the conifers would be bare.

At the pass, hoarfrost furred the ground and the wind was fierce, but Sam pulled on her hat, zipped her jacket, and perched on a rock to eat her lunch and absorb the 360-degree view of the Cascade Range.

When she heard a familiar rustle in the spindly trees, she quickly dug out the sunflower seeds she'd packed. Cocking their black and white heads, the gray jays watched, their shiny eyes eager but wary. She held her left hand above her head, opening it to reveal the seeds. "For Kim."

When she felt tiny bird claws close around her fingers and the tickle of the jays' beaks as they picked up the seeds, she raised her right hand, also full of hulled sunflower seeds. "For Kyla."

It took only minutes for both seeds and birds to disappear, and for tears to streak down Sam's cheeks. Wiping her hands on the thighs of her pants, she sat for a moment more, letting the cold wind dry her face.

Did Troy spend his days with the specters of his wife and daughter? Was he coping better than she was? Was he moving on with his life? Chris was in Alaska fishing.

Was everyone ready to accept that Kim and Kyla's murders might never be solved? Could she ever be okay with that?

Hell, no. How could that ever be okay? Their killer was still out there.

She made an effort to unclench her fists. She couldn't wallow forever. She had to find new hiking companions. Do volunteer work until paid jobs appeared. Paddle with the kayak club. If Chase couldn't come to her, she'd drive to Salt Lake whenever he returned to his condo there. It's not as if anything was keeping her in Bellingham right now.

When she returned to her house, Blake surprised her with a store-bought pizza and news. "You got back just in time to say good-bye. Sophie's leaving us."

"What?" She'd gotten used to having a dog around. And although Simon was still resentful, the cat had finally stopped hissing at the quiet canine.

"I know." Her housemate's tone was mournful. "But check this out. When I heard Troy say that about the dog that traveled across country, I got to thinking."

He pulled out his phone, showed her a Facebook page. Lost dogs, Washington State. In the photo, the basset mix had a red kerchief around her neck, and she seemed to be smiling. *Bring Trixie Home*, said the caption. Home was Tacoma.

Sam blinked. "Tacoma? Trixie?"

The dog stood up from her bed in the corner and looked at Sam, a question in her large brown eyes.

The doorbell rang.

"That's them." Blake walked to the front door.

As soon as the door opened, chaos erupted.

"Trixie! Trixie!" Two girls rushed in, nearly trampling Blake. Their apologetic mother was behind them. The dog bounced up off her bed. She raced first to the kids, her ears flopping, and then galloped in excited circles, skidding on the hardwood floor, baying loudly.

Trixie was a totally different dog than Sophie had been. The mother and Blake and Sam scratched their heads about how Trixie had ended up more than a hundred miles from her home, but the answer seemed irrelevant now. The girls, one on each end of the dog, carried their pet to the car.

The house seemed a little empty after the family had left. Even Simon wandered over to the abandoned dog bed, sniffed, and then strolled away, his tail held stiffly erect, not knowing what to make of the dog's sudden departure.

"Wine is needed," Blake decided, popping the cork on a bottle of merlot. "We'll miss Sophie, and I bet even Simon will, too. But how can anyone argue with a happy ending like that?"

Sam accepted the glass he handed her. She wanted a happy ending, too, but there would never be one for her friends. She needed at least a satisfying resolution. She needed justice.

A few days later, she was in the Kickin' A Saloon, slowly stretching out her beer after the line dance lesson and waiting for a familiar song to come on. She sat with her group of dance friends. Tonight, they were all feeling Kyla's absence so strongly that they could barely stand to look at each other. Conversations would start, then someone would mention Kyla's name, and the talk would grind to a painful halt. Not an elephant in the room, but a ghost. Or maybe a corpse. Make that two corpses, two ghosts. How long would it take for that awkwardness to pass?

The place was, as usual, filled with far more cowgirls than cowboys, so all the patrons had noticed the two new men at the table behind Sam. The high stools were so close that she was practically touching butt cheeks with one of them, a burly fellow wearing khaki pants and a buttoned-down shirt. His companion, a good-looking man with blond-brown hair and a fashionably trimmed three-day beard, seemed familiar.

She ran through the possibilities in her head. Had she met him in the kayak club? She didn't think so. Hiking club? Maybe. Often someone showed up for a hike only a couple of times per year. But she was pretty sure she would have remembered this man because he was around her age, and good looking. Had she taken a class with him at the community college? Was he a regular at one of the local brewpubs? The last seemed most likely; he had a beer in his hand right now.

In a pause between songs on the sound system, billiard balls clacked loudly from the pool table in the corner as a player made a break shot to begin a new game. The television on the wall above the pool table was showing the local news with no audio.

"Oh, no." Her friend Margie grimaced as she pointed at the screen.

An image of Pinnacle Lake was followed in quick succession by photos of Kyla and Kim. Without sound or closed captioning, Sam couldn't tell what the newscasters were saying. When a photo of the trailhead sign was revealed, though, the words TRAIL REOPENED appeared across the top of the screen. So the story wasn't about a new clue, but about the hiking trail being opened to the hiking public again.

"Those poor women," muttered the buttoned-down man behind her, whose stool she was almost sharing.

"One of these days it's gonna happen all over again," said his bearded companion.

"What? How?" her butt-cheek buddy asked. Then he added, "I thought the husband did it."

Sam winced. Poor Troy.

"Maybe," the bearded guy said. "But maybe it could have been, like, target practice that went wrong."

"What?" his buddy asked.

Damn coincidental target practice to kill two women. More like an execution. But then Sam remembered that these guys couldn't share her knowledge of how precise the shots had been.

"You know, like that gal at the picnic who got zinged by a stray bullet from target shooters who were half a mile away."

Sam grimaced. Zinged? The poor woman had been killed in her own back yard.

The bearded guy suggested, "You know how the government says some trails are only for hikers—no bikes or horses or llamas or camels allowed, right?"

"I guess," chuckled his companion.

"So why aren't there trails just for hunters—no hikers allowed?"

The buttoned-down guy grunted. "Would make a lot of sense."

Sam turned to look at the two men again. A memory finally dropped into the appropriate slot in her brain. Sliding off her stool, she walked around the table to the bearded fellow. "Excuse me."

He glanced up from his beer.

"You're Nick Lewis's father, aren't you?"

He sank back on his stool, his expression startled. Sam abruptly remembered that although she'd studied him twice, first in Troy's video and then at the closing ceremony, Lewis had never been introduced to her.

"I saw you with Nick on the last day of the Wilderness Quest session," she hastily explained. "That day was so hectic, I'm not surprised you didn't notice me." She held out her hand. "Sam Westin. I was the field guide in charge of Nick's group."

He grasped her hand with his own. "Tom Lewis. Nice to meet you, Cap'n Sam."

She chuckled. "Just Sam, please. I'm surprised to run into you so far north. Nick said you lived down south in Everett."

"We do. I work for a beverage distributor. I cover a five-county region." He tilted his head toward the bar. "I just convinced this place to give us a shot for some new craft beers."

"Excellent," she said. "The more variety, the better." She took a quick glance at his companion, who was now checking his cell phone.

"This is my new associate, Pete," Lewis said, causing the man to look up. "I'm teaching him the ropes."

After she and Pete shook hands, Sam turned back to Lewis. "How is Nick these days? I think about him a lot."

"We're doing good." Lewis stared into his beer glass. "I think we understand each other better now than we ever have in the past."

His mention of the past brought to mind his odd speech on the last day about leaving the past behind, but this was not the time or place to quiz him on that. She wanted to ask Tom if his son had stopped cutting himself, but Pete was listening intently and she didn't want to reveal any family secrets. Then she remembered the button.

"Tom, this is probably the weirdest coincidence, but that story about the Pinnacle Lake trail just reminded me. I think I have a button from Nick's shirt."

Lewis straightened in his chair, his posture stiffening. "What?"

"Nick has been on that trail, right? You guys have hiked down there."

He wiped his mustache with a finger. "Maybe. I'm not sure. Trails all kind of blend together for me."

Except when a double murder makes one especially memorable. "Well, I was on that Pinnacle Lake trail about six weeks ago picking up trash, and I found a button made out of shell. It had a scrap of red thread in the holes."

Lewis picked up his beer glass and swirled around the last dregs, a clue that she was rambling on. "So?"

"When I saw the shirt that Nick wore when he came to Wilderness Quest, he had the cuffs turned back because the sleeves were too long."

"Yeah?"

"I know that trick because I'm sort of vertically challenged myself, so I do it, too, make French cuffs like that to shorten sleeves. Anyhow, I noticed that the buttons on Nick's cuffs were made out of real mother of pearl, which is not common these days. And there was one button missing, and a piece of red thread dangling where it should have been. Since the shirt was green, that was noticeable."

At this point, his friend slid off the bar stool and headed for the men's room. Creases appeared in Tom Lewis's forehead and his eyes strayed over her head toward the dance floor. Yep, she was definitely rambling.

"So, anyhow, small world, eh?" she summarized. "I'm pretty sure I found Nick's button on the trail there."

"Yeah, small world." He held out his hand. "I can take it now and give it back to him."

"Um, sorry, I don't have it with me." The button was in the glove compartment of her car, but a gremlin in the back of her mind was warning her not to hand it over. "When I saw you, I wanted to tell you about it. I can bring it to your house sometime." She wanted to check on Nick for herself.

He forced a chuckle. "Don't worry about it. It's only a button."

She couldn't insist on visiting, could she? She'd have to drop in uninvited. "Okay," she said. "Nice to meet you, Tom. I really enjoyed having Nick on my crew. And he's a truly talented artist. You should encourage that."

"Of course." The corners of his mouth turned up, but the smile didn't quite reach his eyes.

She trotted back to her stool, took a few sips of her beer and chatted with her dance friends. When the DJ played one of her favorite songs, a bunch of dancers got up, and Sam ended up doing three dances in a row. By the time she finished the third, her beer was lukewarm and her shirt was plastered to her backbone with sweat.

She stepped out the front door to cool off in the evening breeze, and walked to her Civic to get a clip to fasten her hair up off her neck. When she opened the trunk, she was careful not to bonk the kayak strapped into the rack on top of her car.

Next to her Civic, some dinkwad had taken up five spaces by parking a black pickup crosswise with a speedboat in tow. A loud voice called her attention to the far end of the lot. Tom Lewis slapped his friend on the shoulder as they stood next to a Cascade Beverage Distributors van. Pete slid into the driver's seat of the van, then Lewis walked to the black pickup.

Dinkwad identified.

He paused, studying her kayak. "This yours?"

After shutting the trunk, she ran her fingers through her hair. "Yep. I'm too lazy to take it off my car between trips. I see we're both boaters."

"Right." He stroked the fiberglass flank of his speedboat. "I planned to combine business with pleasure on this trip, do a run around the San Juans."

"You'll love the islands," she said. "And the weather and tides are supposed to be decent for the next few days. I plan to get out tomorrow myself."

"I'm thinking of buying a kayak for Nick." Walking to her kayak, he ran his fingers along its side. "Impex," he read from the label there. "Is that a good brand?"

Twisting her rope of fine blond hair, Sam secured it at the back of her head with the clip. "It works for me, but this boat was a Craigslist special. I'm not sure if the company is even in business anymore."

"Craigslist? Good idea, I'll check that." He peered down at her. "Where's your favorite spot to row?"

"You mean paddle. I go to Chuckanut Bay most often, I guess. It's close to my house and more or less protected, and there are multiple put-in spots not too far away. My favorite put-in is Mud Bay, but that only works during high tide. It's named Mud Bay for good reason."

"I get it." He pulled open his truck door. "Thanks for the info. See you, Sam."

"Say hi to Nick for me."

He waved as he slid into the driver's seat of the pickup.

She went back to the dance floor inside the saloon. As she

stepped through Ford Boogie and Booze Cruise, her mind kept returning to the Lewises. The weird conversation about the past on the last day of the expedition. Tom Lewis seemed like a nice enough guy, but his insensitive comments today about the hunters-only trail and the stray-bullet victim nagged at her.

Then there was her recall of Nick's strained relationship with his father. The whole "man up" spiel. Nick's cutting.

Tom couldn't be a truly abusive father, she reasoned, because he'd cared enough to sign Nick up for wilderness therapy. But had he or Nick's mother done something horrible in the past to the boy?

25

The tide at Mud Bay would rise for another hour, and Sam planned to paddle for no more than two, so she knew she'd still be able to load her kayak afterward without having to slog through sticky ankle-deep mud. The evening was a cool and crisp. The hours just before sundown were perfect here, with the wind dying down and the water in the protected bay smooth as satin. She carried her kayak on her shoulder from her car to the shore, then returned to move her car from the loading zone to the lot down the street.

As she slid into her seat, in the distance she noticed a truck towing a boat. A clueless tourist headed for the beach? Not only was Mud Bay too shallow for most motorized craft, but there was no boat ramp and no place to turn around a trailer. The truck turned down a side street. A local, then, returning home. She parked her car, walked back to the beach, donned her life vest and spray skirt, and then paddled away into the quiet.

Kingfishers flapped along the shoreline ahead of her, complaining about her presence as they flew. She startled a great blue heron, who added his or her noisy objections. If only the silly birds would fly back behind her, everyone would be happy. But no, their avian brains were pre-programmed in some way that made them move ahead eighty percent of the time, only to be surprised again when she showed up to interrupt their fishing a few minutes later.

Paddling under the railroad bridge that separated Mud Bay

from Chuckanut Bay, she marveled as she always did that the structure had never been blown up by the anti-coal-train activists. The busy train tracks might be a historical part of Bellingham, but they were ugly scars on the scenic waterfront face of her town.

Kayaking was a form of meditation for Sam. She often mulled over her problems out here. She had to decide what to do about her suspicions surrounding Tom Lewis. After reflecting on what Nick had said about hunting, she'd had Blake call Fish and Wildlife, pretending to be Thomas Lewis asking about dates for his hunting permit. Just as she suspected, Lewis had a license for this season. Only a hunter would have made that "hunters-only trail" comment she'd overheard in the saloon.

Should she call Detective Greene? The woman would probably laugh at her. All she really had was an offhand remark in a bar, a perfectly legal hunting license, and a button, for heaven's sake. No, she argued with herself, she also had Nick's behavior, the cutting, and the odd verbal exchanges between father and son.

Still. All circumstantial, Chase would say.

Nick clearly felt guilty for some reason; something awful was eating the poor boy alive. Maybe notifying Child Protective Services would be a better bet. Would they keep her identity secret?

She chewed on her lower lip, trying to screw up her courage to drive to their Everett address tomorrow and question Nick. She wanted to make sure the boy was okay, but she wasn't looking forward to crossing paths with his father. Despite the man's friendly demeanor, he struck her as a bully. Or maybe a con man. Something off-kilter, anyway.

She decided to drop by around four p.m. Tomorrow was a Monday. School should be out, so probably Nick would be home, but Tom would likely still be on the road somewhere. Maybe she could convince Maya to come with her. Was that cowardly?

Lost in thought, she dipped her paddle too deep and had to

do a hard brace to keep from flipping. Focus on the here and now, she chided herself, taking a deep breath of fresh evening air. Just be.

A sleek head parted the water off to her left. An otter. Feeling blessed by its presence, she stopped paddling and let her kayak glide. Two smaller heads emerged—kits? The family swam toward the shore, sliding out onto a horizontal rock there and then vanishing into a crevice beyond.

Otters. Magical.

A week ago she'd told Chase that she would spend more time in Salt Lake City. There were no otters there. No saltwater bays like this. That was going to be a hard promise to keep.

When the otters didn't reappear, she paddled onward in the shadow of the cliffs, where the soft sedimentary rock had been carved by wind and water into dramatic standing waves. High up on the vertical sides were nest pockets where birds raised their chicks. All those sites were vacant now but marked by white guano stains dripping down from the indentations.

As she reached the point, the wave action picked up, the breeze and current pushing the water in from the southwest, waves banging up against the rocks and islands. Near the small bird sanctuary island in the middle of the bay, harbor seals on surrounding rocks bathed in the last rays of the sun. In the distance, she heard a speedboat zipping up the channel from the south.

Turning her kayak around the point, she drifted into another bay, where the water once again stilled between the cliffs. Locals often called the small inlet Fossil Bay because several large, obvious fossils stood out from the rock wall to one side. An expert once told her that the segmented columns of rock stretched out there were fossilized palm tree trunks, but to her they looked more like the vertebrae of some giant prehistoric creature. She liked to visualize plesiosaurs swimming here in ancient times.

The sound of the speedboat motor grew louder as the craft neared. If the idiot driving it didn't know that rocks lurked only inches beneath the surface, he'd end up shattering his hull. She threw a quick glance over her shoulder and saw the boat zoom into the bay, slowing only a little as it rounded the rocky point.

She quickly looked away, hoping the boat would zip out as quickly as it had slammed in, but instead it just kept coming. Damn it! She didn't want to share Fossil Bay, and the creep was shredding the tranquility of the evening with his macho racing stunt.

A crow took flight overhead, cawing noisily. She dipped her paddle into the water to change course, and caught the flash of white fiberglass in her peripheral vision as the boat skidded into a turn only a foot short of her kayak.

The wave the speedboat kicked up lifted her kayak, slamming her into the vertical wall of rock. Her paddle snapped. Her right elbow crashed into the sandstone. Her forehead was thankfully slowed by glancing off her upraised arm before it, too, smashed into the rock. Everything went white for a slow-motion second as her kayak flipped. Cold saltwater slapped her face and raced down her neck as she turned upside down, her boat rebounding again off the rock. She involuntarily sucked in a mouthful of water before she came to her senses, choking. Bending forward in the dark water, she reached for the grab loop on her spray skirt.

The boat motor was deafening, and for a few horrific seconds, she was terrified she'd feel the blades of the propeller rip into her torso. She pulled on the grab loop. In rescue practice, she'd always been able to easily jerk the spray skirt loose from the coaming and free herself to swim out of her kayak. Now it didn't budge. Hanging upside down, blind in the murky water, she and the kayak bounced off the shore again. This time she smacked her left shoulder against the rock, and she nearly opened her mouth to gasp in pain.

When she yanked on the loop, the front part of her kayak flexed too, the coaming refusing to release the spray skirt. Horror added fuel to her burning lungs as she realized the bow of her kayak was smashed. She was bungee-corded upside down into the resulting flotsam, which continued to crash into and then rebound off the rocky cliff. Her legs were trapped. She might drown here in the heavy duty wash cycle of Fossil Bay.

Pressing her feet upward against the hull, she pushed with both feet while she yanked on the loop. Her lungs were exploding, her throat burning with the need for air. Her right foot slid off the fiberglass into the cold water, and she lost her leverage.

Blindly flailing to locate a solid position for that foot again, she wondered if she should simply abandon the effort and try to pull herself upright with her arms. That seemed unlikely to work, but maybe she could get a breath of air before the debris dragged her down again.

She hit the rock once more, this time with a bit less force. Finally her foot found purchase against the remains of the hull. *Oh God, air, please. Air!* She pushed with both legs and pulled with both hands, nearly folding the kayak around her body.

Finally the spray skirt cord snapped off the coaming, freeing her from the cockpit. Kicking and clawing upward through the floating pieces, she fought her way out of the wreckage.

Coughing violently but finally upright with her face in air again, she drifted for a minute with the debris, clacking against the shore in the waning daylight, gasping for breath, and thankful she was still wearing her life vest.

Cliffs rose on all sides of Fossil Bay. At the shallow end of the bay, she knew there was a small sandy beach, submerged under frigid water now at high tide. Assuming she managed to haul herself on shore before hypothermia claimed her, she'd still have to scramble up the cliff in her wet clothes.

The speedboat had vanished.

26

In her kayak, Sam could paddle from Fossil Bay to the shore of Mud Bay in under twenty minutes, but traveling overland was a whole different experience. Anger kept her warm enough to dog-paddle to the far end of the cove where, shivering and standing in knee-deep water, she shucked her spray skirt and life vest and eyed the best way to ascend the steeply sloping bank. It was the only possible route up out of the bay, but it was covered with Himalayan blackberry bushes, the invasive scourge of the Pacific Northwest, the interwoven spiked branches eagerly waiting to claw her hair and skin.

There was nothing to be done except battle through them. She'd lost one of her water sandals, so she kicked the other one off. She tossed her spray skirt as far as she could up the bank, then started to follow that with her life vest, remembering at the last second to recover her car key from the front pocket, slipping it into her waterlogged bra.

Her right arm felt numb, and she had a hard time controlling that hand. Her left shoulder ached but still worked. The warm liquid that ran down her face had to be blood, but she had nothing to control the flow, unless she peeled off the lightweight shirt she wore. She settled for wiping blood out of her eyes with her shirttail and periodically pressing her hand against the gash she felt at her hairline. Finally, out of desperation, she plastered a fallen leaf against the wound, which was no doubt unhygienic but miraculously served to glue the cut more or less closed. By the time she finally gained the top of the hill, the sun had set.

She checked the lone house there. Not a single light shone through the windows. No vehicles. No sign of life. She remembered reading that the family who owned the property had generously left it to the county as park land. Looked as if the owners had already abandoned it. No help there.

She set off again, still shivering but warmer now from her exertions, climbing along the hillside above the water, forced to hang onto rocks and trees and claw her way along to keep from falling into the bay. The cliffs rose steeply from the water, their vertical sides either slick wind-polished sandstone or obstacle courses of vines, twisted madronas, and ferns barely clinging to the rocky slopes.

She was an idiot. Why the hell didn't she carry her cell phone when she went on these little adventures?

Because they were little adventures, she argued. If she'd been kayaking between islands in the San Juans, she would have worn her wetsuit and dry top and armed herself with a marine radio as well as a cell phone. But this was her back yard; she paddled in Chuckanut Bay all the time. There were usually enough boaters here to call in an alarm if needed, and she'd never landed in trouble before.

Still, she cursed her stupidity as she clawed her way along the steep sides of the bay, crossing above the railroad tunnel as one of the damned coal trains thundered through beneath her, the engine blasting its horn as it went.

It might have been possible to climb up to the houses of the wealthy perched on the cliff top above her, but she was more interested in reaching her car, and even if some kind neighbor there drove her the circular route back to Mud Bay, that would no doubt take just as long. After two hours of struggling along the steep banks and one startling encounter with a fang-baring raccoon, she finally was able to stand upright on the beach at the north end of Mud Bay.

She stomped her way back to her car. There was absolutely no doubt that the attack had been deliberate. Someone had tried to kill her. It had taken her so long to extract herself from the wreckage that he probably believed she'd drowned.

She had no doubt that her attacker was a "he." A "he" with a pickup and a speedboat. He knew both her and her kayak, and she'd foolishly told him about Mud Bay. He couldn't have put his boat in there to follow her, but it was a relatively short drive to the boat ramp in Larrabee Park, and then a speedy trip around the coastline to Chuckanut Bay and Fossil Bay.

He knew she'd found a button belonging to his son on a trail where two women had been murdered. He knew she'd heard his pleas to his son about leaving the past behind. He'd cost her a kayak worth more than a thousand dollars and a paddle worth five hundred. He had intended to cost Sam her life.

In the dark parking lot, she swapped her drowned and torn pants and shirt for the dry clothes she always kept in the trunk: fleece top, yoga pants, dry socks, and running shoes. She was hungry, she was exhausted. Her head hurt, her shoulder and elbow ached, and her hands and feet were on fire, shredded by her trek back from Fossil Cove.

Tom Lewis no doubt believed he had killed Sam Westin, just like he'd killed her friends. She was furious, and suddenly absolutely certain she was right. But the murders still made no sense, and she still had no proof. Nick had to know about the crime—what would happen to him? If Tom was willing to go after her, would he kill his son?

The Lewises obviously had guns in the house. At times during the Wilderness Quest expedition, Nick had seemed almost suicidal. Was he likely to kill himself? Was he already dead? Her imagination produced a terrible vision of Nick's body sprawled in blood across the floor. The clock could be ticking for that boy.

As she started her car and pulled out of the shadows, she considered calling 9-1-1. And say what?

She didn't have time to explain what had just happened and detail all her suspicions; she jammed her ancient plug-in GPS unit into the cigarette lighter and yelled at it to wake up and find the Lewis address in Everett as she pulled onto I-5 southbound. If only the dang thing could make a phone call.

What would get the police to go and check on the Lewis house right away?

She could think of only one thing. She pulled into the first rest stop and called 9-1-1 from the pay phone there. It took five minutes of repetition to explain that it didn't matter who or where she was, she needed the Everett police to check on the welfare of a child at the Lewis address. There were guns in the house and the child could be in danger from his father.

"Who are you in relationship to this child?" the operator kept asking. "Why do you think the child could be in danger?"

In exasperation, she hung up, unsure if the operator had taken her seriously. As she exited the highway on the outskirts of Everett forty minutes later, she passed a police cruiser headed the opposite way. She honked and waved, but the officer driving didn't even glance in her direction as he accelerated onto the on-ramp.

The voice of her grumpy GPS unit guided her through a maze of dark streets to the Lewis house, often issuing directions too late to make the turns, and then chanting "recalculating..." to her annoyance. Twice it ordered her to make a U-turn and backtrack.

The address was on the edge of a newish suburb, down a long gravel side street. The area appeared to be a subdivision in progress, or maybe one that had run out of financing midway. Gigantic white "For Sale" signs sprouted along the roadside, like weeds grown out of control. Wooded lots predominated, with only two houses carved out of the forest bordering the long street.

The Lewis house was the last indication of development in the area.

Lights from within the small ranch-style house spilled out through windows into the dark yard. She parked in the shadows of the forested lot next door, then walked back to the Lewis house. The speedboat, on its trailer, was parked next to a detached garage. She limped toward it.

A security light flashed on.

Shit. Gasping, she dove into the shadows between boat and

garage. She ran her hand along the flank of the speedboat. Dry. Damn.

She gave herself a mental slap; of course it would be dry after Lewis had towed it the same distance she'd just driven. Out of her sight, she heard the back door of the house open.

"I don't see anything."

A wave of relief passed through her gut. Nick's voice sounded small and wobbly, but he was alive.

The security light winked out. Sam stood up, placed her hand on the rollers on the side of the trailer. Tom had wrapped them in terrycloth to protect his precious boat. They were still wet.

"Go check." Tom's gravelly voice.

Crap. She crouched, waiting in the shadows as tentative footsteps neared.

The security light flashed on again, illuminating Nick, who seemed to have shrunk since she last saw him. His face, still with mustache and soul patch in place, gleamed in the bright light, his bruises completely healed.

"Nick," she whispered.

He startled, and for a second she was afraid he might scream. Instead, he slapped a hand over his lips and peered intently in her direction.

She stepped into the light.

His mouth popped open, and for another second, she was terrified he was going to shout a warning to his father. She abruptly remembered that she'd forgotten to check her car mirror. Coated in filth, with wild hair and streaks of dried blood running down her face, she probably looked like she had recently escaped from the grave. In a way, she had.

"Cap'n Sam!" Nick threw himself at her, hugging her fiercely.

His embrace hurt her shoulder and elbow, but she closed her arms around him, glad to see he seemed okay. He stuttered into her neck. "He said ... he said ... you were dead."

"He tried. Why, Nick?"

"It's my fault."

"Nick?" Tom's voice boomed into the quiet evening. "What's going on?"

Nick stepped away from the garage wall into the driveway, swallowed hard, turned his face toward the house. "Nuh ... nothing."

Tom's shadow preceded him. The silhouette of a big man, striding purposefully in their direction.

"Run!" Nick urged, stepping forward to tug on Sam's sleeve.

She stood her ground, wanting to see Tom Lewis's reaction when he spotted her.

She wasn't disappointed. The man's eyes rounded, his mouth dropped open, and he even took a step backward.

He recovered quickly. "So that was you who called the cops, you little bitch. Child endangerment, my ass."

The police car she'd passed must have responded to her 9-1-1 call after all. But Tom had obviously passed their questioning.

"What are you doing here?" he growled.

"I wanted you to see that you didn't succeed." She ignored Nick's insistent tugging.

"I don't know what you're talking about. Nick, come here." Tom slid his hand behind his back and she saw the shadow of the pistol before the weapon itself as he drew it from his waistband. "Nick, come here!"

Nick yanked on her sleeve so hard he nearly pulled her off her feet. "Run!"

Grabbing his hand, she did.

27

"Nick, goddamn it, get back here!" Tom Lewis crashed behind them into the dark woods.

The boy towed her by the hand, dodging between trees, which was a good thing because he clearly knew where he was and her night vision had been damaged by the security light. The ground was uneven and Sam stumbled, feet burning inside her running shoes, blackberry scratches and rock scrapes inflaming her soles. The right arm Nick had hold of flashed a lightning bolt of pain to her shoulder and neck with every tug.

"Dammit, Westin, I'll have you charged with kidnapping!"

A loud boom blasted through the night air, and they both stopped, flinching. But she didn't detect the sound of a bullet whizzing past. She chanced a glance back over her shoulder.

The tall figure of Tom Lewis was barely visible between the trees, backlit by the light streaming from the house. He'd come from inside the house, so Sam hoped his eyes were taking even longer to adjust to the darkness.

"My car," she urgently whispered to Nick. "It's parked in front of this lot."

His voice cracked as he grabbed her arm again. "This way."

The sounds of snapping twigs and thudding footsteps behind them proved his father was closing in. Sam and Nick burst out of the woods onto the road, yanked open the doors of her car and jumped in.

The keys! She couldn't find her keys. Breathing hard, she frantically ran her hands over her clothes, finally located the keys in the teensy front pocket of her pants, and thrust her fingers in. The keys jammed in the crease of her thigh and torso and would come no further. Why the hell didn't she have one of those new keyless cars?

Heart thundering in her chest, she shoved the door open with her left arm and leapt out.

Nick leaned across the seat. "Hurry, hurry! Omigod, hurry!"

As if she didn't already have sufficient motivation.

She yanked the keys out of her pocket.

Tom Lewis thundered out of the woods behind her.

She'd just managed to slam the door shut when the fingers of his left hand clutched at the handle, trying to yank it open again. Clutched in his right hand, the pistol clunked against her window glass, and for a second she was terrified that the barrel would shatter the glass or the gun would fire and she'd lose the top of her head. She pulled on the door handle from her side, afraid to move her hand to reach the lock button.

Tom let go of the driver's door and reached for the back door. Sam slapped at the door lock and heard the clunk of the locks closing, but Tom already had the door behind her open.

"Nick!" he growled.

She jammed the car key into the ignition. Tom's right hand clamped around the back of her headrest, and for once she was thankful that she was petite. Otherwise, he'd have her by the hair or the back of her neck. Twisting the key and pressing the accelerator to the floor, she peeled out onto the road, the tires spitting gravel.

"Nick!" Tom yelled, slipping backward as his feet were dragged on the road. "Don't do this. Sam! Goddamn it!"

And then, with a clunk and a rasp of fabric, the clutching fingers were gone from her headrest. The passenger door banged in the wind. The door open light on the dash kept flashing its red warning in her face, along with the seat belt sign. She remembered to turn on her headlights. The stop sign at the end of the gravel road seemed miles away.

"You okay, Nick?"

The boy hunched over in the passenger seat, his head below

the dashboard, his arms clutched around himself, sobbing, "Oh God, oh God, oh God."

In the rear view mirror, she saw the red flash of taillights as Tom Lewis backed his pickup out of his driveway. Then two high beams came her way at an alarming speed, like a tyrannosaurus bearing down on her.

"You might want to put your seat belt on, Nick." She was approaching the T intersection way too fast.

Like the good kid he was, Nick was reaching for the belt when she slammed on the brakes and skidded around the stop sign, taking a right onto the pavement. They both slid left, Sam banging her elbow on the door, Nick sliding into her, then reversed right, rebounding back more or less into position. The back door slammed shut, and Sam's back and neck cracked. Reckless driving might be a drastic form of emergency chiropractic treatment.

When the tires stopped squealing, she asked, "Where's the closest police station, Nick?"

He sat up and finally jammed the shoulder harness into the buckle. Sam wished she had time and another arm to do that on her side of the car.

"The closest police station?" she prompted again.

"I don't know," he sobbed. "Why would I know?"

They both watched the rearview mirror as the headlights rounded the corner and sped their way.

"Won't that thing know?" Nick pointed to the GPS unit suction-cupped to her dashboard. The blue start screen was on, showing her, as usual, its warning about needing map updates. Like a writer-wildlife biologist-field guide had money to download new data every time any piece of GPS info changed. But he was right, the device should know, and surely police stations hadn't moved around much in the last ten years.

"Nick, press that Skip button."

He did. The screen switched to show multiple options available for setting routes.

"Now what?" he asked.

"Voice command!" she ordered.

Nothing happened except for Tom's headlights getting closer. There was a four-way intersection ahead. Three choices.

"Voice command!" she shouted again.

"Speak a command," the GPS device calmly responded.

"Police station!" she yelped.

"Did you say Lee Session?" the device politely asked. "I found two Lee Sessions."

"That's a person," Nick informed her, checking the screen. "There's a Lee and a Lisa."

Whoever imagined this damn technology would be useful? "Back!" she shouted. "Po-leez stay-shun!" she enunciated loudly.

She was at the four-way stop sign. With no instructions forthcoming, she chose to blast straight ahead. The lights moving at a steady stream in the distance had to be the highway.

"I found two police stations in Ev-er-ett," the device announced.

"Tap the closest one, Nick," she murmured softly so as not to confuse Miz GPS again.

"Snohomish County Sheriff or Everett Police?"

"Whichever is closest!"

The pickup headlights bounced off her rearview, blinding her. She slapped the mirror upward as she sped onto the on-ramp. A feeble horn honked behind her as she cut off a Prius.

"Nick, what will your father do if he catches us?" she asked.

"Drive five miles on Eye-Five," the device instructed.

Tom's headlights swung around the Prius and moved up the inside lane. Sam increased her speed, but there was no way her Civic could match the horsepower of the big pickup. Fortunately, a Mercedes was hogging the inside lane and haughtily refused to respond to Tom's flashing headlights.

Flashing headlights. Excellent idea. She punched the red button in the middle of the dash to turn on her emergency flashers. Now surely everyone on the highway would be on their cell phones, calling in the maniac woman driver speeding down the road with her flashers on. The driver ahead of her switched lanes to the left, further backing up Tom.

"My cell's a lot faster than this thing," Nick murmured, his face blue in the GPS light.

Then why the hell don't you have your cell, she wanted to scream. But who knew how GPS Lady would interpret that.

"Nick," she said again, her voice shaky but soft, "What will your father do if he catches us?"

"In one hundred feet, exit right," the device commanded. "Then keep right."

The SUV driver in back of her had slowed, no doubt alarmed by the emergency flashers, and Tom's pickup slid in behind her, only a couple of feet from her bumper.

"Nick?" she prompted.

He folded over again as if having an appendicitis attack. "Oh God, I don't know! He's my dad."

That didn't make sense, but then not much about the situation did. She peeled off the exit at the last minute, feeling the car's weight shift momentarily onto the two outside wheels as she rounded the curve. With luck, Tom might roll his truck as he screeched onto the exit behind her.

No such luck.

"Drive six miles," GPS Lady told her.

The pickup tapped her bumper. What the hell did Tom Lewis expect her to do, anyway? Pull over so he could conveniently kill her and take his son? Surely he wouldn't shoot into her car while Nick was beside her.

There were cars ahead, stopped at a red light, blocking the intersection. She was going to have to stop.

"I could just jump out," the boy suggested. "Then he might leave you alone."

Like he'd left her alone in Fossil Bay? "No. He might shoot you."

"He wouldn't. He's my dad."

"Well, then he'd have no excuse not to shoot me."

Nick's jaw clenched, his face grim as he acknowledged her logic.

The red light turned green and the cars ahead of her moved across the intersection. The pickup bumped her again. There was no way they were going to make it to the police station before he caused her to crash.

"Hang on, Nick." She careened into the intersection and jammed her foot on the brake, yanking the wheel around. The Civic slid into a turn before halting. The pickup slammed into her left rear fender before sliding off and crashing into a light pole on the corner.

The seat belt forced the air from her lungs, and as she tried to inflate them again, Sam watched Tom open the pickup door and exit, the gun clutched in his right hand. His left was pressed against his head and he staggered, fell to his knees, then got back up again, waving the gun wildly.

Nick was slumped in his seat, but she saw no blood. Had he banged his head against the window?

Above her, the traffic light changed. The Civic was blocking the intersection. As Lewis lurched toward her car, Sam jammed her hand on her horn and kept it there. Headlights from two different directions illuminated the car's interior. Her emergency flashers strobed across the scene.

Whatever was about to happen, there would be plenty of witnesses.

28

Nick Lewis sobbed and crossed his arms, hugging himself. A young boy, trying to be a brave man. Sam, Nick, and Detective Greene were seated in mismatched, excruciatingly uncomfortable chairs as they waited around a scratched metal table in a worn interview room.

The closest police station had turned out to be the Snohomish County Sheriff's headquarters. Sam immediately asked for Detective Greene and was surprised that the officers had complied with her request even though she was wearing handcuffs at the time. A medic cleaned her wounds and plastered some gauze over the worse scrapes and the gash on her forehead.

Her image in the women's room mirror was shocking. Still, for a dead woman, Sam Westin looked pretty good.

Greene, haggard with hair escaping from her bun and a couple of buttons out of place, had arrived shortly before they began the interview. Sam felt empathy toward the woman. It was after midnight, and she'd had an extremely long day herself.

"We were hunting for bears. I didn't want to shoot a bear; I didn't want to shoot anything!" Nick's eyes gleamed with tears as he stared first at Sam, and then at Detective Greene. "But Dad was ragging on me, telling me about how his dad used to take him hunting and how it made him feel like a man to put meat on the table. He told me he'd enrolled me in Washington Wilderness Quest to help me sort things out. Sounded like he was going to ditch me just like Mom did."

Sam wanted to reach out to the boy, but she'd only been allowed into the room on the condition she would say nothing. The detective nodded at Nick, encouraging him to continue.

"So, we'd been trampin' round and round out there and all we saw was a squirrel and a deer, which my dad acted like he wanted to shoot but it wasn't the right time. He said we'd stay out there all day to get a bear if we had to."

He gulped, nervously swept a finger over his sparse mustache, and then returned his hand to his lap. "And then I finally saw something move across the valley on the hillside. I couldn't see it very good through all the leaves, but I could tell it was brown and it looked pretty big."

A tear escaped his right eye and rolled down his cheek. He impatiently wiped it away. "Dad kept saying, 'Well, is it a bear? Is it? Have you got it in your sights? Don't let it get away! Be a man, shoot that bear!'"

Nick paused, catching his lower lip under his front teeth. After a second, he continued, "And so finally, I just pulled the trigger."

He started to rock in his chair. The squeaking of the cheap metal chair was painful in the hushed room.

Detective Greene prompted, "And then what happened, Nick?"

"And then we heard a scream. I wanted to run back to the truck, but Dad said, no, we've got to go see about that, and so we hiked toward the screaming." His nose began to drip, and Nick raised an arm to wipe away the mucus on the back of his sleeve. His eyelashes were spiky with tears. "And, and... and when we got there, a woman was holding this other one and crying. And the one she was holding was wearing a brown shirt and she was wearing a green one, which is really stupid in hunting season."

Anger flashed across his face and then quickly dissipated into sorrow again. "There was blood everywhere, and when we got there, the green woman took one look at us and yelled, 'You shot her! Call 9-1-1! Get help!'"

Raising his hands, he yanked on the top of his hair as if trying to rip out handfuls, and began rocking again. "But the blond woman in her arms had all this blood pouring out of her chest, and there was like this lake of blood spreading out around them. We all knew she was going to die."

Sam's breath lodged painfully in her chest. Kyla's death had not been instantaneous.

Nick paused to swallow and wipe his nose again. "The woman screamed at my dad, 'You murdered my daughter!' and then..." A strangled sob slipped from his lips.

Sam could see the blood, she could feel the terror. Her throat was closing up, and she pressed a fist to her lips and bit down on a knuckle to prevent the same strangling sounds escaping from her mouth.

"...then Dad looked at me and we both knew I'd done it." Nick slapped a hand against his chest. "I killed that lady. And then..." He froze and his eyes went blank as he stared at the scratched metal table top.

"And then..." Detective Greene murmured.

Nick's eyes were fixed on the table. He took a ragged breath, the sound loud in the quiet room.

"And then?" Greene asked again.

"And then my Dad pulled out his revolver and shot the screaming lady, right in the head." Nick raised his face then, his gaze moving from Sam to Detective Greene. "There was this echo that went on forever; it still wakes me up at night. Then it was super quiet for a little bit. And then my Dad shot the bleeding one in the head, too, just to be sure, I guess." Picking up the water bottle from the table, he took a swallow.

Greene asked, "What came next?"

"We just hiked back to the pickup."

No wonder the kid wanted a do-over.

"Do you still have the casings from those bullets?" Greene asked.

Nick shook his head. "Dad ejected them from the guns and then told me throw them out along the roads, one at a time. So I did."

Clasping both of his hands together as if praying, he turned to Sam. "I didn't know they worked at Wilderness Quest. Dad didn't, either. He never let me watch the news or read the paper or even use the Internet before I went there."

By the time Nick's interview was over, all the adrenaline had drained from Sam's system and her tortured muscles had stiffened. She was certain she was shambling like Frankenstein when she walked out of the interview room with Greene. The detective offered her a cup of coffee.

"Can I have a bottle of wine instead?"

The detective laughed. "I can't help with that, but maybe you'll take this." She gestured down the hall, where two familiar figures waited.

Blake, dressed in his late evening sweat pants and stretched-out sweater, gave her his hands-out, what-the-hell stance.

Maya's expression was unruffled, as usual. "You look like you've been run over by a truck," the girl observed.

"It was a speedboat and a pickup." She joined them for hugs, wincing when Maya embraced her enthusiastically. "Not so hard, please."

"Simon wanted to come, but he had an appointment with a mouse," Blake told her.

Behind them, the door to the men's room opened, and her housemate continued, "But we found a stand-in."

Chase gently enfolded her in his arms. "*Hola, querida.*"

He kissed the top of her head, then raised his head to pluck a shred of bark from his lower lip. "Still using the same shampoo, I see."

She gazed up at him. "What are you doing here, Chase?"

"I've been in the area for a few days."

"And you didn't even call?" She was stung.

"I wanted to surprise you with something, but as usual, you stunned me instead."

"Actually, Chase," she told him, "I'd love to quit doing that."

Examining each of their faces, she asked, "What are you *all* doing here?"

Chase said, "Blake called me when you didn't come back from kayaking."

Her housemate added, "Another boater found what was left of your kayak. I thought you were dead."

"Then, when Blake told me you'd asked him to impersonate Tom Lewis with the state wildlife agency, I figured you'd gone after Lewis." Chase crossed his arms.

Sam turned to Maya.

"Don't look at me," the girl said. "I knew you wouldn't die that easy. I just came along for the ride. And then some cop called and said you were here and you needed a ride home."

Sam put a hand on Chase's arm. "What were you going to surprise me with, anyway?"

Detective Greene was back, standing beside them, Sam's cup of coffee in her hand.

"Later," Chase murmured.

"Since I'm not going to inherit the house, again." Blake theatrically grimaced. "Since it's another false alarm, again, I'm going back to my bed." He pulled his car keys from his pocket. "Coming, Maya?"

"And miss the drama?" The girl turned to Chase. "Can I catch a ride back with you?"

"Sure." It turned out Chase had driven his personal car from Salt Lake, further deepening the mystery of his presence.

Detective Greene directed a disappointed Maya to the waiting room, and then invited Chase and Sam to watch the interview with Tom Lewis. She gestured for Chase to precede her down the hall.

"I was right," Greene whispered over her shoulder. "He is a hunk. If you don't want him, I do."

"Hands off," Sam told her.

When confronted with his son's confession, Tom Lewis broke down. Sam and Chase watched the proceedings piped into an adjacent office from a video camera in the interview room.

"When Nick shot that woman, I knew I couldn't let him take the rap for that. He didn't mean to. I shouldn't have been yelling at him to take the shot. Why the hell was she wearing brown? And the other one had on green and her hair was brown. It was hunting season, for chrissake!" He pounded the table with both hands, his handcuffs banging metal against metal. "It was so stupid! Nick's only fifteen, I couldn't let his whole life get ruined, and I could tell that other woman wasn't ever going to say it was just an accident."

He paused to take a breath. "And then, I'd already enrolled Nick at Wilderness Quest to toughen him up, because he just couldn't seem to get over his mom leaving a year ago. And then after ... well, it seemed like an even better idea to send him then, help him move on, you know? How was I supposed to guess those Quintana women were part of that? When I met him, the Director's name was Johnson. What kind of woman doesn't even use her husband's name?"

Kyla normally used a hyphenated version of her parents' last name, Quintana-Johnson, but Sam had noticed that the Johnson half had often been omitted in news articles.

"And Summer Westin?" Detective Greene asked Lewis.

Tom glared at the detective, his eyes blank.

"Cap'n Sam?" Greene suggested.

"I could tell that Sam was figuring it out. She wasn't going to let it be. I knew she'd get the truth out of Nick sooner or later." He tried to raise his hands to sweep them over his beard as he usually did, but was brought up short as the handcuff chain hit the end of the link attached to the metal table. He settled for clasping his hands together, fingers interlaced, his knuckles turning white. "Why couldn't everyone just leave it alone?"

Greene prompted, "So you went after Sam Westin."

Tom sniffed and nodded. "She forced me to. Nick and me, we would have been okay, but she just couldn't leave it alone!"

He leaned toward the detective. "I did it all for Nick. You understand, right? A father would do anything for his son."

* * * * *

Sam, Maya, and Chase waited with Nick in a cell until the juvenile authorities arrived to take charge of him.

The deputies allowed Nick to say a brief goodbye to his father before Tom Lewis was taken away in handcuffs. The poor boy was exhausted and tear tracks scarred his cheeks, but his expression was almost relieved, the burden of secrets finally lifted from his narrow shoulders. Watching Sam's face, he asked, "What's going to happen to me now, Cap'n?"

Chase answered for her. "They'll take you to the juvenile section and hold you for arraignment. Tell the authorities everything that happened with your dad and ask them to call your mom."

Nick made a face. "Oh God, my mom! She won't want anything to do with this. She doesn't even act like I exist. And she'll hate me even more if I cost her money."

Sam patted his arm. "You'll get a public defender."

"And an advocate, probably, to help you through the whole process," Maya added.

Nick bowed his head and pressed his hands to his face. "My life is over. And I deserve it. At least in prison I'll have someplace to live."

A scoffing noise came out of Maya's mouth. "Don't be such a drama queen. Your life is not over. Trust me; I know a lot about the juvenile justice system. You wanted a do-over, right?"

"This is *so* not what I was talking about."

"Whatever," Maya told Nick. "This is what you get. You'll be fine."

A woman officer in uniform, presumably from the juvenile detention center, arrived to unlock the cell door.

The boy stood up, turned to Maya. "Thanks. I think."

"Nick, if your mom won't take you after juvie or whatever they do to you, you might end up in foster care. I know a lot about that, too." Maya pulled a slip of paper from her pocket and tucked it into his shirt pocket. "That's my number. We can talk any time you need to."

29

"Surprise!" Chase waved a hand at a small house a few miles outside of Van Zandt. Clumps of moss spangled the buckled shingles of the roof, and the place sorely needed paint, but the location was lovely, down a wooded road, backed up to the steep forested hills of the Chuckanuts. A tall maple dominated the front yard, its glorious scarlet leaves dancing in the autumn sun.

He'd refused to tell her why he had insisted on driving twenty miles east from Bellingham to show her this. The front door, made up of solid vertical planks of what looked like cedar, creaked as he pushed it open.

"What's going on, Chase? Who lives here?" She stepped in, eyeing a dilapidated couch with a threadbare quilt thrown over it, an easy chair with stuffing sprouting from its back, and a sagging bookshelf full of moldering books. "Correction: who lived here?"

It was clear nobody had inhabited the little house for quite a while.

Off the small living room was a compact kitchen and dining area. The table and chairs filling that space were handmade; she could see the fine craftsmanship even under the thick layer of dust that coated them.

Turning to him, she put her arms around his waist. "Tell me! Does this have something to do with a case you're working on? Did you find a mummified corpse in here?"

"The old lady who owned the place," he said enigmatically,

then, "I never met her." His clear brown eyes were twinkling. He gestured toward the couch. "Have a seat. Back in a second." Leaving the door open, he went out.

She perched carefully on the old sofa. The cushion sagged beneath her weight. A spring poked her in the left butt cheek, she shifted over a few inches. Not much better, but at least she wouldn't have holes in the seat of her jeans.

Dust motes danced in the low afternoon sunlight that streamed in through the open front door. What she could see of the house was dirty and uncared for, but beautifully built.

The walls were polished wood paneling of some kind, old-fashioned but handsome, and the ceiling was supported with thick wooden beams. Even the windows were framed in wood, their sills now stained by years of moisture. Stairs off the kitchen area led to a second floor, which she presumed contained bedrooms.

"Ta da!" Chase reappeared with a bottle of champagne in one hand and two glasses in the other. He popped the cork on the champagne, and then plopped down beside her on the couch to pour. A cloud of dust rose into the air.

Sam sneezed. Then sneezed again. Wiping her nose with her hand, she took the glass of champagne he offered. Suddenly an unnerving idea streaked through her brain: Was Chase about to propose? Oh jeez, was he going to ask her to marry him?

She'd just started a new job with the Bellingham Herald writing outdoor features for the Sunday paper. She wasn't ready for marriage. He wasn't ready, they couldn't possibly—

"You're looking at the new owner of this chateau." He clinked his glass against hers.

She sneezed again. "What?"

He grinned at her, his teeth white against his olive skin and whisker-shadowed chin and cheeks. Where most Native Americans had difficulty growing beards, Chase's face showed the Hispanic genes he'd inherited from his Mexican father. He'd have to shave and suit up before he went back to work, but she liked this easy-going flannel-shirt-clad man sitting beside her right now.

He took a sip of his champagne. "I bought this place."

She gulped from her glass. Was it coming now? The proposal? "It's beautiful, Chase, but it clearly needs a lot of work. When would you work on it?"

"I hoped *we* would work on it. It comes with twenty acres, and there's an old barn out back. We could have horses if we want." He drained his glass.

She drained hers. "Chase, did you quit the FBI? I never asked you to do that."

"I know, Summer. And I appreciate that." He stood up. Grabbing her hand, he pulled her from the couch, then collected the champagne bottle and glasses. "Come see the upstairs."

Following him up the steps, she stewed on the possibilities. He had quit his job for her because she was too stubborn to move to Salt Lake City to be with him, and eventually that would come back to bite her because he loved the FBI. He was waiting to spring the proposal on her until they were upstairs for some reason. Would there be rose petals strewn across a bedspread or some other grand romantic gesture?

Nope. A double bed with a hand-crafted headboard filled most of the bedroom on the right at the top of the stairs. Ordinary pillows and a modern comforter covered the mattress. Chase placed the champagne bottle and glasses on a bedside table.

"The bed is conveniently made up." He flopped down onto the mattress and patted the space beside him. "I slept here last night."

"Chase!" Kicking off her shoes, she climbed up and sat next to him, her back against the headboard. "Spill it! What's up?"

He poured another glass of champagne and handed it to her. "I didn't quit the FBI. But I'm moving here."

She leaned in to give him a quick kiss. "That's wonderful! But the commute to Seattle will be a killer, won't it?"

"No, I mean I'm moving here." He pointed to the bed beneath them, but she knew he meant this house.

"You quit the FBI?" As far as she knew, there was no Bureau office north of Seattle.

"You're looking at the new head of the Northwestern Washington Safe Trails Task Force, headquartered in Bellingham."

"Safe Trails, like hiking trails?" Her thoughts immediately flashed to Kim and Kyla.

"Don't ask me why they call it that hokey name. It's a program to work with local Indian tribes to combat drugs and gangs and casino violations on reservations. Turns out it can be useful to be an urban Indian after all. Or at least an FBI Indian."

"Don't you mean Native American?"

"Whatever." He clinked his glass against hers. "Despite the grandiose name, I am the whole task force, the FBI side of it, anyway. The rest is the various tribal police heads."

Her face hurt, she was smiling so hard. "So you're going to be here all the time."

"Actually, I have to drive to Quinault tomorrow."

She rolled her eyes. The Quinault reservation was all the way over on the Olympic Peninsula; it would take most of a day just to get there.

"But when I'm not working, I'll be here, *querida*." He kissed her.

"Halleluiah!" She clinked her glass with his and then took a sip.

"One last time," he said solemnly, raising his glass again. "To Kim and Kyla."

Her throat tightened. "To Kim and Kyla, may they rest in peace."

After taking another gulp of champagne, she kissed him again. "Thank you for that, Chase." She sat back to study the small bedroom. "What's this about us working on this place?"

"Well, I know you have skills, and—"

Something clomped across the ceiling above them, rolling noisily from one side to the other.

They both looked up at the beams and planking overhead. The sound repeated.

"There's a bowling alley in your attic?" she asked.

He raised an ebony eyebrow. "I heard that same sound several times last night. Squirrels?"

Sam snorted. "I'd say thirty pounders, with masked faces and bushy, striped tails."

Chase tipped the champagne bottle toward her glass. "To new adventures in our lives."

"With hammers and raccoons."

"And love," he answered.

Love and adventure and wildlife. Kim and Kyla would approve.

~ END ~

Author's Note

The state of Washington is blessed with 15 national park units. These include the stunning Olympic, North Cascades, and Mount Rainer National Parks, several national recreation areas, and multiple national historic sites. In addition, the state boasts hundreds of thousands of acres of spectacular national and state forest lands and scenic islands and coastlines.

Washingtonians treasure our public lands, and in much of the state, hiking is a popular activity for residents of all ages. Our beautiful landscapes and hiking trails are also tourist attractions, and outdoor recreation is an important source of income for many businesses.

I choose to call this state home because I love the natural environment here. I am an avid hiker and kayaker. Despite the many hazards present in the wild, deaths are rare in the backcountry, and for this reason, every death that occurs here affects the entire outdoor community. Accidental deaths due to avalanches and falls and drownings are tragic, but the deaths that occur at the hands of other humans are unforgettable.

The murder scenario presented in *Backcountry* is fictional, a creation entirely of the author's imagination. The story, however, was inspired by two very real, very tragic events in the Cascade Mountains of Washington State. I have combined aspects of these two tragedies for my novel.

In August of 2008, Pamela Almli, 54, a resident of Oso, a small town near Arlington, was on a day hike up the popular Sauk Mountain trail in the Mount Baker-Snoqualmie National Forest, when she was shot by a 14-year-old hunter who mistook her for a bear. The 14-year-old who killed her was accompanied only by a 16-year-old hunter, which, unfortunately, continues to be a perfectly legal situation in Washington State as well as in many others. The teenage killer was convicted of second degree manslaughter.

On July 11, 2006, on the Pinnacle Lake Trail off the Mountain Loop Highway, just outside Granite Falls, Mary Cooper, 56, and her daughter Susanna Stodden, 27, were murdered, each shot in the head with a single bullet from a small-caliber handgun. Although their clothing was in disarray, the women were not raped or robbed. Their bodies and packs were left in plain sight alongside the trail.

Mary and Susanna had no enemies. The murders appear to be completely random, and to date, this case remains unsolved. Someone, most likely a local man who happened to be on the trail with a gun in his pocket, is getting away with murder. If you have seen or heard anything that might offer a clue, please call the Snohomish County Sheriff's Office tip line at 425-388-3845.

Acknowledgments

Every author needs help to polish a story. I owe a big THANK YOU to the following people who gave their time and expertise to make *Backcountry* a better book:

Jeanine Clifford, astute reader of a multitude of books

Cherie O'Boyle, author of the entertaining
Estela Nogales mysteries

Gordon Whitesmith, author of *The Random Access Murders*, a vintage computing mystery

Jeanette Hubbard, author of *Secrets, Lies, and Champagne Highs* and *Chasing Nathan*

Books by
Pamela Beason

The Summer "Sam" Westin Mysteries
Endangered
Bear Bait
Undercurrents
Backcountry

The Neema Mysteries
The Only Witness
The Only Clue
The Only One Left (coming soon)

Romantic Suspense
Shaken
Call of the Jaguar

The Run for Your Life Young Adult Suspense Trilogy
Race with Danger
Race to Truth
Race for Justice (coming soon)

Nonfiction E-books
So You Want to Be a PI?
Traditional vs Indie Publishing: What to Expect
Save Your Money, Your Sanity, and Our Planet

Keep up with Pam on her website:
http://pamelabeason.com

About the Author

Pamela Beason is the author of the Summer "Sam" Westin Mysteries, the Neema Mysteries, and the Run for Your Life Young Adult Trilogy, as well as several romances and nonfiction books. She has received the Daphne du Maurier Award and two Chanticleer Book Reviews Grand Prizes for her writing, as well as an award from Library Journal and other romance and mystery awards. Pam is a retired private investigator and freelance writer who lives in the Pacific Northwest, where she escapes into the wilderness to hike and kayak and scuba dive whenever she can.

http://pamelabeason.com

Made in the USA
San Bernardino, CA
15 June 2017